For Roger

love

Susen French-Dawn

Susan lives in Wiltshire and cares for her husband Geoff who has MS. She is Chair of the Salisbury MS Branch and the Salisbury Writers group. She loves gardening, painting and drawing, walking her dog and reading crime thrillers. She has worked as a psychiatric nurse, home help and senior care worker.

Susan is currently working on an anthology of poetry and her next novel, 'Generation Q'.

# By the same author

The Seventy-Nine Series (Vanguard Press)
ISBN 978 1 843861 0 62

Yesterday's Wrongs (Vanguard Press)
ISBN 978 1 843862 0 85

# BEYOND BELIEF

Susan French
───────────────────────────────

BEYOND BELIEF

Vanguard Press

VANGUARD PAPERBACK

© Copyright 2011
**Susan French**

The right of Susan French to be identified as author of
this work has been asserted by her in accordance with the
Copyright, Designs and Patents Act 1988.

**All Rights Reserved**

No reproduction, copy or transmission of this publication
may be made without written permission.
No paragraph of this publication may be reproduced,
copied or transmitted save with the written permission of the
publisher, or in accordance with the provisions
of the Copyright Act 1956 (as amended).

Any person who commits any unauthorised act in relation to
this publication may be liable to criminal
prosecution and civil claims for damages.

A CIP catalogue record for this title is
available from the British Library.

ISBN 978 184386 700 5

*Vanguard Press is an imprint of
Pegasus Elliot MacKenzie Publishers Ltd.*
www.pegasuspublishers.com

First Published in 2011

**Vanguard Press
Sheraton House Castle Park
Cambridge England**

Printed & Bound in Great Britain

*To my husband, Geoffrey Down,
whose support has been invaluable.*

# Chapter 1

## *Calvin*

The circle of jeering faces edges closer to me. I am trapped. I see their eyes. They hate me. Ginger Foster, the biggest boy in the school, has brought his gang to sort me out. They don't seem to notice the rain, or the spreading puddle under their feet.

'Fat pig!'
'Effin' posho!'
'Bleeding spastic!'

*These boys are going to kill me.* My fear rises as they move closer like a many-headed animal. Thumps, kicks and punches replace the taunts. I cower down, trying to curl up. One of them stinks of stale urine.

Ginger grabs my hair and jerks my head up. 'Effin' poufter's cryin'.'

I bite my lip to try and stop the tears. Someone punches me on the jaw and my teeth crunch horribly into my own soft flesh. The bitter metallic taste of blood fills my mouth and trickles down my chin.

'It's bleedin' 'uman! Look, real blood.' Yells of harsh laughter greet this.

'What's it got in its posh levver satchel?' Barry Dobbs sneers.

'Flowers for its mummy!' Ginger snatches my bag from Bobby Parrish, tipping it out on the wet ground. My books, pencils, lunch box and a packet of toffees are scattered in the mud.

Barry kicks my books into the puddle, makes a grab for the sweets at the same time as several other filthy hands.

'I bleedin' saw 'em first.'
'Eff off. They're mine.'

I begin to crawl away. The path smells of damp earth. There is a sudden yell. I've been spotted. Someone lands on my back. They are wearing heavy boots. I see a picture of a lion on top of a zebra as my face thuds into the mud. I am silent. There is no one to help.

'What do you think you're doing?' A different voice.

I open one eye. Not the bleeding cavalry. Tiny Ruth Diamond is standing there with her hands on her skinny hips; like a delicate butterfly among stampeding cattle; the idiot. What can she do against this lot?

'Get her, lads!'

'Picking on girls now, are you, Jimmy Foster? Is that all you're good for?'

'Nah, wouldn't bovver with them meself.'

'So it takes nine of you to fight one first-year boy?'

'I only need one hand to pick you up by your silly hair and throw you over the park wall.'

Ruth stands there glaring at him. 'And what would that prove, Jimmy? That you'd had spinach for breakfast?'

There's a titter from the gang. I keep quiet.

Jimmy's losing face. That narks him. 'You little…' He grabs for her thick ponytail, but catches thin air as she dances out of reach.

'Scat!' yells the boy keeping cave on the wall. 'It's Mr Lee!'

I hear swearing, scuffling and thuds as the gang scramble over the wall and out of sight. I sit up, looking round for the hefty PE teacher. There was no sign of him.

'You okay Calvin?'

'I'll live.' To be rescued was one shaming thing. To be rescued by a girl was… humiliating.

'You look a bloody mess.'

'You ain't supposed to swear.'

'I was using the word as an adjective. "Bloody" as in covered in blood.'

'Clever clogs,' I say, knowing she was. Wondering who'd she'd tell first about me sitting like Job on his ash heap.

'Don't worry, I won't tell. Bet they won't either. Not that they let a girl cheek them and get away with it.'

Her confident smile annoys me as I start to stand up, and grunt as bits of me complain.

'You sure you're okay?'

'Course I am. And you ain't got away with it neither,' I snap. 'There's always another night, another morning. Whenever they like they can get you back. You can't win, neither.'

'You can't just give in to them like that.' Ruth is picking up my books, wiping them with a tissue, which is useless, they're so wet.

I snatch them off her, cramming them in my satchel. 'I didn't just give in to them. They've been using me as a punch bag for so long. I've tried everything. They just go on doing it.'

'But if you stood up to them...'

'Don't talk such ... rubbish. I ain't no David and he ain't no Goliath. I ain't got a chance against him.' I am miserable. I know I will get into trouble about the muddy books, twice: at home and at school. 'So where's this teacher that was coming?'

'That was only Matthew, saving my bacon again.'

I say what I think of Matthew Farnsby under my breath. It would be him. Sneaking off with the bullies so's he'd not be picked on. Though I wish now I'd done the same, which makes me feel worse.

'Pardon?'

'I said I see. That's all.'

'Didn't sound like that to me,' Ruth says, all high and mighty.

I turn my back on her. I don't know what to say. Perhaps it ought to be "Thank you for that", or some such thing. But it didn't matter anyway. Once Ginger's lot had finished with her she wouldn't be so eager next time.

I feel her watching me as I cross the playing field. But when I look back, I see she is walking back into the school.

When I get home, my mother is standing in the doorway with her arms folded.

'Calvin! What time do you call this? The main prayer meeting is tonight.' She stops as she sees the blood, the mud, and my torn clothes. 'And you've been fighting again! Just you wait until your father comes home. He can deal with you, my lad.' She grabs my collar and marches me through to the bathroom. 'Strip,' she says.

I pull off my things, hoping she'll say something about the bruises, the cuts, something. But she just bundles up my clothes and turns away without a word. I run the bath and climb in. At least the water is hot tonight. I hear her putting my clothes into soak in the scullery. Tomorrow, she will boil the old copper and do her daily hand washing, rinsing and mangling of our clothes.

She opens the scullery door to call up the stairs; 'Don't be too long. Your father will be back in half an hour.'

I wince. The belt or the cane? It wasn't much of a choice.

I am lying in the corner of my room, beside the radiator, listening. My parents are in the dining room below. Adam is asleep; I can hear his deep breathing. My father's voice vibrates through the pipe work.

'No, Elizabeth, you may not go out to work. It is not biblical practice.'

There is a short silence. I lean towards the radiator, straining to hear my mother's reply.

'I just thought that maybe it would help? We don't appear to have enough money.'

'You have enough. There is no need for us to give in to materialism. We do not need television or washing machines – they are the tokens of worldliness.'

Mother clears her throat, and then in a subdued voice I hear her say: 'I agree about the television; it would be a bad influence on the boys. But surely it would help if I learned to drive? There would be many ways I could be of service if I could –'

'No, Elizabeth. Your duty is to be a keeper at home. That is your God-given calling. I do not wish the boys to learn either – it would be too much of a worldly pull, owning a car and being free to go who knows where.'

'They will grow up, perhaps go to university?'

'No. I have decided. I am to begin a theological college for the children of the Truth. I have had enough of the godless teaching that the State Schools offer. Not only that – they teach blasphemy. This is what I must do next: protect the children of the Truth from the lies of the Devil.'

I shiver in the darkness of my room. There was to be no escape for us. Mother's voice is almost inaudible now.

'It sounds a daunting task, Saul.'

'My children, all those that God puts into my care, will have the best grounding in the Truths of the Gospel that I can give them, God willing.'

'When are we to begin?'

'It has already begun. I must prepare the sermon for the Elders Gathering next week. The five Congregations will begin to organise the funding.'

'When are the next two Congregations to begin?'

'We plan one new Congregation each month – there is scope, if we use our resources carefully. And we all contribute, every one, working as part of the Body of Christ. You are privileged, Elizabeth, to be here at the centre of the work, knowing all that is happening as those in The Truth prepare for His return.'

'I am, Saul. You go and prepare. I have some kitchen work to do before tomorrow, if I may?'

'It is your God-given duty. I will be in my study.'

I hear the sound of the dining room door close and the creak of the study door. It closes like the door of a prison cell on my mind.

I stretch my fingers, still sore from the caning, and begin to stand up. Then I pause. There is another sound from below. I listen carefully, not knowing what such a soft whimpering could be. Then my heart knots painfully. The sound is my mother crying.

## Chapter 2

### *Ginger*

I run up the alley between the posh houses by the green. My feet hammer the tarmac, making the noise echo back and forth until it sounds like a dozen pairs of running feet; not just one. I like the noise, but I slow, turn to look over my shoulder, just in case. There's nobody there. I hate this time of day. Like in that film, *Dr Jekyll and Mr Hyde;* I am two people, Ginger and Jimmy, changed – not by a fizzy drink, but by where I am. I feel myself shrinking as I see those same grey council houses. The curtain at the front window twitches. I've been seen.

The red painted front door jerks open. A large, red-faced, white haired woman wearing a caftan sways into view.

'Jimmy Foster, yew lazy good for nothing bastard, get your filthy effin' hide in 'ere.'

'Yes, Gran.' I try to duck past, but I'm never quick enough. A meaty fist catches the side of my head, knocking me headlong onto the living room floor. I lay stunned for a moment, then roll sideways as my grandmother turns, slamming the front door hard. The vibrations run through the ancient floorboards beneath the cold faded green linoleum where I am sprawled.

'Yew wet the bed again yew filthy little animal. Get yourself up there and change the effin' sheets yourself. I've a good mind to make yew sleep in 'em.'

I scramble for the stairs, and am rewarded by a hefty kick on the backside as I go. While I strip my bed, I think of school. It's a good thing the boys at St Mark's don't know about gran. None of them would believe it. But it isn't Ginger, it's Jimmy who cries.

I look out at the rubbish filled backyard, wondering if I could shimmy down the drainpipe and escape. But I'm hungry, and to get some food, I have to toe the line. My mattress is covered in a bright red waterproof sheet. It smells of ammonia and rubber. *Why do I do it? Why can't I stop?* I roll the sheets wet side in and carry them down to the kitchen. The wash copper is empty, so I half fill it with cold water and light the gas underneath. While I stir in a cupful of Daz, I feel gran watching, listening, like her cat at the mouse hole. I rinse my bedding at the sink before dumping the soggy mess into the water. I jump as the copper lid slips from my wet finger with a clatter to the floor.

'Can't yew effin' be bloody quiet?'

'Sorry, Gran.'

'When yew done that yew can get the coal in.'

Two hours later I sit down to a plate of baked beans on toast and a sausage. I eat as quietly and slowly as I can, 'minding my manners'. Any step out of line and the plate would be snatched off me and Gran would eat it in front of me. To teach me: life did no one no favours.

*I know, I've learned. She hates me; I am so bad.*

Granny Foster sat watching the boy. He has the same eyes, the same bright hair and pale skin as his father. Even the way he turns his head makes her think of Jimmy. Then she feels there's this emptiness somewhere. An ache. The pain makes her angry with him. His father had betrayed her. And with that slut Rose Barrett. This unwanted bastard was made of the same stuff. He needs more discipline, that's what. He would go the same way, come to a bad end. Not if she could help it. She plonked a half cup of water in front of him.

'Drink that, and no more afore bed. Maybe yew might act your bloody age and stay dry tonight for once.'

I look at the water. My mouth is dry. But I shake my head. 'I'm not thirsty, Gran.'

'Mind you don't sup nothing else. I want yew in your bed in half an hour.'

I climb the stairs and stand looking at the bed. I would have to do something.

I lie pretending to be sound asleep when she comes up to check. I breathe slow and soft until she closes and locks the door.

When I hear the click, I sit up, and pull the thick wad of newspaper from under the bed, then spread it on the floor. The pillow should be okay... then granddad's greatcoat on top, from the cupboard. This might just save my ringing ears from another belting. The lino is cold, the floor is hard, but I fall into a deep sleep.

Sometime around dawn, I dream of Ruth Diamond shouting at me, tossing that shiny hair of hers back. But the voice is my grandmother's, using words that Ruth Diamond had probably never heard of.

I jerk awake, stiff and cold, the wet newspaper clinging to my skin. I sit up, wondering what to do next. Newsprint has come off on my skin. There's a damp patch on the floor. But I feel a slow smile spread over my face. My sheets are dry. No need to skip breakfast and run today.

Almost cheerfully, I roll up the soggy mess of newspaper and drop it out of the window leaving it open for air. I hang the coat out of sight, and put my pillow on the bed.

I hear gran climbing the stairs, I have to hurry. But by the time she opens the door, I'd got myself sitting on my bed fully dressed.

'Off.'

I stand up.

Gran pulls the blankets right back, I see her surprise; the bedclothes are dry.

'I coulda sworn yew was wet – it stinks in 'ere. Go and wash, it must be yew.'

I scuttle from the room quick. Out in the back scullery, I do my best with some carbolic, a rag and a square of towel.

The porridge was hot. I had two mugs of tea. For once gran was quiet. I shot out on my newspaper round, and dumped the wet newspaper in a dustbin three doors down on my way past. My papers are in the bus shelter for me to collect, and I whistle to myself as I drop papers through letterboxes.

Mrs Atkins looks up as I hang my empty bag behind the storeroom door. I know she had wondered if it would be a good thing giving me the round. But I'd heard her tell Mr Atkins yesterday, 'He has an awful reputation as a bully, but he has done his first week well.'

So I hoped I'd done all right; that I could keep the job.

'Well, Jimmy, here's your first week's money.'

I take the coins, and gaze at them. I don't believe my eyes.

'Thanks, Mrs Atkins.' I turn toward the door, but turn back. 'Are there any old newspapers I can 'ave?'

'Sure, help yourself – lots by the back door.'

I stagger back with an armful.

'Take your bag; you can bring it in the morning.'

'How much?'

'How much for what?'

'The newspapers, Mrs Atkins.'

'I don't want paying for old newspapers. You can take as many as you like.'

'Thanks, Mrs Atkins.'

Mrs Atkins is taken aback as suddenly the lad's face is transformed, as if lit from within.

Jimmy Foster is smiling.

# Chapter 3

## *Ruth*

Secret Journal. Thursday 6th.

Calvin was being bullied again today. Jimmy Foster's gang has got it in for him. I wonder what makes them do it. I managed to break it up but don't think it'll make any difference. I wonder if I should tell a teacher? Dad always says that it's not telling tales, especially if someone is being hurt. But it's so hard. I know they'll get me for it if I do. It'll be more than 'goody two shoes' and 'tell tale tit, your tongue'll be split…'

Secret Journal. Friday 7th.
This all began last night, when I came home from my singing lesson.
'Ruth, it's supper time.' Mother's voice comes from the bottom of the stairs.
'Coming, Mother.' I go down, hoping that dad will be home, but he's not.
Mother notices me glance at the study door. 'Your father is at an important meeting in London, Ruth.'
I don't feel hungry then, and I eat a little of the shepherd's pie she has made with the remains of yesterday's roast.
'You'll never grow big and strong if you don't eat, girl.'
I play around with the food on my plate, putting eyes, nose and mouth on the potato with peas. I look at the piano where my brother Daniel's photo looks out at the room. If only he hadn't died, maybe things would have been different.
Mother sees what I'm doing. 'Don't behave like a two-year-old, girl. You can stay there until you've cleared your plate, Ruth Diamond. There are starving children in the world who would be grateful for that good food.'

I open my mouth without thinking first. 'You could send it to them, I don't want it.'

'That's enough from you, you ungrateful, sinful, wretched creature. Despising the good gifts of the Lord! Spare the rod and spoil the child! How true. Your father shall hear of this when he gets home. He's far too lenient with you.'

I can't eat now. My throat has gone all tight. I feel my face burning. I know I am a sinful creature. I don't deserve this food at all. Mother clears the dishes, but she is watching me all the time through the serving hatch. I sit staring at the plate until the food turns into a fuzzy shape. The pea lips seem to move, speak.

'Sinner, sinner, won't eat her dinner.'

It is hours before I get the greasy cold mess past the great lump in my throat.

As soon as I force the last mouthful down, mother snatches the plate. 'Bath and then straight to bed.'

I run up the stairs, turn on the bath taps behind the closed door, and bend over the toilet bowl. Just in time. The food tastes even worse as my stomach rejects it. I stand up, feeling giddy, put the toilet lid down sit on the pink cover.

The large poster, coal black print leers at me from behind the door.

THOU, GOD, SEEEST ME.

I hide my face in my hands.

Mother is calling from the bottom of the stairs. 'I trust you are in the bath, girl. I shall be up in five minutes to check you've washed thoroughly. And remember not to waste water.'

I am in bed at last. My room is under the eaves, and though I should close my eyes and pray with my mother, I watch the large elm tree swaying in the breeze outside my window. Some starlings are squabbling among the branches. What would it be like to fly?

My mother has been praying for my lost soul for so long, I can't keep listening to it. I feel so bad. I hear the sound of my father's car on the gravel. Mother has heard it too, and after a few more long words, she says Amen at last.

'Think hard about your immortal soul, Ruth. It is never too early to think of eternity.'

How I wished I could answer her like Jane Eyre had answered Mr Brocklehurst, when asked how she would avoid falling into hell.

'*I must keep in good health and not die.*'

Her fate was to be sent to Lowood School, and she was far less of a sinner than me. What terrible fate would come my way should I answer my mother like that? A half smile came on my lips as I noticed I was thinking like Jane Eyre.

'This is not something to grin about, child.' She turned to go, and then paused. She turned, pecked my cheek, and said, 'God bless you, child.'

'God bless you Mother.'

I fall into a fitful sleep, in which I am climbing among the elm tree branches, trying not to tread on plates of cold shepherd's pie, and as my feet land on them, the peas are huge green marbles that roll under the plates. I claw at the branches where my nightdress has caught in the twigs. Mother will be so angry if I tear it.

The wind is cold on my body. There are raindrops dripping off the leaves, making the branches slippery. How am I to get down from here? The ground is a long way down. How did I get here in the first place?

That's it. I must be dreaming. I must open my eyes. But there is no difference when I do. I am standing on the long branch that often taps my window. My nightdress is still caught on the twigs.

I scream. There is the sound of feet on the stairs inside. This is not a dream. My father is at the window. His face is white with fear. I have never seen it like that before.

'Ruthie! Don't move!'

'What's the matter with her?'

'She's been sleepwalking again. Something must have upset her.'

My mother appears at the window, totally calm. 'Ruth, just come back the way you got yourself out.'

I edge towards her, slowly, trying to get back to my room.

There is a loud crack behind me, the branch gives way and I plunge down, down towards the ground. I hit my head on something. There are coloured lights like fireworks, and then there is silence.

I hear someone calling through the silence. It is dad. I answer.

'You are safe in bed now, Ruthie; the doctor says you aren't hurt. Just sleep now.'

I wake in the downstairs guest room. I have a dressing on my head, and bruises. It was not a dream. I have been sleepwalking again. I go back to my own room tonight, but they are putting bars up at the window. My window.

# Chapter 4

## *Oliver*

Oliver sits in the corner of his room, watching. From this position, he can see the street outside, the whole of the living room and most of the kitchen. This corner is safe. His drawing paper and coloured pencils are right beside him. The blue baby quilt that he takes everywhere is folded underneath him for a cushion. He pulls his knees up under his jumper to keep them warm. He can hear them talking about him in the next room.

'He just sits there all the time. It's not normal for a child his age.'
'I shouldn't worry, it's just a stage he's going through, you'll see.'
'What about the way he rocks when he sings?'
'That'll pass when he starts school.'
'That's another thing that worries me. He doesn't talk much either.'

Oliver rocks a little. It feels good, comforting. But they are watching him. Better not do it if they can see. Maybe go into the middle of the room, sit on the sofa near the television. It is all right to sit on the sofa by the television for hours. Maybe he could do that a bit, when the doors were locked against the outside.

'Do you suppose he's autistic?'
'I don't know. I'm just worried about him starting school. What if he ... you know, what happened at the nursery.'
'He's older now, he won't do that again.'
'Still, they wouldn't take him back after that.'
'You worry too much.'

Oliver rocks himself to and fro. He does not like the pictures that come when they say the word 'Nursery'. He takes his pencils and begins to draw them; first, a picture of a little girl in a blue dress, her hair long and golden; crying. A pair of scissors. It had been so easy. But the teacher takes the scissors away, makes him stand in the corner.

The next picture is red and angry.

'Maybe you're right. He's fine now when we go to the supermarket. Even sings a bit when we drive there.'

'He's fine at Sunday School. Mr Diamond said as much to me. Let's see how it goes.'

'You don't think I should take him to see someone?'

'No, that's a bit drastic; you know it will go down on his record. He might get labelled; you know how people's expectations limit children. They'd be watching for the next odd thing he did.'

'I'm afraid for him.'

There is a strange sound from the next room, one that Oliver recognises. He draws a figure wearing a dress, with lots of blue teardrops flying everywhere. She does this a lot. Oliver can make her do it. Easy. Pull the tablecloth onto the floor, spill the flowers, watch the water drip onto the chair seats, soak into the cushions and trickle onto the carpet.

Oliver's pencils move busily over the paper, sketching in the picture. Yes, that was how it was. The mark on the carpet had looked like a curled up cat. Oliver draws eyes on the mark. They are very large and green with black stripes across the centres. For a moment he debates about whiskers, but gives it bloody teeth instead.

Then he draws the cat tearing up the letters that come in the mornings.

Oliver sits huddled up in the chair. They are talking about him again.

'I know, but the school insisted on the referral.'

'Have we no rights as parents?'

'Dr Hall is the best in his field.'

'I don't care if he is ploughing champion, I don't want Oliver labelled as some kind of freak.'

'In a way, I'd be glad to know what's wrong – especially now.' She puts her hand on her stomach.

He covers it with his. 'I know, but try not to worry.'

Oliver does not like it here. The woman behind the desk has fierce eyes. They are taking people into other rooms around the sides of this one. He grips his quilt tight to his chest. They wanted to take it away, but he screamed so much they let him bring it. But screaming doesn't work for everything. They had still brought him here. The fierce woman had taken him into a room away from the people. It had toys in it. But Oliver does not touch the toys. He fears the great blank window close to them. He moves far away from it, and sits on his quilt in the corner. The room is watching him.

The fierce woman comes to fetch him again. She takes him into another room, where his people are. There is another blank window in here; a big white blind covers it. Oliver wonders if the man who sits behind the desk feels it watching him.

'Hello, Oliver, I am Dr Hall. I am pleased to meet you.' The man gets up from behind the desk, and Oliver cannot believe how tall the man is. Oliver looks up; the man's head is near the light on the ceiling.

'Sorry, I am a long way up.'

The man suddenly drops to the floor, sitting on the carpet next to Oliver. It was confusing, the way he changed shape. 'Is that better?'

Oliver didn't know if it was.

The man asks him lots of questions, but Oliver takes his mind out of the window and sits on the sill, looking out over the park, like the pigeon that sits there too.

His people talk to him instead. The man gets up and sits on the desk. He writes lots of things on the paper, but he makes no pictures. When the man stands up, and they go out of the little room, Oliver thinks it's over. But no, they come to this place again and again. Oliver would not have minded it, but the room was watching him. Even when he smashed the toys against that terrible window, they still made him go back.

His home place changed. She had changed shape a while, then she went away. When she came back a strange woman came with her. They carried two white quilts wrapped round something. They made Oliver come and look at them.

'Your sisters, Oliver. Say hello to them.'

Oliver looks at them. Strange creatures with toothless mouths and waving hands. He doesn't like them.

There is a lot of noise from the new creatures the woman brought back. They scream differently from Oliver, but they get all the attention. When Oliver screams they tell him to stop. These creatures are allowed to scream, even in the night.

That last night, they scream so much that Oliver has to throw things at them to make them stop. His people come in and drag him out, shouting at him to stop. They shut him in his room and lock the door. Oliver sits in the corner rocking. There is a lot of noise; something with flashing lights comes outside and he sees mother climb into it with the creatures. At least they are not screaming. Father comes and lifts him into the bed. He is shaking and he does not look at Oliver. He tucks the blue quilt in beside him and closes the door.

Next day when he is eating cornflakes in his corner, the fierce eyed woman comes and takes Oliver away from his people to a strange place. He does not have his people any more. He only has his quilt.

# Chapter 5

## *Adam Crouch*

English Essay. *What I am going to do when I grow up.*

*I am going to be famous one day. Not like a film star, better than that. I will be famous like Charles Wesley or Billy Graham. I am going to be a preacher, like my father, Saul. He is a very important man, and he has a very big church where lots of people go twice every Sunday.*

*Our church is a wonderful place of worship. It has a large glass dome at the centre of the main building. It is very beautiful, and shows Christ preaching his Sermon on the Mount. I want to be like Christ and preach the good News of Salvation to lost sinners.*

*I shall lead the prayer meetings, and teach the Sunday school. I shall love to teach the children the wonderful hymns and choruses that I know, and play the piano for them. I shall study hard, and lead the Bible Study for the grown-ups.*

*It will be part of my calling to hold marriage services, although I do not think I shall marry. I shall also have to hold funeral services, which will be sad for those left behind, but a time of rejoicing for those who have been called into the presence of their Saviour.*

*When I am old enough, I aim to go to Bible College and learn as much as I can, ready for the important task to which God has called me.*

The headmaster put the exercise book down with a sigh, and looked up at the worried teacher who sat on the other side of his laden desk. 'It is, as you say, a very unusual essay.'

'So what shall I do about it Alan?' the young man leaned forward, earnestly.

'Nothing, James, nothing at all.' The headmaster shrugged. 'We've been here before with the True Gospel Members.'

'But the lad seems ... brainwashed. We can't just leave it!' He stood up, pacing toward the window.

'I know James. The True Gospel Church has an incredible grasp of its members. The teaching is, shall I say, thorough. My advice is simply to correct his English, his grammar and punctuation, and leave it at that.' Alan shivered. The room seemed smaller and darker than usual, the cracked green paint and the much marked magnolia emulsion seeming to crowd in on him.

'The poor kid doesn't live in the real world.' James paced back to the bookshelf, picking up a tattered copy of *Great Expectations*. 'I set homework on this the other week; the children were to watch the film on BBC2. *Great Expectations* is our set book this term, and I got a letter back from his father saying they did not have such a worldly appliance in their home, and please would I refrain from setting such tasks in the future.'

'It doesn't surprise me at all. What does surprise me is that they still allow their children to attend state schools at all. I would have expected them to set up their own schools, to protect their young from the worldly influence of a godless environment.'

'It seems incredible in this day and age.'

'At least he knows where he's going. There is no doubt that these children are a benefit to the school, punctual, tidy, polite and hard working. Without them, our examination success rate would drop sharply.'

'It's not natural.'

'No, and his father would tell you that he is not in the business of catering to fallen human nature.'

'I feel I should talk to him...'

The headmaster stood up. 'James, no, my advice is to steer clear of tangling with him. He has powerful friends; his influence is everywhere. In my opinion, and don't quote me on this, in this town that family is the spiritual equivalent of the Dysons.'

James Linton looked at his friend in astonishment. 'It makes them sound like the Mafia.'

Alan nodded. 'That's it, but they're not physically violent, it's more an insidious take-over of the individual, a kind of mental hijacking which people don't notice until it's too late.'

James picked up the blue exercise book and paused, glancing out of the window. 'What the heck's going on down there?'

Alan came across to look. A large crowd of children were gathered round a tall, thin boy who was standing on an upturned milk crate.

James opened the window. They could hear the lad's voice clearly, soft and musical, even above the rest of the playground noise.

Adam Crouch was holding an open air service in a corner of the playground.

Several children were sniggering, some were embarrassed, and some seemed entranced. The preacher did not seem aware of his audience at all. Several missiles had been thrown, half-eaten sandwiches, a tomato and a paper dart, but there was not even a flicker of an eyelid to show the lad had noticed.

'Can we allow this in the school playground, Alan?'

The headmaster looked at his friend, a frown of anxiety creasing his forehead. 'I don't think we can. But I'm afraid we are going to have terrible trouble in preventing it. We are, when all is said and done, a Church of England School. We can't be seen to oppose the teaching of Christianity.'

James looked down at the scene below him. 'I see what you mean. We can crack down on things like smoking behind the bicycle shed, the drawing of graffiti on the walls and the dropping of litter.'

'But this is a whole new ball game.' Alan turned away from the window. 'To cap it all, the lad's father is on the board of governors, and there are four more of his members to give his vote weight.'

'Why so many?'

'Because most of the other parents would rather stay at home watching television than join a committee, James.'

'That's a little unfair.'

'No, I don't think so. Most things that require effort in any community are done by a few; and those few are usually doing sterling work on several committees. It's the rule of creeping apathy. Nobody thinks they can make a difference any more. Even voting has become a half-hearted activity.'

'So we are left open to a few activists?'

'I don't think we can stop it. The opiate of the people has changed, *EastEnders* and *Casualty*, *Richard and Judy* and *Inspector Morse*; all these are more real to Mr and Mrs Average than their own next door neighbours.'

'God help us.'

'Saul Crouch would say Amen to that. Would you ask young Adam to come up and see me after break?'

'Sure. What are you going to say to him?'

'I haven't got a four letter clue,' Alan said, as the two minute bell for the end of recess sounded, 'but I have serious doubts about the True Gospel Church movement.' He bent to open a desk drawer, taking out a slim fluorescent pink file; 'Take a look at these clippings and tell me what you think when you've read them through.'

'Are the contents as lurid as the cover?'

Alan laughed. 'Almost – those files were a cheap job lot.'

'I can see why.'

James took the folder home that evening. Dee was cooking supper. He put his arms round her as she stood at the cooker, kissing the soft skin at the back of her neck and breathing in the smell of her. 'Hello scrumptious.'

She leaned into him with a sigh. 'Good day?'

'Better now. What are we eating?'

'Spaghetti Bolognese.'

'Great. Can I help?'

'Wash the salad for me? Though I'd rather you stayed right where you are, I need to start the spaghetti.' She turned towards him lifting her face to his for a kiss.

James worked beside her and soon they were sitting down together.

'Much marking to do tonight?' she enquired, passing him a large helping.

'Some. I'm fairly up together. I've a file on the True Gospel Church to wade through though.'

'They're a weird bunch. What started you off on that?' She sprinkled parmesan liberally over her plate.

'Adam Crouch. He was preaching in the playground today.' James took the proffered parmesan from her.

'It doesn't surprise me at all. At the playgroup, we did Halloween masks once. We had a communication to the effect that we were not to teach such evil superstitions to the young people.' She wound spaghetti deftly onto her fork. 'So when we've finished supper, you'll want to do your bits. I've got my Open University assignment to do.'

So together later in their bright clean living room, she sat at the computer table, he settled down with the file beside the fire.

The first clipping seemed quite innocuous:

*'The True Gospel Church has today opened its five hundredth church. Speaking at the ceremony, the founder of the movement, the Right Reverend Saul Crouch, said that the Nation was spiritually hungry in these materialistic days, and that the True Gospel Church offered the original Gospel of salvation, which the established churches no longer espoused. This is the reason God has blessed our people.'* Alan had written 'The Daily Standard, April 10, 1985' on the bottom of the cutting. The by-line was Paul Markham.

So they were getting big. Nothing worrying there, James thought, turning to the next page. This was a longer piece, entitled '**College or Monastic Cult**?'

*The simply named 'Theological College' of Crow Lane, London EC4, has attracted a number of criticisms of late. The students have, it is reported, to spend four hours of each day performing household duties, from cooking and cleaning, to laundry and gardening. They also have to spend two hours daily in prayer and meditation, and eight hours in study, with an additional half-hour compulsory Meeting at six a.m. and an hour at nine p.m. for teaching. It is also alleged that the students have a very poor diet, causing lethargy and extreme weight loss. One wonders whether the students have much time to eat or to sleep properly when following this regime. When asked if the college received funding from the 'True Gospel Church', the Superintendent refused to comment. It is a known fact that a high proportion of the College students go on to minister in 'True Gospel Churches'.*

As James read on, he found the hairs on the back of his neck beginning to prickle uncomfortably. The newspaper headlines were increasingly antagonistic toward the movement:

**'*True Gospel Church; Sect, College or Cult?*'**

*Questions have been raised after the deaths of several of the young people studying at the Theological College, Crow Lane. The Superintendent, Reverend Amos Firth, denied that the deaths were suicide, claiming that there had been a viral outbreak at the college. Tests were being carried out to ascertain whether it was a strain of meningitis. Asked whether the regime at the College was, as reported, spartan, he replied that the students had all that was required in order to live according to the Teaching. When asked what the rules of the Teaching were, the Superintendent said, 'The Teaching is a biblically based discipline of life which cannot be understood by those that are spiritually dead or sleeping. To comprehend the Teaching, an enquirer must suspend conventional knowledge and accept the practice in faith and humility.'*

*Police are currently investigating various allegations regarding conditions at the college.*

James stretched and yawned, 'Fancy a coffee, love?'

'Please. This TMA is a tough one.'

'You'll do fine; you've never scored less than 90%, to my knowledge.'

James made them both coffee and sat down to continue his reading.

***True Gospel Church Finances under the spotlight.***

*It is reported that the members of the True Gospel Church have been encouraged to sell all their possessions and give them to the church in order to promote the Gospel. Members are living in communes within the churches, where many still work at outside jobs and give all their income to the cause.*

*The church is rumoured to have a turnover in excess of twelve million pounds a year, some of which has been spent on a large country house in Wiltshire, renamed 'The Retreat', where many of the church members are now living.*

Some time later, James looked up, the last clipping in his hand. He shivered. The list had gone on relentlessly. Were there arranged marriages? Was it teaching or was it brainwashing? What did the movement do with such vast sums of money?

That the church was successful there was no doubt. What was disturbing was the list of prominent people that Alan had clipped to the back of the file. Politicians, judges, policemen, all of whom had some connection to the movement. But was its growth benign or malignant?

With a sigh, he picked up a pile of red notebooks. Form 4b's history essays would look tame after this. Later, tucked up in bed with Dee, he told her of his discoveries. Her last words as she dropped into sleep reverberated in his mind for some time before he too fell asleep.

'They sound frightening and dangerous, don't they?'

Unknown to James, while he had been reading the contents of the lurid pink file, not far away, a certain Minister of the True Gospel Church was writing in a hard-cover notebook.

### Journal, Saul Crouch.

*There has been a sustained attack on the Truth over the past weeks; several of our members have been corrupted. There had to be a purge by the Joshua group. Brother Amos has fulfilled his duty efficiently, although I find these acts of judgement alien to my spirit. There was adverse publicity in The Daily Standard, mostly by a young man called Markham. It has been arranged for him to lose his job with them, so that may be the end of his campaign of evil words. The policeman was another matter; Brother Amos and I could not decide how to treat him. He was polite, respectful and professional. I'm not sure he was convinced by our explanations. Sergeant Cooper is an unusual policeman.*

*My children are growing in number; I have placed several 'family' groups in suitable homes; I have some excellent Sisters to care for them. And it is a joy to my heart to know that very soon they will not be tainted by worldly education. Our school is about to open its doors. The young people will be protected throughout their most vulnerable years. Praise the Lord.*

In a backstreet, Ayesha Muhktar lay gazing at the ceiling. It seemed strange that her family wished her, as a Muslim girl, to attend school, whilst all the time, planning for her to marry as soon as she was sixteen. Her cousin, Ahmed, especially, frightened her with his furious denouncement of all Western practices. He wants to change the country, she thought. But have we the right to impose our ways on these people? I suppose the Imams are right; after all, they know the Teachings.

'O, Allah, be merciful, that I may be able to love the man chosen for me,' she whispered fervently into the darkness.

# Chapter 6

## *Ten Years Later*

Sunday 1st March

Reggie was soaked through to the skin. It would be several hours before he could go back to his rented room. In any case, there was nothing to do there, no television. There was no point going to the pub, he owed money to the barman who'd laid his last lot of bets for him. Then he spotted the church lights blazing out like a lighthouse in the wet. At least it would be dry inside. Bit like the sermon, like as not. He caught a glimpse of the large name board outside. In bright purple lettering it proclaimed 'True Gospel Church', Minister; Rev Adam Luther Crouch. Underneath in smaller type on a notice board were the times of services. There seemed to be at least three every day. Morning Service must just have started.

Reggie sneaked in at the back, with a hymnal from the shelf in the foyer, standing uncertainly beside a row of coats. He moved slowly sideways with one hand busy searching the pockets behind his back, whilst mouthing the words of the hymn. His eyes flickered over the congregation, and as the hymn came to an end, he began to edge toward the exit.

Calvin Crouch had seen the man come in, and moved silently to stand beside this new brother who was too shy to come right into the congregation. Brother Adam was getting into his stride now, his lovely voice both holding attention and pleasing to the ear.

Adam saw Calvin move toward the newcomer, and his handsome face seemed to radiate an inner joy as he smiled. 'Welcome, Brother, welcome! Brother Calvin, bring him into the company!'

Reggie found himself propelled to the front and seated on a hard bench covered in hessian matting. As the preacher resumed his sermon, Reggie tried to wriggle along toward the edge of the seat, his eyes fixed on the door and escape. But the hand on his shoulder was linked to a very muscular arm. He was trapped, but it would be easy enough to sit out the service and vanish afterwards. He tried to relax on the uncomfortable bench while the preacher thundered above his head. The musical voice went on and on while his thin flesh went numb. He'd known softer prison mattresses. Then, as if at a hidden signal, the congregation rose to its feet and launched into song: 'Just as I am, without one plea, but that thy blood was shed for me...'

Reggie lurched to his feet a fraction behind the rest, clutching his hymn book, but before he could open it, he was marched forward to a long cushion.

'Kneel,' said the man called Calvin.

Reggie knelt.

The preacher launched into a long prayer for those who had come forward in faith, urging others to come, in a long and heartfelt plea that would have melted even a prison warder's heart.

The penitents were each joined by one of the congregation, and then they were led away through a small side door. Reggie was borne along with them and into a cell-like room. He looked round, desperate to escape. There was no window. Reggie backed toward the wall as Brother Calvin locked the door and pocketed the key.

'Don't be afraid, Brother. You're very good. Almost as good as me.' Brother Calvin emptied his own pockets. Three wallets, several pens, Reggie's blood pressure pills and his room key were tumbled onto the table beside a big black Bible.

Reggie stood up, overcome with admiration for Brother Calvin. 'Blimey! I never felt a thing! Where'd you learn to nick like that?'

'Never mind that, Brother?'

'Reggie, Reggie Foster.' He swallowed convulsively. 'It's a fair cop, guv.' That was it, back in the nick and only outside for a week. Bloody stupid, that's what.

'Brother Reginald, I have a proposition for you.'

'A what?'

'Listen.'

Reggie listened, and his jaw dropped in amazement.

Brother Calvin took a note from each of the wallets, and handed them to him, but pocketed the wallets. 'I shall return these to their owners. Now, remember the rules, Reginald, and we shall do very well together.'

Then Brother Calvin unlocked the door, and led him up the stairs into a long hall, where cloth-covered trestle tables were set for a meal. Reggie was handed a plate, and joined a queue beside a serving hatch, where his plate was loaded with meat, vegetables and gravy. He was guided to a table where Brother Calvin sat at the head. Reggie sat beside him, suppressing feelings of confusion between a school dining hall and the prison canteen. They were joined at their table by another man, whom Brother Calvin introduced to Reggie as Brother William. When their table was full, Brother Calvin gave thanks. 'Tuck in, Brothers and Sisters, before the food gets cold.'

A grinning Reggie did just that. Whoever said there was no such thing as a free lunch? His fingers felt the notes in his pocket, he was comfortably warm, and he was no longer hungry. Things were definitely looking up; so much so that when Brother Calvin suggested he help with clearing the tables after the meal, it didn't take away the glow he was feeling.

Even when the preacher came to have a quiet word with him, he just answered in the way that Brother Calvin had told him to, though he couldn't bring himself to pray like these folk did, out of thin air.

Brother Adam patted him on the back. 'Bless you, Brother Reginald. This is a truly happy day for you.' He had the perfect voice for a preacher, something like Richard Burton. Every word the man said sounded like a phrase from a poem or Shakespeare.

One Week Later.

Ruth sat in her usual seat for the morning service, her stomach churning. She had eaten a heavy meal and it was weighing like a heavy conscience on her spirits. There was that feeling again, was it a foreboding? She shivered, and tried to ignore the irrational thoughts that were running through her mind. It felt like the shedding of blood.

Matthew watched her from the pew behind; preoccupied by the way the sun caught Ruth's lovely hair into a halo of light. Even that severe hat she wore could not entirely eclipse it... 'A woman's crowning glory.' At her slender throat was the white cotton scarf he had given her. There were dark circles under her eyes again; he hoped she hadn't been working too hard at the hospital. A hymn was announced, and the young man brought himself back to spiritual things with an effort of will.

Ollie knew suddenly that he had had enough of all these people, who were so sure of themselves, so very clean, and so smug, sitting in their neat little rows singing. Why should they sing? The whole world was full of bad things. They were watching him, he was sure of it. That one at the front, he looks just like that trick cyclist from the hospital: him that always treats me as if I were a maggot. It was clever to get away. It was so easy, they think I'm stupid. It's a good thing to let them think that. Then you get to hear things.

I must find the man. He is the most important, then the others, if I can. I have to punish him. The voice said I must.

I don't like this. They are taking people away, out of the side door. Why? Where are they taking them? Perhaps they are taking them to the hospital? I don't want to go back to the hospital. They make me take pills and sleep all the time. I want to see mother. Not that other one, she likes her new ones more than me. When she got them she didn't want me any more. What are they doing to those people they take out the back? What are they going to do to me? Ollie felt the panic start at his feet, trembling its way up until he could only rock to and fro in his seat.

The woman beside him put a comforting hand on his arm. Ollie shrugged it off and screamed, 'No, I won't go back! You can't make me!'

Suddenly, all those faces turned together, the sea of eyes were all staring at him. They wanted to hurt, Ollie knew that, had expected it. That's why he had the knife, to protect himself.

He took it out and held it up so they could see. 'Leave me alone or I'll use this!'

The woman had gone from the seat beside him. Ollie stepped carefully into the aisle, began to walk to the front of the church. He had to find out where they were taking these people. Then somebody stood in his way. He ignored him. The voice said, 'This one!'

Ollie felt the knife move in his hand; it was alive, it sang to him of blood. He obeyed the voice. He looked for the others. He saw one, and struck again. Then he could smell the blood, and terrible fear all around him. He struck out at every one of those faces, those plump bodies, watching the red blood blossom behind the knife.

Ruth felt her father move, and before she could grasp his arm to hold him back, he was sprinting down the aisle toward the man with the dripping knife.

'Dad, no! Don't!' But her father was gone.

Ollie was standing by an empty pew.

'Give me the knife, young man,' Ben Diamond said.

Ollie hesitated. He knew this man from somewhere. A bright room long ago where there had been singing? Yes, that was it, the photograph. He was one the voice had said must die.

'Give me the knife, son, you don't need it anymore. You're quite safe here.'

Ruth ran softly along the now empty pew to her right, then toward the pulpit, where Adam was standing mesmerised by what was happening. She ran across the front of the church, her footsteps sounding hollow as she moved over the concealed baptistery beneath. She was behind the man. Her father gave no sign that he had seen her.

Ollie looked at the man, and almost gave the knife to him; he seemed so calm, his eyes were gentle, like still pools of water. Then the voice spoke again, 'This is the true enemy!' He felt a terrible rage shooting up through his body, into his arm, and along to the knife. He moved quickly toward the man, the knife raised.

At the same instant, Ruth launched herself at the man, aiming for the knees since her light weight would have little effect. But she was just too late.

Ruth heard the soft noise as the knife struck her father. It seemed to be such a long drawn out sound for so short an action. Ruth's momentum carried her forward, the man saw her, slashed at her arm, and then the man tumbled to the floor with the impact of Ruth's body. He dropped the knife as he fell, and her father kicked it away with a force that impaled it in the wood of a pew further down. In seconds, the man was overpowered.

Ruth crawled toward her father. Bright red blood was seeping from his shirt. With shaking fingers, wishing she could wake from this nightmare, Ruth tore the shirt open, swallowing hard at the sight of the terrible gash and the amount of blood that was pouring from it.

'Steady, that's my Sunday best,' her father smiled.

'Don't talk,' she said, wrenching the white scarf from her neck and folding it into a thick pad to press against the wound.

'Ruthie, you're a brave girl,' he grimaced as she put pressure on the wound. 'Where's your mother?'

'She went into the counselling room with the lady in the checked coat.' To Ruth, it seemed to have happened in another life.

'Tell her I love her.'

'Don't be silly. You can tell her yourself.' Ruth looked down at her hand. It was already covered with his blood.

Ruth heard the familiar sound of an ambulance siren approaching.

'Thank God. They've got here quickly.'

'Brother Adam, could you help that woman there? Put something against the wound to stop the bleeding?'

'I phoned from the vestry.' Brother Adam seemed not to have heard her, but, thankfully, somebody else had. Adam looked down at the blood seeping through Ruth's scarf, and passed out cold.

David Davies was uneasy as he drove his ambulance toward the little chapel on the outskirts of the town. First, he'd been two moves from checkmate against Willey Foley, his co-worker, when the call had come in. Second, he would be breaking a thirty-year-old promise the minute he stepped through that Chapel door. Lastly, there was the death of his young Morgan to consider. Never did believe it was a virus, and never would. With any luck it would turn out to be a hoax.

'It looks the business, Davy; there are two police cars outside already.'

'There's Tessa's ambulance coming over the roundabout too,' Davy added.

Willy and Davy unclipped their seat belts as they came to a halt, and dropped quickly to the pavement. A few moments later they were ready with a stretcher and their bags. A woman beckoned them, and they followed her into the chapel.

Willy and Davy stepped through the chapel door from an ordinary Sunday morning into a nightmare that would haunt them both for the rest of their lives. There was blood everywhere, splashed over the pews and the pale lemon walls. He'd seen blood before, of course, plenty of it. It was the place and the silence that seemed to make it worse. Chapels should be safe places. Two police constables were kneeling beside a woman, giving her CPR.

The two paramedics glanced round, their first question always; whose need is most urgent? But this time Davy found himself glancing behind. Where was the lunatic who'd done all this? He shook the question away, and knelt beside a young woman kneeling in the aisle, holding a very bloody cloth to a chest wound.

'Let me have a look, young lady,' Davy said, aware of more paramedics coming in, 'who is the patient?' He winced inwardly when he saw the depth and positioning of the wound, caught Willy's eye as they swung into action.

Ruth sat back on the floor with her back against the end of a pew. 'He's my father, Benjamin Diamond. He tried to stop the man with the knife.' She lifted her hand to push back her lovely hair, and the second paramedic noticed that her arm was bleeding at the same moment that she seemed to notice it herself. He unwrapped a large dressing with a flick of the wrist, and had rolled it round her arm and taped it firmly into place before she had time to register the depth of the cut.

'That'll stop the bleeding until you can get it stitched,' he said, in a cockney twang.

Ruth read his name badge, and said, 'Thank you, Mr Foley.'

'Willy. What about the man behind you, love?'

'Adam Crouch, our Minister. He fainted when he saw the blood.'

'Must be a Pisces,' Willy grunted, feeling for a pulse. 'Nice strong heartbeat. He'll wait.'

'Will, we need to get a line in fast; this man's lost a lot of blood.'

'Right.'

Ruth watched them work. It was so very different when it was someone you loved being treated; so very much worse. She was stirred into action as Davy spoke to her.

'Hold this, love; just keep it raised while we move your father onto the stretcher.'

Ruth held the bottle of liquid as her father was moved. The side door was swinging open; someone must have gone to tell those in the counselling rooms what had happened. She saw her mother stumble into the church as the men lifted the stretcher. Ruth unconsciously ground her teeth as she beckoned her mother to follow the stretcher to the ambulance.

Her mother said nothing until they were in the ambulance, aware of the emergency siren and the speed at which they were moving. The paramedic was attaching equipment, monitoring, constantly on the alert for any change in his patient.

'Tell me what happened, Ruth.' Her mother was holding one of dad's enormous hands. The fluid drip bottle swayed unevenly as the ambulance sped over the bumpy roads.

Ruth grabbed a handhold to steady herself. 'There was this man,' her voice cracked as she tried to speak. She took a deep breath before continuing, 'This man, with a knife, suddenly screamed and started stabbing people. Dad went to stop him, asked him for the knife. I tried to stop him, but he took no notice of me.' The smell of antiseptic was making her feel sick.

'He wouldn't.' Miriam pursed her lips.

'So I ran round behind them. Tried to stop the man as he went for dad.'

'What on earth possessed you? That was a very dangerous thing to do.'

'I had to try,' Ruth's voice was low, apologetic.

'There's nothing of you – how did you think you'd have the strength to take on a grown man?'

Was that anger or derision in her voice, Ruth wondered?

'She brought him crashing to the floor, in spite of her light weight.' Ben Diamond had opened his eyes.

A weird dancing of lights and shadows behind Ruth's eyes made his pallor seem more intense.

Willy Foley was watching the monitor anxiously. 'Don't talk, and just lie quiet until we can patch you up, sir.' He was standing feet apart, to keep his balance.

'You can't keep a preacher quiet long.' Ben tried a smile.

'Someone's had a good try, sir.'

It was odd, Ruth thought, how people always seemed to call her father 'sir'.

Raymond Le Measurer straightened his tie, watching the auto cue carefully. The 'on air' sign flashed and he began. 'Good afternoon. Here is some breaking news. This morning a man was arrested following an incident at The True Gospel Church in Watery Street, Salisbury. Several people were taken to hospital after the disturbance in which a man is believed to have run amok with a knife during morning service. Dominick Draper is at the scene. Dominick, can you hear me?'

'Yes, Raymond, I am here, outside this normally peaceful chapel, where at least one member of the congregation is believed to have been killed, and several others injured, one seriously. It is thought that their attacker was a man who absconded in the early hours of this morning from a secure psychiatric unit at Betterstone, a mile from here. I have with me now the Minister of the True Gospel Church, the Reverend Adam Crouch, whose uncle, Benjamin Diamond, was among those injured.'

The camera panned to the left to reveal a handsome blond-haired man wearing a cassock and dog collar.

'Reverend, what is your immediate reaction to the attack on your congregation this morning?'

'Of course we are all deeply shocked and distressed by this unfortunate incident. But while our hearts go out in love and in prayer to those injured and their families and friends, we must also reach out in love and understanding to the young man who felt driven to commit this dreadful act.'

'Where were you when the attack took place?'

'I was in the pulpit. At first, it just seemed as though someone was taking exception to my sermon, but when I glanced up and saw the knife, I realised that it was a potentially dangerous situation. Before anyone could prevent him the man ran down the aisle toward the front of the church, stabbing at anyone in his way. My uncle, Benjamin Diamond, very bravely approached him, and tried to persuade him to hand over the knife. My cousin Ruth, his daughter, also tried to help. Unfortunately they were both hurt, Benjamin seriously, and another was killed, but we are waiting to inform his family before releasing his name. I ran to the vestry and phoned for the police and an ambulance immediately.'

'Will you be cancelling services until further notice?'

'No, we will not. Although we cannot use the church, evening worship will go ahead as usual. We have already arranged for an open air service tonight at the Castle Road football ground, beginning at six-thirty God willing.'

'Thank you, sir. That was the Reverend Adam Crouch, who intends to hold evening service as usual. This is Dominick Draper returning you to the studio.'

The camera panned to the cleric standing solemnly beside the notice board; the service times showed distinctly in large black letters. Below, a large text in bright red proclaimed:

'Without the shedding of blood, there is no remission of sins.' The reference was below camera height.

Adam pressed the remote to switch the set to standby. It had been an exception to their usual Sunday rule, but they felt it necessary in the circumstances.

'There will be a lot of people there tonight, Brother.' Calvin's eyes glittered in the dark room.

'Yes, I must prepare well; it is a God-planned opportunity to reach the lost.'

'I must get ready too. What time are the vans due with the folding chairs at the ground?'

'In an hour; Brother Matthew is organising the sound system, and the full choir is to turn out. I do pray that Sister Ruth will still be able to sing.'

'I shall ask her. It is important that the service is the best we can offer to the Lord.'

'Amen, Brother, Amen.'

## Chapter 7

Sunday 8<sup>th</sup> March

Ruth sat in the waiting room, a plastic cup clutched between her fingers; the coffee inside it had cooled long ago. The dressing on her arm smelt clinical. The wound had begun to throb but she was hardly aware of the pain. If only she'd been quicker. If only she'd been stronger. But God's will was right. So why would it be right for her father to die? What good would that be in the scheme of things? Ruth's grip on the cup tightened fractionally, and the plastic split suddenly, spilling the oily liquid over her hand and onto her coat.

'Do be careful, Ruth!'

Her mother's sharp tone and the small sound of cracking plastic roused Ruth from her blasphemous thoughts. *Serves me right* she thought. Ruth put the cup onto the floor, where a pool of brown grew round it like a lake round a tower. She mopped her coat with a few tissues, and then went to find something to clear away the mess.

Back in her seat, she remembered how excited her father had been at his retirement dinner.

She could still see it, hear the words:

'With the proceeds from the sale of my business, I intend to establish a foundation to educate young people from deprived areas, to help them through college or university. I intend to set up a nationwide youth scheme and to put in place workshops where these young men and women can gain useful skills: such as car maintenance, computer skills or catering, in the evenings and at weekends. This should keep them off the streets, away from the dangers of drink and drugs. I also intend to set up several drugs rehabilitation units throughout the country.'

A man had stood up at this point, and said, 'I thought you were retiring, sir?' The room had filled with laughter at this point; Ben Diamond was a workaholic.

When the laughter had subsided, her father had continued. 'Not being entirely selfless, I would like to see the Holy Land; something I have been too busy to do until now.

'I would also like to announce that 'The Retreat' is fully operational now, I've, I mean the church, has bought the Manor House, the Old School and the adjoining Matrimony Farm. The tithe barn is to be our place of worship.'

Another man stood at this point. 'Mr Diamond, could you describe for me the function of 'The Retreat'?'

Ruth had recognised him as a well-known journalist.

Ben Diamond had smiled broadly. 'Mr Markham, I am glad the *Daily Standard* has taken the trouble to ask me, rather than hazard more guesses in its columns.'

The journalist grinned.

'The establishment of The Retreat is the result of many years' work. There, the plan is to enable those members who wish to do so, to live as part of a community untainted by the modern world and its shoddy values. We shall establish a boarding school for the children of parents who are on missionary service, and for those whose parents wish them to be given a truly Christian education.'

The journalist stood again. 'Are you saying that children are not being taught the basics of their faith within the state system?'

'No, they are being given facts about world religions. They are not being taught the truths of their own faith.'

The journalist stood up again, but everyone in the room was suddenly on their feet and applauding. Ruth had watched her father raise his hand for silence.

'Friends, I don't need your applause. What I would ask is your help and your prayers, only then can we achieve anything in God's name. I'm always aware of the fact that "Unto whom much is given, much shall be required".'

Then he had led a room full of hard-nosed businessmen in prayer.

A trolley bounced past the open door and it was with an effort that Ruth became aware of the hospital waiting room. It didn't make any sense for her father to be injured at this point when he was doing so much for the Lord. But she would have to wait and see what God had in mind through these things.

Her mother sat beside her, hands folded, and head bowed in prayer. Ruth knew that attitude. Miriam could maintain that stance through a three-hour prayer meeting without wavering or falling asleep.

Ruth looked up and saw her father standing in front of her. For a moment, she didn't think anything of it, except that a feeling of intense joy came to her as he bent to kiss her hair. Then he was gone.

Miriam looked up at the same moment and saw the familiar shape of her husband as he bent to kiss his daughter's hair. His dark brown eyes gazed into hers; Miriam began to speak his name, but he vanished. There was only a doctor walking toward them.

'Mrs Diamond?'

'Yes, Doctor?'

'We did all we could, but I'm afraid we lost the battle. Your husband died a few moments ago.' The doctor had seen many people faced by similar news in this drab room, but never before had he seen a reaction like Miriam Diamond's in all his years of casualty work.

She simply sat and bowed her head, silently.

The daughter stood immobile. The doctor suddenly recognised her; he had never seen her out of uniform before.

'Nurse Diamond?'

'Dr Ferguson. Thank you. Can you tell us when my father is ready for us to see him?'

'I'm so terribly sorry, I didn't realise it was your father.'

'There's no reason why you should.' Ruth sat, suddenly feeling light-headed.

Dr Ferguson's bleeper sounded, and he hurried back into the corridor.

After a few minutes, Miriam Diamond stood up. Ruth followed her to where Dr Ferguson was replacing a telephone on a wall mount.

'May I see my husband's body now?'

Her calm was astonishing, thought the doctor, as he led the two women to the door of the crash room. 'Would you like a nurse to stay with you?'

'No thank you. That won't be necessary.'

Ben Diamond didn't look any different from usual. But he would never have been able to lie so still in life.

Ruth stared at the body of the man that she'd loved so much. But he wasn't here. 'He said to tell you that he loved you.' Her voice was unnaturally loud in the uncarpeted room.

'I knew that,' Miriam said softly. 'I knew that.'

Brother Robin was waiting in the foyer to meet them when Miriam and Ruth left the hospital. Motioning them to silence, he guided them through the crowded entrance to where he'd left his car in the car park, and when they were seated, he spoke.

'Brother Benjamin has been taken home?'

To an outsider, this might have sounded as though Benjamin would be waiting for them back at The Retreat.

'He is with his Saviour,' Miriam said quietly.

'We must give thanks to Him for His gracious and boundless mercy.'

The three of them bowed their heads where they were in the car, to the consternation of the parking attendant, who was in the process of checking the ticket displayed on the windscreen. After the prayer, Brother Robin drove them to The Retreat, where they were offered a meal, which neither of them was able to eat. It was a relief when Ruth was called to the choir rehearsal soon afterward. With an empty heart, Ruth pulled on the heavy blue choir gown and joined the choir in the main hall. To show excessive grief would be a poor witness. She must be strong.

It was not often the church had television advertisements for its events, but that was the effect of the news item; the football ground where they were to hold the evening service was crowded to capacity.

Ruth climbed the narrow steps of the stand. She concealed herself in a corner, wrapping her cloak round her for warmth, though she thought she would never be warm again. There, in the shadow, she gave herself up to the misery of her loss. Here, unobserved, she wept soundlessly into her sleeve while the orchestra played. The choir filled the stand to overflowing, and they sat in ranks in front, on the pitch as well. The crowd's faces shifted like pebbles on a beach as the Minister approached the staging where a pulpit had been installed. He lifted his hand, a hush fell over the crowd and it became a congregation. Adam leaned toward the microphone.

'Brothers and Sisters, we gather together tonight to share the wonderful news of the Gospel. We will also remember those who have been called home to their Lord today: Brother Benjamin Diamond, Brother Harold James and Sister Hope Briggs. Let us rejoice with them, they have run a good race, they have kept the faith.'

There were shouts of 'Amen!' and 'Praise the Lord!' from the crowd.

Adam held up his hand, and signalled to the choir, who stood in one movement. They sang:
'Safe in the arms of Jesus,
Safe on his gentle breast
There by his love o'er shadowed
Sweetly my soul shall rest.'

The service continued, and Ruth sang the words although her mouth felt full of sand, hot and dry. The sermon was delivered in that musical and hypnotic voice, and people streamed to the front for counselling. They were led to a group of marquees that had sprung up on the tennis courts and the playing field. Ruth watched the crowds idly, for once not paying any attention to the preacher. What were Brother Calvin and Brother Reginald doing among the crowds? They seemed to be working their way along the rows of people. Then she was summoned to the front. They wanted her to sing. She protested, but in vain. Ruth had the best soprano voice they had; and she must sing to the glory of the Lord.

*Even on the very day when my father has been murdered?* Ruth thought, and was shocked by her sudden self-will. So she stood there for a moment, feeling her anger begin to burn until the conductor signalled for her to sing. I shall sing, she thought, but not for you. I shall sing for my father; his favourite hymn, to the music of the Londonderry Air. She ignored the chord the orchestra gave her, and launched into a different hymn.

'I cannot tell why he whom angels worship
Should set his love upon the sons of men
Or why as Shepherd He should seek the wanderers
To bring them back, they know not how or when...'

Ruth sang unaccompanied, with tears in her voice, as she had never sung before. Her voice soared among the crowd, and her tears were reflected in hundreds of eyes and felt in hundreds of hearts. When the hymn was finished, there was a long pause, and the congregation erupted into sudden and spontaneous applause. Not in all her years of singing at services had this happened to Ruth, and she stood stunned, amazed. What would Brother Adam say? Applause? At a service? Unthinkable!

But Brother Adam simply bowed his head and waited. When there was silence, he said, 'Thank you and God bless you especially for singing for us this evening Sister Ruth. For those of you who don't know, it was Ruth's father, Brother Benjamin, who was taken to be with His Saviour this afternoon.' The hush that fell over the stadium at that point was eerie in its intensity. Brother Adam began to pray, and people streamed down to the centre of the pitch where there was a makeshift penitent's bench. Hundreds of them, a thousand? Ruth could not believe it as she sang the hymns that followed each prayer in a long cycle. At last there were no more penitents, and Brother Adam led them in a closing prayer.

But still it was not over, as the congregation began to sing, the choir took up the strains, and the sound was glorious, swelling, reverberating, even the ground seemed to tremble beneath their feet. It was well past midnight when they dispersed, still singing as they went, even though it had begun to rain.

Ruth sat on the edge of the staging, watching the stadium empty. Her mother was talking to several people she had taken to the counselling tent. How could she just go on, as if nothing has happened? As if nothing had changed when everything had changed? Ruth's fingers clutched the rough wood of the edge of the staging. I should be able to do it, but I can't. I can't go on with it without dad. Before she was aware of her own movement, she was on her feet and running over the grass toward the fence, where she scrambled over as she had often done as a child, but less easily in the heavy choir gown.

Out into the lane, through the rain-wet streets to the church she ran. Avoiding the police cordon, she went around the back of the building where the dustbins and the central heating oil containers made a heady mix of smells. Set against the wall was a long fire escape. Ruth's feet clanged against the rusting metal as she climbed. The steps were sheltered as they angled to and fro across the side of the church, like an ugly metallic scribble. The seventh flight ended at the parapet.

The cold air at the top slapped her face. Her choir cloak billowed around her as she walked out onto the roof. The stained glass dome was lit from below. There were people still inside, distorted into wild multicoloured shapes by the curved sections of window. It was still magical, even from the wrong side. How often she had helped to clean the glass with her father beside her, then they'd go down the steps to the old kitchens and make hot mugs of soup, or drink cool lemonade up here on hot summer days.

She turned quickly away from the memories. The whole town was visible from here; the cathedral glowed in its floodlights against the dark sky.

'I won't look down, that's all, just won't look down,' she said, over and over like a mantra, to nerve herself. The wind was terrific up here tonight. The sound of it answered the tumult in her head, as she stood there, shaking with sobs.

'Why? Why him? It doesn't make any sense!' A flash of light made her half-turn, but it was only a car parking in the street below. Distracted, she looked down, and her world span out of control. She gripped the stonework to steady herself.

'I shouldn't have come! I should have waited for dad to finish evening service.' Then the pain of the loss hit her again, and she called out in her anguish. He would never come up here again with her.

The parapet was very thin, very easy to climb up. Slip over, and fall into nothingness, into peace. Her hands were chilled by the rough concrete. It was gritty under her fingers. Wet seeped through her coat as she swung her legs over the edge. She heard a sound behind her, turned her head toward it, her hair billowed out by the wind. Then she fell.

# Chapter 8

12.40 a.m. Sunday March 8<sup>th</sup>

Inspector Cooper looked at the bloody scene in front of him. The church was silent except for the forensics team. Even they seemed subdued. The atmosphere of the place had affected them even more than the horrific events earlier that day. He had six men allocated to take statements from all those who had attended the morning service. The rooms to the side of the worship area were slowly emptying; people were going upstairs, where the sounds of cutlery on china and the smell of food made a surreal accompaniment to their grim task. The white forensic suit the inspector was wearing rustled as he moved, counting the pews and drawing a rough sketch of their layout. Under his arm was a floor plan of the church.

A policeman also swathed in coverall suit and gloves came toward him, his attire looking as incongruous as swimwear worn at the Ritz.

'I found these on the seat that the assailant was sitting in, sir.'

'Thanks.'

Cooper took the plastic bag and peered at the contents. Inside were three photographs. He drew in a deep breath.

'Allsopp?'

'Sir?'

'We need to investigate whether there was any connection between the deceased and the man, Oliver Brown. If you could follow that line of enquiry for me, I shall speak to the psychiatrist at Betterstone.'

Joshua waited, pencil in hand, knowing there would be more.

'How are you at church attendance, Allsopp?'

'Not my cup of tea, sir.'

'Nor mine.' There was another pause. 'My granddaughter has joined this church; her mother is very worried about it. I think we'll make a visit to Castle Road stadium tonight.'

'The football stadium, sir?'

'They're holding an open-air evening service there.'

Sunday Afternoon.

Cooper headed through the all-too-familiar Betterstone Psychiatric Hospital grounds. It was a bizarre mix of buildings from different eras; some wards were simply rows of terraced houses knocked together. A few purpose-built modern wards stood out; the admission block was all gleaming floors and UPVC double glazed windows. It overlooked a gloomy two storey locked ward.

Dr Hall was in his consulting room, surrounded by several piles of case notes. He stood up as Cooper came in, holding out a welcoming hand. 'Do sit down, Inspector. May I offer you tea, coffee?'

'No, thank you, Doctor Hall. I mustn't take up too much of your time.' Cooper shook the outstretched hand. 'You work on Sundays normally?'

'I often catch up with case notes at the weekends. But I was expecting you to come as soon as I heard what had happened at the church.'

'Tell me about Oliver Brown.'

'I've written a short summary of his illness and life so far, which should help you. But there's something more about this "escape" that bothers me.'

Cooper leaned forward in his seat. 'What's that, Doctor?'

'He couldn't have escaped by himself. It wouldn't have been possible from the ward he was on.' Dr Hall placed a plastic carrier bag on the desk. 'This was found hanging from the upper window of the secure ward early this morning.'

The bag contained a long rope ladder, rolled up.

'I assure you, Inspector, we don't stock these at the hospital shop.'

'And he didn't have this when he was admitted?'

'If he had, it would have been put into safe keeping. We always list the contents of a patient's suitcase and all their personal effects on admission. Two members of staff are present.'

'So why would someone help a very sick patient to escape from a psychiatric hospital?'

'Whoever did it was very irresponsible. Or did so with malicious intent, Inspector.'

'May I see the ward, and his room?'

'I'll show you myself.'

The ward was brightly painted and clean, but it had that unmistakeable institutional smell: a compound of cooking, close living people and disinfectant. Cooper kept his eyes on the doctor's back, avoiding the gaze of the few patients who were slumped on chairs or pacing the floor.

'Most of our patients are at occupational therapy or the sheltered workshops,' the doctor explained, unlocking a door and leading the way up the stairs. Cooper closed the door behind him and it clicked shut with the finality of a cell door.

The walls of the room were papered with posters. Religious texts, films such as the *Life of Christ*, vied with the *Lord of the Rings*. There was an enormous crucifix over the bed, and there was a monk's habit on the back of the door. Cooper shivered. 'Was this the room he escaped from?'

'No, all these rooms have secure windows. He made it out of the new bathroom window at the end – the security bars haven't been replaced since the renovation.'

Cooper followed him to the bathroom, which turned out to be one of four in the middle of the block. He gazed out of the window, noting the scratch marks on the sill. The ground below was tarmac paving. 'Would he have had much difficulty getting out of the hospital grounds from here?'

'It wouldn't have been all that easy in daylight; the hospital is surrounded by high walls but a fit and active man could have managed it. We think that Oliver escaped very early in the morning while the nurses would have been busy getting the older patients washed and dressed.'

'How many nurses are there on the ward at night?'

'Two, usually.'

Cooper thought about spending a night locked in this ward and shuddered. A prison cell would be preferable. 'May I speak to the nurses involved?'

'Certainly. They may be on duty again tonight – we'll check the rota as we go out, if you've finished here?'

'Yes, thanks.' Cooper longed to be in the fresh air again.

'There's something that Oliver will need.' They returned to Oliver's room, and Dr Hall lifted the pillow. 'I thought as much.' He withdrew a tattered blue nylon cot quilt, and handed it to Inspector Cooper. 'He will miss this as soon as he begins to feel vulnerable or threatened. It will calm him better than drugs.'

Cooper stared at the quilt. It felt light and warm in his hands: incongruous in this setting.

'That reminds the poor bastard of the only time he ever felt safe and loved,' Dr Hall said, turning toward the door.

Cooper put the quilt carefully into the bag on top of the rope ladder. What on earth had possessed the man to leave this behind?

'I need to have a quick look at his things, Doctor Hall.'

The psychiatrist turned. 'Be my guest. I'll be waiting for you in the ward office.'

In Oliver's room, Cooper sat on the bed and gazed intently around. There were no books. There was an expensive radio with combined tape and CD player, some CDs and cassettes. The posters, the crucifix and monk's habit were the only other signs of Oliver's presence. The drawers held clothes, mostly jeans and T-shirts. The small wardrobe held a raincoat and two pairs of dirty trainers lay at the bottom. Cooper was on the point of closing the door when he noticed a small shelf above the clothes rail. There were three tapes pushed to the back. Cooper reached for them. They were blanks for home recording. He put them into an evidence bag, and went to look at the tape holder on the shelf beside the radio. Two more of the same type of tape joined the others in the bag. Cooper went to the window again. The hospital was going about its business as usual. He glanced down at the huge old-fashioned hot water radiator that he had been warming his hands against. There was something stuck to the wall behind the piping.

Cooper's large hands had some difficulty detaching it and holding it up to the light. It looked like a small and very expensive bugging device. What the hell was it doing here?

Cooper waited until Dr Hall had finished his phone call before tapping on the door.

'Inspector, take a seat. Have you finished for this afternoon?'

'Just a couple of questions, Doctor Hall.' Cooper sat on the uncomfortable looking chair, whose stuffing was bursting out of its red vinyl cover. 'Do you know what this is?' He held out the silvery object from behind the radiator.

Dr Hall took it, frowning in puzzlement. 'Never seen anything like it in my life. Where did it come from?'

'Behind the radiator in Oliver's room.' Cooper put the disc back into its plastic bag. 'Secondly, would you have expected Oliver to be violent?'

The doctor swung round on his chair. 'If you had asked me that yesterday, Inspector, I would have said no. The only thing that would make him violent is if he were frightened. The one time he was violent cost him his home.'

'How was that?'

'His twin sisters were crying one night, and his parents only rescued the babies in the nick of time. He was throwing things at them.'

Someone was clattering crockery in the ward kitchen behind them.

'Surely that was childish ignorance and jealousy?'

'Oliver was diagnosed as autistic before his sisters were born. He was taken into care because his parents were afraid of what he might do next time. With the right home environment, there might have been some improvement, but not in the so-called care system. He didn't have a chance.' Dr Hall sighed. 'His being in hospital was more a case of Oliver being protected from the world, rather than the world being protected from Oliver.'

A large woman in a flowered apron tapped the door. 'Tea, Doctor?'

'Yes please, Gladys. Would you like a cup, Inspector?'

Cooper looked at the enormous grey metal teapot, the huge white jug of milk and the pile of pale green cups. 'No, thanks, Doctor, I must get on. Thanks for your help.'

Outside again, Cooper walked through the hospital grounds, wrestling with his conscience. It won. The women's ward was shaded by a row of copper beech trees. Lillian was quiet today, looking up at her visitor with mild interest. Cooper placed the packet of drawing paper and pencils on her lap. They were opened with a cry of pleasure. She began to sketch with them immediately. He did not look back as he closed the door. The woman in that room was not the woman who had been his wife.

As Cooper made his way toward the entrance, he caught sight of Dr Hall coming towards him.

'Inspector, I'm glad I caught you. Just one thing I thought you might be interested in. I've just spoken to the man whose room's next to Oliver's. I thought nothing of it the first couple of times he mentioned it, but in view of what's happened I think you ought to know. He says, *"I wouldn't like to have Oliver's voices. They are far worse than mine."* So I asked him why they were worse. The answer was, *"Because I can hear them right through the bedroom wall, Doctor, and they are evil".*'

'Thank you, Doctor, is there any chance there might have been someone in the room with Oliver?'

'No, Inspector. Oliver has few visitors – his father comes sometimes, but they always go to the hospital canteen for a cup of tea together.'

'Can I speak to this man?'

'He's gone to the Sunday film – he'll be a couple of hours in there.'

'I'll leave it then. Thank you Doctor.

5 p.m. Sunday 8th March.

The prisoner had begun to throw things around the cell. His shouting and banging could be heard from the front desk. Sergeant Sam Barry was worried; the man was violent; and he had a duty to his staff not to put them in any unnecessary danger. But his duty to the prisoner was to prevent him injuring himself.

As he hesitated outside the cell, he heard a familiar footfall behind him. 'Inspector, we've got a real problem here.'

'I may have the answer.' Cooper produced the quilt, and placed it in the sergeant's enormous hands.

'This, sir?'

'So the psychiatrist tells me.'

Sam put the quilt on the sliding hatch, opened it and pushed it through. At the sound, Oliver turned, and a look of relief crossed his face. Slowly, he crossed to the door, and cuddled the quilt to his face.

Cooper spoke to him, 'Oliver, Jesus says it is time to rest now, and after that he wants you to tidy the room for him.'

Sam watched in amazement as the man curled up on the bed, with the quilt against his chest and face. 'Well I never did!'

'Comes to something when all you've got is a cot quilt,' Cooper said. 'Was there anything interesting in his pockets?'

Sam's face lightened. 'Yes, sir, some photographs. Come and see; I left them on your desk.'

The photographs were crumpled and torn, but still recognisable. They were of one of those killed at the church, Benjamin Diamond. There was also one of the front entrance of the True Gospel Church, showing a giant scripture text.

'Now where the blazes did he get these, and why was he carrying them?' Cooper placed the photos found at the church on the table beside them as Josh Allsopp came into the room.

Josh looked at the pictures.

'These were in Oliver Brown's pocket,' Cooper told him.

'Oliver Brown went to Sunday School at the True Gospel Church,' Josh said. 'He was in Ben Diamond's class.'

'Any links with the other injured or dead that you've been able to trace?'

'The only thing they seemed to have in common was the church, sir.'

'We'll need fingerprints off these pictures, Barry, if you'd take them to forensics for me.'

6. 15 p.m. Castle Road Football Stadium

Cooper stood, as usual, observing. Sometimes he felt as though he was also observing himself: his reactions, from a distance of thought. The size of the crowd worried him somewhat, and he had called for some additional police presence among such a gathering. For a moment, he thought he recognised a prison-grey face among the shifting shapes in the crowd, but couldn't be sure.

Reggie Foster almost dropped the wallet he had between his fingers when he caught sight of the inspector. He stood still in front of an enormous woman in a floral tent of a dress until his panic subsided. Then he calmly returned the wallet to its owner, minus a crisp note, confident that he'd be difficult to nail down in such a crowd.

Paul Markham sat uneasily at the front of the crowd. The man in the wheelchair beside him sat very still.

'Are you okay, Dan?'

'I think so. It's just – it brings back too many memories. Mother's over there, and Ruthie's in the choir.'

Paul scanned the massed choir, but couldn't see Ruth among them.

'They surely don't expect her to sing, tonight of all nights?'

'Do you want to bet on it?'

Joshua Allsopp was an unhappy man. His wife Alicia was due to give birth any day. He wanted to be there, with her, where his real world began and ended. He tried to concentrate, to think like a policeman. What could the inspector expect to find out here? His mind went back to the church building, the marked outlines of the places that bodies had fallen, the witness statements he had taken. There was a lot of paperwork waiting to be done. But Cooper seemed absorbed by the proceedings, making notes as he watched.

Then the girl began to sing, and Josh was suddenly aching with the beauty and the sadness of her singing. It mesmerised him, drew him to itself, the melody wakening a longing to know what lay behind the loveliness of her song. Never had he heard such music; lamenting and pleading for him to come, now was the time. He began to go forward, but Cooper put a hand on his arm.

'Steady, Josh.'

If it hadn't been the inspector, he would have shaken his arm free of the restraint, answered that call. Josh shook his head for a moment, as if waking from a dream and then found himself blushing.

'Don't worry about it. Listen, Allsopp, I need you to go down there, but be aware of what's happening, use your eyes and ears. Report back to me at the car. You won't find me in this crowd.'

'Yes, sir.' Josh tried to remember how he had felt a moment ago, but it had evaporated like steam into the air. He made his way carefully to the front, wide-eyed and perceptive, to where hundreds of figures were kneeling. As soon as some were led to the marquees, they were replaced by more from the crowd.

Cooper watched, and then detached himself from the crowd as the singing and the prayers continued, heading toward the exit. 'Must get out before the end or it'll take an age to get back to the station,' he told himself.

As he approached the Castle Road exit, a man stopped him. 'Inspector Cooper?'

'Yes. Can I help you?'

'I think I can help you.' The man held up a large supermarket carrier bag; inside was a bulging folder, its ghastly pink cover beginning to tear under the pressure of its contents. 'Here are all my cuttings and all the information I've gathered about the True Gospel Church over some years. They might help you in your investigations.'

'Thank you, Mr?'

'I'm Alan Bleakman, headmaster of St Mark's School and this is my colleague, James Linton, who's head of English.'

'I see.' A memory of a girl with lovely auburn curls surfaced. She had married a Linton. Cooper focussed on the man in front of him: 'I remember Adam Crouch was a pupil of yours.'

'More a pupil of the True Gospel Church.'

'You had considerable trouble with his father, Saul Crouch.'

'You have a remarkable memory, Inspector.'

The crowd behind them began to sing.

'If you need me at any time, my card's inside the file.' Alan Bleakman began to walk away. His friend looked at the policeman for a moment, as though asking himself a question, and then he followed the headmaster through the gates. Cooper took the file to the car and sat in the passenger seat, beginning to read its contents systematically. Some time later, an exhausted looking DS Allsopp flopped into the driver's seat beside him.

'Anything useful?' Cooper enquired.

'There's a group of ex-cons among the church membership – Reggie Foster, Willy Smith, Rickie Murgatroyd and his brother Mick.'

'Turned over new leaves, have they?'

'They certainly looked the part. I've been given the times of induction classes at the church; it seems there are to be several groups running concurrently. Do you want me to go to them?'

'Yes, I'd like someone on the inside, so to speak. Give me your impressions. You'll need to read this file too.'

'That's not one of ours.'

'No, I was given it by the headmaster of St Mark's school a short while ago. It's very interesting. The preacher, Adam Crouch, was a pupil there.'

'So he's a local boy?'

'Yes. In the early days of the True Gospel Church, their youngsters attended state schools. There was a long running battle between the school and the Church. Darwin's theory, Religious instruction, sex education – it was a nightmare for the Local Education Authority. Now the churches run their own schools, but it's not necessarily a good thing. The children don't have any contact with the real world.' Cooper sighed, 'And those that join them are encouraged to separate themselves from the evils of the modern world.' Cooper passed Josh the car keys. 'Even their own families are off limits.'

'It sounds like the Moonies, sir.'

'Far worse than that, Allsopp; far worse. But let's get you home. Your lovely wife will be missing you.'

The outside broadcast team packed their things into their van and headed back to the studio. 'That girl has some voice,' observed Dominick Draper, as they negotiated the entrance to the studio.

'I've not heard anything like it since Charlotte Church,' one of the cameramen said.

'Did you see old Max Waterman's face? He'll be after her,' the driver said.

'Recording contract? I wonder how the True Gospel Church will view that.' Dominick stretched his long legs as far as the van would allow. 'I could do with a long drink, anyone else coming?'

Paul Markham was worried. Dan had been sitting with his head in his hands ever since Ruth had sung. He parked the wheelchair beside the van, unlocked the door and unfolded the lift. At last, Dan moved, reaching for the control switch that would bring the lift down.

'I wish I could help her, Paul.'

'We both know just how dangerous it can get. It's taken a long time for us to establish our new personas. We mustn't risk everything until we're sure of winning.'

'At least they don't know I'm still here.' A brief smile lit up his handsome features. 'For once, the Joshua Group bungled an assignment.'

'Let's keep it that way as long as possible. It's best you stay dead, old chap.'

# Chapter 9

Sunday night 1 30 a.m.

There were only a few members gathered in the marquee. Brother Adam had taken a full minibus back to the retreat, leaving Brother Calvin and some of his special helpers to do the final clearing-up. When all the chairs were stacked and the litter cleared, they retired to a smaller tent, and with Willy Murgatroyd keeping watch, they emptied their pockets onto a table. Willy's task was taken by Reggie while his takings were added to the pile. The men set to counting, and there was only the sound of their breathing with the chink and rustle of coins and notes.

Brother Calvin stood, his usually dour face flushed and excited. 'The best yet, brothers, the best yet. A twenty pound bonus to each of you tonight.'

There was a general buzz of satisfaction as bundles of notes were passed around.

'But a word to you, Brother Reginald.'

'Yes, guv?'

'Forget the "guv", you have got to blend with the wallpaper. There must be no sudden 'bloodies' or 'buggers'. You mustn't make any slips, or you'll stand out like Eliza Doolittle when she breaks her pearls at the ball. Understand?'

'Yes guv, I mean Brother Calvin.'

'Practise it until you say it in your sleep. That's all, and don't forget, everyone, no boozing at the pub; get a bottle at the off-licence and take it home.'

The group of men dispersed, but Reggie was held back by Brother Calvin's heavy hand on his arm. He pocketed his precious notes quickly.

'Right, Brother Reginald. Have you any outstanding debts?'

'I owe me rent, a few weeks behind; I owed her when I went inside.'

'How much?'

'Hundred and forty.'

'Anything else?'

'Bookies, sixty quid.'

Calvin handed him two hundred pounds. 'Right, go and pay them off as soon as you can. Tomorrow I need you at Fieldstone market, I'm working up there.'

'What? Pay them off? Guv, I haven't had such good pickings in a long time.'

'Brother Calvin to you, Brother Reginald. You'll have more. Pay off these debts. You must look like a reformed character. Stay sober, at least when you're out. Now, pop up to the Chinese and get your supper – Lee will give you a discount if you mention my name.'

'They'll be closed by now.'

'Go to the back door and whistle.'

Reggie grinned, revealing yellow teeth. 'Yes G – I mean, Brother Calvin.'

'And buy yourself a toothbrush, Brother, cleanliness is next to godliness.' Calvin swept the piles of money still on the table into a large cloth bag.

Madge Briggs heard Reggie come in. It was early for him. She had the late night movie on as usual; she didn't sleep well these days. She expected the footsteps to pass and the sound fade as Reggie's feet met the carpet on the stairs. But they stopped outside her door, and he knocked. Never in all the years he'd been lodging with her, between spells inside, had he ever knocked on her door. She'd thumped on his a few times when the rent arrears got too much. Blood out of a stone it was with Reggie. What on earth could be wrong? She opened the door, keeping the chain on, just in case.

He was looking unusually smart. He took an envelope from his pocket, and his dog-eared rent book. 'I've come to pay me rent, Madge.'

Her jaw dropped. 'A couple of weeks off then, is it?' she asked, cautiously.

'Nah, the lot, and a fiver for interest,' Reggie said, beginning to enjoy himself.

Madge took the rent book and the envelope through the narrow gap that the chain allowed and opened the envelope. She was surely dreaming. Her fingers lifted out the thick wad of notes and held them up to the light. They were real all right. Best ask no questions though. With the ease of long practice at the bingo hall ticket office, she counted the notes.

Reggie watched her reflection in the mirror, and couldn't resist another grin.

Madge made up the book to show nothing owing, and brought it back to the door.

Reggie examined the book with satisfaction, 'Looks good, that "paid to date".' He turned toward the stairs, but paused. 'By the way, could you get my water heater fixed for me? It'd be nice to 'ave a bath.'

Madge stared at him. That boiler had been broken for years. 'Why, yeah, I'll get Johnny onto it in the morning.' Madge watched him climb the stairs. It wasn't only the rent and the sudden interest in bathing. He had a tube of toothpaste and a new toothbrush sticking out of his pocket. Reggie whistled a tune as he rounded the corner of the stairs. That tune – she'd heard it before, a long time ago, in Sunday School.

Ruth lay on the wet roof looking up into Matthew's anxious face.

'What on earth were you thinking of, climbing onto the parapet like that?'

Ruth couldn't answer. The wind that had blown her light frame back onto the church roof had been like a giant hand pushing her back towards life. God didn't want her to die yet; that was clear. She was shaking; her body felt colder than she had ever known it possible to be.

Matthew looked down at her dark eyes, startling in her chalk white face, her lips blue with cold.

'Come on Ruthie, you must stand up.'

She staggered obediently to her feet, but they began to slip on the treacherous surface of the roofing. He lifted her then, and began to carry her. He balked at the thought of all those steps to negotiate, but one look at Ruth's ghostly face told him that it was the only way. It seemed like climbing down Everest in the dark. Although she was not that heavy, he was staggering under her weight by the time he reached his car. He could feel her shivering convulsively in his arms, and wished he had something hot to give her. He rested her feet on the ground as he opened the car door and sat her in the front seat. Once he had her settled, he sat in the driver's side, switched on the engine and put the heater on full blast before driving away.

Matthew glanced at her anxiously; she was so very still, her breathing soft as a child's. Then he thought of how light her body was, and began to worry again. Did she realise that she looked as thin as an anorexic? The question brought a sudden pain to his chest, just as when his grandfather had died. If that was the reason, she needed help. Maybe she was ill in another way? I'm worrying without reason, he told himself, she's always been thin. He pulled up outside The Retreat, and looked at her beautiful face at rest in sleep. But there were hollows forming in her cheeks where there should be healthy flesh. How he longed to kiss those full lips. But this was not the time.

Ruth had watched him as he drove, idly wondering where he was taking her. The heat was like a balm on her face and hands. She closed her eyes, and drifted into a half-sleep.

She woke when the engine was switched off, and looked round in confusion.

'It's all right, you're with me.' Matthew's voice brought back the memory of the church roof and the sudden impulse that had almost ended everything.

'I'm sorry, Matt; I didn't mean to frighten you.'

'I'll live. But what possessed you to go up there? Heights have never been your thing.'

'I used to go there with my father. He loved the view from up there.' Ruth's self-control was such that, although she was crying, she held her voice steady.

'I can't believe it's happened. It seems like an incident I saw on the news, rather than something that's happened to us,' he said.

'Up there. Just for a moment, I meant to jump. Away from those images that keep appearing every time I close my eyes. I hadn't thought it through. It was the height, it sort of pulled me.'

Matthew felt helpless; the usual trite words that sprang so easily to the lips when it was someone you didn't know were useless to him now. Ben Diamond was as true and good as his name. It would have been better had it been a certain other Crouch. Matthew recoiled from his own bitter thought; how could he have wished such a death on anyone?

Ruth looked round at him, her eyes over large in her pale thin face. 'It felt as though a giant hand was pushing me back onto the roof.'

'Thank God it did.' Matthew leaned across and put his arms around her. 'I can't offer you any comfort, darling, save that I'm here should you need me.' The word was out before he could censor it.

'Matthew?' She looked up, her eyes puffy from crying.

'I'm sorry – it just slipped out. Forget it.'

Ruth put her hands on his cheeks, turning his face towards her own. Under that open gaze, Matthew felt suddenly light-headed. She raised her lips to his, and he lowered his head towards hers until their lips met. Time seemed suspended for those moments. Then she was crying in his arms as though the world had ended.

When her sobbing had subsided, he lifted her face to his and kissed her again, tasting the salt of her tears on his lips. 'Come on, you need something more than kisses to warm you.' He helped her out of the car and into The Retreat. The kitchens were deserted, but there was some soup left in a large pot in the fridge.

'I can't eat anything. Not now.'

'No such thing as can't.' He heated some and set the steaming bowl in front of her. 'Eat.'

She bowed her head in a silent grace, and then lifted the spoon slowly, as if she'd forgotten how to feed herself. The bowl was only half eaten when she put the spoon down. 'That's enough.'

'When did you last eat?'

'Breakfast.'

'And that was?'

'About six, I think.'

'I bet it wasn't a full English one either.'

'Half a grapefruit and some coffee.'

'In that case, you finish that bowl of soup, sweetheart. There's no point in wasting it, is there?'

'I shall probably be sick if I force it down.' It was Ruth's turn to regret words slipping past the censor. On any other day it would never have been said.

'Tell me.' Matthew's expression was not, as she'd imagined, one of disgust.

'It began with mother making me eat everything on my plate, even when I wasn't hungry, or not well. It was soon after Daniel... Then it would just happen, I couldn't keep it down. Now I have a job keeping food down.'

Matthew looked at her, and he could imagine the loveless meals taken with Miriam. He thought carefully about the problem before speaking. 'Never mind about the rest of the soup. I'll finish it for you, and you must go to bed.'

'Thanks. But I must do my evening meditation and prayer before I go up.'

Matthew looked at the dark circles under those lovely eyes, and thought of the hour-long ritual. 'No, I don't think so. Bed is the best thing for you just now. And don't set the alarm for early prayers either.'

'But I ought to.'

'Ruth, darling, go to bed, now!'

She came to him like a child needing comfort, and he held her close. 'Goodnight. I shall keep a double prayer and meditation for us both,' he said, as she climbed the great staircase. He went to the chapel and stayed there for a long time. He came out as confused as he had been when he went in.

Miriam moved out of the shadows at the back of the church and slipped out of a different door.

2 a.m.

Cooper had been working late on some paperwork in order to clear his desk. Then he began a new flip chart. The cover title was in red felt tip; True Gospel Church – Murders?

He wrote in the names of the victims, and coloured in a red link between Ben Diamond and Oliver Brown. Ben Diamond, Hope Briggs and Harold James had all been involved with church finances; linked in green; Treasurer, Assistant Treasurer and Accountant. Other people whose names appeared on his chart would have been surprised to see their names on there at all. From time to time, Cooper referred to the file that Bleakman had given him. A list of those who had died at the True Gospel Church service, those at the College and yet others linked with the church who had died suddenly.

Morgan Davies, Becky Elliot, Lee Fong, David Garnet, John Hammond, Serena Lawrence, Kirin McDonnell, Mary North, Yvonne Parsons, Chan Sung, Michelle Verin, Anatoly Warner, Wayne Mosoto, Katy Smith.

He made a note to look up the post-mortem reports on all these, and then sat looking at his handiwork for a long time. One of the news cuttings led him to begin another list: 'Missing church members.'

Then he wrote the word 'Motive?' at the top of a new sheet.

Power, greed / financial gain, fanatical commitment skews judgement, revenge, or silencing someone, unprovoked attack by mentally disturbed patient.

The file he had himself begun on the True Gospel Church as a young policeman was on the desk; he had not yet reopened it. He pushed it away.

Cooper sat for a few minutes longer, trying to plan his next line of enquiry, but his eyes began to droop. Time to get some sleep.

# Chapter 10

Monday Morning.

Ruth was picking at her breakfast when Calvin sat in a vacant seat opposite her at the long table. He looked so untouched by yesterday's events that Ruth wondered if the man had any real feelings. He seemed a very different man from the boy who had been so bullied at school.

'Sister Ruth, I trust the Lord granted you some rest last night?'

'A little, thank you.'

'You were not at morning prayer and meditation today?'

'No, I was not.'

'You must remember you have a duty to set an example to the younger members in the truth.'

'I am aware of that, Brother Calvin. I won't make a habit of it.'

'I'm glad to hear it.' Brother Calvin paused. 'There is another matter I need to discuss with you, Sister Ruth. I will wait in the main meeting room for you to finish your meal.'

Ruth made her way to the room, to discover she had been called to a full council meeting. It took her a minute to take in all the faces around the table. The heavy red curtains were opened to reveal rain pouring down the church-like windows in this room. Her heart began to race uncomfortably.

Brother Saul stood to speak first.

Ruth could see his reflection in the gleaming oak of the table she had so often polished.

'Welcome, Sister Ruth, we have much to discuss this morning. Let us pray, brethren.'

There was a rustle of robes as the men stood, bowing their heads.

Ruth found it impossible to concentrate on the prayer. She looked down at the worn red carpet beneath her feet. On any other day, her father would have been part of this group: the most powerful men in the church.

After the prayer, an agenda was passed around. Ruth saw, with some puzzlement, her name as item one.

'Well, Brothers, we have an important issue to decide first. The recording agent, Max Waterman, was at the meeting last night and has offered Sister Ruth a recording contract. We had a short discussion after the service and he sent this by messenger this morning. It is a difficult issue, since it involves a very worldly organisation, and we must consider the spiritual danger to our Sister if we were to permit this contract to go ahead.'

Ruth watched Brother Saul's mouth form the words. It felt as though she were watching a ventriloquist's dummy, speaking someone else's words.

'It would be a good means of spreading the gospel to those who would not otherwise hear it,' Brother Adam said.

'True – and it would also raise revenues for the work of the church,' Brother Calvin said.

'What are the terms of the contract, Brother Saul?' asked the Rev Amos Firth, leader of the theological college.

'A five year contract to produce two albums a year. The remuneration would, it seems, depend on sales, although there is a lump sum payable on the signing of the contract,' Brother Saul answered. 'Overnight I sent a directive to all our UK congregations and I have votes from five hundred and sixty-two of our Brother ministers. It remains for us to cast our votes and count the result.'

Ruth watched as the men solemnly cast their votes, and the secretary, Brother Robin, took them to a side table where there was a computer screen flickering. He counted the slips of paper he had in his hand, and added them to the totals on the screen.

'The vote has been in favour of permitting the contract to be signed,' Brother Robin announced.

'Sister Ruth, it is the decision of the eldership that you will sign the recording contract with Mr Waterman. We trust that you will bring many the good news through this new ministry of song.'

Ruth swallowed hard. 'But what about my nursing, Brother Saul?'

'This will be your ministry. It will remain to be seen if the one will rule out the other. I was never in favour of your training in the first place. The Council's decision means that the recording work will come first.'

'Item two on the Agenda, to arrange a marriage partner for Sister Ruth. Have there been any enquiries for her hand?'

'Three, Brother Saul,' the secretary said.

'Have there been any recommendations from the council?'

'One, Brother.'

'Any from her father?'

'Brother Benjamin made no provision before he was taken home.'

'Let us vote, all in favour of the council recommendation?'

All the members raised their hands.

'Then that is decided. Sister Ruth, you will unite with your chosen marriage partner at morning service in three weeks' time.'

'But who is it to be?' Ruth asked, desperately.

'That will be revealed on the day. You may begin your morning duties.'

'But,' Ruth began.

'Sister Ruth, I understand that you are still in shock from the sudden death of your father, so I will overlook your behaviour this morning. Go to your morning duties.'

Ruth suddenly wanted to scream at them, to ask what right they had to rule her life in this way. She stood and began to turn toward the door, when she saw Brother Calvin begin to smirk. The look so angered her that she turned back to the table.

'What right have you to take decisions on my behalf?'

There was a stunned silence. Then Brother Saul stood. 'Sister Ruth, go to the solitary wing. We will decide how long you need to remain there. We act as your parents now that your father is dead. As your parents, we must discipline you.'

Ruth looked at him in horror. Some people had been kept in solitary for months. She left the room, feeling as though the floor was soft beneath her feet, that it moved and made her steps unsteady. Access to the solitary wing was on the far side of the building by a narrow flight of stairs that led to the attic bedrooms. Once they had been servants' quarters, now they were bare rooms where people went to meditate and pray. Or so it had been proposed. It had become a punishment block for those who stepped out of line. Whether this had been the intention all along, Ruth couldn't say, but now people avoided mentioning the subject.

Ruth went to her own room, and picked up her journal and her Bible, some spare clothes, towels and her wash bag. Slowly, she placed the items in a carrier bag, and began the walk to the solitary wing.

Sister Barbara, who was deaf and dumb, kept the wing. Silently, she led the way to the room Ruth was to occupy, held the door open, allowed Ruth to pass, and then locked the door behind her.

The room had bare white walls, a high window that showed only sky, a narrow bed and a washbasin. There was a commode beside the bed.

Ruth sat on the bed and wept.

# Chapter 11

Ruth was asleep when the door was unlocked seven hours later. The meal was placed on the window sill; the nun that brought it simply went out again. If it hadn't been for the smell of the food and the click of the key being turned, Ruth might have slept on. As it was, she woke with a start, looking in confusion round the room. With awful clarity, the events of the last two days came back to her; was it still Monday, or had she slept longer?

The room swam around her as she sat up; her legs seemed to have forgotten how to function as she attempted to stand. It was too long since she had eaten. The food was plain steamed fish and vegetables but welcome all the same. Here, in the quiet, it was possible for her to eat as slowly as she needed to. The silence was profound.

Outside the meeting room, Max Waterman was pacing up and down, his mobile phone clamped to his ear. He switched it off at last, and turned toward the doorway he had been watching for so long. His footsteps echoed in the large hallway, and he felt distinctly spooked by the quiet figures that ghosted past him from time to time. It was unnatural, he thought, for youngsters to be so subdued. No make-up or jewellery on the girls, whose full length drab coloured dresses just revealed soft indoor slippers. The boys wore similar drab colours; some of the older ones sported monks' habits in dark brown, yellow or white.

There was no music in the hallway either, and Max found this silence unsettling. All day, every day, there was music in his world, a constant background in the restaurants, in the lifts, in the studios, in his car. In this silence he could hear his tinnitus howling. He did not like this silence. It was as if it were listening to him. He became aware of an odd smell drifting from a partly open doorway. It dragged his thoughts right back to that damn church he'd attended so long ago. 'I don't want to go there...' he moaned softly under his breath. The memory, so long buried and thought dead, had awoken with the smell of incense.

A vision of a puffy face beneath greasy black hair, breath that smelt of whisky and a thick red neck encircled by a clerical collar. Father O'Leary: the priest from hell itself. He shook his head to clear the image from his mind.

Max tried to creep towards the door, but his steps were faithfully echoed by the polished wood beneath his feet. He pushed the door gently, and looked in. It was full of figures, seated in the lotus position, eyes closed, hands turned upwards and sitting so still they could have been made of wax.

He jumped convulsively as a hand touched his shoulder, spinning round to see who it was. Father O'Leary used to do that to him. But it was not the priest. It was the young man he'd spoken to this morning. Max had never seen such compelling blue eyes.

'Mr Waterman. Welcome to The Retreat. I am Brother Adam. I am minister here. I do apologise for keeping you waiting. I have been meditating in another part of the building, since we do not all fit in one. We will, when the worship section is completed.'

Max stood gaping down at this handsome man wearing a monk's green habit, trimmed with dark brown. He took the hand that was offered him, and shook it automatically. He struggled with his sense of dreaming this, only managing to stutter: 'Pleased to meet you, I'm sure, Brother Adam.'

The minister turned. 'Follow me, Mr Waterman. The other council members are waiting for us.'

Max lifted his briefcase and followed the man into a large room, where there was an enormous table, surrounded by men wearing various pale-coloured robes.

'Do take a seat, Mr Waterman. Can we offer you water or a herbal tea?' Brother Adam stood with his hands inside the wide sleeves of his robe.

'Nothing, thanks.' Max couldn't recall the last time he'd drunk water.

'May I welcome you to our meeting, Mr Waterman. I am Brother Saul. Would you be so kind as to read the terms of the recording contract to us, section by section, so that we may question you about them?' The man wore a spotless white robe trimmed with gold, and a gold tie about the waist. His hair was silver, his face clean shaven, and the eyes shone like blue lasers in a barely lined face.

'Why, yes, of course.' Max hefted several copies of the document from his case, and passed them to the man in a grey robe next to him. The man rose silently and distributed copies. His feet made no sound on the polished floor.

'Thank you, Brother Robin.' Brother Saul sat at the head of the table. 'Let us begin, Brothers.'

Max had never spent an evening like it. The men were sharp, he had to admit it. But Max had one thing he would not concede.

'The girl must sign the contract herself, or it won't be valid.'

'We can sign as her proxy,' Grey-Robe Robin said.

'Not unless she's a minor or you have power of attorney,' Max said.

There was a general stir among the robes: the first sign of any emotion at all.

'Will you wait outside for a moment, Mr Waterman?' Brother Adam said.

'No problem.' Max retrieved his briefcase and scurried out of the room. He'd felt like a cockroach in the Royal kitchens in that group.

Some half an hour later, Ruth was startled to hear a knock at her door. She had no time to respond before the door opened, and Sister Barbara beckoned her to follow. Ruth made to pick up her things, but the nun shook her head, and beckoned her again.

She was escorted to the meeting room again. The room was exactly the same as it had been that morning, save that the curtains were drawn and the ornate chandelier lights were on.

'Sister Ruth. I trust you have benefited from your day of solitary observance.' Brother Saul was at the far end of the room.

'Yes, thanks be to the Lord,' Ruth replied automatically.

'We have called you to sign the contract for the recordings. The agent, Max Waterman, is a worldly man. He does not understand the nature of the True Gospel Church. He insists that you sign the contract.' Brother Saul was gripping the end of the table so tightly that his knuckles showed white.

Ruth had never seen him so tense before. 'I understand, Brother Saul.'

'Good.' Brother Saul paused. 'Brother Adam, please call Mr Waterman in, would you?'

Brother Adam glided out and returned with Mr Waterman. He was a very ugly man, thought Ruth, as she watched him collapse onto the chair beside her.

'Pleased to meet you, Miss Diamond,' Max said, offering his hand. Ruth took it, and found it very soft, hot and sweaty.

'Please call me Sister Ruth, Mr Waterman,' Ruth said, looking with amazement at the contract and the sums of money involved.

As soon as she'd signed the paper and the witnesses had added their signatures, Ruth was escorted back to the room in the attic, clutching the copy of the contract that Max Waterman had insisted she have.

After she'd spent an hour in meditation, she opened the contract, and a letter addressed to her in handwriting she did not recognise, fell onto the floor. The noise was so loud in the silence that Ruth looked behind her in case it had been heard.

11a.m. Monday 9$^{th}$.

Cooper had been late into the office this morning. He put it down to advancing years, since he had never felt the lack of sleep before. The office was chilly since the heating system was on the blink again and a white frost still covered the ground. He opened the cupboard and hauled out the heater he stored there for such emergencies. There was a sound in the corridor, the glass panelled door opened to admit Allsopp, looking hollow-eyed.

'Sorry I'm late sir.'

'No problem. It was a late one. Got anything for me?'

'Fingerprints have come back with some prints on the photographs, sir. Some were Brown's, but none of the others were on record unfortunately.'

'Could be useful later,' Cooper said. 'Sit down and listen to this, Allsopp.' The inspector pressed the play button on a dusty old machine.

*'Oliver. I hope you are listening to me. You are a good boy, I know that. Now I need your help in something that must be done. There are evil men at the True Gospel Church. They are doing evil things. Will you help me, Oliver? I need someone who isn't afraid to bring judgement on these evil doers. Listen again tomorrow, Oliver, I will tell you more. This is a secret. You must tell no one, the evil ones will hear of our plans to destroy them. Nothing must stand in our way. They shall be destroyed.'*

Josh sat gazing at the tape recorder as though he'd never seen one before in his life. 'Who the hell was that?'

'Oliver Brown's voices – the voice, to be more accurate. It's muffled to cover identity, but the man has a local accent – the boffins identified that much. They've taken copies of them all – I found five tapes in Oliver's room, to see if they can gain any more information from them.'

Joshua found himself following the line of the cracks in the coffee-coloured wall, in an effort to get his mind round this. 'Are you saying that someone pretended to be Brown's inner voice in order to get him to … to kill the people in the church?'

'Seems like it.' The inspector put the shiny thing he'd found in Oliver's room on the desk.

'What's that, sir?'

'An expensive gizmo. It transmits and receives over two hundred yards, apparently. I found it in Oliver Brown's room, hidden behind the radiator.' The inspector got up to warm his hands at the heater.

'So they were instructing him?'

'Looks possible; I don't think they thought he'd tape the transmissions, though. He obviously wanted to hear them more than once. If they knew he'd kept these, they would have vanished very quickly. As it happens, it's the first real break we've had. Right, son, let's listen to the lot. I've got them in sequence. Make notes of any ideas you have while we listen. I'll do the same. We'll milk this evidence dry. I want to catch the bastard who did this. It's obscene.'

# Chapter 12

## *Matthew*

I must walk slowly along the corridor and keep my eyes lowered. Even though it seems my thoughts are loud enough to be heard by anybody in a mile radius. I will pray as I walk.

Lord,

I haven't been so worried about anything since... no, I won't think about that. I've been looking for Ruth all day. Although I've been at every meal and managed to join two of the most likely devotional groups, there's no sign of her anywhere. The effect of her absence on my inner peace is like a car alarm howling during prayer. I am making my way to the kitchens by the longest route I can. But Lord, I can't ask anybody where Ruth is, since the rule of silence is absolute in all the corridors. I ask you to quiet my spirit, and entrust her to your care. Amen.

The kitchen is busy as usual; the great bowls of next morning's bread dough are being put to rise overnight in the ovens. The temperature is set very low. I help to carry the dishes, help clean down the work surfaces and wash the floors. Someone is breaking the silence rule and singing under their breath.

I bring myself to order; I must meditate as I work. 'Why should someone missing spoil my inner peace?' But I know only too well why it does.

I had been eight years old. Digger had woken me as usual; his rough wet tongue licking the soles of my feet. The house was unusually silent.

'Stop it, you horrid dog!' Digger wagged his tail, and trotted to the door.

'All right, I'm coming.' I didn't often wake before my parents, but I must have, since Digger was asking to be let out. I thundered down the stairs, enjoying the rhythm, like drum beats.

I hauled the chain off the front door and Digger shot out to have a wee straight away.

'Good dog. Come on, let's get some breakfast.' I feed myself and Digger, and then go up to dress. The silence is beginning to bother me, so I make a lot of noise to break the quiet. Then, with a thudding heart, I creep along to my parents' room. I hold my breath as I knock softly. There is no answer. I knock again, more loudly, and when the third and loudest knock brought no response, I put my hand on the doorknob and open it slowly and quietly.

I jump in shock as Digger bounds past me, pushing the door wide. The room is empty. The bedclothes are neatly folded back, as though someone was about to get into bed. But no one had. I look in the bathroom; my heart pounding now. Digger is sniffing under the bed, but there are only dad's slippers tucked under his side. Mum's pink ones are on the other side. But where were the feet that belonged in those slippers?

'Come on, Digger, where are mum and dad?' The dog wagged his tail, but made no move. I sit on the bed, shivering. There must be a reason. What would Sherlock Holmes do? He would search the house thoroughly for clues. So I go from room to room, until I'd searched the whole house. As I reach the kitchen again, I feel that familiar shudder of unshed, bottled-up tears.

Don't be stupid, Matthew Farnsby. You're eight years old and too big to cry. The sound of the post crashing onto the hall mat makes me jump again. Digger rushes off, barking loudly, beginning to attack the letters. This never normally happens, since the hall door is kept strictly shut to keep dog teeth out of the post.

'Leave it! Bad dog!' I say, in as fierce a voice as I can manage, and I am amazed when he drops the letters. I gather up the post and carry it into father's study, where the post is usually tackled while my parents had that disgusting midmorning herbal tea.

I don't know what to do next. I find myself looking at the secret place. Maybe I should look in there? I could hear my father's voice saying, 'If ever you need help, open the secret place.' But is this the time? Father always sorted the post, and some of the letters went into the secret place. Others went into the filing cabinet, others into the safe. I'm not sure about the difference, but I know Brother Saul doesn't know about it. Just in case, I look at the post. The bills I recognise, and leave them on the desk, but there are two envelopes marked confidential. I open the secret place and tuck the letters in on top of the papers crammed inside. Only papers? What help could they be?

At that moment, I hear the sound of a car pulling up outside. I slam the secret place shut. Heart thudding with hope, I run to the window. For a moment, I don't recognise Brother Saul because he's wearing an ordinary suit, not his white robes. He comes up the path with one of the nuns from The Retreat.

I open the door to them.

'The Lord be with you,' Brother Saul says.

'And may His peace attend you,' I reply. 'My parents aren't here, Brother Saul. I don't know where they are.' It's hard, but I keep my voice steady.

'This is why I have come, Matthew. Your parents have been called away on the Lord's business, and I am here to care for you with Sister Barbara.'

The nun smiles, but says nothing.

'But, they didn't say anything,' I begin.

'There wasn't time.' Brother Saul walks past me into the hall and leads the way into the study. 'Do sit down, Matthew.' He sits in father's chair, which annoys me.

'They would have made time,' I protest, not sitting down.

'The Lord's work comes first, Matthew. Before everything else.'

I face him, standing in front of father's desk. 'They will write to me then.'

'That will not be possible at the present time.'

'Why on earth not?'

'Because it has been decided, Matthew. You must apply yourself to the rule of obedience: of deference to your elders. You must get yourself ready for school as usual, and Sister Barbara will take you.'

'But I want to see them. They would never leave me without saying goodbye, and when they'll be back!'

'That is enough, Matthew. Do as you are told!' Brother Saul stands up to his full height and bellows at me, his blue eyes bright with some inner ice that seems to freeze my spirit.

'Get ready and go to school. Now!'

The habit of obedience wins, and I fetch my school things. The nun follows me. I put on my coat, and make my way down the path, although it's too early. After a few minutes, I try asking Sister Barbara if she knows where my parents are, but she just goes on walking as if she doesn't hear me. That morning is the longest of any I remember. When I have eaten what I can manage of my lunch, I sneak out of school through the gap behind the cycle shed. At home, there's still no sign of my parents; the car is gone. Cautiously, I go round to the windows one by one. In the kitchen Sister Barbara is cooking a meal, and I can see that she has put our washing out on the line. My parents' bed sheets have been changed. There is nobody in the dining room, sitting room or the library. The study window is a little higher up, and I have to scramble up the tree outside.

Brother Saul is in there, among a turmoil of books and papers. Every drawer has been emptied, everything from the safe has been taken out, and all father's books are stacked on the floor. Brother Saul is shaking each one before replacing it on the shelves. Brother Robin suddenly stands up from the desk and replaces a bundle of papers in the safe.

'Nothing among these, Brother Saul,' he says.

'It must be here somewhere. Keep looking.'

My eyes scan the room. My heart leaps with relief. They haven't found the secret place. Neither will they if I can help it.

Brother Saul stands and comes to the window. I duck behind the leaves and stay stock still while he opens the window. His expression at that unguarded moment reminds me of the sparrow hawk that had taken a chaffinch outside the kitchen window one morning. I had watched it consume the entire bird save for a few feathers. The eyes were cold and the beak cruel.

My father, standing beside me, had said, 'There are people like hawks, Matthew. They strike when you least expect it.'

The words had made me shiver at the time.

Back at school that afternoon I narrowly avoid a detention for daydreaming in maths, but my teacher gives me the benefit of the doubt, and I make myself focus on my work, to avoid thinking about what was going on at home.

Sister Barbara is waiting for me outside the school. Still, she doesn't speak, but beckons me to walk with her.

One of the teachers sees her, and asks, 'Excuse me, Sister, is there anything wrong with Matthew's mother?'

Sister Barbara walks on, as though she hasn't heard. I blush crimson at the rudeness of it, but follow in the nun's wake.

Home is never the same after that. Digger vanished. Brother Saul comes to the house every day and uses my father's study. Sister Barbara cooks meals for me, and that weekend, five other children come to live at the house, with another nun, Sister Anna, to help. As soon as I can, I take all the children for a walk through the wood, half-thinking I saw Digger ahead sometimes. At my tree house, we sit round and talk. They too had lost their parents in the same way I had. Only their homes had been sold and they'd come here. Why had my home not been sold? I ask.

The eldest boy, Jacob Reed, says, 'Maybe your father didn't give his property to the church. I know mine did.' He sits holding his younger sister Martha's hand. 'I got into trouble, asking a teacher about my parents. They phoned Brother Saul.'

I ask, 'What did he do?'

'He put me on punishment for two weeks for disobedience to the rule. He told them my parents were fine, on missionary work in Canada.'

We talk long and hard about what might have happened to our parents, but none of us could understand where or why they had gone so suddenly.

Steven and Thomas Kirkham sit together, their young faces pale. Their sister, Rebekah, was not convinced easily of anything, and questioned all our thoughts as though she were a terrier with a bone.

'There's no use talking about it,' she says, finality in her tone, 'we've just got to put up with it until we can find out something. As carefully as we can – and keep each other informed if we find out anything.'

Sister Anna is different, and that night I plucked up the courage to ask her about my parents, and Digger. 'I don't know anything about them, Matthew. Just trust in the Lord and He will reveal His plan in His own time.'

This was the kind of answer I had come to expect. 'Why does Sister Barbara never speak?'

'Because she is deaf and dumb. It is a cross she bears with grace.'

After everyone was in bed that night, I slipped down to my father's study. I wanted to take the papers from the secret place. Sister Barbara was in the kitchen, but she wouldn't hear if I made a noise; only if I thumped the floor would she pick up the vibration.

Carefully, I turn the handle. The door is locked. I never do find it open in all the years that follow.

I come back to the present, to the bright glare of the fluorescent tubes, Jacob washing the floor, his sister Martha working on the vegetables for tomorrow's lunch. Nothing has changed. This time I'm not going to put up with it. I'll find Ruth, whatever it takes.

Rebekah Kirkham comes in, her yellow robe grimy from the greenhouses where she'd been working. 'May the Lord be with you, my Brothers and my Sister,' she says, standing with her back to the Aga for warmth.

'And may His spirit guide you in all things,' we chorused, using the set response for the day.

'Brother Matthew, there is a request for you to attend on Brother Saul after morning meditation.' She bowed in my direction before leaving by the kitchen stairs, which led to her dormitory section.

So that is why she'd broken silence. Jacob and Martha looked at me anxiously.

'Don't worry, I'll be fine,' I say, in order to avoid them breaking silence. I would have to confess it tomorrow; best if they didn't get themselves into any trouble for my sake.

They nod, and fold their hands in an attitude of prayer.

I'll need those prayers if I'm to get any sleep tonight. I'm rather afraid I shall dream of searching for lost people again.

# Chapter 13

## *Ginger*

Ginger stopped whistling as he went up the front path. He could hear Gran shouting. Ma Foster was as formidable as ever, but unable to aim a blow at him from her wheelchair. Arthritis had not improved her temper. He dumped his thick wad of leftover newspapers from the shop on the step and put his key in the door.

As he stepped into the hall, he felt gran's powerful voice reverberate through the fabric of the building. 'Yew comes back 'ere after all this time and fink I'm goin' ter welcome yer with a cuppa tea. You got anovver fink comin', Reg Foster, an' no mistake.'

Ginger stopped in mid turn, the door key in hand. Reggie Foster. His father? What the hell was he doing here? He lifted his papers into the hall and closed the door quietly. Gran was still shouting.

'What about that tart that left yew with Ginger? Not a word nor a penny from either of yew all these years. I don't want nuffin to do wiv yer. On yer bike.'

Ginger stepped closer to the door to hear the man reply. His voice was much softer.

'I want ter make up fer it now, Ma. I know it must 'ave bin 'ard on yew and the boy, but I'm 'ere now, an' I've got a good little number, plenty o' money. I can 'elp now.'

'I don't need none o' yer 'elp.' Ginger could hear the wheels of the chair squeal as she did one of her handbrake turns in it. 'An' 'ow long will it be afore yew lands inside agen wiv this "good little number" might I ask?'

'I want to see my boy.'

Ginger hesitated. How often had he longed to know his father, to do the things that fathers and sons did, like going to a football match or fishing or whatever. He wasn't too sure what real fathers did. His had been a "waste of space" according to Gran, more often in prison than not. 'Hell,' he muttered, 'I don't even know what he looks like.'

'That you Ginger?' Gran's hearing was as acute as ever.

'Yeah, Gran.'

'Come on in, don't 'ang about out there. Yer dad's turned up like a bad penny ter see yer.'

Ginger opened the door. His father was smaller than he'd thought he'd be. A small, wiry looking man with thinning ginger hair like his own stood in front of the empty fireplace. They stared at each other for a minute, the same blue eyes sizing each other up.

Reggie put out his hand awkwardly. This young man was a stranger; so like himself, and yet, so very different. 'Hello, Jimmy.'

Ginger looked down at his father's outstretched hand as though it was a snake, and then looked away. 'Hello, Dad.' He turned away from him. 'I got some nice chops at Pritchett's Gran, I'll go an' put 'em on.'

'I done the spuds, they're on the stove.' Gran followed him into the kitchen.

'Right.' Ginger busied himself unwrapping the meat.

Reggie stood in the doorway. 'I could get us a takeaway.'

'No thanks, Dad. We got our dinner. I only got two chops, thinking as we'd be on our own as usual.' Ginger kept his voice level, but his anger was only just under the surface. This was the bloody sod who'd abandoned him.

Reggie tried another tack. 'What you doin' now, then son?'

'I'm a shop manager. When I was a kid, I got this paper round, then I took on two, 'cos I needed the money.' Ginger slapped the two chops into the grill pan. 'Then when Mrs Atkins expanded the business, I got a job be'ind the till at weekends. Then we thought we'd buy the empty shop next door and run a supermarket and restaurant at the back.' Ginger added salt to the potatoes and switched on the gas. 'I worked at everything what was needed. I been to college. Mrs Atkins made me manager last year.'

Reggie couldn't help his heart swelling with pride. This was his son, doing all right. 'That's ... flippin' amazin', son.'

'I reckon it was, considerin' I was left to fend fer meself and gran.' Ginger reached into the freezer, 'Peas 'n' carrots, Gran?'

'That'll do, luv.'

Ginger put the packets of frozen vegetables on the worktop and reached for a couple of pans. 'As far as I'm concerned, I don't need nuffing from you.'

Ma Foster turned her small bright eyes on her son. 'You 'eard what 'e said. We don't need nuffin from yew.'

Reggie hadn't anticipated his son's anger. To be honest, he'd never given him a thought for much of the time he'd been away. No point, really, he couldn't give the boy a home. In his mind, the boy had stayed that red-faced scrap that screamed most of the time. Stupid, really. Of course he'd been growing up while his back was turned.

'I'd better be off then.' He reached into his pocket and dropped a bright yellow printed card on the table. 'I can be found here any meeting night,' he said as he went down the tiny dark hall without looking back.

Ginger did not look up as he filled the pans with water at the sink. The front door closed and he and gran were left alone again as usual.

Gran picked up the card. 'True Gospel Church,' she read out, 'it gives the times o' the services.'

Ginger turned the chops, thinking, where have I heard that before? Yes, that was it. 'That's the church where that lunatic ran amok wiv' a knife a couple days back.'

'Well, what's yer dad doin' at a church of all fings? 'Ope it ain't nuffin' goin' ter make trouble fer yew at the shop.'

'Nah, Mrs Atkins knows all about me dad. Says yew can choose yer friends, but family's what yer born wiv' – I reckon she's right.'

'Too right, luv. I got ter put up wiv' yew.' Gran's eyes twinkled.

'Cuts both ways, that.' Ginger threw a tea towel at her which she caught deftly in one arthritic fist.

'I 'spose yew wants me to do summat wiv' this?'

'I got a few ideas.' Ginger grinned.

Gran thwacked him on the behind with the cloth.

Ginger put two plates in the oven to warm. 'Yew can make yerself useful and set the table.'

As Gran set the cutlery on a tray, Ginger put the card in his pocket. Wouldn't do no harm to take a look at that church. Where the murders happened, like.

# Chapter 14

## *Ruth*

She sat staring at the letter for some time, and then moved to the door where the peephole was. There was no one in the corridor. But she felt as though her every move was being watched, so just in case, she went into the corner of the room and sat on the floor before opening the envelope.

A key dropped out onto her robe and began sliding to the floor. Afraid it would make a noise, she caught it before it slid to the bare boards. Then she smiled. Sister Barbara wouldn't hear that. But maybe someone would, whispered her inner caution.

Ruth had never felt alone at The Retreat. Somehow she always felt that someone was observing her everywhere she went. It hadn't helped that even small misdeeds had somehow been 'known' by the Elders that ruled the chosen. How they knew these things could not be entirely explained by the 'Duty of Revelation' – that each member be aware of shortcomings in the others and should confess it to their mentors.

There was another envelope and a typewritten letter inside the first. Her name, written in her father's familiar scrawl, was on the outside of the second envelope.

'For Ruth, to be opened in the event of my death, Ben Diamond.'

The letter was from her father's solicitor. Nigel Bishop.

Sunday evening.

My Dear Miss Diamond,

I was indeed very sad to hear of your father's untimely death today. He was an extremely talented and good man. I shall miss him a great deal.

What I have to say to you now may distress you further, but I must tell you these things. Some two years ago, your father came to me with certain worries he had concerning The True Gospel Church and the way it was being managed. I know he was investigating certain aspects of the administration and the movement of members, especially some in high positions who suddenly left their homes without making any attempt to say goodbye to relatives or even to their own young children.

I advised him to be extremely careful, since I had heard a similar worry expressed by David Farnsby shortly before they left in the same manner. I did have a very odd letter from him soon after he disappeared, which didn't quite put my mind at rest. I even spoke to an Inspector Bradley about it.

Since then, I have kept this letter and the key your father left with me on your behalf, and enclose it. I may say that I have your father's will safely here. If you would make an appointment to see me, we can discuss this matter further. It was his wish that you should see me without your mother present.

I have given this to Max Waterman, who is also a client of mine; so that I could be sure you would receive this letter and the one from your father.

I trust I will see you at the interment.

Sincerely....Nigel J Bishop.

Ruth put the letter on the floor beside her, trying to make sense of the contents. What was it her father had been worried about? Surely there was a simple explanation for the movement of staff – sometimes they were needed elsewhere quickly. The 'rule of obedience' applied throughout the community after all. Then, why would he want her to see the solicitor without her mother present? It didn't make sense, knowing how close they'd been. And why wouldn't he be sure I'd get the letter if it came in the post as usual?

She lifted the letter and read it again. Obviously the solicitor didn't understand the way the community worked. But that didn't explain the fact that father had gone to see him, worried about something in 'the way the church was managed'. But what on earth could it have been? The church accounts were audited by an outside firm; the management by the elders was excellent, beyond doubt. Nothing disturbed the smooth day to day running of The Retreat, the College or that of their many churches that dotted the country.

A niggling thought arrived: what about those deaths at the College? Ruth could recall how worried dad had been about that. He'd gone to see the College for himself. Brother Saul had been angry with him about that – not part of his remit. Then there was Matthew; he had never found out where his parents were – it had weighed on his mind so that he had been kept back in his growth; he was still wearing a novice robe after all this time. He couldn't resist asking questions about his parents whenever an opportunity arose. He had failed in obedience; in accepting authority.

She turned the key over in her hand; it was a Yale, the sort that opened an outer door. What door and where was it? Ruth stood, and walked slowly around the room, and glanced quickly down the corridor through the peephole. Sister Barbara was passing through, with a woman in worldly clothes close behind her. It would be safe to sit on the bed, since if Sister Barbara was kitting out a new recruit she would be occupied for some time. She peeled back the envelope without tearing it and lifted out the contents.

The paper was covered in a sequence of numbers; the first group read; 417, 11. 1447, 7. 1725, 7. 851,12. 1718, 3. 1929, b4. 924, b1. 793, 2. 737, b4. 566, 4. 722, 19. 1742, b17. 1932, 9. There were just these four closely typed sheets, with hundreds of groups of numbers on them. Ruth blinked back tears. She had expected something more than one of father's ciphers to work out. She looked again in the envelope, and there was a short note in father's handwriting. She grasped it with trembling fingers.

My Dearest Ruth, I haven't much time before catching the train. But I had to leave this message for you in chambers with Nigel Bishop. With any luck, the contents of this letter will never be in your hands. But if they are, I will not have destroyed them, my doubts and worries will still have not been resolved and I will have died as a result of a growing threat to the church, a terrible evil thing that has grown up in its shadow. It is not impossible that I will have died of natural causes, in which case I will leave it to your good sense to destroy all evidence of my concerns. Keep all secret until you are sure. Your mother will not hear me on this matter – she is fiercely loyal to her family.

Do not trust anyone until you are completely sure of them. I mean anyone. Especially the Joshua Group.

May God bless you, and keep you safe – Dad.

Ruth sat immobile for some time. It was as though she had been given permission to think things that she had kept firmly in the back of her mind for many years. The sort of questions that would land one in solitary, or on hard tasks, or would lead to... vanishing from The Retreat. She shivered as she remembered all those she'd known and daren't ask after. She had a sudden memory of *Watership Down*, one of the books which she had read secretly over the years. There was a warren where nobody dare ask 'where'. Ruth shuddered. The terrible unspoken word was apostasy; those that went back into sin and rejected the truth. A pang of fear went through her as the thought of her father in that state at death came to her. If he had harboured wrong thoughts about the Brotherhood, it would have been a grievous thing, 'An evil heart of unbelief'. The words always came to her mind as if spoken by Brother Saul. A brief smile touched her lips; not spoken, as such, more *thundered.*

There was only one thing to do; she must burn the code, before his sin could affect any more of the Brotherhood. Then there came a second, chilling thought. What if father was right, and there was something truly evil going on under the cloak of spirituality? The room felt suddenly cold, alien, as though the very words she had been thinking had woken some dark presence. She shook off the fancy, and opened her Bible. It was often the answer to her father's riddles. Some time later, she stretched and sighed. She was on the wrong track; none of the numbers were biblical references. This one was very different from dad's usual ciphers.

What had her father meant by the 'Joshua Group'? The name was vaguely familiar; where had she heard it?

Ruth knelt on the hard floor and spread the letter and code on the bed, and began to pray for guidance. There was always a comfort in this for her, but this time she felt nothing but confusion and unanswered questions. She stood and paced the room, then knelt again to wrestle the problem out. It was only the smell of food from the corridor that roused her from her trance-like position. There was just time for her to slide the papers between the leather backing of her Bible and the cardboard stiffener before the door was opened. It would need sitting on to flatten it, she thought.

Sister Barbara smiled to see Ruth on her knees with her Bible. The Solitary was obviously doing her good. She placed the tray of food on the bed, signed a blessing, and left as soundlessly as she'd come.

Ruth ate slowly and carefully. The thought of vomiting into the commode did not appeal; it would be only too obvious if it happened. Questions would be asked. The loss of privacy was bad enough already. It was a case of eating only a little at a time so that her stomach didn't reject it.

Just as she'd rebelled at the thought of an arranged marriage, again she felt the stirrings of a terrible conflict of emotions. Her duty of obedience struggled with her feeling that the choice of a husband was something deeply personal. She also knew that she was not ready for such a relationship. How could she marry with this sickness problem draining away her energies? How could she keep it from someone who shared the most intimate parts of her life? That part of her life that most shamed her, that made her feel worthless, stained, much less than perfect. She pushed the tray of food aside, half eaten. She could take no more. She threw off her clothes and climbed into bed. The tears came then.

She fell into a fitful sleep in which she dreamed of starving children with swollen bellies and mournful brown eyes. They reached out for her food. She tried to give them the food from her plate, but they seemed unable to take it. A voice was saying: 'No, not from her, she is not worthy.'

Ruth woke, weeping again.

# Chapter 15

## *Annabel*

Inspector Cooper hated staff appraisals. So he had set himself to get them out of the way as soon as he possibly could in order to get on with his real job – catching criminals. The third candidate was just about to take a seat when Allsopp interrupted him for the fifth time that morning.

'What the hell is it now, Allsopp?'

'I am sorry to bother you, sir –'

'Not sorry enough or you wouldn't do it.'

'It's just there's this woman wants to talk to you. She used to be a nun at that Retreat place, run by the True Gospel Church.'

Cooper drummed his fingers on the desk. 'All right, Perkins, you're saved by the bell.' He heaved his tall frame from the seat that had contained him for far too long and strode after Allsopp.

'Interview room two, sir; a Miss Annabel Harman.'

The woman was about fifty, still attractive, her hair still blonde and her body wiry rather than thin. She turned shrewd blue eyes toward the inspector, and stood up, extending her hand in greeting.

Cooper felt a strange excitement at the touch and almost pulled his hand away in surprise. 'Miss Harman, how can I help you?' He motioned her to sit down.

'I hope I can help you, Inspector. I heard about Ben Diamond's death and I came to tell you what made me leave the True Gospel Church.' Her voice was soft and musical.

'Has that any bearing on his death?' Cooper perched himself on the edge of his seat, his voice taking on the crisp tone that showed he was interested.

Allsopp stood beside the door, observing and taking notes.

'It may have. I just feel it's time to come forward with what I know, and what I suspect. Before this, I have a feeling that I would have been written off as some kind of neurotic having a spiritual crisis of some kind – menopausal hysterics or something along those lines.'

Josh saw the Inspector's lips twitch slightly. 'Try me, Miss Harman.'

The woman reached into her bag for several notebooks. 'These are my daily notes – I still keep it up even though I no longer attend the True Gospel Church. I left without warning and changed my name, kept away from them completely,' she paused. 'You see, I was afraid to leave openly after what I'd seen happen before.'

'Go on.'

'There were several young couples that belonged to the Church, Mr and Mrs Kirkham; they had three children, Rebekah, Thomas and Steven.'

Cooper glanced round; nodded when he saw Allsopp writing the names in his notebook.

'Then there were the Reeds, their two children Martha and Jacob, then the Farnsbys, they had one little boy called Matthew. Over a period of six months, all their parents vanished, leaving their children with the Church. The Kirkham's and Reed's homes were sold soon afterwards; I was chosen to care for the children at the Farnsby's home, with another Sister, Barbara, who is deaf and dumb.'

The buzzing of a bee at the window punctuated her words.

'Here are all their names and dates of birth, and the addresses they were living at before the houses were sold. The Farnsby house is still owned by the Church; Saul Crouch still uses it as an office, away from The Retreat.'

Cooper reached out to take the folded paper, passing it to Allsopp to keep with his notes.

'Now, for a long time, I was uneasy about it, especially as the children were terribly unhappy, not knowing what had happened to their parents. Then I became worried as there were more 'disappearances' – one was an older couple; the wife had developed dementia. It was suggested they sell their home and move into sheltered accommodation. I saw them both on the

Sunday. On the Monday morning, the house was empty and there was no sign of them ever again.'

'Are their names on the list?' Cooper asked.

'No, I didn't think to put them down – Victor Morris and his wife Gladys. They lived in Rampart Road, number 23.'

Josh wrote quickly in his notebook. He felt a tingle of excitement running through him. The bee buzzed as if in tune with his mood.

Cooper was leaning forward, 'Did you ask about them?'

'Of course, I never had a straight answer from anybody. The line was that they were being cared for, our task was to follow the Rule of Obedience.'

'The Rule of Obedience?' Cooper asked.

'It seems so innocuous, but it binds one completely. I can remember most of it still. She fixed her eyes on the wall in front of her and began:

'The True Gospel member must at all times observe the Rule of Obedience. Avoid talking in the corridors, for it will disturb tranquillity. No unnecessary talk in tasks, for this will disturb concentration. No questioning of Eldership decisions, for this will sow discord. No telephone calls, radio or television, for this will bring in worldly disturbance. No relationships other than those approved and arranged by the Eldership, for the avoidance of sin. The members must at all times avoid all sleeping quarters save their own at all times. The membership does not require money or possessions. Alcohol is forbidden at all times, that my Brother may not sin.'

'Sounds like a prescription for a medieval monastery,' Cooper said.

Miss Harman smiled. 'When one is involved, it all seems proper, correct. Any stirrings of discontent are soon squashed as sinful pride and resentment, quickly confessed and put aside. It is very difficult to think clearly when one's days are taken up by a strict timetable of duties and religious observances. It was an exhausting regime, Inspector. I became very underweight, and it is so hard to think when one is under such pressure to conform.' A shadow passed over her face. 'Would you mind if we let that poor bee out, Inspector? It reminds me of how I felt in my last months in the True Gospel Church; struggling against something I couldn't see, and yet I knew was there. A shiny glass prison.'

Cooper stood up and let the bee fly free. It went straight up, and vanished from sight.

'And did you have difficulty escaping your prison?' he asked gently.

Miss Harman's words were no longer cool and deliberate; they tumbled over one another. 'My sister and her husband came to see me and took me home with them. Sister Barbara had ignored the rules and called them, helped them take me out of the back gate. I was running a temperature and almost crazy with delirium. I was very run down. It took me months to shake off the rule; I had become an automaton Inspector. At first I believed I should go back. If you talk to any of the membership, the answers you will get come straight from the rule. And, believe me; they will know nothing apart from what they have been told.'

'Who is the main leader?'

'The Reverend Saul Crouch. His ministry began some twenty years ago, under Billy Graham, I believe. His two sons, Calvin and Adam have a good deal of power – Adam was given the pulpit at the local True Gospel Church – Calvin seems to be a sort of treasurer. The Eldership runs the whole thing. Nationwide –'

'Nationwide?' Cooper interrupted.

'Yes, nationwide. There are hundreds of branches run by Elders appointed by this church – this is the British headquarters.'

'There are churches abroad?' Cooper enquired.

'Yes. In America, Canada, France, Germany, Australia and New Zealand at the time I was with them.'

Cooper drummed his fingers on the table. The problem was knowing what to ask. 'What made you begin to doubt the Church, Miss Harman?'

'It was the way those children were abandoned. Even for people totally dedicated to the cause, it was decidedly odd when they vanished without even a last kiss for their own children.'

'Thank you for coming forward, Miss Harman.' Cooper held out his hand. Her small, cool fingers in his again gave him that frisson of excitement, but this time he was prepared, and showed no sign of it.

'There is one other thing that bothered me. There is something called "The Joshua Group".' Miss Harman shivered suddenly. 'A kind of police, I suppose, in the Church. That's all I know about them. Except that mention of them frightened folk.'

'You have been very helpful, Miss Harman.'

She flushed under his gaze. 'Is there anything else I can do?'

Cooper thought for a moment of candlelit dinners, but pushed the ridiculous thought aside. 'I'm sure there will be – but at the moment I'm not sure what the questions will be. I can contact you?'

'Yes, of course. I did write my own name on the paper.' Her smile reminded him of sunshine on sunflowers.

'I will be in touch. Thank you again, Miss Harman.'

'Annabel,' she said, and was gone, leaving a slight hint of freesias on the air.

Cooper went to the open window, gazing out across the city streets awash with traffic. The tiny figure walking to a blue Nissan parked at the front paused, looked up, and waved. Cooper returned the gesture awkwardly, acutely aware of Allsopp beside him. When he closed the window, Allsopp was sitting at the desk, scanning his notes.

'Where do we start with this sir?'

'The missing persons, perhaps they were reported missing? The houses – the solicitors that dealt with the sales, neighbours, I'm afraid it'll be shoe leather stuff, Allsopp.'

Allsopp met his gaze. 'Nothing I like better sir. I'll go back to the office and make a start, then sir. Are you going on with the appraisals?' The innocent look did not deceive the inspector.

'I'll do yours next, young man, if you're not careful.'

Allsopp grinned. It was odd, but he was sure that the inspector had been rather taken with Miss Harman.

Much later, on his way home, Cooper found himself buying a small bunch of freesias to put on his desk. They have the most wonderful smell, he thought.

# Chapter 16

## *Mrs Diamond*

Miriam was angry. Her temper was something with which she had struggled for many years and now she desperately missed Ben's steadying hand and voice. That Ruth had answered the council back was unforgivable. The meditation group was silent, but there was no quiet to be found while this anger at Ruth's behaviour disturbed her inner calm. She tried to picture her tranquil lake scene, but it kept blowing up a violent storm. Then there were the images of Ben's face, the blood, the cruel knife…

Brother Saul watched his cousin from the comfort of his room; the screen showed a well-ordered group. But Miriam was not at peace; her facial muscles would not relax into their usual calm pose, although her straight back and posture were perfect. He flicked a switch to observe Ruth; she was at prayer. Good. She had been off screen in the corner of the room for a while, and he had thought to ask Sister Barbara to look in on her.

Saul pressed his intercom switch. 'Peace be with you. Sister Doris, would you ask Sister Miriam to come to me after meditation?' He pulled his white robe closer round him. There was a chill in the air today.

'May the Lord guide your steps aright, Brother Saul, I will go to her now,' Sister Doris replied.

Miriam followed Doris silently through the corridors to the council room. Doris went to her seat in the corner. There was a robin outside the window. Red was the colour of anger, and of blood.

'Peace be with you, Sister.'

'May the Lord guide your steps aright, Brother Saul.' She watched the bird fly away.

'You may be seated, Sister.'

Miriam sat, and waited with her hands folded in her lap.

'Sister Ruth is progressing well. She is not yet ready to rejoin the members, but there is improvement.' Saul straightened some papers on his desk.

Miriam nodded. 'As the Lord wills.'

'I think we may postpone the marriage for a week or so, since there is the Celebration of Life service to come for Brother Benjamin.'

Miriam's face clouded for a moment, until she gained control of her feelings once again. 'The Lord has given wisdom. Has the day been chosen?'

'On Friday, Sister.'

'I will be ready, the Lord willing, to give sound testimony. Is the marriage partner chosen for Sister Ruth to be here?'

'He will be. Since you brought the problem of her closeness to Brother Matthew to my notice, I have been able to keep them separate. It was a blessing that you saw them together, we were able to act quickly. Brother Matthew has not grown as he should; he would be a great hindrance to Sister Ruth. The council have chosen a more mature partner.'

Miriam longed to ask who had been chosen, but the rule of obedience demanded that she obey without question. It still rankled with her stubbornly independent spirit.

'You are not at peace, Sister. Speak freely.'

Miriam had not expected this, and her thoughts began to spin dangerously out of control for a moment. She must be careful how she spoke. 'I am troubled by the loss of my husband after so many years together.' Miriam felt her control slipping, and stopped speaking.

Saul nodded his understanding. 'Naturally, Sister. But there is more, is there not?'

'Yes, Brother. The way my husband was taken has shaken my spirit deeply.'

'As it has us all. The Lord tests us in many ways, but never beyond our strength.'

'The policemen coming into The Retreat – it seems to have left a taint of the world outside.' She paused. 'Then there was the man Max Waterman, and the contract for Sister Ruth to record some songs.'

'This also brings in the outside. This we understand, but it was felt the outreach would be a new ministry; it may reach many who will not attend a service.'

Miriam stopped her tongue on the words that shot through her mind; *You mean you felt it would be profitable.* Instead, she said, 'I am afraid for Sister Ruth. She is not strong.' The anger was simmering somewhere in the region of her stomach.

'We will take every care of Sister Ruth.'

'As the Lord wills. When shall I visit her?'

'Not while she is in solitary, Sister Miriam, you know the rule.'

The question had been a mistake. Miriam gritted her teeth for a minute, then said, 'Forgive me, Brother Saul. I was speaking as a mother first, and not as a Pilgrim.' She watched his face carefully, was he angry?

'I prescribe two hours weeding the front drive. The third section is being done this week.'

'As the Lord wills.' Miriam seethed. A novice's punishment!

'Peace be with you.' Saul stood to give the blessing.

Doris and Miriam stood, and said Amen together. They bowed their heads and walked out, Doris closing the door behind them with a soft click.

Miriam stood still for a moment, gathering her self-control again with an effort.

Doris paused beside her, placed a gentle hand on her arm, smiled, and was gone.

Miriam's control broke, and she leaned against the wall, covering her face with her robe for a moment to hide her tears.

From his desk, Brother Saul watched her carefully as a pimple faced novice approached her, and placed a garden bucket at her feet. She looked up at the sound. Now, how did he know so quickly? Miriam lifted the bucket and followed him out of the front entrance and down the drive.

From the second floor, Matthew saw her go, and wondered what breach of obedience Miriam could have committed to earn a weeding session. Matthew felt his fingers, rough and calloused from many hours spent on his knees out there.

Saul sat at his desk, deep in thought. It was needful to allow plenty of space for the Celebration Service; there would be many outsiders present. The football stadium would not have the right air of dignity, and the main church, even had it been allowed by the police, was not big enough.

He stood, opened a cupboard to reveal a telephone. He plugged it in, and dialled a number. 'Good afternoon, may I speak to the Bishop, please? The Reverend Saul Crouch. Of course I will.'

Some minutes later, he put the telephone back in its hiding place, unplugged it, and closed the door. He hummed a tune under his breath as he lifted the funeral service book from the shelf. Time to prepare for the very best of services. Brother Benjamin deserved nothing less. The others, Sister Hope and Brother Harold deserved it too. But Brother Benjamin was indeed a special case.

His lingering smile was reminiscent of a contented tiger.

Miriam knelt with the other penitents as they worked their way toward the open gates. For a moment, she had a sudden urge to run through them; leave this place behind. But where would she run? There was no home to go to since their family home had been sold, and the money donated to the church. Even had she somewhere to go, there was no spiritual hiding place.

In the silence of the driveway, she could hear her husband's words, all those doubts he had, and all the questions he had been asking. Miriam thought of the words of a hymn to try and smother the seeds of doubt that had begun to grow in her heart. But it was useless. The questions began again. What if Ben had been right? What if they had silenced him as he had thought they might? And who were they? Who could she turn to for help? Only at times like these did she long for her son's strength. But the Lord had taken him; perhaps as He had taken Ben, in order to keep her walking close to him and not to fallible loved ones.

She began to recite the psalms under her breath, beginning at the first.

## Chapter 17

Max Waterman had taken the corner into The Retreat too fast, and had to stamp his foot hard on the brake to avoid what looked like a prayer meeting in the drive. The briefcase on the seat beside him shot to the floor as the car stalled and bumped along the verge for several yards. What the hell were these people doing? The kneeling figures had scattered, but were now kneeling again, one by one, as though nothing had happened. They were hand-weeding the drive, for God's sake!

Max sat for a few moments, swearing roundly while his shattered nerves righted themselves. Then drove much more slowly the rest of the way toward the house. Dealing with this place was so damnably frustrating. No telephone, in this day and age? It was unbelievable. Come to think of it, there was no sign of a television aerial or dish on the roof either. It was positively mediaeval.

He rang the doorbell; even that was muted. To his surprise, Brother Saul opened the door.

'Peace be with you.'

'Er, yes, thank you,' Max said.

'You wished to see me?'

'Yes, we need to arrange a couple of days for Ruth Diamond to come to the recording studio.'

'That will be easy to do. Sister Ruth can come to you tomorrow and Thursday but Friday she has a choir engagement, her father's Celebration of Life Service.'

Funny way to describe a funeral, thought Max. 'Can I pick her up at eight in the morning?'

'I will relay the message to her. What time will she be back with us?'

'Depends on the traffic, but around five.' Max shifted uncomfortably on his feet. He wasn't used to being kept on the doorstep like some cold-call salesman.

'May the Lord bless your work, Brother.' Saul closed the door.

Max swore again, and coloured as he turned and saw the shocked look of one of the robed figures passing with a bucket of weeds. Remembering, he drove more slowly past the group of gardeners, then, with a feeling of immense relief, put his foot down to put distance between him and that truly weird place.

Josh Allsopp rang the doorbell of the second house on his list – there had been no one home at the first. The door was opened by a young woman wearing a long blue robe. 'Peace be with you,' she said, putting her hands out as though offering a gift.

'Police,' Josh said, awkwardly showing his warrant card.

'But you are a Brother, I remember you, at the service.'

'Yes, that's right.' Josh flushed slightly. 'I have a meeting this evening.'

'But do come in, Brother Joshua. May I offer you herb tea or mineral water?'

'Mineral water please.' Josh followed the girl into a comfortable family room filled with well-worn sofas and armchairs.

'Do sit down, Brother Joshua.' She went through into a kitchen, returned a few minutes later carrying a glass of water, and followed by another older woman in a yellow robe. 'Sister Veronica will sit with us while we talk.'

'Thank you.' A chaperone, thought Josh, taking the glass. The water was cool and refreshing.

The girl sat with her hands folded, waiting for him to speak. Sister Veronica sat in the corner by the window, mending a pair of child's jeans.

'I am investigating the disappearance of the couple who used to live in this house.'

'But Brother David and his wife Stella own this house.'

'A David Farnsby? He had a son, Matthew?'

'Yes, Brother Matthew is at The Retreat; his parents are serving the Lord elsewhere.' The girl's calm gaze met his with no trace of guile.

'So you know where Mr and Mrs Farnsby are?'

'No, I didn't say that – I only know that they were here and are now serving somewhere else. The rule of obedience means we may be called to a new place of service at any time. We must obey without question as part of discipline. A foot soldier must obey orders, or there is no winning the war.' She smiled, as though this was so simple it was a wonder he had not understood it at once.

Josh was taken aback. He tried another tack. 'What service are you called to do here?'

'I am caring for the children whose parents have been called to serve elsewhere. I have seven in my care at the present time.'

'It's very quiet.'

'They are at school or College for the day.'

Josh took a long drink of his water. It was hard to know what to ask. 'Did you care for Matthew Farnsby at the time?'

'No, of course not – I was far too young. Sister Barbara and Sister Anna were here then.

Josh referred to his notes. 'This house wasn't sold – I see the homes belonging to the other families were sold?'

'Mostly, our members sell their homes and donate the money to the church.'

'Then why wasn't this one sold?'

'I'm not sure – it is big enough to hold a small group of children away from the Main Retreat, they don't disturb the members while here.'

'That wouldn't do, now would it?' Josh muttered under his breath.

'Brother Joshua, you have much to learn of obedience.' The girl's words were sharper than the gentle expression that went with them. 'I think you should ask these things of Brother Saul, or one of the council members.'

'I am sorry, Sister?'

'Sister Martha.'

Josh looked up quickly. 'Martha Reed?'

'Why, yes.'

'So you were one of the children who came here after Mr and Mrs Farnsby left?'

A shadow crossed the girl's face. 'Yes, my brother Jacob and I came to this house when our parents were called away.'

'Where are they now?'

'That is a question that I must not ask; obedience is the first rule of the foot soldier.' Martha looked at Sister Veronica, as though for guidance.

'You were left here alone?'

'No, not alone, my brother Jacob and the other children were here.' The girl folded her hands together as if in prayer.

Josh found this difficult to grasp. 'So it was like a boarding school, you saw your parents in the holidays?'

'It wasn't necessary.'

Josh couldn't believe that these children's parents could simply leave them.

The older woman stood. 'I think Sister Martha has answered your questions, Brother Joshua. If there are any others, you must ask them at the meeting this evening. Your tutor will advise you.'

Josh was being shown the door – something that went against the grain. Especially as he was getting some answers here. 'But I need to ask…'

'This evening, Brother Joshua. One of the eldership will be better placed to answer your questions.' Sister Veronica gestured to Sister Martha, who went into the kitchen. Josh was propelled down the hallway and out of the door.'

'Peace be with you, Brother Joshua.'

Before Josh could reply, the door was firmly closed behind him.

Ruth was confused, she knew she had been in solitary. Now she was searching her father's study for a book. It had to be a particular book, quite large, judging by the numbers, and easily available – but not as obvious as the King James Bible. The solution had to be harder than that – since Ben Diamond wasn't going to make it easy for the wrong person to decipher the message. She kept looking over her shoulder – who was it that her father had feared? Would they come looking for her here? There was a noise outside; she looked round, the door handle turned. The door opened revealing a dark-robed figure with no face. She woke, sweating and shaking. Who was it that her father had feared?

In spite of her dreaming, Ruth was beginning to feel a little better. The routine of The Retreat went on without a pause beyond the solitary wing, an eighteen hour day that usually stretched her to the limit. Here, she had slept long hours between small meals, and apart from choir practice, nothing to do but think, pray and read. Her only reading was her Bible, but the letter and code that her father had left occupied her waking and sleeping thoughts.

There was a tiny sound outside before the door was opened. Sister Barbara was carrying a tray, which she placed on the bed beside Ruth. The child was sleeping too much, she thought, pursing her lips. Without a sound, she signed a blessing and left.

Ruth felt quite hungry for a change, and ate the vegetable soup and cheese salad with relish. The apple she put aside for later. It was only as she lifted the plate with the apple on it that she saw the folded paper.

'Peace be with you, Sister Ruth. You are to be ready to go to the recording studio tomorrow morning with Sister Amelia at eight. You may be away for the day, and again the following day.

'On Friday, at ten in the morning, the Celebration of Life service for your father, for Sister Hope and Brother Harold will be held in the Cathedral. The choir will be in attendance.

'May the Lord make his face to shine upon you and be gracious unto you.

'Brother Saul.'

Ruth sat for a long time gazing at the wall in front of her. The next two days would be very busy: a good thing. She was dreading Friday.

# Chapter 18

Calvin faced his father across the desk. His yellow robe itched against his skin. 'I wanted to know whether my proposal had met with Eldership approval, Father.'

'You must remember to address me correctly, Brother Calvin. It is part of the rule.' Saul stood, tucking his hands inside the sleeves of his robes. 'We did give your proposal a good deal of thought and prayer, but we decided that it would not be a suitable match.'

'But F- I mean, Brother Saul, why not?' Calvin felt the old anger and frustration at the way his father controlled everything. 'We are of an age, and in The Truth. I can see no problem with it.'

'Brother Calvin, the Eldership has decided. Ruth is too close to you as a first cousin. For breaking discipline, you will spend the morning breaking the ground for the new potato crop in the upper field.'

'Father! All I did was ask!'

Saul's voice became soft: a dangerous sign. 'Brother Calvin, you will follow the rule of obedience as the rest of the community does. Go and begin your task, and may God be your guide.'

'I don't know why you don't buy a tractor.'

'Brother Calvin, you will go to your task for the rest of today. And one more act of disobedience will earn you a week in solitary. In the sweat of thy brow shalt thou eat bread.'

Calvin hesitated. He could not afford to be locked up for a week – there were too many things he needed to do. It was bad enough having to spend a day in the potato field. 'May God be with you, Brother Saul,' he managed through gritted teeth.

'And with thy spirit, Brother Calvin.' Saul sighed and sat at his desk again. Calvin's behaviour was a niggling problem, like Paul's thorn in the flesh, he never allowed his father to relax.

Calvin headed for the stables, where there were several shire horses kept for the heavy farm work. A few minutes later, a red-robed figure could be seen ploughing the upper field, where other blue, orange and brown-robed figures were also at work.

Saul watched on the screen for a few minutes and then went back to his work. What he didn't see was the jeans clad figure of his son emerge from the rear of the stables, riding a bicycle down the back lane to a group of sheds. Minutes later, a silver sports car roared out of the last shed and out of sight.

At seven a.m., Ruth was singing scales to keep her mind off the morning to come. Unusually, she had managed some of her breakfast, which had arrived at six. The time passed too quickly. What would they think at the studio when she turned up dressed in her blue robe? She imagined all the fashionably dressed young men and women she would meet staring at her. The sound of a car in the driveway made her leap to her feet, bag in hand. Then there was sound of footsteps approaching, the door opened and Sister Barbara beckoned. Ruth felt giddy as she stepped out of the room. The air was cool, the smell of cooking had floated up the stairs and the sound of the water tank in the roof above was suddenly loud.

To Ruth's surprise, she was taken to Sister Barbara's room. The elderly woman pointed to a navy suit with white blouse and a long pleated skirt which lay over a chair. Ruth put it on. Sister Barbara walked round her, tutting under her breath, feeling the looseness of the waistband with her bony fingers. Ruth found herself up on the chair whilst Sister Barbara stitched two darts into the waist. There was no mirror, but this did not worry her – that she wasn't to wear the blue choir robe was enough.

Max Waterman waited in the hall; the church-like smell of the place and the silence made him fidgety. Several brown-robed figures were wax polishing the staircase with great energy and care in an eerie silence. A sound made him look up. Ruth, dressed in an old-fashioned navy suit, was coming down, accompanied by a green-robed older woman. At least she wasn't wearing the blue robe thing.

'Ruth, how good to see you again.'

'Good morning, Mr Waterman. I am ready. This is Sister Barbara.'

'Pleased to meet you.' Max extended his hand.

Sister Barbara simply bowed.

Max withdrew his hand awkwardly. Was this old bat coming too? A chaperone in this day and age? He moved toward the door, and the two women followed. Max sighed as he removed the papers and files from the back seat and put them into the boot. At the studio, he found a seat for her in the control room, where she sat like a nun at prayer for the whole morning. Max felt as though a living censor was keeping tally of his expletives.

'Who's that?' asked his PA, Diane.

'Chaperone.'

'Well, boggle my ghast,' Diane muttered, heading for the door.

The studio was smaller than Ruth had expected. There were no musicians that she could see anywhere. Then she met Diane, who was not much older than herself, wearing ancient jeans and a T-shirt that said 'It's not my fault' across the front.

'Can I get you anything? Tea, coffee?'

'No thanks.'

'I'll get you mineral water. You'll need it.' Diane smiled.

Ruth sipped the mineral water and put on the headphones she was given.

Diane passed her a pile of sheet music. 'When you're ready, we'll make a start. I've marked the ones that Max wants you to do.'

Ruth read the sheets of music, gently singing the words of the first one.

'I see you know that one,' Diane said.

'No, I've never heard it before.'

Diane looked up in surprise. There was more than met the eye in this girl – that was certain. 'We'd better run through it a few times then, to get it right.'

But there was no need, once Ruth's head filled with the music, she sang without hesitation. Max grinned at Diane, who shook her head in amazement.

'Told you she was good, didn't I?'
'You should have said brilliant.'

At the end of the morning, Ruth sat with a cheese and salad roll while the others tucked into an enormous lunch. Max fetched a large bowl of raspberries with some Greek yoghurt for her. Ruth realised with a shock not only that she was enjoying the meal, she had forgotten all about her father's death. A pang of guilt shook her. How could she have forgotten so soon?

'What's up, Ruth?' Diane had noticed her sudden change of colour.

'Nothing really. I just forgot ... about my father.'

'Nothing wrong in that, you're only human after all.' Diane had watched the newscast about the 'Massacre at Morning Service', with horror.

Ruth looked at Diane in surprise. Being human was to be in a state of sin. 'I should keep him in mind.'

'I don't see how, when you're learning new words and music there isn't room for anything else.'

Ruth tried to suppress a giggle, but it escaped. She'd had a mental image of her mind full of words and music dancing around.

'That's more like it. Now, we need to get some pics for the cover.'

'Pics?' Ruth looked puzzled.

'Photographs. You need a new outfit and a hairdo, and then we'll be in business.'

Ruth swallowed hard. Photographs and hairdos were frowned on as worldly things – this earthly body was but a shell for the immortal soul. 'I'm not sure…'

'Don't worry – you'll look stunning.'

'That's what I'm afraid of.'

Diane gave her another puzzled look. What planet did this girl come from?

An idea was forming at the back of Ruth's mind, and turning so that Sister Barbara couldn't see her lips, she said, 'I need to see my father's solicitor.'

'I can drive you there. No probs.'

'It's just that I need to go on my own.' She nodded at the robed figure sitting beside her.

Diane looked across at Sister Barbara's unsmiling face. 'Leave it with me – I'll see what we can do – maybe tomorrow?'

A few miles away, Calvin had overdone the whisky. He swallowed his third black coffee before setting off for The Retreat. It had been a good day, apart from his father's refusal to let him marry Ruth. The whisky had not eased that ache at all; neither had it improved his temper. He drove with the roof down and his favourite music thumping in his ears. But neither the speed nor the music could ease the emptiness he felt. A few raindrops splashed on his face, and he reached over to close the roof. That was a mistake.

The bend was nearer than he'd thought, and he lost control of the car as he rounded the first half of the double bend. His speed carried him onto the wrong side of the road, where a small blue mini van was coming toward him at speed. Calvin wrenched at the wheel and pumped his brakes in rising panic. He couldn't believe the noise of the collision. It seemed to go on for ever until there was a terrible darkness. He fell into it.

## Chapter 19

Ruth was lost in a warm haze of impressions, of new music and of new words to songs. Echoes of musical phrases alternated with snatches of conversations and new faces in her mind. The countryside was a blur of green as the car purred on towards The Retreat.

'Did you find the recording session hard?' Max asked, feeling his spirits lift, as he always did, when driving his powerful car at speed.

Ruth considered the question, tilting her head to one side as she did so. 'The music, the singing, that wasn't hard. But meeting all those people was a bit ... loud, I suppose.' She glanced at Sister Barbara, who was half asleep in the back seat. 'It is very quiet at The Retreat.'

'I know. I find that hard to take myself. Too used to music and noise about me.'

'I suppose you're used to it. Loud, I mean.'

Max had never considered his world as 'loud', but chuckled to himself. The kid was right. 'Yep, used to it loud... That's me. Whoa! – What the hell!' Max skidded to a sudden halt. Ruth was jerked out of her warm cocoon as she saw an incredible sight ahead of them in the road.

Calvin opened his eyes and wiped the sticky stuff away from his eyes. He looked confusedly at his fingers. The sticky stuff was blood. He closed his eyes then opened them again, the blood was still there. Gradually he remembered. There had been another car. He had crashed into it. Where was it now? He eased himself up, but was prevented by the roof of the car. His legs were twisted awkwardly under the steering column. For some moments, he regarded this phenomenon with profound curiosity. The odd shape of the space where he was lying did not allow him to sit up. The air bag lay like a giant squashed balloon, splash-patterned with something red. So that's what they look like, he thought.

Then, as if a light had been switched on in his brain, the scene connected into meaning and sense; car crash, air bag, blood. He explored the cut on his head with his fingers, and then moved his limbs carefully. Nothing appeared to be broken. A draught came from the crushed front window, through which a narrow slit of light filtered. Tiny shards of glass were scattered all over him. There was a dull ache around his ribs and his neck was sore. Peering around him, he realised that the car must have turned over at least once because the roof was well crushed down. His seat belt was still in place, and he struggled to reach the catch. He was lying sideways, on a slope, with his head hanging toward the passenger door. He couldn't move. Panic began to rise from somewhere in the region of his stomach.

Then there was a movement somewhere near his feet. A voice sounded outside.

'Jeez, Spanner, no one could live in that. Let's run fer it.'

'We ought to look, Kev, – just in case, like.'

'Whatever.'

Calvin kicked as loudly as he could on the roof, now usefully close to his feet.

Two voices swore loudly at the sound.

'Best get the hell outta here, Spanner!'

'Bog off then. I'm getting him out.'

Calvin breathed a sigh of relief at this.

'You'll never open those doors.'

'Wanna bet?'

'Nah.'

There was a short pause and then there was a tremendous grinding sound. Someone, perhaps Spanner, was using a crowbar on the crumpled passenger door. Calvin could feel the metal tearing under the pressure.

'Why dontcha do the ovver side?'

'Coz I want to pull 'im up this side. The damn thing'd roll on me if it shifts. I can see 'is bum. Grab the other crow bar and 'elp, or sod off.'

'Keep yer 'air on.'

It was some time before the door swung open, and Calvin saw a broad face leaning in behind a quiff of hair cut Mohican style and dyed bright pink, orange and green. The sides of the head were shaved. Both ears and the nose were well studded.

'You 'urt much?'

'I don't think so.'

'Bleeding miracle, that.' A muscular arm tattooed with a bright red dragon reached over to the seat belt. 'Stuck.' The arm vanished and then reappeared with a hammer clutched in the beefy fist. The noise was appalling in the confined space. Calvin had opened his mouth to protest when the seat belt catch capitulated.

The arms were round his waist and pulling. His ribs hurt so much at the movement that he yelled. The sound was barely out when he landed doubled up on the grass. For a few minutes he sat where he'd landed, then rolled over and vomited on the grass. Calvin was still kneeling when there was an ominous noise from the car. It began to slide down the slope away from them.

'You was right, Spanner. It would've landed on ya.'

They watched in silence as Calvin's pride and joy bounced away down the slope and into the lake at the bottom. It seemed to move in slow motion. Even the bubbles that closed over it as it sank seemed to be reluctant to burst.

'Wow.'

'Bleeding shame that, Kev.'

'You could say that.'

Calvin felt as though he was floating above the field.

His two rescuers exchanged glances, and then moved across to where their own vehicle lay, the front concertinaed in and the wheels splayed apart. Calvin didn't register what they were doing until their van tumbled its own erratic way down to the lake. It teetered for a long moment on the bank before sliding gracefully into the water and disappearing from view.

'Nice one, Spanner.'

'Yep. No sweat, Kev.'

'Why?' began Calvin.

'Joy-riding, son. Now, you won't say nuffing neither. No tax disc? Likely no insurance neither. Let's call it quits, shall we?' The exuberant quiff of vibrated.

'All right. What about that?' Calvin pointed to the hole torn in the hedge.

'I'll stick some green stuff in it.'

Calvin had thought of asking for some compensation for the loss of his car, but thought better of it now. He had not taxed nor insured the car, nor had he passed a driving test. It was high time to work his way around his father's rules and do it.

Calvin staggered behind his two rescuers back up the grassy slope, but whether his giddiness was down to the whisky or the accident or both he wasn't sure.

At the road, once the gap was roughly camouflaged, they began to walk toward the next village. The road was deserted, and Calvin stumbled out into the road, away from some vicious overhanging brambles. A car appeared suddenly from around the bend behind them and skidded to a noisy stop, stalling a few inches from Calvin's rear. So much had happened that Calvin just turned and stared at the gleaming bonnet.

Max leapt out of the car. 'What the blazes do you think you're doing in the middle of the road, you steaming idiot?'

'Walking back to The Retreat,' Calvin said carefully, since his tongue suddenly felt too big for his mouth.

Ruth wound down her window. 'That's my cousin, Calvin Crouch,' she announced. Though why he was covered in blood and walking back to The Retreat at this hour she could not imagine. He should have been leading group four meditation.

Calvin thought the fact that Ruth should be in the car was only right in the surreal world that he found himself living in. He almost wished to be back in the safety of The Retreat, where everything was predictable.

Ruth caught a brief glimpse of a weird figure running away behind the hedge, with a shadowy echo of a shape behind. Was that a kind of hat he was wearing? Fancy dress, maybe.

'Be more bloody careful in future. I only just damn well missed you.' Max climbed back into the car and started the engine.

Ruth suddenly realised that Max was about to drive on. 'You can't leave him here, Mr Waterman. He's bleeding, and it's miles to The Retreat.'

'He's filthy – bleeding – he'll mess up my car!'

Ruth looked at Max. He was incredible. Could anyone seriously put a car before someone's need? He must be joking. She tried a smile, and got out. She took Calvin's arm and opened the back passenger door. Calvin climbed in with some difficulty, obviously stiff and sore.

Sister Barbara looked at him long and hard as the car began to move, then leaned over to fasten his seat belt. What on earth had Calvin been doing this time? She could smell whisky on his breath. This would mean trouble. Had he been fighting? Those creatures that had vanished into the field looked violent enough.

Ruth looked in the vanity mirror. Calvin looked ghastly. He would be in the soup if he turned up at The Retreat in that state. But there seemed little she could do. There was a long silence in the car until they approached the outbuildings on the edge of the land belonging to The Retreat.

Calvin seemed to wake up at this point. 'Let me out here, please.'

'We're still a good way from The Retreat,' Max said.

'I know. I'll make my own way from here.' Calvin began to open the door.

'Bloody hell, man, wait till I stop, for God's sake.' The car lurched to a halt and Calvin got out like an old man.

Sister Barbara followed him.

'It's all right, Sister, I can manage,' Calvin said, angrily, turning toward her since the Sister could only read his lips.

Sister Barbara stood her ground, pointing to the wound on his head.

Calvin shrugged and set off for the nearest shed.

Sister Barbara glanced at Max, signing him to wait, and set off after Calvin.

Max looked after them. 'What the hell did that mean?'

'She's going to wash and dress that cut on his head and wants you to wait for her,' Ruth explained.

'What does she think I am? A bloody taxi service?' Max protested, but he switched off the engine and lit a cigarette.

Ruth got out of the car to avoid the smoke, and then set off to find the other two.

The shed door was ajar. Inside, it had been made into what Ruth could only describe as a squat; a picture of one had appeared in a Christian Outreach magazine that she had once read, until Brother Saul had banned it as unsuitable reading.

Sister Barbara looked up as Ruth came in, and gestured to the little first aid pack that she had taken from her bag.

Ruth set to helping: opening some sterile wound cleansing swabs to pass to Sister Barbara. The wound needed sutures. 'You ought to go to casualty with this, Brother Calvin.'

Sister Barbara nodded in agreement, watching their lips carefully.

'No, I'll have to get back as soon as I can – before my father misses me.'

'He will have already, surely?' Ruth said.

'No.' Calvin winced as Sister Barbara cleaned the wound, 'Someone is covering for me. But I don't know how long they can carry it off.'

'So you've been playing truant?'

'Something like that. You were lucky – your father let you do nursing. I've been kept tied to the family firm all my life.'

'He had quite a disagreement with Brother Saul over it, I remember.'

Sister Barbara taped a large dressing over the wound, and stuffed all the swabs and paper waste into a plastic bag. She closed her bag on it with a snap of the catch and turned to go back to the car.

'I'd better go, Brother Calvin. God Speed. But I don't know by what miracle you're going to hide that dressing, Cousin.'

'I'll give it some thought,' Calvin said.

# Chapter 20

## *Wednesday*
## *Saul*

Journal

I have been working since five this morning since sleep has eluded me. This time of the year is always hard. I hadn't known how much Elizabeth meant to me until the morning I lost her. It is something I am not able to understand. It is incomprehensible to me that God should take my helpmeet away just when the work to which we had been called was bearing fruit. The thick burgundy hard-back notebook I wrote in at the time is opened at the page as usual. I will read it again this evening: the anniversary of our parting.

The old Journal.

Elizabeth has been taken from me this morning. The boys are at school as usual, I have not informed them as yet. I must make preparations so that the cause of truth is not harmed. I was unprepared, but I should have been ready for the attacks of the evil one – none other could have been responsible for such an act. I must bury her memory. It will be possible, with some careful organization, to carry on with the plans. I cannot raise more of my own children since the Lord saw fit to take that from me, but His plan was larger than my vision. I will have twenty-seven to raise in The Truth by the end of the month. I need Dr Harold's help immediately.

Saul leaned back in the black leather office chair. The entry was fine. What had happened was still painful. The boys had been inconsolable, and then there was Calvin's conviction that he'd heard Elizabeth crying during the night. But Elizabeth had never cried in all the years they had been together. He stood to replace the burgundy notebook and returned to the current navy one, sitting at the desk again; continuing to write under the neatly written date at the top of the page. 'My room is silent save for the scratching of my pen and the tapping of a branch on the window. I am at peace.'

Had he looked up, his mind would certainly not have been at peace, for he would have seen his son walking past in his bright red robe; if Calvin was in group four meditation, he could not possibly be walking in the grounds as well.

Josh was surprised to find himself in a queue at the church. An anxious looking blue-robed figure worked his way along the queue, sorting them into six lines.

'Bless you, brother, what colour were you given at the meeting?'

By the time the man reached Josh, he'd found the little blue ribbon, and held it up.

'Bless you, brother, join line one.'

The lines moved quickly, each diverging toward a different desk beside a door where people were given badges and were buying packages.

'Bless you, brother. Your name is?'

'Joshua Allsopp.'

They found his name on their list and handed him a name badge. *Joshua Allsopp. Christian. Blue Group A261.* He was moved toward more robed helpers.

'Brother Joshua, would you like to purchase a basic starter pack or the complete pack tonight? The basic is fifteen pounds, the complete is thirty.'

'A complete one, please.' He reached for his wallet, paid, and was given one of the larger packs.

'The Lord has blessed you with a wise choice, brother. Take a seat inside, and welcome to The Life of Truth.'

Josh went inside and sat at the back of the room. The door and walls were painted blue. There must be over two hundred in this group alone, he thought. He was aware that other rooms were in use, equally crowded. If each queue led to a room, that was twelve hundred people. Curious, he opened his pack. Inside was a large black leather bound King James Bible, with a zip round the edges to protect the pages. It smelt of new leather and fresh print, it was beautiful and comfortable in the hand.

Underneath it was a hymn book in the same style. There was a smaller book of dated daily readings and teachings, and another large book entitled 'Measure; the growth of the spirit in the individual'. There was a loose-leaf file with two packets of A4 lined paper inside. There was a pen, inscribed with a biblical text. 'Study to be a good workman, rightly dividing the Word of Truth.' The last item was a diary with three meditation sections for each day, the subject printed in.

Josh looked up; people all around him were looking at the contents of their packs. He made a note of the names of as many as he could. He fingered his own name badge self-consciously. He wrote: 'The organization seems astonishingly well run', then he looked up as an imposing white-robed figure strode to the dais.

'God be with you, Brothers and Sisters in Christ.'

Another man, wearing a green robe, stood and announced. 'Our teaching begins, Brothers and Sisters. When a blessing is given, the congregation always responds. The reply to this is "and with your spirit", Brother Saul will repeat the blessing, and you will respond.'

A smiling Brother Saul repeated his words. The group responded raggedly.

'Bless you, my children. I welcome you to the best life that can be lived: the Christian life. In these classes you will be guided onto the path of truth. The lessons will be hard at times, but I pray you will persevere. It is a strait and narrow way that leads to eternal life. I pray that you will use the means of grace that are available to you, attending the teachings, reading your new Bibles, using the readings list and observing the meditations. Attendance at Worship Services is a Grace, a Duty and a Witness. I urge those of you who have only the basic pack to invest in your spiritual health by purchasing the supplementary pack next meeting. May God give you the light of understanding.'

Green Robe stood and said, 'And may His spirit guide us all.' The group responded with more assurance this time.

'Amen. Thank you, Brother Adam.' Brother Saul stepped down and a blue-robed figure opened the door for him. Josh could see him enter the next room and mount the dais, which was at the end opposite to this room. Green robe then began the teaching.

'Please open your files and insert the paper so that you can take notes, Brothers and Sisters.'

Josh's pen flew over the pages, he was conscious of others doing the same.

Rule of life or 'measure'. The activities which show the measure of spiritual growth.

1. Each day the believer must read the appointed scripture.
2. The believer must refrain from alcohol.
3. The believer must discontinue with unhelpful relationships...

At this point, someone put up a hand to ask a question.

'Yes, Sister Roberta?'

'What do you mean by unhelpful relationships?'

'You must prefix your question with my name, Sister,' Green robe said, smiling. 'An unhelpful relationship is one that hinders your spiritual growth. For example, a man might be in the habit of going for a drink with his friends several nights a week, but finds it hard to resist the temptation to drink alcohol with them. So it would be better in this case for him to cease these friendships for his own sake.'

'Thank you, Brother Adam. But what if the Christian were to witness to these people in that situation? Would that not be a good thing?'

'Sister Roberta, it would be hard for a new Christian to do that. They are still uncertain of the way themselves. It is necessary for them to grow in spiritual strength before taking on such a venture. I point you to the teaching on page sixty of your guidance notes, "If meat maketh my brother to offend". This is a teaching from the early church. Some meat sold in the meat market or shambles had been offered in ritual sacrifice. The new Christians were not sure whether to eat it or not. The teaching was to avoid it if any Brother Christian would be led astray by it.'

'Thank you, Brother Adam.'

'May your spirit be led into understanding, Sister Roberta.'

'Brother Adam, what if our families are opposed to our faith? Must we separate ourselves from them?'

'That is a difficult problem, Brother Andrew. It requires much prayer and spiritual strength on the part of the new believer. The Lord will speak to them. Have faith and ye shall move mountains.'

    4. Believers should attend all means of grace. These are worship services, meditation, classes and prayer meetings.
    5. Believers shall learn the benefits of tithing.

A hand was raised near the front. 'Brother Adam, could you explain "tithing"?'

'Thank you, Sister Amy. I would be delighted to do so. Tithing is the biblical practice of giving one tenth of your income to God.'

There was an audible sound as many of the congregation gasped.

'It seems a lot to give, when you have other commitments. But there is no compulsion to this rule – it is something that the Brethren and Sisterhood learn at their own pace. I have found that God blesses those who put his work first among their priorities in every aspect of life. If this is something hard for you, leave it to one side for now.'

'Thank you, Brother Adam.'

    6. The believer shall live simply. Whole natural foods and natural fibre clothing is preferred.
    7. The rule of obedience is set to enable believers to learn self-discipline; wife to husband, child to parent and believer to the Elder brethren.
    8. Robes must be worn in The Retreat and for closed services. The colour of the robes indicates the standing of each disciple.

Josh's mind began to reel as the list, the questions and the explanations went on. At a quick calculation, if every member in that room was on twelve thousand a year, the income would be astronomical. And this was not the only room, nor the only True Gospel Church congregation.

Josh staggered out into the street at past midnight clutching his new blue striped robe and feeling strangely euphoric. There had been meditation, singing, more teaching and more meditation. The prayer session at the end had been electric, people praying aloud in strange languages while Brother Adam translated. Josh watched a group of girls dancing down the street and singing hymns. The burden of guilt that he had carried since he had discovered what and who his father was and what he had done seemed to have eased, leaving him...happy. Home and bed seemed an excellent idea. Then he remembered his wife, and he broke into a run toward his car. Alicia would be so worried. Then there was the baby, due soon. His tired mind played over the hymn that they had sung at the end, played too fast with the rhythm of his feet:

> 'Just as I am without one plea
> But that thy blood was shed for me
> And that thou bid'st me come to thee.
> O Lamb of God I come – I come.
> Just as I am and waiting not
> To cleanse my soul of one dark blot
> To thee whose blood can cleanse each spot,
> O Lamb of God I come – I come.'

Earlier that same evening Calvin had waited behind the boiler room door for his alter ego to appear. The plan had gone badly wrong since he had been so very late. He just hoped that Willy Murgatroyd had remembered this fall back meeting place and had managed to carry things off during meditation. He had only been to two sessions. It would be better if his special group did more classes and meditations. They'd fit in better. He had a sensation similar to the time he had tried to juggle eggs and his father had come in and caught him. He had been made to eat the resulting mess – scrambled. To this day he could not face scrambled egg – the gritty bits of broken shell had been disgusting, along with bits of dirt, hair and dust from the floor.

His mind was foggy with exhaustion, shock was making him shaky and the drink hadn't helped. He tried desperately to think of a plausible excuse for his injuries.

Calvin shrank back against the wall as steps came closer. The door opened to reveal Willy's red-robed figure.

'Cor, guv, wot 'appened to yew?'

'Smashed the car up,' Calvin said, handing Willy his yellow robe.

'Bad?'

'Sank it in a lake out of sight. Beyond repair.'

'Yew all right?'

'Headache. But I need to work out a cover up. How can I explain this?'

Willy scratched his arm, where there were several angry looking insect bites. 'It'll have to be good to get past yer dad,' he said slowly, gazing up the steep steps he had just descended.

'I know that.' Calvin's head thumped painfully as he raised his voice.

'Got it!' Willy said; 'Yew fall down the bleedin' stairs. I find yew.' He held up the red robe. 'Afraid I tore it an' got it a bit mucky too. So you tripped on the bit that's dangling and went a whopper down the back steps.'

Calvin considered the idea. The back steps were uneven, concrete, and dirty. 'Right. Give us the robe.' He lifted the dressing from his head and squeezed blood down the front of the robe. He changed into the dirty robe, and headed for the back steps. He kept the dressing on the cut, which was bleeding freely again, until he reached the steps. At the bottom, he stood and let blood drip onto the stones, and then went slowly up them, dripping all the way.

'Yer dad's bound to smell that whisky on ya!' Willy commented from behind him.

Calvin chuckled, 'No, dad, I mean, Brother Saul, can't smell a thing.'

'Yer kidding?'

'He had some kind of virus. Wiped out his sense of smell.'

Willy shook his head in disbelief, half admiring and half worried at the amount of blood that was being lost all over the floor. 'That's enough guv; yew'll pass out in a minute.'

Calvin did feel very groggy, but his fear of his father and the consequences if his other life was laid bare kept him on his feet. He reached into his pocket for the clean handkerchief that he always kept there. It was filthy.

'Sorry, guv. Had to use it.'

Calvin gestured to the yellow robe that Willy was wearing, 'In the pocket, there'll be a fresh one.'

Willy passed it to him, and Calvin held the handkerchief to his head, leaning against the wall. Then he made for his father's study, his heart thudding uncomfortably and his head throbbing painfully in rhythm. He hoped this would work. His father would have been out at the new classes tonight, and was probably on his way back.

Saul was just hanging up his cloak when his son staggered in, supported by Brother William.

'God be with you, Brother Saul.'

Willy was amazed that Calvin could follow the rule when he must be out on his feet.

If Saul was surprised, he didn't show it. At the door, he sent someone for Sister Miriam. As she bathed and dressed the wound, he listened to the explanation in silence. He gestured for Calvin to remove the soiled and torn robe, while Willy helped Calvin into a clean one.

'Go to your room, Calvin, I will join with you there for prayer and Sister Miriam will bring Dr Harold to look at you.'

'Very well, F- Brother Saul.'

When his son had gone, Saul plugged in the telephone and called the doctor before examining the robe. Certainly covered in blood and both torn and dirty. He put it into the laundry chute on his way along the corridor toward the back stairs. Slowly, he descended them, noting drops of blood and the pool of red at the bottom. A handrail would be a good idea.

Perhaps the lad was telling the truth, for once.

Brother Matthew came in from the gardens. 'What on earth's happened? Sorry – God be with you, Brother Saul.'

'And with your Spirit. An accident. Would you clean these steps, Brother Matthew?'

'To the Glory of God, Brother Saul. Would it be good to spend task time tomorrow as I have kitchen duties this evening?'

'It would. I will send you some penants. May your labour be fruit to your spirit.'

Matthew's heart pounded in his chest so that he thought Brother Saul must be able to hear it. He took a deep breath and spoke.

'May I ask an audience, Brother Saul?'

Saul looked up in surprise – never had Matthew asked to speak to him privately. 'You may. What troubles you, my son?'

'Sister Ruth. I am concerned about her health. She is very thin.'

Saul wondered if this was a ploy to discover where Ruth was, but, seeing the young man's genuine concern, he said, 'I will ask Dr Harold to see her. Sister Miriam also expressed concern for her. "In the mouths of two witnesses, a thing shall be established."'

'Amen,' Matthew said, and took flight along the lower corridor.

As Saul climbed the stairs and entered the hall, Dr Harold came in, closely followed by Sister Ruth and Sister Barbara. The two women stood against the wall, hands folded, waiting for the men to take precedence. As he greeted the doctor, Saul's eyes took in Ruth's pallor, her hollow cheeks and the way her clothes hung loosely. The child was far too thin. How had he not noticed one of his children's ill health?

'I have two patients for you, Doctor; my son Calvin and Sister Ruth.'

Ruth looked up in surprise from her demure pose, gazing at the floor.

Saul beckoned them to follow, and the four of them gathered in his office. After he had examined Ruth, Dr Harold sent her to wait outside.

'I'm not sure about this – it may be the loss of her father, but it may be something worse. I shall need to do some blood tests. She is certainly worryingly underweight. I will send her some special drinks to build her up, but I want to find the cause of her weight loss.'

'Do the tests as soon as you can.'

Doctor Harold opened the door. 'Sister Ruth, would you attend clinic for a blood test at eight tomorrow morning.'

'Yes, doctor.'

Harold watched her walk behind Sister Barbara up the stairs. She climbed very slowly, as if it were a great effort. 'You were right to call me, the child is sick.'

'With God's Guidance. Follow me; my son is in his room.'

Dr Harold followed Saul to Calvin's room. The head-wound was deep. He noted the smell of whisky on the young man's breath as he examined him, but only said, 'You'll be a bit groggy for a couple of days, young man.' Turning to Saul, he said, 'Best to send him to casualty for an X-ray; by the feel of it, he's got a couple of broken ribs, there may be other injuries. Could you phone for an ambulance? Here's my phone.'

'I see.' Saul took the mobile, and dialled expertly, to his son's surprise.

'Did you lose consciousness at all, young man?'

'Yes, I did, I think. And I was sick after...'

'Bed rest for a couple of days when he gets back from the hospital, I think, Saul. They may keep him in overnight for observation.'

As they walked down the long staircase together, Saul asked, 'Are Calvin's injuries consistent with falling down stairs?'

'You mean ones like this?'

'No, stone steps onto a concrete floor.'

'Possibly – he is very bruised. The head wound was caused by something fairly solid and jagged. Not these smooth wooden steps, certainly.'

Saul opened the door to the back stairs and the doctor looked at the long steep flight in horror.

'I wouldn't like to fall down those.' Absently, he pulled at a piece of red cloth that was caught on a nail at the top. Saul took it from him with the air of a detective at a crime scene.

'A handrail, Saul?'

'I have put it in hand already.'

'Good. See you in the morning.'

Ruth was so tired that she lay on the bed fully clothed and slept straight away. It seemed only moments before there came a knock at the door and it was morning.

# Chapter 21

Thursday Morning.

Ruth sat up, bleary-eyed, as Sister Barbara brought in a tray. On it was a note beside her breakfast which read, 'Dr's clinic, eight a.m, recording studio car, eight thirty.'

Had she really slept all night in her clothes?

The Bishop sat looking out at the cathedral. The sight of the soaring seven-hundred foot spire usually lifted his spirits. This afternoon, it was bathed in sunshine, people were sitting around on the grass, and overhead the kestrels that nested high up on a ledge were in residence; one was hanging as though from a thread just within his field of view. It had probably seen something in the water meadows for lunch. The Bishop sighed, turned back to his desk and the problem in hand. The others would be here in fifteen minutes; time for some quiet prayer in a corner of the cathedral before the event.

At the same moment, Ruth was singing softly whilst sight-reading a piece of sheet music in the studio for the third time. 'This isn't right, Max, I'm sure this should be in 'F' sharp, the natural jars so.' Her heart thumped painfully; perhaps she shouldn't have said anything?

'That's what's printed?'

'Yes.' Ruth felt a sudden surge of confidence. 'Listen – I'll sing it as printed, and then in 'F' sharp; see what you think.'

Ruth's voice at full volume filled the room, everyone listening intently. Max watched and listened to the girl more closely than anyone. What a talent – and musically literate too! 'Leave that one till the end, Ruth; I'll get someone to check it out before we record.'

Max passed the music sheet to Diane. 'Run this past Sandy, will you? He understands musical hieroglyphs better than anyone.'

'Except maybe Sister Ruth; she staggers my psyche every time I see her.'

'Me too,' Max said absently as Ruth began to sing again.

The Bishop rose from his knees, feeling the all-too-familiar arthritic pain in the joints. Nowadays he understood all too clearly the point of that line in the Remembrance Day Poem. Age was definitely wearying.

Archdeacon Wise flapped toward him like a grounded crow. 'Your Grace, the first of your visitors has arrived.'

'Thank you, Bertie. I shall go to the meeting directly. I do not wish to be disturbed.'

'There is that problem in the North Transept, Your Grace.'

The Bishop looked at his colleague's anxious face. 'I know, bless you for reminding me. If leaving it will not cause the Cathedral to fall I will come and take a look myself this afternoon.'

Bertie looked at the Bishop in some puzzlement. He could never tell whether the Bishop was joking or not.

'Very well, Your Grace.'

The Bishop smiled as he watched him flap away into the cloisters. If only all his flock were as committed as Bertie.

The meeting room was beginning to fill by the time the Bishop returned. He gestured them to sit down at the long, well-polished oak table.

'Thank you all for coming this morning. Do help yourself to refreshments; they are available on the far sideboard. We will wait five minutes for any latecomers; then we will begin with prayer.'

Someone brought him tea and he sipped at its warmth gratefully; the Cathedral was cold even in summer. At the five minute deadline, he stood to begin, every head bowed and there was a hush. Into the hush came the crash of the swing doors flying open and the local Baptist minister, John Black, almost fell into the room.

'Welcome, Brother, I am glad you could join us.' The Bishop's lips twitched in amusement as the poor perspiring cleric hurried to a seat.

'Thank you, Your Grace, terribly sorry to keep you all waiting; I was held up by a late funeral.'

The hush returned; the Bishop prayed for clear guidance and mutual understanding of the difficult issue before them.

'Do be seated, gentlemen. You will find an agenda under the paper set in front of you.' There was a rustling as a dozen pairs of hands reached for the agenda. What was this extraordinary meeting to be about? The Bishop took the opportunity to place a cup of tea in front of the Baptist Minister, who jumped in surprise and smiled his thanks.

'Now, to business, Gentlemen. Our point of discussion this morning is The True Gospel Church. We will begin. Point one. Within the diocese we have built up an ecumenical spirit which has blessed us all and our congregations. Now, I wish to hear your real feelings on the effect the True Gospel Church is having on the health of the spiritual community. Father Murphy?'

'I am seriously worried by this movement, Your Grace. Many of my congregation have joined this group and have been instructed that The Roman Church is not beneficial to spiritual growth, that they should withdraw from the church and any relationship which would hinder them from leaving the church.'

There was a murmur of agreement around the table. The Bishop wrote the comment down and then asked: 'Pastor McGregor, have you any concerns?'

'Very similar ones, Your Grace. There is also the matter of a family that has simply – gone.'

There was a gasp of astonishment at this.

'Gone, Pastor?'

'Yes, one of my flock; he had joined this True Gospel Church, but had still come to meetings quite regularly. But then a few weeks passed and I had not seen him, neither had my wife seen any of the children at school – she teaches – so I called round to his home. It was empty, and a for sale board stood at the gate.'

'There must be a simple explanation, Pastor.'

'That's just what I told myself. I called on his sister who lives a few streets away. She knew nothing about it either.'

Pastor Black from the Methodist Church looked really worried at this. 'I'm afraid the same pattern of events has been repeated twice in my congregation.'

Pastor McGregor passed a letter to the Bishop, who read it with increasing concern.

'This is from Rabbi Solomon. Apparently, a family whose son was of age for his Bar Mitzvah, simply vanished.'

The Bishop made copious notes as he asked each of the group in turn what problems they had with the True Gospel Church.

After two hours of discussion, he stood to adjourn the meeting. 'Thank you, brethren. It seems that the problems we face are tremendous. I had hoped I was mistaken. I have noted, and I share, your concerns. I shall be taking this matter to the Archbishop. I will be very grateful if you keep in touch with me if you have any problems before our next gathering – I take it you wish to meet again over this issue?'

There was a murmur of agreement.

'Let us close in prayer. Pastor McGregor, would you lead us?'

The Bishop's heart warmed as the Pastor prayed fervently and from the heart for guidance over the coming days. Theirs was the same God.

The Bishop sat at his desk with his notes, black coffee at his elbow. The computer screen showed his list of documents. He selected one entitled 'TGC'; opened a new file and began to type.

Private and confidential; to the Archbishop:

Minutes of the Ecumenical Committee. Extraordinary General Meeting.

Points of concern...

About thirty minutes later, the Bishop finished his spell-check and printed out the document. This he placed in the hard-copy file of the Ecumenical Committee. Then, he emailed the minutes as an attachment to the Archbishop. He felt bone-weary. As he had typed up the minutes, the scale of the problem had become clear; before, there had only been vague uneasiness. Now, he was afraid in a way he had not been since serving in the trenches during the war. He glanced at the case containing his VC and smiled grimly.

There were no medals given in this kind of war.

## Chapter 22

Ruth ate the fish in parsley sauce slowly. It seemed so strange to be here alone today – there had been no one available to come to the studio with her. It must be the to-do with Calvin's arrival in solitary this morning. She'd caught a glimpse of him through the open door of his room. The bruising looked awful.

Diane came across. 'When you've finished, we'll go out to the hairdresser, then we'll call in at Hadley's. We can pop into that solicitor's too, if you'd like?'

'If that's all right with you,' Ruth said, pushing her plate aside.

'No, you finish that. I'm off to fetch some chocolate cheesecake. Want some?'

'What's chocolate cheesecake?'

Diane looked at her in amazement. 'You've never eaten choccie cheesecake?'

'I don't think so.'

'Well I'll be f- I mean snardle-whacked.'

'You'll be what?'

'Gob – I mean shocked.' Diane shook her head as she went to the sweet trolley.

Later, as they threaded their way through the weekday traffic, Ruth said, 'I can't have anything done to my hair, you understand.'

'Why not?'

'A woman's hair is her crowning glory. A gift which a woman must cherish.'

Diane put her hand up to her cropped curls. 'My hair would look a mess if I grew it long.' She pushed the salon door open, 'Come in. They'll do something with it that won't involve cutting.'

Ruth had never been in a salon before. She gazed around at the customers. One woman was sitting with her hair in strange rolls under a stranger-looking lamp; another wore a plastic cap with her hair pulled through in little strands. There was a sweet chemical smell in the air, bright coloured bottles lined the shelves and posters of young women with hair that looked uncombed gazed down from the walls.

The woman who came to sit her in front of a mirror had blonde hair with red streaks in it. Ruth tried not to stare as she undid the clips and pins holding her own hair in place. It fell four feet over the back of the chair, almost reaching the floor.

'Wow! What lovely hair you have.' The hairdresser reached for a brush to tidy the mass of glossy waves, 'I have never seen hair like it.'

'Ruth doesn't want it cut,' Diane said.

'I don't blame you. But you could do with these split ends taken off – they're so tangled and thin. Then I can pile it up on top for you; let the curls hang down.' She lifted the offending bits to show Ruth. It was the bits she called her 'rat's tails' – so awkward to comb through.

She suddenly felt rebellious. 'Yes, cut those bits off, please.'

Some time later, she emerged with her hair arranged in a style she'd never imagined possible. The dress that Diane bought her was a simple white full length gown that clung to her figure, though Ruth insisted on having a size larger than she needed to reduce the clinging effect.

The solicitor's office was in a converted medieval town house. The flagstone floor had been retained, large oak beams supported the ceiling and an enormous staircase curved up to a gallery above.

Ruth found herself staring at the receptionist: a woman that looked so masculine that she looked like a man in woman's clothes.

'Miss Diamond?' this apparition said, in a deep husky voice.

Ruth blushed and stood up.

'I'll wait here for you,' Diane said.

'Thanks.' She followed the figure up the stairs and was shown into a spacious office. A tall, thin, balding man stood up and came toward her, hand outstretched.

'Ruth, I'm so glad you managed to get away to see me. I hope it wasn't too difficult.'

'I'm at the recording studio on my own today – Calvin had an accident and Sister Barbara had to stay at The Retreat.'

'Recording Studio?'

'I'm recording some hymns for Mr Waterman. I'm enjoying it. It helps me... to forget for a while.'

'I'm so sorry about your father, Ruth. The cloak and dagger with the letter may not have been necessary, but I thought it safer. Now, I'll read you the letter I had from David Farnsby – I was going to send it to you, but I left it out by mistake.

'Nigel,

If you don't hear from me, please go to the police. I am very concerned about what's been happening at the church lately.

David.'

'Is that all he wrote?'

'Yes. Now, I did take it to the police – I spoke to an Inspector Bradley. A few days later he telephoned me to say that he'd spoken to David Farnsby's doctor. He had been admitted to hospital for psychiatric care, and his family had gone to Scotland to live with relations.'

Ruth stared at the solicitor, looking like a rabbit caught in headlights.

'Ruth, are you all right?' Nigel Bishop stood up, looking worried.

'Yes – if I could have a drink of water?'

The solicitor pressed a buzzer on his desk. 'Bring a glass of water for Miss Diamond, could you please, Danielle?'

The masculine receptionist placed a glass in Ruth's hands and left.

'Sorry about that,' Ruth said, when she had taken a few sips of water. 'It's just that Matthew Farnsby was brought up with us, at his home. It was never sold. But he never knew what happened to his parents.'

'With us?'

'By the True Gospel Church. Two of the sisters cared for several children who were without parents. Matthew was one of them. He never went to Scotland.'

'Are you sure?'

'Yes.' Ruth sipped her water; her hand was trembling as she held the glass. 'He was at school with me.'

Nigel Bishop was silent for a moment. Something was definitely wrong somewhere. 'I'm not sure what to do next, Ruth. You're saying that David Farnsby and his wife disappeared, leaving their son behind.'

'Maybe we should talk to the police again?'

'I'm not sure we have too much to tell them – nothing concrete.' He moved to look out of his window, hands in pockets.

'I think we should tell them what we know,' Ruth said slowly.

'I will, then.' He sat down, and opened a large blue folder on his desk. 'The other thing is your father's will. He has left half of all his investments and Rectory House to you. The keys are here.' He put a bunch of keys on the desk. 'There is also some money in a building society account for you. To be used if you need to get away.'

Ruth stared at the solicitor for a moment. The words 'If you need to get away' echoed in her mind. Why would she want to get away? There was money, a house, some investments. All things he should have given over to the church; hidden from his wife. She picked up the keys. 'Rectory House?'

'Yes. It's in a village near here. It has been rented out for several years. The current tenants are on a two year contract, which ends this summer when they move – he's in the army. The rental money is paid into your Building Society account monthly.'

'I didn't know,' Ruth said faintly, 'not even about the building society account.' Why would her father hide so many assets? It was so unlike him to be secretive. Either he was not the man she'd thought him, or he was so convinced that there might be something so amiss with the church that he felt he had to make provision for her. Just in case. But in case of what?

'I don't know why your father planned things as he did, but I am more than ever concerned that he may have been right to be worried about the church. You will be careful, won't you?'

'Oh, don't worry about me – I'm just part of the church furniture.'

The intercom on the desk buzzed. 'Your next appointment is here, Mr Bishop.'

'Thanks, Danielle. Ask them to wait, and offer them a drink. I'll be a few moments yet.'

Ruth stood up. 'Thank you,' she began.

'Do sit down again, Ruth. I have something else for you.' He went to a safe in the corner and took out a small enamelled box. 'These belonged to your grandmother, and she left them to you.'

With trembling fingers, Ruth opened the box. Inside were several smaller boxes. The first she opened contained a three-string necklace of natural pearls. 'But I'm not allowed to wear such things – it's external adornment.'

'That's why they weren't given to your mother.' Nigel Bishop gave a wry smile. 'Your grandmother didn't want them sold; they've been in the family for five generations.'

Ruth gazed down at the pearls and then slowly opened the other boxes; there were diamond earrings, pearl earrings, silver and gold bracelets, an emerald pendant and a gold watch set with tiny diamonds.

'Then I shan't sell them either, since that's what gran wanted. But I can't take them back to The Retreat; they would take some explaining.'

The solicitor took the box from her and placed it in the safe again. 'You may want to place them in your own bank when you get things organised. Here are details of the bank and building society accounts that your father opened in your name. I must add that there was a very odd request regarding your brother's accounts. He kept them open after Daniel died. He has also left him half his investments and a property in Coombe Bissett.'

'Why on earth did he do that?'

'I have no idea, Ruth. He asked me to continue adding interest to them as if he were still alive, until such time as he asked me to cease doing so.'

Ruth gazed at the carpet, her eyes taking in the complex pattern of interlinking squares. 'It's a bit like a chessboard,' she said.

'More like a Chinese puzzle.'

'I need time to think about all this.'

'I'm sure you do. And I must see my next clients.'

'I should have made an appointment...'

'I know how difficult it was for you to get here on your own.' He reached across the desk and shook her hand.

'Thank you for all your help.'

'All part of the service. Take care,' he turned and picked up a Harrods carrier bag. 'These are yours; your father left them with me for you.'

Ruth felt the weight of several books and a couple of files in the bag. She put the keys into her pocket and stumbled toward the door.

'I'll keep in touch; give me a call if you need me.' Nigel Bishop had followed her to the door and opened it for her. 'I shall be at the funeral tomorrow.'

Ruth nodded, she had managed to keep all thought of the funeral at the back of her mind and the reminder was almost a physical pain. She made her way down the stairs like a sleepwalker. Diane stood up. 'You look as though you've seen a ghost. Come and have a coffee.' Ruth was steered into the café two doors down the street, where she was presented with a hot chocolate and a currant bun. Ruth sipped the drink cautiously at first and then enjoyed it. 'This is good; I never tasted it before.'

'You haven't lived, Ruthie! You've got a bit of colour now. I hope it wasn't bad news.'

'No, not bad news as such. Just... worrying.'

'Put it out of your mind for now – we'll have to get back to the studio – the photographer is due at three-thirty.'

It was a relief to return to the bustle of the studio, to the strangeness of posing for photographs, and of listening to her own voice on record. It was only as she sat on the narrow bed in her solitary room with the Harrods bag at her feet that the day's happenings crowded in on her. Ruth sank to her knees in prayer beside the bed, where she was disturbed an hour later by Sister Barbara with a tray of supper.

Over her arm was Ruth's long black dress, which she put carefully on the bed.

'Bless you, Sister,' Ruth said, getting to her feet, which were cramped from kneeling so long. Sister Barbara nodded, made the sign of blessing, and left Ruth alone with her grief.

Archbishop Pringle stared at the file printout from the Bishop of Salisbury for a very long time. Then, turning back to his computer he sent a copy of the minutes to all his fellow archbishops and to his own bishops. Then he consulted the phone book, and telephoned a certain Inspector Cooper.

Nigel Bishop had a busy afternoon, and it wasn't until after five that he was able to telephone Inspector Bradley's Office; but a stranger answered.

'Inspector Cooper.'

'Ah, Inspector, I was hoping to speak to Inspector Bradley, it's Nigel Bishop here.'

'Afraid he's living it up in Spain; retired now – can I help at all?'

When Nigel had finished speaking, Cooper sat thinking for a long moment. 'Could you have the letter ready for my sergeant, DS Allsopp, to collect? I'd very much like to see it.'

'No problem. Goodnight, Inspector.'

Cooper hung the phone by its wire for a few moments, watching it untwist, before replacing it. This would not be on computer yet; he set off for the file room.

'Job for you Bertie, I need a missing person report for a David Farnsby, in Bradley's time, around fifteen years ago.'

'Thanks a bundle, Inspector,' Bertie grumbled, 'I was just off home for me Lancashire hot-pot.'

'Tomorrow will be fine,' Cooper grinned.

'Never leave a job until tomorrow, that's my motto, and you know it.'

Just as Cooper opened his office door, the phone rang. 'Archbishop, how can I help you?' His expression was grim as he listened to the measured voice at the end of the line.

'I'll get to it right away, Your Grace, thank you for sharing it with me.'

The email attachment was larger than he'd expected. He printed it out, taking it to his comfortable chair. The door opened, Bertie's dour face appeared, in his hands a faded manila file.

He placed the file on the desk. 'Just sign the receipt form and I'll be on my way, sir.'

'Quick work, Bertie.' Cooper signed the docket.

'I know me files, sir. Not like them damned computers, they don't get lost, not tracked proper like.'

'Thanks.'

'Goodnight sir.'

Cooper stood beside his flip chart and began to fill in more names on his missing church members' list. It was getting worryingly long.

## Chapter 23

Friday Morning.

The Bishop woke with a headache and a feeling of impending doom. His morning devotions were not the usual peaceful communion he was accustomed to having with his maker. He felt unsure of His guidance; and a dream still haunted him. He had been in a small canoe, tossed about in fast flowing rapids toward a precipice of Niagara Falls' proportions, with only a broken stump of a paddle to fend off disaster.

'Up the creek without a paddle,' he murmured under his breath.

'Your Grace?' Archdeacon Wise must have come in quietly after the Bishop had knelt.

'Nothing really, Bertie. How are the preparations?'

'About finished, I think. I wasn't sure about setting out all the chairs the Reverend Crouch suggested, but I've done it. I had to borrow some.'

The Bishop turned to look at the sea of chairs. 'You've done well.'

'They sent some... men to help.' The Archdeacon sniffed. 'More like a group of community service workers than church elders.'

The Bishop laughed. 'Did you check the plate afterwards?'

The Archdeacon blushed. The Bishop clapped him on the back. 'Never mind, let's do Matins; are there any takers?'

'Mrs Williams.'

'That'll make three: "Where two or three are gathered together", Bertie. I just wonder sometimes if we need so much room for them.'

Bertie fell into step beside the Bishop, puzzled as usual by his Grace's comments. He noticed a cobweb on one of the seats and brushed it away as he passed. It seemed somehow to be significant, and he shivered.

Outside, the first of many coach loads of robed figures were walking silently, two abreast, toward the main doors, observed by curious onlookers and the newsmen already gathered for the event.

Daniel and Paul were escorted through a side door which avoided the steady stream of people pouring through the front entrance. They sat in an area shadowed by an enormous tomb with a knight atop it and a little dog at his feet.

'Isn't this too much of a risk, Dan?'

'Would you miss your father's funeral? Anyhow, they'll never recognise me in this wheelchair, wig in place and dark glasses on. I wouldn't recognise myself.'

'You look like an actor from a second-rate spy movie.'

'Thanks pal.'

At The Retreat, all was quiet bustle after morning meditations. All were dressed in full robes except for Ruth and Miriam. Ruth had not been able to speak to her mother, since they were in separate groups. Ruth climbed aboard the first choir coach and huddled into a corner of the long rear seat. Simone Brooke, the music Sister, found her after a long search, and asked the Sister beside Ruth if she would sit elsewhere.

'How are you, Sister Ruth?'

'I am well, thank the Lord. And you?'

'I am truly blessed, Sister. Will you be able to sing today?'

'With God's grace I shall.'

'Then let us look at the order of service together before we arrive.' Sister Simone took a folder from her briefcase and opened it. 'It is indeed unfortunate that you have been otherwise engaged during choir practice, Sister.'

'I have been singing to the glory of the Lord. Many souls may be touched by the music, God willing.'

'I pray it may be so, and that no damage comes to thee from coming so close to worldly things, Sister Ruth.'

'I thank you for your prayers.' Ruth opened the folder, changing the subject to the music for the service. She was called back to the present when the coach stopped outside the True Gospel Church. Brother Adam stepped onto the coach and called her forward.

'Sister Ruth? There is a car to take you to the service.' When Ruth reached him, he helped her down the steps and led her to a large black car. Parked in front of it was a hearse. Inside was a coffin covered with flowers. The coach moved away and Ruth was suddenly alone, facing the reality. This was a real funeral. This was her last goodbye to her father.

Brother Adam opened the car door and Ruth climbed in, to find a black clad figure seated in the back.

'Mother!' Ruth moved to hug her, but Miriam pushed her away, gently enough, but it was a rejection nonetheless.

'Sister Ruth,' Miriam said quietly. 'How are you?'

Ruth could not answer for a moment. 'I am well, thank the Lord. And you?'

'I am truly blessed, Sister.'

The hearse ahead moved out, the traffic giving way to the two cars following behind. It seemed to take no time to reach the Cathedral. The crowd outside was enormous, the television outside broadcast van stood incongruous in this setting. In a daze, Ruth followed the men carrying her father's coffin.

She should have been prepared for the size of the congregation. There must be choirs from every True Gospel Church near enough to travel, she thought. The aisles were full of robed figures, the choir stalls were crammed full; there were many standing at the back of the nave. Ruth stepped gracefully into the space Sister Simone indicated; her mother sat in the front row of seats, her back ramrod straight.

Her father's coffin was placed between the two others that had already been carried in: Sister Hope and Brother Harold. Ruth felt a guilty pang as she realised that she hadn't given these other two brethren a thought; too selfishly bound up with her own loss. The strangers along this front row must be their family members.

The service began with prayer, and a welcome from the Bishop. Then the choir stood in one swift movement and the enormous building was filled with music. It echoed back and forth under the high arched roof, loud, sweet and clear. Sister Simone conducted them and Archdeacon Wise fell in love with her music.

At the back, Reggie and the rest of Calvin's group were lined up in order with the collection plates that the Murgatroyd brothers had acquired from somewhere.

'Remember, two each side of the door and smile,' Willy Smith whispered, 'as soon as they carry 'em out.'

The service continued to unfold like a dream to Ruth. She stood to sing the solo parts she had been given like an automaton. Only when she sang did she seem to waken from her trance. The experience of singing with such a choir was thrilling. There were readings, a sermon from Brother Adam, and eulogies from Brother Saul. And in between all, there were hymns, psalms and solos sung. At last, all was over, and Ruth followed her father's coffin once again toward the hearse and the drive to The Retreat's churchyard for the interment.

Nobody noticed the small dark blue VW van that parked nearby, nor the two figures that looked on through a thin place in the hedge as the service progressed at the graveside.

It was a quieter gathering, but still very crowded. Ruth dropped a little earth on the coffin and turned away, feeling completely empty. The faces in front of her seemed to blur and sway. Matthew caught her before she fell.

'It's over now, love.'

'I'm sorry to be such a poor witness, Brother Matthew.'

'You were simply amazing.'

She looked at him in confusion. 'Amazing?'

Brother Adam appeared at Matthew's elbow. 'We must help her into the car. She will be better for some food and drink at the retreat.'

She stumbled as the two men helped her to the car, which smelt of peppermints. It seemed to be travelling above the ground as she floated, weightless, over the soft cushions.

Matthew placed his arm around her shoulders and then she felt grounded again.

But the sense of unreality returned as she floated into the main reception room at the retreat, where food was laid out for guests. Matthew found her a glass of milk with two plain biscuits, thinking that she might be able to cope with this plain fare. Ruth was unaware of it, but all the reception rooms had been pressed into service to cope with the numbers. And at each gathering, invitations to service were being given out to those not wearing robes.

Outside the Cathedral, other leaflets were being distributed. Max had worked overnight to get them ready. 'Give them to the ones in ordinary clothes; not the choirs, I doubt they have money or CD players.'

The leaflets bore a glossy photograph of Sister Ruth, the cover of the CD, and 'Out soon, a magical compilation of sacred songs' £1 off cover price with this coupon.

The newsmen began to pack up. Inside the Cathedral, men were removing the TV cameras and folding up the chairs. The Bishop caught sight of a disreputable group working together, and caught the Archdeacon's eye.

'No doubt about it, an odd bunch. Even with the suit, I recognise Reggie Foster from my parish days. Perhaps they're the ex-cons' prayer group.'

The Archdeacon sniffed. Then he almost ran down the aisle toward a robed figure. The Bishop recognised her as she turned; the one who'd conducted the choirs.

No wonder Bertie wanted to speak to her. The music had been simply amazing. That girl who'd sung the solos had a voice fit for heaven. How she had managed to sing when it was her own father lying there he'd never know.

By the entrance, the Bishop paused to pick up a piece of paper. His jaw dropped as he read the advertisement. How mercenary could they get, giving these out at a funeral?

He stood at the entrance, saying goodbye to a last few stragglers. Then he went back inside, feeling the need of a quiet spot in which to pray.

Back at The Retreat's churchyard, Daniel sat beside the newly filled grave for a long time, his eyes fixed on the flowers. Paul had become impatient, walking among the other stones and reading the inscriptions.

'You okay, old thing?' he said, seeing his friend stir, as if waking from a trance.

'I wish I'd been able to talk to him before he died.'

'Cruel, that. Life gives no second chances. You've a namesake buried here, by the way.'

'No, that'll be my grave. It'll have the date of my "Accident" on it,' said Dan.

Cooper sat at his desk facing the darkness outside. Even having divided the various ministers between them, they'd both had quite a long day of it, especially having attended the service between visits. The question troubling him was not easy to answer. Was the evidence sufficient to widen the investigation and would the Chief Constable give him more resources to pursue this?

# Chapter 24

Friday Morning.

Calvin woke to a silence that was profound even for The Retreat. For a moment he felt a panic rising within; had the last trumpet sounded and he been left behind? As he came to full consciousness, he laughed at himself for his childish fears. Brainwashed, that's what he'd been. Brainwashed. There must be someone about. He got out of bed. The pain and stiffness was ample reminder, if he needed any, of his narrow brush with death. He pulled on his robe and went in search of food. As he neared the kitchen he heard laughter. Someone not observing the rule of silence? He opened the door quietly. The room was awash with strangers working at the stove and carrying dishes out into the reception rooms.

A man in a white jacket and blue checked chef's trousers spotted Calvin and came over to him. 'Good morning, sir. Can I help?'

'I wouldn't mind some breakfast. I seem to have been forgotten.'

'No problem. Sit down at the table and we'll sort you out.'

Calvin sat and was rewarded with a full English breakfast. Quite a change from the usual wholewheat muesli.

'How come they forgot you?' the chef said, whipping the empty plate away and replacing it with a pile of hot toast.

'In bed – I had an accident.'

'So you missed the funeral.'

'So that's where everyone's gone. I'd forgotten all about that.' His heart skipped a beat; he hoped the men had behaved themselves. He'd not thought to give them any instructions.

'We've been called in to do the wake food. All the cooks are singing in the choir this morning. There are some of your mates helping in the dining rooms.'

'Thanks.' Calvin had no intention of finding his 'mates'. He finished his third slice of toast, emptied his cup and stood up too quickly, forgetting his injuries. He had to grab the table edge for a moment.

'Steady, mate. Not as spry as usual.'

Calvin managed a grin. 'No. I must make a note not to fall down stone steps in future.'

'When I do it I'm usually well out of it and I seem not to hurt myself much.' The chef grinned and headed for the sink with the dirty dishes. 'See you.'

'Thanks for the breakfast. It was very good.'

Calvin was suddenly in a hurry. It would be a long time before he had such a chance again. How much time did he have until his father got back? He headed for his father's study and began to search the drawers and filing cabinets very carefully indeed, replacing things exactly as they had been.

Friday Evening.

Inspector Cooper was in a quandary. He sat alone in his favourite Italian restaurant, but that was not his problem. His problem had just arrived at the entrance and was waiting to be seated. There was no vacant table for her, but Cooper was at a table for two. His heart thudded uncomfortably loud as he nodded to Paulo.

'You are ready to order, sir?'

'Yes, I mean, no, the lady waiting, she is welcome to join me if she wishes to do so.'

'That is very kind of you, sir. I will ask her.'

Cooper watched as the waiter spoke to the newcomer. He found he was biting his lip, something he hadn't done for years. He stood up as she approached, the waiter pulling out her chair with a flourish.

'Inspector Cooper, how very kind of you.' As she leaned forward to take his hand he was aware of that subtle perfume and the way her black dress clung to the outline of her breasts.

'Not at all. The pleasure's mine. Can I buy you a drink?'

'A white wine, please, Paulo.'

'I bring your usual, Miss Harman.'

'Make it a bottle, please, Paulo. I could do with a drink after today.'

'Has it been a bad one?'

She tilted her head to one side, examining him, 'Yes, I'd say it's after funeral malaise. I've been there too – hence the black dress. It's not easy for me, hearing all that again, being among them.'

'Were you quite safe, I mean, would they try to get you back if they saw you?'

'They would indeed. But,' she stooped to take something from her bag and placed it on her head with a flourish, 'maybe they had some difficulty?'

Cooper laughed. The grey wig was so awful that it looked like an unkempt floor mop. 'I suppose they did.'

She put it back in her bag. 'I felt a bit like an alcoholic in a brewery, though. The sheer hypnotic pull of it, the familiarity and the joy of the singing.'

As they talked and ate, Cooper forgot his work for the first time in years, and the ugly murders he was investigating faded to the back of his mind. He forgot the time and his loneliness and the problems he had been turning over in his mind. He was unaware of the food or the other customers around them. He could only see Annabel.

He only remembered his world when he was opening his car door for her outside her home and his phone rang in his pocket. 'Cooper,' he said, automatically, 'right, straight away.'

He put the phone back into his pocket, and looked up the steps at Annabel. She smiled, 'I see your work has caught up with you. Thank you for a lovely evening.' She put her key in the door.

'Can we do this again?' He did not want to let her go.

'Phone me,' she said, and was gone.

Ruth could not sleep. She lay on the bed gazing at the ceiling, images of the day's events flitting through her mind. The way her mother had pulled away from her. The crowded Cathedral. The interment and the crowded reception afterwards. After several hours, she sat up in bed and took out her father's letter and the pages of code. She took the first of the books her father had left with the solicitor and began to work with it in relation to the code. It was often something to do with biblical references, but that hadn't worked. She tried various combinations of page number and chapter number on three of the books that were in the bag and then she tried the Chambers Dictionary. As she linked pages and references, the words on the page began to make written sense. Her heart pounded, so that she got out of bed and looked down the corridor. No one was stirring at this hour, but she had that uncomfortable feeling of being watched again.

She was right, of course, but never imagined that her actions, along with many others, were shown on the monitors in Saul's study. But Saul was fast asleep, and so was Brother Anthony who should have kept watch when Saul was otherwise engaged.

The letter that emerged did not immediately impact on Ruth's consciousness, since she was preoccupied in finding and writing down each word as she marked it off on the page of typed numbers. The chapel bell tolling six warned her to put the sheets of paper together and tidy the books away. The letter was deciphered. Ruth sat on the bed, painfully aware of the papers hidden under her pillow, but she dare not read them yet, she must wait for her breakfast.

When she had eaten, Ruth placed the deciphered letter sheets inside her bible and began to read it properly for sense.

Ruth,

These are the things that concern me.

(1) There are couples in the Truth who have vanished.
David and Hannah Farnsby. Mr and Mrs Kirkham, John and Mary Reed, Geoffrey and Sarah Warner. Tom and Barbara Hughes, Archie and Betty Wainwright.

(2) There is a system of surveillance in The Retreat. Many things have happened to convince me of this, but I have not found out how it is done.

(3) Not all the funds that are raised are declared in the accounts. For instance, all the houses belonging to the couples listed above were sold except the Farnsby's – the deeds probably mislaid – but the proceeds were not listed in the accounts.

Hope Briggs and Harold James were investigating this with me.
(4) Calvin is not to be trusted. He leaves The Retreat regularly. He seems to have created a clique of ne'er do wells around him and it makes me uneasy.
(5) I have put aside money and a home for you and your mother should you ever be in need of it. If my suspicions are unfounded, you are welcome to give it to the True Gospel Church, as you think fit.
(6) There is a plan called the 'Day of Revelation', which worries me greatly. It seems to be set for a time when the True Gospel Church is under threat of some kind. There is a letter and a box in every church to be opened on that day. I have not been able to discover their contents.
(7) What is the purpose of the Five Hundred Group?
(8) The Joshua Group may be a kind of police run by the church. I have not found who runs it, where or how they operate.

Be very careful, Ruth.
Your loving Father.

# Chapter 25

Saturday Morning.

Saul turned off the television set and closed the cabinet door carefully before plugging the telephone into its socket.

'Brother Samuel, we need to have an urgent meeting of the five hundred group. A general election is imminent.' There was a short pause before Saul spoke again. 'We must keep this from the church membership, Brother; but maybe it would be unwise for them to gather at The Retreat – try one of the large conference centres and then it will be easier for the group to remain incognito.' Saul paused, tapping his fingers on the desk while listening.

'I know, there will be domestic staff, but we can organise things around that. Good; make it Monday of next week, Tuesday at the latest. We must be ready.'

Saul replaced the telephone in its hiding place and went to open his safe. From it he took out a large red folder; inscribed Authorised Brethren Only. Below this was written in bold black letters:

**Agenda for Change; the True Gospel Church Political Objectives.** As he opened it, Saul smiled. It was an unpleasant sight.

Ruth opened her eyes and stared at the ceiling for some time. A surveillance system, her father had written. She lay still, really looking around the room for the first time. Where was the camera hidden? She shivered, to think that someone might have watched her most intimate moments. Thank the Lord that she had not been sick during her time here. Then it struck her that her sickness had not been discovered before; so the bathrooms were probably off screen. She sat up in bed and reached for her Bible. There was no sign of any camera lens overhead. Her gaze was apparently on the book in front of her, but she was looking at the lower part of the walls. She could see nothing suspicious. Ruth read the day's portion of scripture and knelt beside the bed in prayer. Her mind was a chaotic jumble of thoughts.

'Lord, help me to be clear in my thinking and guide me aright. I have been given a task and I don't know what I should do. Those that I have loved and trusted may not be what they seem. I must decide whether my father was mistaken. I trust that I shall prove a worthy servant. In thy precious name… Amen.'

Ruth continued to kneel for some minutes. Her Bible had fallen open at the parable of the tares. 'Let the wheat and the tares grow together until the harvest.' It seemed like an answer to her prayer. So did she have to do anything? It could be argued that it was in God's hands; that God knew who was His, and would take them to be with Him at the end of days; the wheat or the chosen.

Her head throbbed with the uncertainty of it as she went to the corner of the room to use the commode. As she sat, she saw the camera lens. It was on this wall, and was set between two pipes. She could not be seen from this position. She craned her neck around as she covered the commode. There was no doubt. A cursory glance would ignore it as part of the plumbing. She must not make it obvious that she knew of the glassy eye observing her every move. For everything normal, she must be in view. She washed her hands at the sink, jumping nervously as Sister Barbara brought in a tray of breakfast for her.

'Bless you, Sister.' Ruth took the tray from her and sat on the bed. It was an unusually substantial meal: cereal, scrambled egg, toast and marmalade. Beside the dishes were three little cartons. She turned one over, reading the 'directions for use'.

'Nutrisip', for use in convalescence, in cases of prolonged loss of appetite, a complete vitamin balanced formula in a pleasant tasting drink.

'I suppose this is Dr Harold's prescription,' she told the empty room, beginning with the scrambled egg before it got cold. Cold food always made her retch, she couldn't risk it here.

'I need to talk to Matthew about all this. How on earth can I contact him without being seen?'

Sister Barbara returned to find food still on the tray. She shook her head, and gave Ruth soap and towels, beckoning her to follow, which Ruth did eagerly. A bath or a shower would be very welcome.

Matthew had finished scrubbing the steps with the six penitents he had been assigned. They had not been cleaned for years, judging by the thick layer of greasy dirt that had clung to them. He gazed down at the floor that led to the garden door and to the boiler rooms. They could also do with a clean, and the group had two hours more penance to do. The fact that Matthew had set them eight steps apart on the staircase had meant that they had all been working the whole time.

'We'll begin on the corridor at the far end and work down towards the doors.' The group of robed figures gave a muted collective sigh, and set to work.

Calvin stood at the top of the steps, muttering under his breath. He could not get to the boiler room whilst all this cleaning was in progress. Therefore he could not get out today. His exit was blocked.

'It's not that important, is it?' Willy asked him as they climbed back up to the library.

'It's something I lost at the accident, a book.'

'No worries then.'

'It has my name in it.'

Willy swore under his breath.

Josh looked at the gap in the hedge that the farmer had pointed out to him, and asked:

'What made you suspicious, Mr Parrett?'

''Twas the lines across me field, Sergeant. I got out of me tractor and went to have a look. Come along of me.' The farmer strode down the slope towards a lake.

'Look here, now.'

Josh looked. There were large marks gouged into the bank in several places, some tyre prints and bits of broken glass. 'I see what you mean, something has gone in here.'

'I reckons there'd be two in there, son. They didn't come straight down here off the road. There's a spot a bit of the way up I'd like you to see.'

The old man set off up the slope at a pace that left Josh panting to keep up. 'Here, look at that.' He pointed to a mess of tyre marks, glass and a bumper that lay among the brassica seedlings. 'I reckon someone was sick as a dog over there.'

'You're right. And if I'm not mistaken, there's some blood over here.'

'That'd be some more over there too, son. What you going to do?'

'Find out if there is anybody in the lake with whatever else went into the lake.'

'I thought as much. Spose it can't be helped. Try and keep them in one line and not all over my beets, will you?'

'I will, Mr Parrett. Thank you for calling us. You did the right thing.' Josh called for backup and began making notes for his report on the incident. It was a nuisance, since there was so much to do on the Gospel Church case, but it couldn't be helped.

Soon there was a crane in the field, first lifting out a very badly damaged silver sports car and then a blue mini van that had obviously hit something head-on. The police divers were still leaving trails of bubbles on the muddied surface of the water. Josh moved forward with the team, anxious to know whether there was anybody in the vehicles. He let out a long sigh of relief when he saw the empty seats, only then aware that he had been holding his breath.

The divers had brought a pile of items to the surface. An old bicycle, a shoe, and what looked like a hymn book. Josh wondered how they had got there, and shivered as he remembered the Rex King case. He had a mental image of a chess piece, a black knight, trodden into mud. 'Don't go there!' he murmured under his breath. He picked up the book by one edge. It hadn't been in the water for very long, since the print was still legible. It was leather bound in red, and had once had those gold-edged pages that were often seen on expensive Bibles. The shape was familiar.

Joshua peered at the spine. 'True Gospel Church Hymnal.' He opened it carefully to see an up-market version of his own hymnal. It was inscribed to 'Calvin Crouch, on the occasion of his eighteenth birthday'. The text beneath said:

'O make a joyful noise unto the Lord, all ye lands.'

Joshua put the book into a plastic bag, and watched the divers until it grew too dark to see. 'Give it up now, lads; I don't think there's anyone in there in need of urgent help.'

'Thanks guv, see you down the pub?'

Josh hesitated, 'No thanks, I'd best be getting back.'

'Not like you, Josh. What's up?'

'His missus is about to drop one any minute,' chuckled the other diver.

'Come down with the cigars later then.'

Josh waved as he climbed wearily into his car. Should he or should he not go to the pub?

He remembered guiltily how little he had seen of Alicia this past week, how she felt trapped indoors at this late stage in her pregnancy, ordered to rest and bored out of her mind. Her grandmother was due to visit next week; meantime, she was on her own. He'd best write up the report on the accident, leave a note for Inspector Cooper about the hymnal, and go home.

No pub tonight; after all, the teaching advised against it.

# Chapter 26

Sunday

Morning service was over, but Brother Saul had asked everyone to remain seated for a few moments. He stood on the dais, a striking, near biblical figure, his white robe moving slightly in a breeze from the open window.

'Brothers and Sisters in Christ, I have a work that must be done before Tuesday Morning. All those of you not involved in essential tasks will be needed. We will use the meditation rooms, and in your groups you will be given your part of the task to perform. May the Lord be with you.'

'And with your spirit, Amen.'

The sound of the enormous congregation in response was almost deafening.

Ruth wondered if she was to be included in the task. She headed towards the exit, where Brother Robin seemed to be selecting people for his own group. He beckoned her across. The group were all in advanced robes – Deacons, Elders, Archdeacons and disciples. As Brother Robin led the way, Ruth could almost hear the unspoken questions in the air between them.

Outside one of the larger storerooms, they halted. There they were each given a trolley containing several large cartons. When it was Ruth's turn, Brother Robin handed her a small instruction sheet,

'Here's the outline of your task, Sister. You are to oversee group six in the blue meditation room. You may take the trolley up in the lift. Make sure that the room is locked behind you whenever you leave it.' He handed her a key with a blue tag, 'Come to me with your finished files at the end of each session and I will give you more supplies when they are needed. May God grant you and your group speed and accuracy, Sister.'

'Amen, Brother Robin.'

Ruth pushed her squeaky trolley towards the lift, wondering at the change of routine and what it meant. When she reached the blue room, a quiet line of robed figures were waiting for her. One stepped forward to take the trolley from her as she unlocked the door. Ruth read aloud from her sheet.

'We shall need eight tables arranged around the walls of the room, with enough space to walk behind them. The men to do this please. When I open the boxes on the trolleys, please will some of you take them and place them beside tables according to the numbers marked on them. There should be five boxes to each table.'

There was no fuss, the things were organised swiftly and silently.

'We are to assemble the pages in the order we have set them out. When you have completed a batch, pass them to the next table and so forth. The last two tables are to place the sheets in the folders and check that the pages are complete. I am to be in charge of one final table; Deacon Robert the other.'

Ruth read the titles on the folders as she helped Deacon Robert to lift them onto the final tables: Agenda for Change; Political Objectives; the True Gospel Church. She thought nothing of it until she saw the index pages that were already printed on the inside of both covers. The Five Hundred Group: names and telephone numbers. Authorised personnel only.

She could see the words scribbled in her notes of father's letter. The Five Hundred Group existed. She was drawn back to the task in hand as a novice in a blue striped robe placed a completed batch of pages beside her. It flashed through her mind that the pace of work would prevent anyone from reading the contents of the files, and only those at the final checking stage would see the complete document. With no chance of taking in the contents. Why was such secrecy needed?

She must have a complete copy for herself. Where was the surveillance in here? She tried to look around, but the pace of work was such that it was impossible.

Mathew had not been included in the task; he was on kitchen duty. At least Ruth had looked a little better in morning service. He rinsed cutlery and crockery before placing them beside the sink for washing up. It didn't need much thought, and his mind wandered to the special task that had been set for the day. What could it be?

The trays from the solitary wing and sick rooms arrived. Matthew recognised Ruth's tray with its little carton on the trolley. He took it to deal with first, enjoying this small contact with her. As he did so, he noticed a folded sheet of paper under the cereal bowl. He placed it in his robe pocket in a smooth movement while continuing to clear the tray. If it was a message from Ruth, it was pure chance that it had not been intercepted. Why had she taken such a risk from solitary? What was wrong?

Josh Allsopp was late into the station that morning. Not that it was after the time he should have been there; he was habitually an hour early. But it felt wrong; he always enjoyed the sensation of getting ahead with the day's work.

Perkins was on the desk. 'Afternoon, Gov.'

'Leave it out, Perkins. I was at the hospital in the early hours.'

'Has she had the baby then?'

'No such luck. A false alarm. She's back home now. Is the Inspector in?'

'Yes. But I can't make him out this morning.'

'Why's that?'

'He was singing to himself in there.'

'You're having me on!'

'Scout's honour, something about Berkeley Square.'

Josh was smiling as he knocked and entered the office. 'Good morning, sir.'

'Morning, Allsopp; get the crew in here and we'll all have a look at this.'

It took a few minutes for all the team to assemble, most leaning against the wall, some on the desks, a couple sitting on the window sill.

'This device was found in Oliver Patton's room. It is an expensive piece of equipment. I'd like you, Melhuish, to try and find out where these can be obtained. This was used, I believe, to instruct Patton to carry out the attacks at the church. This is

165

confirmed by the contents of these tapes found in his room. The experts are still working on the voice.

'Right then, this is how things stand at the moment.'

Next was one of the inspector's usual flow diagrams. Cooper pointed out three names underlined in red: Hope Briggs, Ben Diamond and Harold James.

'Those three were the treasurers for the True Gospel Church here in town. Each TGC has three people responsible for the finances of that church. But it seems to me that there are things missing from the income columns – such as the donations of new converts' property.'

'How did you get the accounts, sir?'

'I asked for them. I had expected a refusal or at least a delay. They simply said, "No problem, how many copies do you need?" it took me by surprise.'

'Nothing to hide, perhaps?'

'They may honestly believe that. It makes them all too convincing.'

Josh swallowed a retort. This was an investigation. His own feelings about the church were irrelevant here.

'What really brings this to my notice is this fact; all three treasurers are dead. Was this in order to silence them about something they were about to make public?'

'It is suspicious,' Josh acknowledged.

'There is something else that has been bothering me about the growth of TGC.' Cooper turned over his flip chart to show a page titled 'Ethnic Cleansing Murders'. 'For those of you who haven't had any direct contact with this investigation; the murders involve members of varying ethnic groups, seem to be racially motivated and are always absolutely clean forensically.'

'What connection could there be between the church and these murders, sir?' DS Barry asked.

Cooper lifted a page. Underneath was a map. 'The red stickers are for the EC murders, the blue ones show the positions of TGC buildings.'

Josh swallowed hard. The stickers made neat little clusters. 'The ethnic cleansing murders were thought to be the work of the BNP, sir.'

'Neat diversion, I think. They were religious leaders in their communities. I have been through the list of victims carefully. Apart from a high percentage of drug pushers of any nationality, there were imams, rabbis and priests. One woman puzzled me on the list, though, a Mrs Rowena Heggarty.'

'Unconnected, perhaps?'

'She turns out to have been a medium.'

Josh stared at the map for a moment. 'The teaching at the TGC contains a warning to believers to avoid all such superstitions as evil. It includes horoscopes, fortune tellers, spiritualists and mediums, sir.'

'Could you bring me all the literature you have been given?'

'Yes, sir.' Josh felt uncomfortable as all eyes turned towards him.

'Allsopp has been doing undercover work at the local TGC,' Cooper added.

The eyes looked away.

'Now, I want you, Barry, to begin a list of all the children who have apparently been abandoned by their parents in the TGC. It's not going to be easy, since you are going to be asking questions over a wide area. Miss Harman has given me some names and addresses to begin with – relatives of the vanished, so to speak. Take PC Hope and WPC Tallish to help you. Good luck.'

'Sir, that call from the farmer, Mr Parrett, I've put my report in your in tray,' Josh began.

'Spit it out, I know it'll be relevant.'

'Briefly, we found two vehicles in the lake, both impact damaged, no bodies we could discover. But there was a TGC hymn book belonging to a Mr Calvin Crouch among the debris.'

'I thought they didn't have worldly things like cars?'

'Only of necessity; I don't think Mr Crouch had necessity, if you see what I mean, sir. The vehicle was not taxed and Crouch does not have a driving licence.'

'But was he the driver. Allsopp, was he the driver?'

'I'll see what I can do, sir.' As Josh left the office, he heard an odd, rusty sound. Inspector Cooper was singing under his breath.

The Prime Minister sat looking out at the rain, an equally overcast expression on his usually cheerful face.

'Wilson, how can we sanction such policy changes? It will alienate an enormous number of voters.'

'With respect, sir, the focus groups seem to be unanimous on these policy points. The cessation of Sunday trading bill has reared its ugly head again. Then there is the Religious Education reform bill – I can't see how it will wash with the NUT, but they might have to swallow it under pressure.'

The Prime Minister groaned. 'How can I forbid them to teach evolution, and avoid teaching anything but Christianity in a multi-ethnic country? It would be political suicide. As for closing all but Christian faith schools, it's impossible. There would be riots.'

'Did you read the proposals for the eradication of prostitution?'

'I did. And the proposal to ban contraceptive advice to all but married couples, the compulsory adoption of all illegitimate children by married couples and the mandatory jail sentences for truanting, vandalism and drug abuse.'

'The prisons would overflow, Wilson. Mind you, it's tempting to think that such draconian measures would work. Especially the death sentence for drug trafficking. But I'm convinced the civil liberties and Human Rights Lobbies will throw the proposals out.'

'According to the focus groups, there will be little chance of electoral success if these are not on the agenda.'

'What on earth is happening to progress in this country? We seem to be going back to the dark ages.'

'I don't know, sir. But it frightens me; there will be a terrible backlash from the religious minority groups over these proposals. There will be riots, I'm sure of it.'

'There may be anyway if these murders continue, Wilson. Is there any progress on that front? Is it the BNP, or do we look elsewhere?'

'MI5 will have a report from our man undercover tomorrow. And I have a friend in the police force, a Chief Inspector Cooper. I think you should speak to him, sir. He has a theory which seems, to say the least, improbable, but if he's right, he'll need our help to gather the evidence he needs.'

'I'll talk to anyone with half an answer.'

'I've taken the liberty of arranging an appointment for you with him on Tuesday at six p.m. It avoids your other commitments.'

'Not my marital ones,' the Prime Minister said, glumly.

Matthew sat in the toilet to open the note. It was very short. 'I need to see you urgently.' Underneath was a diamond drawn under a tree, with a number five slashed through. Only Ruth could have sent this. It was years since they had met under the hollow oak. Half past five, when they were at private meditation. This, as Ruth knew, could legitimately include a walk to release tension and quieten the spirit.

'I only hope it's not pouring with rain, Ruth,' he said under his breath, 'It'll look rather odd if I march out into a downpour.'

# Chapter 27

Sunday Afternoon.

Ruth made her way toward her rendezvous with Matthew with a fast beating heart and a terrible urge to look over her shoulder to see if anyone appeared to be watching or following her. The sun made long shadows over the grass. A blackbird hopped along; his own shadow enormous for such a small bird. Were the shadows she saw also far bigger than their causes? Her heart skipped a beat as she observed Matthew approaching the oak from the far side and vanishing from sight.

She joined him inside the hollow trunk a moment later. He looked anxious.

'What's wrong, Ruth? You're not ill, are you?'

'No, Matt, nothing unusual for me; I'm taking the drinks Dr Harold has prescribed. It seems to be helping me keep my food intake up.'

'No more sickness?'

'Not if I eat hot things and don't force food down past being full. No, it's not that. Read this.' She passed him the sheets of paper on which she had written the deciphered letter from her father.

Matthew read in silence, his face registering shock and disbelief. 'Surely, this isn't your father's writing – you've copied it?'

Ruth handed him the cipher. 'This is what I had. It took me a while. The note at the bottom; 'A message in Chambers' was the key; the numbers refer to my father's copy of Chambers' Dictionary, with a list of numbered names on the fly sheet.'

'Not the usual Biblical references?'

'I think it was an extra precaution – any King James' Bible's references would be the same, but only that particular copy and edition would have deciphered the whole message. He left it with the solicitor.'

'A double meaning; Chambers in chambers, typical of your dad,' Matthew smiled.

Ruth's spirits lifted for a moment, 'Yes, he loved puzzles and word-games. He even used to watch a programme called *Countdown* with a neighbour, much to mum's annoyance.'

'Television? Your father?'

'Yes. He often said we couldn't understand the world if we cut ourselves off completely. That's why he insisted I do my nurse training. Not that I shall be allowed to do that anymore under Brother Saul's guidance. I believe he was right; I understand the outside world a lot better than many of those born in the Truth. But it's still like a foreign country to me.'

'For those who attend True Gospel School it'll be another planet.' Matthew looked at the papers in his hand again. 'So, are we really being watched?'

'Yes, I'm afraid it's true, the camera lenses are usually hidden in the plumbing. I've only discovered one in my room. It's hard to avoid looking at them, I warn you, be careful, now you know.'

'Well, I'll be Job in his ash-heap. And the other things?'

'The Five Hundred Group seem to be a political action committee. The special task we've been doing is assembling copies of their policy document: "Agenda for Change".'

'Seems a good thing to do – we need to be an influence for good in the world. But Calvin's group have always bothered me – kind of separate from the rest of us. I wonder what they're up to.' Matthew gazed out through the surrounding shrubs and the intervening grass. He could see the paths where robed figures were walking in twos and threes in silence.

'What do you think of the vanishing couples?'

Matthew's face clouded. 'I don't want to think about that.'

'No more do I. Nor the horrible thought that my father was treasurer and the others that died were his helpers.'

Matthew gasped. 'I hadn't thought of that. It's a bit of a long shot to call a coincidence, isn't it?'

'It's what I was saying, we're too naïve in the Truth. Anyone outside would see it straight away.' She paused for a moment. 'It's because we're not taught to think for ourselves.

171

Obedience, the rule of silence, faith, nothing that we are expected to do asks us to think for ourselves.'

They heard the warning chime for six o'clock prayer.

'What do you want me to do?' Matthew asked, handing her the papers.

'Pray for me. I don't know what I should be doing.'

Matthew put his arms round her and kissed her gently. 'I will, love.'

Ruth pulled away from the warmth and safety of his embrace. 'I'm not sure I should be close to you; Brother Saul has chosen a marriage partner for me.'

'There are times when I cannot find it in my heart to be charitable toward Brother Saul. Pray for me, Ruth. I fear an evil heart of unbelief is growing in me.'

Ruth looked into his eyes. 'I fear it for myself these past months. We must be strong together.' She ducked out of the hollow trunk and walked toward the chapel building.

Matthew followed some minutes later. Ruth was right, he thought. Hard not to keep looking around when you knew you might be watched.

Fox waited at the drop point for an hour, but there was no sign of his man. Working for MI5 was not the glamorous life that fiction cracked it up to be. He was longing for a cigarette and only too aware that it was twenty-six days since he'd had his last one. The café wasn't busy at this time on a Sunday afternoon. Fox took his cup to the counter and asked for another.

'Quiet this afternoon,' the plump, stocky man behind the espresso machine commented. 'You a writer?'

'How'd you guess?'

'The notebook, on the table; journalist or novelist?'

'Murder mysteries. It's better down here away from the missus and the kids. No interruptions.'

'Rather you than me, mate, I'd rather cook.'

Fox returned to his seat. He began noting things in his book – car registrations, the comings and goings in the street outside, descriptions of people. He didn't look up as a man came in.

'Excuse me, could you tell me where Union Street is?'

'It's a bit complicated, let me write it down for you,' Fox offered.

The stranger took a notebook from his pocket and Fox wrote: 'Ten a.m., point four Tues', followed by rhubarb, rhubarb, rhubarb.

The man took it and examined it. 'Thanks a lot,' and headed for the door. Fox pushed the envelope that had arrived on the table under his notebook.

'So much for not being interrupted, mate.' the man behind the counter chuckled. 'Fancy a freshly made doughnut on the house?'

'Thanks.' Fox remained in the café for another forty minutes before closing his notebook and heading back to the office. The report must be on Wilson's desk in the morning. Someone was smoking upwind of him. It smelled so good; he breathed in deeply as he passed. Did passive smoking count when giving up? His route took him through the local park, where he was surprised to see his contact sitting on a wooden bench, his hat down over his eyes, apparently asleep. Fox slowed, his eyes only moving as he passed the slumped figure. His whole body tightened like a coiled spring as he took in the patch of red on the chest, the knife which impaled the body to the bench and the opened jacket. The notebook was missing.

He walked on as if nothing had happened, although every nerve in his body shouted 'Run'! This life wasn't glamorous. It was either bloody boring or damned dangerous. Out of sight, he took out his phone and sent a text message. Then he went into the gents' toilets. If anyone had been watching, they would not have seen the brown-suited man reappear, although a man in an odious green and yellow checked overcoat emerged some minutes later.

As Annabel let herself into the house, she could smell baking. She put her coat in the closet and went into the kitchen.

'Sister, how was Evening Service?' Elizabeth asked, her long grey hair coming loose from its pins.

'Brother Saul was not there, the service was led by Brother Adam. It seems that Brother Calvin has had an accident, falling down some steps.'

Elizabeth looked up sharply. 'He is badly injured?'

'No, it seems not, don't be concerned.'

Elizabeth sat at the long scrubbed kitchen table, which was laden with fresh-baked bread. 'Look at me, working so on the Sabbath.'

'The men at the homeless shelter will be grateful for it. Shall I help pack it?'

'Let it cool a while. I have the soup made ready. We can have some for lunch, Sister.'

'Have you made a decision about speaking to the Inspector?' Annabel asked, gently.

'I can't make up my mind. It seems like a betrayal. All the years we both gave. I cannot think we were so wrong, Sister? It was just that I was not strong enough to follow the path chosen for me.'

'It may be that we are on our predestined path now, Sister. We can only follow where it leads us.'

'I don't know. Often, I still feel as though I should return.'

'Elizabeth, as far as the True Gospel Church is concerned, you are dead.'

The older woman covered her face with her hands. 'I knew that would be so. I just didn't think it would be so hard to leave my boys.'

'They leave flowers on your headstone. I have seen them do so.'

'I have a headstone?'

'Yes. I went to your funeral, Sister. That is why I was so shocked when I saw you again. I don't know who was buried, if anyone, but it was a heavy box that was lowered into the ground that day.'

Elizabeth groaned. 'What am I to do?'

'I think there is only one thing to do: talk about your fears to the Inspector. It will relieve your mind. He may say it is all fevered imagination, but at least you will know how it sounds when you tell an outsider. We cannot tell what the world will say about these things; we do not know.'

'Yes, I will talk to the policeman. This has been a burden too long on my spirit.'

Annabel put her arms round her friend. 'Bless you, Sister. I am sure it is the right thing to do.'

'As long as you use the telephone, Sister, to arrange a time with the Inspector; I cannot bear using the machine.'

'You can take the Sister from the True Gospel Church, but can you take the True Gospel Church from the Sister?'

'Not in my case, Sister Annabel,' Elizabeth said wearily.

## Chapter 28

Monday

Saul was unable to sleep. He gave up and dressed at four a.m., poured boiling water on a herbal tea bag and went to his study. He reached for his journal and began to write:

'It is near the end times. The Day of Revelation approaches, the signs are there: earthquakes, wars, pestilence and catastrophic weather change. I welcome it, yet I am afraid of the coming judgement. So many of my people are not ready and so many more have never heard the message. I feel I have failed, yet I must trust to the Eternal Wisdom. He knows who His chosen ones are. I fear for my children.'

He knelt in prayer for a long while and then stood gazing out of the window at the mature oaks that dotted the grounds. Capability Brown had designed the landscape, he'd been told by the agent when they'd been shown around. He grunted in satisfaction at the memory of the man's expression when he'd said: 'God designed it, man is simply the gardener following in the steps of Adam.'

Saul replaced his journal on the shelf and went to check the monitors in the hidden chamber. His people were sleeping; save for one who was at prayer. There were three messages on his new answer phone, one from Brother Amos. Dr Harold had been right to suggest the new machine.

He lifted the receiver and pressed a pre-programmed number. 'Brother Amos? Glad to see you're keeping good hours.' The clock tower showed ten past six, and already robed figures were out on their way to morning meditation.

'Will you be at the meeting of the Five Hundred Group, Brother? Yes today. Bassett Conference Centre has confirmed our booking.'

Saul played imaginary scales on the table as he listened. 'No, it won't be a problem. We have had to use an outside venue

– The Retreat is very full, and so are you at the college. It will also be more secure for our members' identities. It is essential that no one links them with the Church yet. Is there any news of the two that absconded?'

Saul's fingers began to mark out arpeggios, leaving marks on the polished table top. 'I'm sorry about that, it must be in the Lord's will. Are the joint gatherings of the Revelation and the Joshua groups to go ahead as planned tomorrow? Good. And the police suspect nothing at all? Excellent. God be with you, Brother.'

Saul stood for a moment, considering his Brother's attitude. Since they had been boys together in the Truth, Saul had always been uneasy in his presence, there was something cold and cruel about him. The memory of finding Amos pulling feathers from a live blackbird he'd caught in the raspberry cage came back to him. Sometimes Saul felt as though he was being plucked when those eyes fastened on him. The discipline at the college was harsh, to say the least. But Amos had always said 'Spare the rod and spoil the child', whenever Elizabeth had pleaded for a little more gentleness with the younger ones. He suspected that the two latest children to go missing were running from some over harsh punishment. Or simply the gruelling regime that Amos had instituted at the schools and colleges.

He shrugged off the thought of Elizabeth, and pressed another button on the telephone. 'About the arrangements for the Conference, Brother Samuel, shall we confirm the final details?'

Later that same morning, Ruth was working at the end table assembling the contents of the red folders and placing them ready to be packed in the cardboard boxes that had been supplied for the purpose. Somehow, she had to know what was in these files. There was a radiator, level with the tabletop opposite where she sat. Her gaze flickered to it from time to time. Would a file slide down behind it? Could she do it unseen? As one of the helpers came with another completed batch of contents, she realised there was about ten seconds when the end of her table was obscured by the helper from the watching lens. If she was to do it, that was her chance. Her heart thudded and her hands shook so that she thought someone might notice her anxiety. The first and second opportunity had passed before she nerved herself to push several files toward the table edge. The top one teetered and stopped, but the one underneath slid on. The top one vanished from sight, the rest were spread unevenly across the table. As calmly as she could, Ruth straightened the pile and continued to assemble files; her mind niggling away at the problem of retrieving her prize without being seen. By late morning, the group had finished their task.

Ruth led them in prayer and meditation until lunch. Locking the door behind her and putting the keys in her pocket, wearily, she pushed the last trolley load toward the storeroom. As she approached, she saw around a dozen dark-suited figures moving boxes away from the store. They looked identical, save for the colour of their ties: red, blue, yellow and orange. It was almost a uniform, she thought, as she passed them. One smiled at her in passing, so she lowered her eyes and shivered. Suppose he was her chosen marriage partner?

Her boxes were counted in and signed for. As the Brother clerk turned away, a novice approached her. 'Sister Ruth, you are to join Blue group for lunch today. Brother Saul wishes to speak to you after meditation this evening. May His grace attend you, Sister.'

'And the blessing of peace be with you, Sister Angela.' Ruth watched the girl hurry away down the corridor. She looked anything but peaceful. Then she took in the meaning of the message. What did Brother Saul want with her? Was it about her marriage arrangements? Or was she to be released from solitary? Or... had someone seen the file fall behind the radiator? Her mind ran on, finding more things to worry about: the books and her father's letters, or her meeting with Matthew. Ruth leaned against the wall for a moment. How had she come by such an uneasy conscience? Then, as the storeroom door closed, her heart pounded in sudden fear. The blue-room keys were still weighing heavily in her pocket.

Fox waited in the ante-room at Number Ten. Wilson had said nine a.m., but the clock showed twenty past already. So absorbed was he in refining his notes that he jumped nervously when the door opened.

'The Prime Minister will see you now.' Wilson looked ill, great dark shadows beneath his eyes contrasted with his pale skin. A bit like a plant kept too long in the dark, thought Fox.

The Prime Minister came towards him, hand outstretched. 'Mr Fox, I am so grateful for the sterling work you have been doing on behalf of your country.'

'Thank you, sir. It beats playing draughts,' Fox said wryly, while the word *creep* resonated in his head.

'I was so sorry to hear about the incident yesterday. Are you sure your cover isn't compromised?'

'I can't be absolutely certain sir, but it seems reasonable to continue.'

'What do you make of the message he left?'

'It's straightforward as far as the activities of the BNP go – no sign of any new clearly defined political agenda at all. But Hughes must have been on to something; that number he wrote on the outside of the envelope is beyond me.'

'Foxed, eh!' The Prime Minister chortled.

Fox managed a thin smile. 'For the present, sir, but we'll crack it, given time.'

'Well, keep up the good work.' The man looked suddenly exhausted under the veneer of charm and energy. 'Don't get yourself killed.'

'I don't intend to, sir,' Fox said, wondering what point there had been in the meeting at all as his hand was shaken again and he was shown out.

Wilson put a hand on his arm and guided him into an alcove. 'Contact this man – I'm sure he can be of assistance, he's cleared security wise. I've arranged for him to see the PM tomorrow at six p.m.'

Fox took the card he was offered. When he looked up, Wilson was gone.

The Prime Minister gazed down at the report on his desk. 'He seems genuine enough, Wilson. I don't think he's the type to stab a colleague in the back.'

'No, sir, efficient, careful and trustworthy, that's Fox. I worked with him for a while in the army.'

'I shall have to put this aside. I hope someone finds out why that number was worth killing an agent over. What are the things on my agenda today?'

'Apart from questions about the sex life of the member for Oswald North in the House this morning, the bill for Amendment of Sunday Trading is up for a second reading.'

'Beats me how the Reformation Committee have done it; the retail industry are up in arms about it.'

'So are many shoppers. But their other Sunday legislation, no pub opening, no sports fixtures – even Sunday television – it beats me how they got this far.'

'I'm booked to see someone from the Reformation Committee this afternoon; a Reverend Samuel Burgess.' The Prime Minister almost scratched his head, but avoided the toupee just in time.

'As long as he doesn't bring MacLean with him, sir.'

'Not even Martin Luther the first, just someone called the Reverend Saul Crouch.'

'Is there anything else, sir?'

'Just organise those files for me while I'm gone – those can be put away, and arrange meetings with the people on this list as soon as possible.' The PM stood up and stretched before taking the briefcase Wilson handed him. 'Once more into the breach, dear friends.'

Saul was already on the train, in an otherwise empty first class carriage, when Brother Samuel boarded it at Reading. 'Peace be with you, Brother.'

'And with you, Brother Saul. Here is a copy of the agenda, first for the Prime Minister, then one for back at the Basset Centre for the second part of the meeting of the Five Hundred.'

Saul took the folder of papers. 'Pity we'll miss the morning session.'

'They'll be going through the Agenda for Change this morning. We know all the contents of that. This afternoon we can be with the focus groups and the final planning session.'

Saul opened the folder. After reading the contents, he looked up at his companion. 'It seems to be correct. How much opposition to the scheme do we have?'

'There was a serious problem with Grant, from Oswald North, but he is likely to resign this week; the press have somehow discovered his unfortunate sexual habits.'

'Any others?'

'A few, but most have been dealt with. I'm confident we'll win the vote.'

Saul saw the attendant approaching, and gave his companion a warning glance while sliding the papers out of sight inside the folder. 'Breakfast, I believe.'

## Chapter 29

Monday Afternoon.

In the United States, the enormous crowds outside the White House, the Capitol Building and Congress had dispersed at four p.m., ending a long vigil of prayer, song and preaching that had had the President preparing to go out and join them; after all, there were thousands of voters out there and he was nearing the end of his first term; although it might be safer to remain neutral. He had certainly advised the British Prime Minister that he'd best ensure the passing of the bill amending Sunday Trading. Its counterpart was a certainty here, as far as anything was certain in political life.

Outside the Vatican, the crowd filling St Peter's Square was listening to a preacher, the third in the rotation of speakers. Prayer followed hymn and preaching followed hymn. The Pope was away on one of his foreign trips, and so was spared the decision of whether to go out and add his blessing to the gathering on his doorstep.

One thing that surprised the young policeman, Giovanni, was the absence of any litter at all when the enormous crowd dispersed.

The crowd outside Number Ten was eerily quiet; every head was bowed in silent prayer. Among the group there were women and children. On the stroke of eleven, they began to sing psalms. At the same moment, outside Parliament, another crowd launched into song. Outside the Welsh Assembly, and the Scottish Parliament, the same scene was repeated.

Inside the Parliament building, the Chief Whip was taking a long swig from his hip flask. His advice to the Prime Minister had been to support the bill. He could understand his objections to it, but it would be better to avoid a defeat. It had been worse even than the Whip had thought. The worst trouncing that a government had ever had. He moved slightly in order to see the white-faced Prime Minister standing at the despatch box. How such a rebellion of back benchers had arisen, it was impossible to tell. The Amendment of Sunday Trading Bill had been passed into law by an overwhelming majority.

The news had filtered outside. A white-robed figure stood to address the crowd.
'Brothers and Sisters in Christ. The bill has passed. The Sabbath is restored.'
There was a roar of jubilation from the crowd. Brother Saul raised his hands and a profound silence fell.
'Let us pray.' The man, looking like an actor from a film on the life of Christ, lifted his hands to heaven.
'O loving Heavenly Father we thank Thee for this victory over the evils of capitalism and those many Sabbath-breakers. We pray that this will free more souls to observe Thy day and seek the true happiness and peace that only comes to those who love Thee and keep Thy commandments. May other victories follow in the battle against the evil one; may we not flinch when we are called to war in thy name, Amen.'
The responding amen was like breaking thunder.
'Hymn 206; "Fight the good Fight",' announced a blue-robed figure
The crowd began to sing. The music swelled like a tidal wave in its force and intensity. A policeman on duty felt suddenly, deeply, afraid. He could not tell why.

Not far away, a mob of counter demonstrators were being held back by police. Though less well organised than the crowd that had taken the main ground in the early hours of the morning, they were an angry and determined group. The police line was breached in several places and the streets seen from above in the police helicopter looked as though they were flooded with a fast moving tide of brightly coloured insects.
'This is real trouble,' the pilot said.

'You're not kidding. We need to put the hospitals on alert, and bring in reinforcements to calm this lot down.'

The Prime Minister had tried to leave by his usual exit, but had been warned of the breaking riot outside. So he took the emergency route back to Number Ten.

The news team was set up on a rooftop. From their vantage point, they could see absolute chaos below as the mobs from the side streets ploughed into the True Gospel Church gathering.

'This is Dominick Draper here with your on-the-spot newscast. Today, the Sabbath Act has become law. As you can see, behind me there is mob violence as protesters attack the True Gospel Church members and the hundreds of other church groups gathered here.'

The cameras turned and panned over the crowd below.

'As you can see, the True Gospellers and their supporters are offering no resistance whatever, which seems to have infuriated some, and nonplussed others. Police are overwhelmed at the moment, but reinforcements are on their way. Our only prayer, and prayer it must be, is that there are not too many casualties tonight.

'This is Dominick Draper returning you to the studio.'

Inspector Cooper sat dumbfounded at his desk. Annabel Harman and Elizabeth Crouch sat opposite him, their backs ramrod straight, their feet planted firmly on the floor, as though they were ex-soldiers waiting for their orders.

'Tell me from the beginning. You are?'

'Mrs Elizabeth Crouch. I was – am – married to Saul. We had two children, Calvin and Adam. When I left, as is the custom, I was declared dead. I was unaware just how far they took that, but Sister Annabel has told me.'

'I attended a funeral service for Sister Elizabeth. Her two sons were there. They believe she is physically dead.'

'So there was an interment?' Cooper's pen hovered over his notepad.

Sister Annabel looked at her friend. 'Yes, there was.'

'Was there a body in it?' Cooper asked.

'I don't know, Inspector. It was closed. But it was heavy.'

'So it had something in it.' Cooper wrote another note. 'Do these burials happen often?'

'Only when there is a death, Inspector.' Annabel was smiling.

He couldn't help a grin in return. 'I mean these 'empty coffin' burials for those who leave the TGC?'

'Any lost member is mourned in this way.' Sister Annabel looked at the floor.

'So, a member who has left may be in physical danger from the TGC members?' Cooper enquired.

'I don't believe that, Inspector,' Elizabeth said. 'It's just that if we're found, we are brought back into the Teaching. I am not strong enough to pursue the Teaching. So I must avoid them.'

'It's the Joshua Group, Inspector. Their task is to rescue the lost sheep of the fold.' Annabel looked ...frightened, thought Cooper.

'Yes, Inspector, they return the backslidden to the True Gospel fold.' Elizabeth sat with her hands folded.

Cooper noticed that there was flour under one of her fingernails. 'And if they don't wish to return?'

'There is no choice, Inspector. They bring us home, whether we like it or not.' Annabel shivered. 'I pray they never find me, Inspector.'

'Are they violent, Miss Harman?'

'They're more subtle than that, Inspector.'

'Could you write me a list of those burials, Miss Harman?'

'Those that I know of, certainly.'

'I remember many that might be included, shall I write them for you?' Elizabeth volunteered.

'That will be useful, thank you.'

Joshua was just climbing the stairs to the upper office when Cooper caught sight of him.

'Just the man I needed to see. Bring a couple of those awful machine coffees with you to the office, would you, Josh?'

A few moments later, he handed the inspector a plastic cup of hot liquid, and sat on his desk, sipping his drink.

'Take a look at these lists,' Cooper said, passing two sheets of paper.

'Empty burials, sir?'

'The TGC, it seems, don't like to lose a member. So they have a funeral for the ones that get away. Complete with coffin.' Cooper drummed his fingers on the desk.

Josh stared at the list.

'So we have several missing people, and people buried who aren't dead at all,' Cooper continued.

'My God, sir! It looks like a system for disposing of unwanted corpses. None of the people who have left the church would be back to question their "burial", and if they did come back, they'd be told it was a symbolic burial. No questions asked.'

'Do you think we've enough for a few exhumations, Allsopp?'

Josh's heart sank. All the peace that had come to him since joining the TGC drained away. 'We've got to try for it, sir.'

# Chapter 30

Monday

Ruth was terribly afraid. The angry mob surged round and through the lines of the choir and many of them fell. She tried to help some of them up, to follow Brother Robin's lead towards a side street, but the crowd was too dense.

Daniel pulled himself up against a pillar. 'Can you see her, Paul?'

'It's difficult in this mob – but she was only about twenty yards away so we should have a good chance.' He swallowed his own doubts, and continued to look for Ruth's distinctive mop of curls. 'I'm going in there – stay where you are, Dan.'

'Don't, you'll be killed!' But his words were lost in the tumult around him. Somehow, people avoided his wheelchair, wedged as it was in a doorway. He flopped down into it again. 'Damn, I hate being so helpless.' Then he thought, maybe I can do something. He pulled out the sports whistle he used to call Paul when he needed him. He began to blow short blasts on it.

Paul heard it as he struggled to keep on his feet as the tightly packed crowd surged unsteadily. He called Ruth's name over and over.

Ruth heard someone calling. She was holding Sister Angela's hand, but they were pulled apart. She stumbled, fell painfully to her knees. Someone pulled her to her feet. She looked into pale blue eyes.

'Ruth, come with me.' Paul was in no mood for small talk.

'But who are...?' Her question was cut short as she was knocked off balance again. She landed brutally hard on her already bruised knees. Somebody trod on her foot, someone else on her thigh.

Two strong arms lifted her again. 'No time for buts – let's get you out of this!' But which way was out? He hesitated – the noise and the sheer number of moving people disoriented him.

Then he heard Daniel's whistle. 'This way!' he shouted above the noise, 'toward the sound of the whistle.'

Ruth held onto this saviour; whoever he might be, he was the only option at that moment.

They were thrown up against a brick wall, like flotsam in a stormy sea. Ruth followed as Paul inched his way toward a doorway, lost his balance and fell into the lap of a man in a wheelchair.

'Sorry, old thing – Ruth, squeeze in behind the chair while I open this door.'

Ruth staggered, grabbed the pillar beside the chair, narrowly avoided falling again and pulled herself out of the flow of bodies with difficulty.

Paul put a silvery Yale key into the lock behind Daniel, and opened it. Daniel propelled himself backwards, quickly followed by Paul, who pulled Ruth in after him and slammed the door shut as fast as he could.

They looked at each other for a moment and then the two men laughed. 'Who would've believed it? Rescued and kidnapped in broad daylight!'

Ruth looked frightened at this, glanced at the closed door in panic.

'No, don't even consider the possibility of thinking about going out there!' Daniel said, quickly. 'You're quite safe with us, honestly.'

'Who – who are you?'

'Daniel Diamond and Paul Markham.'

Ruth stared at them both, staggered back against the wall and slid gracefully to the floor in a dead faint.

'Should've been a bit more tactful, Dan.'

'Don't think there's an easy way to resurrect a dead brother.'

'I'll sit her on your knees and we'll put her on the sofa,' Paul said.

Matthew was on duty in the kitchens, preparing tomorrow's vegetables, but rumours of the day's happenings had filtered even as far as here. He peeled potatoes like an automaton, his lips moving in silent prayer for all his friends and his Ruth. The enormous pans of water and potatoes looked like great ponds of white, fleshy fish. He heard another coach pull up. He continued to peel whilst looking at the tiny corner of the front drive that could be seen from here. Under the bright security lights, people were walking in twos toward the front door, some had bandages, and some had blood on their robes. One or two needed help to walk. But this was not a choir coach. There had been two already, but no sign of Ruth. Matthew bowed his head to his task again. He dare not pause; for who knew where the camera was that was watching him? The stale smell of cooking in the kitchens sickened him.

Brother Jacob and Sister Rebekah looked at each other; how could Matthew observe the rule so carefully when Ruth might be badly injured? He was certainly an example to them, in spite of still wearing novice robes. They bent their heads again, Jacob to his carrots and Rebekah to her sprouts.

The Retreat clock chimed eleven as a barn owl flew low over the cemetery. Brother Saul was in his room, a plaster over one eye and a bandage on his wrist. 'No, I'm fine, thank the Lord. Go and care for the others, please, Miriam, Doctor Harold is holding a clinic in the dining hall.'

'As you wish, Brother.' Miriam withdrew, frustrated that she had been unable to gain any news of Ruth.

Saul limped to uncover his console and check his observation screens. There was general confusion in the dining hall where the doctor was working. Miriam would be best used there. Sister Barbara was already moving among the injured. There were still another two coach loads missing. 'We need to know who's missing,' he drummed his fingers on the table top. He covered the screens, then pressed a buzzer on his desk. 'Sister Grace, will you find Brothers Jude, Nathaniel, Elisha and Simon, please?'

Ten minutes later, the four deacons arrived in their purple robes. 'I need a roll call of all those who are here. Then we need to visit the hospitals where our Brothers and Sisters may be.'

The deacons left to begin their task, which would take several hours.

Saul knelt in prayer. The victory had been great, but the cost had been blood. So it was in war.

Monday Evening.

Inspector Cooper looked at his men. 'Right, Melhuish, any progress on the device?'

'Yes, sir, but you're not going to like it.'

'Fire away.'

'It's MI5 issue, sir, the latest technology. A Mr Fox is waiting to see you about it, sir.'

'Interesting, good work Melhuish. Allsopp, the literature?'

'Sir, I've photocopied the leaflets, and bought an extra copy of some of the books.'

'Barry?'

'We've still got some way to go, sir, but here's a list of the names so far. We've also begun another list – of missing adults.'

'Good work. I have a list of those too. Now, tomorrow, photocopy your lists and give them to Allsopp, Barry, Tallish, Hope, then continue with the missing persons list first thing. Melhuish, stay with me to talk to Fox. Allsopp, I'd like you to go round to the TGC cemetery tomorrow and write down all the names and dates on the gravestones. I doubt we'd be allowed to see their books, but you might not be suspected of loitering, as a member. Goodnight and thanks for your hard work.'

There was a scraping of chairs and a shuffling of feet as the officers disbanded.

A wiry looking man in a vile checked coat stood up from the back of the room and came forward. 'Fox, sir.'

'Good. How can I help you?'

'Well, I thought voice analysis on those tapes you found in the perpetrator's room would be useful.'

'I've got our own men on that.'

'We have more sophisticated equipment, if you'd care to take advantage of it.'

'It would be useful,' Cooper admitted.

'There's something more too.' Fox held a CD case between his fingers. 'The activities of this particular Sect have begun to cause concern in high places.'

'I'm not surprised.' Cooper shrugged, 'The riots in London were terrifying.'

'Quite so. Shall we share our information?'

It was not so much request as an order, but Cooper was intrigued. This was unusual cooperation. 'My office, then. Shall we send out for sandwiches?'

'That would be excellent. Tuna and mayonnaise on brown if they've got it.'

Allsopp reached for his coat. 'Usual, sir?'

'Fine, Allsopp.'

# Chapter 31

Monday Evening.

Allsopp had returned in record time with the food, and a large vacuum jug of coffee. But in that short time Cooper and Fox were sitting in front of the dismembered flip chart. The pages were attached by sticky tape to cupboard fronts, the filing cabinets, chair backs and along the front of Cooper's desk. The pooling of information from the CD that Fox had brought and Cooper's file on the True Gospel Church had made them all sit stunned.

Fox broke the silence. 'I hadn't made the link between the 'ethnic cleansing' murders and the church. They really pulled the wool. We've lost two agents investigating these deaths. Of course, it's blindingly obvious from your map that a church was at the centre of each group of deaths. But, cunningly near BNP groups too.'

'I wasn't aware of the size of the problem,' Cooper said grimly. 'We need to think carefully about our next move. We don't want to lose more men.'

'No, we don't.' Fox drummed his fingers on his lips. 'I can speed up the exhumations if you'd ...'

He was interrupted by a knock on the door.

'Come in,' Cooper swivelled his desk chair round. 'Yes, Harper?'

'The Bishop to see you sir. Says it's urgent. About some church stuff. Says it can't wait.'

'Show him in, then.' Cooper stood to stretch his legs.

The Bishop hurried in, clutching a thick blue file. 'I'm so sorry to disturb you so late. I had a conference in Bristol that I couldn't avoid, or I should have been with you ...' He stopped abruptly as he caught sight of the pages displayed around the office. 'I see you already know. I brought these lists for you, thinking I'd be written off as a silly old man.'

'Your Grace, it's not too late; thank you for coming in. Do take a seat.' Cooper extended a hand in greeting, but the Bishop simply placed the file in his outstretched hand.

'Thank you for seeing me.' The Bishop sat beside Allsopp.

Cooper opened the file. Inside were neatly typed lists of all the concerns of the Ecumenical group with regard to the True Gospel Church. Silently, he stood and began to add more names to the lists on the sheets in front of them. When he had finished, he sat down with the air of someone who had opened a freezer full of thawed and rotting meat.

'Where do we begin?'

Fox turned his chair around so that he was facing the desk, and the others arranged themselves around it. 'Pen and paper each, please, Allsopp,' he ordered.

The four men sat late, consulting the charts, making notes, allocating tasks. As the old Gaol clock showed twelve-twenty, Cooper was climbing the stairs to his bed, Allsopp was making hot cocoa for his wife Alicia, and Fox was telephoning his superiors. The Bishop was in a corner of his study, praying for divine assistance in the task that lay ahead.

Ruth opened her eyes to see a strange ceiling overhead. The mouldings were a series of Tudor Roses that, although the paint was yellowing, were quite beautiful. A movement at her side brought her gaze downwards, to where a figure sat in a wheelchair. A figure, whose face was well known to her, but grown more mature.

'Feeling better?' the figure asked.

There was no doubt. 'You're Daniel.'

'Good to see you again, Sis. It's been too long.'

'But why? What happened? How?'

'It's a long story. I'll tell you over supper.'

'The patient awake? Good. I'm Paul, by the way. I care for your brother.'

'In more ways than one,' Daniel chuckled. 'Have you any other painful bits apart from the grazes on your hands and wrists? We bathed those already.'

Ruth could feel her knees throbbing as she began to sit up. She lifted her robes carefully to see the damage. They were a mess of blood, dirt and bruising, the flesh starting to swell alarmingly. 'These are a bit sore,' she admitted.

Paul went into a room behind her and returned with a bowl of water with diluted disinfectant and some cotton wool, beginning to wash the cuts.

Ruth blushed to have a man do so intimate a task, and reached out to take the swabs herself.

'Sorry, I forgot the rigid rules,' Paul chuckled, moving away, 'but you're more than safe with me.' He passed dressings for Ruth to put on, and as she struggled, motioned Daniel to help.

'All right for a little brotherly assistance, Imp?'

'Thank you.' The pet name came straight out of their past into her present with a wonderful musical sound.

While they sat around the table, eating a casserole that Paul had left in the oven with jacket potatoes, Daniel told his story.

'I wasn't approved,' he began, 'Brother Amos discovered my secret, and the Joshua group sentenced me to death.'

'But, surely not!'

'As surely as they bungled the job that left me in this wheelchair. The man that was buried in my place was a hitch-hiker I'd picked up that morning. Knowing what had happened, I swapped identities with him, putting my wallet in his pocket whilst I was waiting for the fire brigade to cut me out. He had no identification on him at all, which was odd.

'The man who drove the truck into my car from behind was a Joshua group man. I knew him from college, several years older than me and built like a tank. It took months for me to get well. I met Paul in the Spinal Unit – he was researching the activities of the TGC, he spotted who I was quite early on. So I had to explain why I couldn't be known to have survived that smash. I was really worried they might print my photo in the newspaper and that someone would spot it.'

'I was able to help him there, by doing an exclusive on the crash, and making sure that photos of the dead man were printed. Strangely enough, no one came forward to identify him.

'We were lucky to get away with it!' Daniel laughed.

'But why on earth would they want you dead, Daniel?'

'Because they discovered I'm homosexual.'

The words dropped like lead weights into Ruth's consciousness. She closed her eyes, dropped her head into her hands.

'I'm so sorry, Ruth. It's not what I would have chosen. It's just what I am, the way I'm made.' Daniel's voice was soft, pleading.

'But it's a sin, a terrible sin!' Ruth said, tears slipping under her fingers.

Paul took her hand gently away from her face. 'It's just the way we are made. We are only people who love differently.'

'God doesn't make people sinners. There's always choice!'

'I know, Sis, but the right choices I was given were either to live celibate or to live with one partner. I tried the first, but I found it impossible. So, Paul and I have been together for several years now. It's like a marriage.'

'A travesty of marriage!' Ruth shook her head, then wished she hadn't as pain racked behind her eyes.

'No more so than those soulless marriages arranged by the TGC,' Daniel said.

Ruth's mind returned to that council meeting at which she had been told her marriage partner had been chosen. She shivered.

Daniel saw her response. 'They haven't married you off yet, have they?' he demanded.

'No, not yet, but it's arranged. I answered Brother Saul back about it and ended up in solitary. But he couldn't keep me there all the time because he needs me to sing.'

'Bully for you. He needs standing up to more often.'

'It didn't do me any good.'

'I bet you feel a lot better for the rest, it's a wonder anyone can stand the pace they set.'

Ruth realised the truth of this. And also that she had something to tell Daniel about their father and his suspicions. 'Did I still have my carry sack with me when I got here?'

'Yes, it's beside the sofa, I'll get it for you,' Paul said, reaching around behind him, and swinging the cotton bag across the table.

'I've got something to share with you. Father's last letter and his will.'

'How did you get that?'

'Solicitor had them. I went there on my own, as father requested.'

'Well, I'll be – how did you manage that?'

'I have a recording contract, and Sister Barbara couldn't come with me one day. So I went.' Ruth couldn't help feeling a little proud of herself. 'There's a lot more to tell you, but here's dad's letter first.'

'Not one of his codes!' Daniel groaned.

'It's all right; I've decoded it, look underneath, on that piece of paper.'

Daniel read it silently to himself, and then passed it to Paul. 'He wasn't fooled then,' he said.

'Nor do I think he was fooled by your death. He refused to change his will when you "died". He's left you a house and some money.'

Daniel sat back in his chair and laughed until tears ran down his face. 'Not a fool at all!' he said, when he had recovered his breath.

# Chapter 32

Tuesday

Ruth turned over and almost fell from the bed. She had been sleeping close to the edge that was normally against the wall. There was a strange smell of bacon cooking. The ceiling with its Tudor Roses brought back the events of the day before. What Daniel had done was sinful, no doubt, but surely it didn't deserve a death sentence? It seemed incredible that the Joshua Group would be involved in such things. Daniel must be mistaken.

On the other hand, there was her father's letter, his doubts and suspicions, the things that had happened, people missing, people dead. They couldn't have been responsible for that poor madman's actions at that terrible service. Such things happened, like storms and tempests. *Acts of God.* Her mind slid away from such a thought. How could such things as murder be an act of God?

She slipped out of bed and onto her knees for morning devotion, whimpering in sudden pain as her sore knees touched the floor. Ignoring it, she reached for her Bible. No words came as she bowed her head, only a confusion of churning feelings and unanswerable questions. She opened her Bible to the twenty-third psalm, and sang it instead of prayer.

Downstairs, Paul and Daniel stopped in mid-task to listen. The sound was so clear and pure it seemed to the two men that they'd never heard anything so lovely.

'Wow!' Paul said, returning to the left trouser leg that he had been struggling to insert Daniel's inert left leg into. 'I can see why they use her so much for services.'

'Use her is right. Fancy asking her to sing at a service the very day that her father had been murdered? Callous, that's what they were.'

'Pull yourself up on the bar, then we can make you decent.'

Daniel pulled himself up by his now immensely strong arms, supporting his body off the ground whilst Paul pulled his trousers up and swapped the bath chair for his wheelchair. He lowered himself gently into his seat.

'They'll be looking for her,' Paul said, hearing her light step on the stairs.

'Too right. We need to do some planning.'

'Breakfast meeting, then?'

Daniel was already setting the table as Ruth came in. Paul had reached into the oven for a dish of bacon, and had cracked two eggs into a pan.

Ruth suddenly felt very hungry indeed.

When the meal was over, they sat with coffee; Ruth had water because there was no herb tea.

'We need to find out what was in the file that you hid behind the radiator,' Paul said.

'That's going to be rather difficult,' Ruth said.

'You still have the keys to the blue room?' her brother asked.

'Yes, I couldn't think of a way of getting them back without incurring a punishment for carelessness at the least.' Ruth lowered her head. 'I couldn't face it at the moment.'

'No shame in that – they ask too much of you,' Daniel said. 'Mind you, we're asking a lot of you as well. You need to go back and be there on the inside to see what's happening. We are very worried about all that's been going on – you probably don't know the half of it, but Paul has a thick file of stuff. If what we suspect is true, we need to be ready.'

Ruth looked into her brother's eyes, and what she saw there made her suddenly very afraid. 'What sort of things?'

'We won't go into any detail now – you mustn't be "missing" for too long, and I want to get you a mobile phone.' Daniel wheeled himself to a desk in the corner. 'Paul, will you pop down to the phone shop and get a straightforward one? Ruth hasn't used a phone much.'

'But I have – at the hospital.'

'At the hospital?' Daniel swung his chair round to face her.

'I trained as a nurse. Dad insisted I learn something outside the church.' Ruth couldn't help a sinful feeling of pride and amusement as Daniel's mouth dropped open.

'How on earth did he swing that one?' Daniel grinned.

'Probably threatened to withhold funding for some project or another,' Paul said, from the doorway, 'back in a few minutes.'

An hour later Ruth walked into the London True Gospel Church Headquarters. She was awed by the size of the foyer, with its miniature waterfall playing over a tiny stream between flowery banks. The glazed domed roof reminded her of her own chapel with its stained glass dome that she had so often watched sun-sparkle rainbow colours onto the church and congregation below.

'With the Lord's help, can I aid you, Sister?'

Ruth jumped in surprise. A deacon in purple robes stood beside her. His eyes were mismatched, one blue and one green.

'I'm sorry, I startled you Sister: Brother Job. You looked so lost.'

'I am, or rather, I suppose my congregation think I am. The Salisbury True Gospel Church, I'm Ruth Diamond. I was separated from my choir group yesterday.' Ruth was so thrown out of routine that she forgot to add any biblical text to her speech.

'God be praised that you are safe. I trust you are well?'

Ruth recovered her poise with an effort. 'Thanks to the Lord's goodness, I was only cut and bruised, my wrists and knees. Many were worse hurt, I'm sure.'

'That is true. Come.' The deacon led the way through a doorway into a long corridor. Novices were polishing the floor and the wood-panelling.

Ruth felt at home with this, and smiled at the workers. She was escorted into a large office. Inside at the desk sat a Brother in white robes.

'Peace be with you, Sister, do take a seat. I am Brother Joshua Adam.'

A chill went through Ruth as she heard that name, but she answered calmly, 'And with your spirit, Brother Joshua. I am Sister Ruth Diamond.'

'Ah, the lost singer! There has been great concern for your welfare, Sister Ruth. A moment, whilst I contact Brother Saul with the good news of your safe return.' He lifted a telephone on his desk and dialled.

To Ruth's surprise, it was answered. So there was a telephone at The Retreat! Brother Joshua Adam spoke at some length, and then hung up. 'So, Sister Ruth, you must stay with us until a Mr Waterman comes to take you to a television studio, and Brother Saul will escort you home this evening. We have two important meetings today.'

'As you think fit, Brother Joshua.' Ruth bowed her head. A television studio? Her mind whirled. Would she be singing? Brother Saul had obviously permitted it. She looked down ruefully at her muddied, bloodstained robes. 'Perhaps I can wash my soiled robes?' she asked, hoping it wasn't too demanding a request.

'Certainly, Sister, you must represent The True Gospel Church in clean robes. I must be off now; I shall leave you with Brother Job, he will show you to the laundry.' He stood, taking with him a large blue folder that Ruth recognised. The gold lettering caught the light: Agenda for Change.

Ruth became very conscious of the mobile phone in her robe pocket, the keys tucked into her underwear and the task she had to carry out. Her heart began to thump painfully. She would have to conceal them whilst washing the stains out of her robes.

Ayesha hurried along the side street towards the market square. The suitcase slowed her progress, adding to her anxiety. It was early yet, and there were few shoppers about. The Burka she wore made a soft susurration against the day clothes she wore underneath it, the wheels of the suitcase rumbled noisily over the tarmac. She glanced around from time to time. The smell of coffee drifted from the corner café. Several times she thought she had seen Ahmed's turban bobbing out of sight as she looked behind her. Sweat trickled down her back. Her hands were clammy, though the day was quite chilly. Not much further now, and she would be with the one man in the world that she could ever marry. Against her family's wishes: she had never seen her father so angry. The face of the man that they had chosen haunted her dreams, a shopkeeper, short, fat and balding. Ahead, a strange figure in a white plastic suit emerged from a doorway. Ayesha's heightened senses could hear the fabric creaking as the man inside it moved.

Suddenly, from behind her, came the sound of soft soled shoes striking the pavement in a fast staccato rhythm. She threw herself against the wall. Ahmed flew past her and cannoned into the white garbed figure. Someone groaned, gasped for breath.

She thought someone said, 'You'll do nicely,' in a muffled voice.

Ahmed sank to the ground. The white clad figure walked briskly away.

Ayesha looked down at her cousin, the man who had terrified her for so long. Any moment, he would be on his feet and would carry out his vow to kill her for dishonouring the family name. But he didn't move. She saw red seeping from beneath his clothes. He was bleeding. Perhaps he had fallen on his knife?

With shaking hands, Ayesha turned her cousin over. His own knife was still in his hand. But the knife that had caused his heart to stop beating was still protruding from his chest. Those fierce brown eyes gazed at nothing.

For several minutes, Ayesha stood, unmoving, gazing down at the body of the man who had tormented her for so long. Then, she turned and walked swiftly away.

At the entrance to the side street she cannoned into a man coming the other way, murmured an apology and tried to move past.

'Ayesha! What on earth's wrong?'

'Guy!' She dropped her suitcase and threw her arms round him.

Guy held her for a few minutes until she stopped trembling enough to speak.

'It's Ahmed. Somebody killed him. He's in the road, just back there.'

At that moment, a cry went up in the street behind her. 'I think he's been found,' Guy said, 'do you want to go back?'

'No,' she said, 'I don't. He was intending to kill me.'

Guy looked down at her in horror. 'You didn't …'

'Of course I didn't. But I saw who did.'

Guy looked up the narrow street as a police siren howled its banshee wail. 'Did you touch him at all?'

'I turned him over.'

'Then we'll have to go back, there might be traces of you at the scene.'

Ayesha looked at him in terror. 'But, the rest of them, they'll find me.'

'Not if we tell them what's been going on. The truth.'

Reluctantly, Ayesha followed him back towards the gathering crowd.

Ruth had borrowed a fresh choir robe whilst hers was drying in the modern electric machine. Her secrets were still safe, and she was sitting alone in Brother Adam's office. She was using the quiet to meditate, because the thoughts that seethed in her mind did nothing for her inner peace. She looked up as someone knocked the door and entered, carrying Ruth's clean robe.

'Peace be with you, Sister Ruth. I am Sister Josephine.'

'And with your spirit, Sister,' Ruth replied, taking in the tall, grey-haired woman who stared at her so intently that she turned her eyes away in embarrassment. Ruth put on her clean robe.

'I knew your father well.' She sat down, as though suddenly tired of standing. 'Before he was taken from us, he left me a task to perform. I have completed it, but now I cannot give him the results of my research. It has troubled my spirit much over the past few days, that I delayed so long, undecided, and now cannot give these things to him myself.'

'Research, Sister Josephine?'

'He asked me to – no, it doesn't matter what it was. Do you know who is investigating his murder?'

'A Chief Inspector Cooper.'

There was a long pause before Sister Josephine answered. 'Could you give these things to him for me, for your father?' She wrote 'Inspector Cooper' on the package and held it out to her.

'Of course. But… is it safe to do so in here?'

Sister Josephine looked surprised. 'Well, yes, the safest in the building, since you seem to understand the problem of continual oversight. That's why I came to you here.'

Ruth took the package and placed it in her carry sack. 'I will take it to the Inspector.'

'May the Lord watch over your steps, Sister.' As she said this, she stood up and made for the door. As she opened it, she passed a deacon coming in.

'Sister Ruth, a car is here to take you to the studio. God be with you in your travels.'

'And with you in yours, Brother Job,' Ruth responded, following him to the front entrance.

Her sense of unreality increased as the enormous limousine swept through the traffic and through the gates of the television centre. It was another world, full of semi-familiar faces that had peopled the televisions on the hospital wards she had worked in. She remembered vividly her sense of shock as people kissed openly on screen, scenes of bedroom intimacy and brutal acts of violence portrayed in terrible intensity. This was entertainment for so many; she'd found it unpalatable, had turned her eyes away from the flickering screens.

Should she be going on television at all?

# Chapter 33

Tuesday

Cooper strode down the alleyway and ducked under the police tape, showing his ID to the officer on duty. 'Who's scene of crime officer, Wilson?'

'PC Ames, sir.'

'Right.' With a nod of thanks, Cooper looked for Ames, without moving from the spot.

Ames caught sight of him and beckoned him across. The man was lying face-up in the alley, the knife that had killed him glittering in a shaft of sunlight. 'Morning, sir. This seems to be another of the ethnic murders. But this time we got lucky; we have a witness.'

Cooper looked up at him sharply. 'A witness?'

'Yes, sir. She's in the café with WPC Morris. A Miss Muhktar.'

'I will go in to speak to her immediately. Ah, here comes the pathologist now.'

'Good morning, Inspector. Not so good for this poor sod, though. Hmm; Adult male, twenty-five or so, Muslim, perhaps Arabic origins. Easy cause of death.' He stooped down to examine the corpse more closely. 'I'd say someone has turned him over since he died. The knife has been knocked upward and deeper into the chest, consistent with the victim falling forward onto it. Here, there's blood pooled where he fell, and not too much on the chest. He was probably already dead when he was turned over.' He straightened up. 'Looks as though he was ready for trouble, doesn't it?' He pointed to the knife that the victim's fingers still clasped.

'Thank you, Jim. I'll be in the café if I'm wanted.' Cooper could hardly contain his eagerness. A witness, at last!

'Got a thirst on, has he?' the pathologist said, as he knelt by the body.

'No, sir, a witness to the murder.'

'Ah, that explains it. Have the photographers been?'

'Yes, done and dusted. There's one waiting to finish off.'

'Right.' With gloved hands, the pathologist set about removing the knife and placing it in an evidence bag. A separate bag was used for the one the victim had in his fingers. When they were both properly labelled, he passed them to PC Ames. 'Get the photographer to record these; then, shall we bag him up?'

Ames signalled to the photographer and to his officers who were waiting with the stretcher and bag.

In the café, Ayesha turned her eyes away as the policemen lifted Ahmed's body, slid the black bag over him and zipped it up. It took four of them to lift him; he was, or had been, a big man. All that was left to show of what had happened here was a pool of blood and a chalk outline inside a line of police tape. A police photographer was walking around the spot, taking pictures from every angle.

Cooper returned with a cup of coffee. 'Do you feel able to talk to me about what happened, Miss Muhktar?'

The girl nodded, her head barely moving. It was disconcerting, he thought, interviewing a pair of eyes. The young man beside her was tall, blond, and blue-eyed. WPC Morris sat bolt upright, her bright, intelligent gaze taking in everything around her as she sipped her hot chocolate.

'I was walking toward the market square. This man came out of the doorway down the alley. There was the sound of running footsteps behind me. I threw myself against the wall. Ahmed shot past me and ran into the man with quite a thud. Then he slid to the ground. The man in the white suit just walked away.' The girl paused to steady herself. Her whole body was shaking: the Burka seeming to vibrate.

'I turned him over. That's when I realised he was dead and not me.'

'Why should you have been dead?' Cooper asked, gently.

'Because Ahmed had sworn to kill me. He is, was, my cousin. I have brought dishonour to the family name. I wish to marry Guy.' The dark eyes turned toward the blond man beside her. 'I am sure the knife in his hand was intended for me, Inspector.'

There was a silence at the table, punctuated by the sounds of crockery clattering in the kitchens and the traffic on the main road nearby.

'Is there anything else you can remember?' Cooper broke the silence.

The girl looked up. 'The man seemed to say something. It sounded like "You'll do nicely." It was a bit muffled by the white suit.'

'White suit?' Cooper probed.

'Yes, the man who killed Ahmed was wearing a white suit; like the ones the police were wearing.'

'A forensic suit?' Cooper put his cup down with a thud. That would explain the lack of any trace of the killer at the crime scenes so far. Where the hell had the killer got his hands on them?

'Sir,' PC Morris said. 'About three years ago, there was a break-in at the Glasgow works where these suits are made. About five hundred of them went missing, were never traced.'

'I sincerely hope he doesn't intend to use them all,' Cooper said dryly. 'So they were stolen with this in mind.'

'There's something else, sir. They took small, medium and large.'

The woman in make-up looked at Ruth's flawless complexion with awe. 'You don't need much doing to your skin, love.'

'I don't wear make-up. Do I have to have some on?'

'I'm afraid so, without it you'll look like a ghost on screen. It's the lights; they drain the colour from your skin.'

Afterwards, Ruth sat in something called the green room; which was apparently where people waited to go up into the studio. There was food set out on a table at one end, where there was a constantly moving crowd of hungry customers coming and going. There were television screens at one side of the room, showing the programmes that were live at the moment. Her mineral water was fizzy; but she sipped it anyway. The make-up on her face felt greasily unpleasant, but she had been surprised to see how…different it had made her look. The screen on the left flickered and changed.

'Here is a newsflash. A man, perhaps a Muslim, has been stabbed to death today in Salisbury. It happened at around eight-thirty this morning. Police have not named the victim as yet. There is speculation that this is another of the so-called ethnic cleansing murders. Dominic Draper is at the scene. Dominic.'

'Morning, George. The police are not releasing any more information at the moment. All we know is that the man, aged about twenty-five, was stabbed in this alleyway behind me at about eight-thirty this morning. He is thought to have been of Arabic origin, probably a Muslim. Police will be making a statement later today. This is Dominic Draper, returning you to the studio.'

The newsman, Dominic Draper, had been at her father's funeral, she thought. What an awful job, going around the country giving out the news of murders.

## Chapter 34

The chat show's host and his partner had coordinated their notes for the interviews. Although the cues would be there, much of their live show was done by the seat of the pants, as Derek was fond of saying.

'Let's get these God-botherers on the spot and make them wriggle,' he murmured as the studio lights went down.

His wife, Deanna, gentle and patient, just smiled, patting her skirt pointedly. She was a good foil to his more abrasive, sometimes arrogant, stance. She rather liked the girl, loved her singing and so gave Ruth an encouraging smile as the lights came on and the numbers counted down to zero. A red 'On Air' light glowed over the exit.

Max Waterman fidgeted in his seat beside her.

'Good afternoon. On today's show we have a very talented young woman whose amazing voice has enthralled those who have heard her sing. Ruth Diamond is a member of The True Gospel Church, where, very recently, a man ran amok with a knife, killing three of the church members. Ruth, welcome to the show.'

'Thank you.'

'I'm sure the viewers would like to know; what was it like, the morning of the attacks in the church?'

Ruth was taken aback by the question, but, breathing steadily, answered quite calmly. 'It was horrific. I lost my father and two dear friends that morning.' This was like debating issues with her father, as she had so often done whilst growing up.

'Tell me; is it true that you went to help your father defeat the attacker?'

'I tried to help him, yes.'

'And were injured yourself?'

'Only a small cut from the man's knife.'

'You showed tremendous courage.'

'I don't think so. Anyone would have done the same.'

'I would certainly have thought twice myself before taking on a man armed with a knife. What do you think drove him to such violence?'

'I believe he is a sick man. He was a patient in the local psychiatric hospital.'

Deanna put a question next: 'Do you think it's possible to forgive such an act? The murder of your father – it's not something that you can shrug off, is it?'

'Forgiveness is something that comes with love and understanding. Although we are told not to cast our pearls before swine, that is, proffer forgiveness to the unrepentant, we need to set our hearts and minds free from the poison of hate and the lust for revenge. It doesn't help, in my view.'

Deanna digested this for a moment, whilst Derek sprang into the pause.

'What, may I ask, do you think of the political involvement of the True Gospel Church?'

'I believe that the Elders are working for the general good of the people.'

'Some of the changes that have just become law have been described as limiting civil liberties.'

'If that liberty is to do something against the moral law, then it is a liberty that should not be taken, surely?'

'So who is in a position to decide what the moral law is?'

'We are a Christian country, are we not, so it must be the Ten Commandments and the law of love instituted by Christ himself.' Ruth was beginning to relax. She could do this, she thought.

Derek had not expected an answer like that, so he rapidly changed tack. 'Have you any idea of the real world, since you have spent your whole life cloistered in the church?'

'I trained as a nurse at the Salisbury District Hospital. I don't regard that as "cloistered".'

Again, Derek's notes and her reply did not match. 'Surely that is unusual for a member of your church?'

'Others have done so.'

'And were you educated exclusively within the church?'

'No, I went to St Mark's in Salisbury before going to the church college.'

Derek was beginning to perspire. This interview was not going as planned. All his information said that the members of the sect were brainwashed and virtual prisoners of the cult.

'Does the church practise arranged marriages?'

'It is not an uncommon practice for marriages to be arranged. Often others have a better perspective on which members would be best together. Other faiths have practised it for centuries.'

Derek turned, 'Max Waterman, welcome to the show. You are well known for finding new singing talent; where did you meet Ruth, Max?'

'I heard her sing first at an open air service, then at her father's funeral. I knew that she had an amazing talent, so I approached the church for permission to sign a recording contract.'

'Surely, the True Gospel Church would be against such an enterprise?'

'I was aware of no resistance. They took time to consider the proposal, and then they accepted it.'

Derek turned to another man who had been sitting in shadow. 'Mr Markham, as a journalist, what do you make of the True Gospel Church?'

Ruth gasped in shock as Paul's face came into the light. He nodded to her, smiled as though to a stranger, and turned to Derek.

'The True Gospel Church has many aspects. I believe Miss Diamond's life to have been markedly different from many of the other members of the sect – her father was a very powerful and wealthy businessman, and I feel he had more freedom than many within the church to bring his daughter up in the way he felt to be best.'

'In what way?'

'In that she was allowed to do her nurse training. Tell me, Ruth, have you been allowed to return to your nursing since your father died?' Paul's eyes were very blue, Ruth noticed.

Ruth swallowed hard, her hands were sweating. 'No, I have been busy with the recording contract.'

'And will you be returning to your nursing duties?'

'It depends on the decision of the Elders.'

'So you are not free to choose for yourself?'

'It is better for me to be guided by the Eldership.'

'And have you had your marriage partner arranged for you?'

'Yes, I have.'

'And have you met him yet?'

'No, I have not,' Ruth answered, suddenly wondering when this would end.

'Has the date been arranged?'

'In a few weeks' time.'

'I see.' Paul leaned forward in his chair. 'Do any of the young people from the church attend state schools now?'

'No, we have our own schools and colleges.'

'I rest my case, Derek. Although Miss Diamond had opportunities beyond the usual, she is unique among the True Gospel Church membership in that she has had so much contact with the real world.'

Derek turned to him and smiled. 'We're running out of time here. We shall be discussing the impact of the True Gospel Church after the break with the Bishop of Salisbury, the Liberal Democrat leader of Salisbury District Council, Sir Stanhope Short and with Paul Markham. Before the break, I would like to ask Ruth Diamond to sing for us.'

Ruth stepped to the microphone and began to sing, unaccompanied at first, then the small band of musicians joined in. The song came to an end, lights went on, the on air sign blinked out, and everyone relaxed, except Derek, who was deep in conversation with the Bishop and the MP.

Paul turned toward her and winked. Not knowing what else to do, she sat down in her seat beside Max Waterman, who passed her a glass of water.

'Excellent, Ruthie, absolutely spot on,' he grinned.

Meanwhile, at the Bassett Conference Centre, the joint assembly of the Joshua Group and the Five Hundred Group was well underway. The Elders had convened for a few moments to watch the programme on which Ruth was to sing. There was a quick intake of breath when they saw who was lined up to speak against them on national television. Their decision led Brother

Joshua Adam to a telephone. From his little green notebook, he selected a number and dialled.

'Four two six? A 1 here. Activate Code seventeen. I repeat, activate Code seventeen.' His face showed no emotion as he returned with the remaining Elders to the conference room.

At the television studio, the second half of the show got underway with Paul Markham reading out some statistics regarding the True Gospel Church and its activities. Then the studio began to fill with smoke, and an alarm began to shrill.

Derek swore loudly as the camera, sound crew and audience began to evacuate the studio.

'That'll be live,' warned Deanna.

'Well, viewers, it looks as though we have to pause there for a moment. We'll be back to you as soon as we can.' Reluctantly, he rose to his feet.

The producer sprinted over to him. 'Let's use studio thirteen – it's been redecorated and they'll be using it full-time tomorrow.'

Derek grinned. 'Good one. Let's move it!'

The discussion went ahead. If the Elders at the conference centre had been aware of it, they would have been very angry indeed.

Four two six hesitated. Could he do more? He had only been authorised for a Code seventeen. He decided to phone his boss.

'B2? It's four two six. Authorised, code seventeen by A 1, ineffective, I repeat Authorised, code seventeen by A 1, ineffective. Instructions required. Instant.'

For several minutes he waited beside the telephone, anxiously glancing over his shoulder. How long could he afford to be away from his post?

Brother Joshua Adam was unused to being called to the telephone. He was even more unused to things that didn't go the way he planned them. 'Not effective? What does the idiot mean? That code would have emptied the studio. What is he playing at?'

'I could ask him, but it might reveal his position if he were overheard.'

'I'll get on to it. I will contact him direct. Thank you, B2.'

Brother Adam switched on the television set in the lounge. The screen flickered into life. The unholy bunch of gossips was still at it. Brother Adam dialled four two six. 'A 1. Code fifty. I repeat, A 1, Code fifty.'

The oily looking presenter was saying smugly, 'No fire alarms to interrupt us here, gentlemen. The reports of ill-health and deaths among the True Gospel Church College students have been many and very worrying. What have your researches shown, Paul?'

'That seven students died last year, and there were twenty-one cases of severe illness, put down to an outbreak of viral meningitis.'

'That seems unfortunate rather than culpable?'

'It does, until you realise that such outbreaks have occurred at all the colleges throughout the country. It's my belief that the eighteen hour regime of duties, prayer rituals and the poor diet contributes to the high incidence of ill-health amongst the students.'

'Miss Diamond, let me ask you as a graduate of the True Gospel College. Did you find the regime there particularly hard?'

Ruth swallowed hard. It was going to be a difficult question to answer truthfully without bringing disrepute on the church. 'It was a hard discipline, but it is necessary to work hard and subdue self-indulgence. The young have much to learn.'

'Were you ever hungry at college, Miss Diamond?' Paul Markham asked.

'Of course. It's natural to be hungry when one is young.'

'Let me put it differently. Was your hunger ever satisfied when you had finished your meal?'

Ruth took a deep breath. 'No, but that was the rule. Always leave the table feeling as though you could eat a little more.'

'Did any of your college companions become ill whilst you were there?'

'Yes, several were unwell.'

'Did any of them die?'

Ruth's answer was lost in a blur of sound, dust and confusion. Bright stars flickered and she fell into blackness.

Brother Joshua Adam gave a grunt of satisfaction as the screen went blank, and then flickered into advertisements. He strode back towards the conference room. Just as he did so, a small party of men entered the foyer. He paid them little heed as the door swung gently to behind him.

Wilson was not far behind the Prime Minister as they stepped into the foyer. The face that he glimpsed momentarily gave him a jolt of surprise and fear. Whilst the Prime Minister was talking to the manager, Wilson peered obliquely through the glass of the door. What were all these men, many of whom he recognised, doing here? Trade union leaders, politicians, high-ranking army, navy and air force personnel, rubbing shoulders with judges, senior police officers and ...

'Wilson, could you get a message to my wife? Tell her we'll be an hour later than we thought.'

Wilson reached for his phone as the Prime Minister went up in the lift with the Home Secretary, discussing something intently.

Before he could dial, the phone rang in his hand. 'Wilson.' He listened, aghast at what he was being told. 'Right, I'll inform the Prime Minister at once.' The call to Number Ten forgotten, he sprinted for the lift.

Ruth opened her eyes. For a moment, she could not make any sense of what she saw. There was something looming over her which looked like a concrete pillar. Her mouth was full of dust and she was lying on the remains of a chair. She shifted her position, aware that she was covered in tiny cuts and abrasions. Whatever had happened, she was able to move. Nothing seemed to be broken. The pillar above her began to slip, creaking eerily as it did so. Gingerly, she slid herself along on her bottom in the cramped space until she could turn over. The pillar was caught in some cables which were slipping, stretching and snapping under its huge weight. Ruth began to crawl, whimpered as the pillar slipped again. A wall of debris either side trapped her under sentence of death. Desperately, she scrambled forward. A small space opened out beside her. Wriggling through the narrow gap, she stood up, taking deep breaths of dusty smoky air. The pillar finally won over the strength of the cables and fell with a splintering crash as it crushed the things still beneath it.

Ruth fell to her knees in an attitude of prayer, giving wordless thanks to her saviour. Then, for the first time in her life, she had an answer. Or, rather, an order. 'Use your skills here, daughter.' So clear was the voice that she opened her eyes to see who had spoken. There was no one there.

The studio was rubble. Her gaze took in the chaos before she could make sense of what she was looking at. Then her brain registered. There were injured people lying amongst the debris, others standing dazed by the blast. She scrambled over the rubble and began to examine the nearest victim. She tore strips off her white under robe to put pressure on bleeding limbs, working furiously from one to another.

The air was rent by the sounds of sirens approaching. Ruth bent to her task, clearing the airway of a man who wasn't breathing, and beginning mouth-to-mouth. It wasn't until he opened his eyes that she recognised Derek.

'Must be my lucky day,' he coughed painfully, looking into her eyes.

Ruth blushed and turned to the woman who lay beside him. No pulse. Ruth closed her eyes gently and moved on.

'Well, now, we mustn't make a habit of meeting like this, Miss Diamond.' The paramedic grinned.

'Mr Davies.' Ruth straightened her aching shoulders, 'There's one woman dead, she can wait a while, but the man over there looks in a bad way with internal bleeding, I've only been able to slow the blood loss from his legs.'

'Will do, Ma'am.' The second paramedic, whom she recognised as Willy Foley, gave her a case of equipment. 'I bet you can make use of this.'

It seemed to Ruth that she had been kneeling beside the victims for hours when the helpers began to make an impression on the number of casualties. The two paramedics picked their way towards her.

'I think it's time you went to get yourself checked over, Miss Diamond,' David Davies suggested.

'But we're not finished yet,' Ruth protested.

'Tough as you are, young lady, you were caught in an explosion.'

'Were there many killed?'

'Probably four, but we're not through here yet. They're bringing in dogs to see if there are any still buried.'

'Was Paul Markham all right?'

'The journalist? I haven't seen him. He might have been taken by another crew. Don't worry, Miss Diamond. He's a tough one. They couldn't kill him in Iraq.'

Ruth's vision blurred. 'I could do with a drink of water,' she murmured.

The two paramedics exchanged knowing glances and supported her under her arms as she stumbled over the rubble, suddenly feeling exhausted. Someone wrapped a blanket round her and a cup of hot sweet tea was placed in her hands. So bemused was she that she drank the strange liquid without a protest.

# Chapter 35

Wilson burst into the room where the Prime Minister was just taking a sip of whisky; the Home Secretary was opening a laptop.

'Sir – there's been an explosion at the BBC Television Centre.'

'Put the TV on; let's see what news there is.' Stuart Winter was not easily ruffled, but the sight of the pile of rubble in the studio where he had been interviewed so often chilled him. He gulped the rest of his whisky and put the glass down.

The newscaster was talking to some of the survivors.

'Were you in the studio when the blast happened?'

'Yeah, I was, like. The programme was going on abaht this church what's causing all the bovver, like, then, bang! The place blew apart. I was lucky, like, 'cause I was behind one of them big pillars. Chap next to me was blown outside.'

'You had a lucky escape.'

'Yeah, right. Seems someone didn't want the programme to go out, like.'

'Why do you say that?'

'Stands to reason, dunnit? First there was this fire in the other studio, so they move the whole shebang over in this studio, then, bang, no programme.'

'So the programme was stopped, restarted, then this blast stopped it completely. You think someone wanted to prevent the programme being broadcast?'

'Yeah, mate. It's obvious, innit?'

'Thank you, that was Fergus Ashworth, who survived the unexplained explosion in the studio behind me.' The interviewer turned towards the camera. 'No one knows for sure what caused the blast here today, there was no warning and there are four known dead. Dog teams have been brought in to search amongst the rubble for survivors; the injured have been taken to several hospitals around the capital. If you have concerns for loved ones who may have been caught up in this terrible incident, the helpline number will be on screen shortly. The programme on air at the time was 'Derek and Deanna'. Today's topic- 'The *Real* True Gospel Church'. There are speculations about the cause, as you have heard just now. At the moment the exact cause of the blast is not known, and no one has claimed responsibility. This is Dominic Draper returning you to the studio.'

Wilson pressed the remote when the Prime Minister waved his hand. 'Any ideas, Wilson, Leggat?'

'I don't think it's one of the usual terrorist groups, sir,' Wilson said, 'the target's wrong – unless they were after the True Gospellers, that is.'

'It's a possibility.' The PM sat deep in thought for a moment. 'Did you know that the True Gospellers have a multi-million pound annual budget?'

'Is that worldwide, sir?' Leggat asked.

'No, just the UK.'

Wilson sat heavily on the sofa. 'I've just seen a very worrying thing, sir.'

The PM's head twisted to face him. 'What?'

'That Brother Joshua Adam. He's here, holding a conference. I saw him go in and stand up on the stage with some others of his ilk.'

'So?'

'It's the people I saw with him, sir. Just a minute, I'll write down the names of as many as I can remember.'

The room was silent save for the scratching of Wilson's pen. He handed the sheet of hotel notepaper to the PM, who scrutinised it closely.

'What the hell are they up to?' He stood up, went to the window to look out over the countryside. This was usually a quiet place to get things done. He had been looking forward to a peaceful meal with his wife and the two men he had with him. Instead, there was yet another crisis. He was beginning to wonder if this job was really what he wanted after all. He smiled at the thought; he'd be bored witless having nothing to do but write his memoirs. Not ready for that yet, he decided.

'Wilson, we need someone on the inside at that meeting. We have to know what's going on.' He gazed at the list with unfocussed eyes. 'We can't use anyone that's known to any of the group here. It's going to be tough. Maybe we should use bugs?'

The Home Secretary looked up. 'We did have some at a meeting of this group, sir, but they found every one of them. Report says that one of them was used in that church killing, to convince the perpetrator that voices were telling him to kill the people in the church.'

'But the attack was on the church itself. Stolen by them, used against them? It doesn't make sense,' Wilson said.

'It would if you wanted to make it look as though outsiders had killed some of your members that you wanted rid of. Neat trick; suspicion drawn elsewhere and no one looking at the church itself for the guilty party.' The PM turned away from the window. 'Get Fox here, and that policeman who's dealing with the knife murders. I want to pick their brains.'

'Yes, sir.' Wilson reached for the telephone.

'Right, Leggat, what about these prison reforms? The budget's too tight to do anything major, but we can't risk any more early releases. It'll lose us votes.'

Ruth sat in the ambulance with a man who'd lost an arm in the explosion; the paramedic had persuaded her to come to the hospital to be checked over. Her ears were ringing, presumably the effect of the blast; everything seemed muffled. The many small cuts were beginning to smart, and there was a tender area across her back which throbbed with each beat of her heart.

The man on the stretcher looked towards her and smiled with difficulty, the cuts and bruises on his face were ugly and swollen. 'You're that girl who sings, aren't you?'

Ruth nodded.

'Would you sing something for me now? It would take my mind off the arm a minute.'

Never had Ruth felt so reluctant to sing. Her mouth was dry, her ears ringing. But she smiled and asked the paramedic for a drink of water. She began to sing.

'By cool Siloam's shady rill
How sweet the lily grows
How sweet the breath beneath the hill
Of Sharon's dewy rose…'

# Chapter 36

Calvin was in no mood to follow rules. He had read the file, 'Agenda for Change', and had kicked the door of his room so hard he'd left a dent in the woodwork and bruised his toes in the process. Retreat shoes were not designed for such activities. In the boiler room, he changed into his outdoor shoes, wincing as his ribs protested at the movement. He was supposed to be painting the new handrail on the steps as 'light duties', but he would not be able to settle to it.

This 'Agenda for Change' would ruin things for him.

Adam was talking to a couple whose arranged marriage was to take place this weekend. They looked ridiculously young, sitting opposite him in his study. Not for the first time, he wondered about the wisdom of the practice. He was distracted by a figure cycling up his driveway. The man wore jeans and a red T-shirt. For a moment, he didn't recognise him. Then he knew. How was Calvin able to come to his home, where had he got those worldly clothes and, of all things, a bicycle?

'Sister Anne, Brother Thomas, here are the guidance notes for your wedding; and the books "The Christian Witness Through Marriage", and "Disciplined Sexuality".'

'We are indebted to you for your help, Brother Adam.'

'Are there any questions?'

They looked at each other confusedly. The True Gospel Church did not encourage a questioning attitude.

'Well. I shall see you again for prayer before the ceremony. God bless you both.'

'And you, Brother Adam.' They bowed and walked out, their robes billowing out behind them in the draught from the open front door. Calvin never could close a door. All The Retreat ones were self-closing, to avoid noise.

He found his brother in the kitchen, tucking into a large cheese sandwich. 'What on earth are you doing, Cal?'

'Eating.'

'I can see that. But what of your afternoon duties? And where did you get those awful clothes?'

'That's not important. Have you read this?' He pulled a large blue folder from a plastic shopping bag and pushed it across the table.

'I've helped assemble them. But I wasn't cleared to read the contents.'

'Have a read whilst I go and look at your TV set. Sister Ruth is on *The Derek and Deanna Show* this afternoon.'

'Is she? Be careful no one sees the set, I'll be through in a minute.' The file was probably just another of those long-winded theological tracts that father was so fond of producing.

By the end of the first page, he was frowning. By the fourth page, he was looking pale. He was into the political section when Calvin shot through the door, looking white as Saul's Robes.

'It's Ruth. There's been a bomb at the Television Centre. In the studio where she was being interviewed.'

Adam noticed a tiny piece of cheese caught on his brother's chin and a small patch of blond stubble he'd missed whilst shaving. It couldn't be true. One of Calvin's inane jokes. He followed him through into the lounge. The doors concealing the set in its recess were wide open. There seemed to be a demolition site behind the announcer who was holding one of those woolly microphones.

Calvin pressed the volume control.

'This terrible event has shocked everyone here today. Police dogs are helping to search for survivors among the rubble. It is known that four people are dead; around thirty are being treated for injuries sustained in the blast. There is still no information about the cause of the explosion.'

A bloodstained figure on a stretcher was carried past the reporter.

Calvin looked round as there was an odd thud behind him. Brother Adam had fallen in a dead faint. 'He never could stand the sight of blood,' Calvin said, as the newsflash came to an end, he switched off the set and closed the doors.

The PM sat back in the leather chair. Fox, the Chief of Police Sir Tristan Flint, Cooper, Allsopp, Leggat, and Wilson arranged themselves around the room on the sofa, the window sill, and the desktop.

'Thank you all for coming here at such short notice. There are three things I want to discuss this evening. First, the explosion at the Television Centre, second, the latest ethnic murder, and third, the meeting downstairs of the Five Hundred Group. Wilson?'

'Latest reports indicate a bomb behind one of the studio walls. Oddly, it seems to have been built into the fabric of the building. Detonated by a remote control device.'

'A sleeping bomb? With personnel on hand to detonate it if and when required?' The PM jiggled his knee up and down, as he did when under stress. 'We need to arrange a check of all public buildings as soon as possible, Tristan, how soon can you get it underway?'

'Quickly if we can use army personnel, a bit tight staff wise.'

'Do it. What about the motive for the blast?'

'It may have been the True Gospel Censorship Department,' Cooper said, dryly, 'they weren't getting a very good press.'

'It could well have been them – but we have no proof of anything at the moment, sir, no one has claimed responsibility,' Fox added.

'Does anyone know what happened to Sister Ruth, the singer, who was being interviewed?' Allsopp enquired.

'That's a point; would they sacrifice such a PR asset? She's bound to earn them a packet in record sales, as well,' Leggat said.

'That's a conundrum. Now, the murders. I must tell you all that Cooper was selected to investigate these murders because there are, have been, grave suspicions about security at the Met recently. There may be True Gospel Members working undercover amongst our men. Cooper, is there any progress?'

'Yes, sir, I have been working on this latest death all day. Seems to have been much as the others, except that this time we had a witness.'

'Description?' The PM looked up eagerly.

'Unfortunately not; the man wore a forensic suit, believed to be one of five hundred in assorted sizes stolen some time ago. One thing that has confirmed my suspicion that these are more than simple random killings is what the witness heard the killer say.'

'Which was?'

'You'll do nicely.'

'Just that?'

'Yes, sir, as though the killer was looking for someone to fit particular criteria – sees the right type, says, "You'll do nicely".'

'I suppose it's progress,' the PM said glumly. 'So the crime scene is always clean as a whistle, there's no link between killer and victim, just looking for somebody in the wrong place at the right time. I don't envy you that task, Inspector.'

Cooper smiled. 'They always make a mistake in the end, sir. Always.'

'I wish I had your confidence. Now, the meeting downstairs. We need some ears. Any suggestions?'

'I've been thinking about that, sir.' Fox stood up, hands in pockets. 'I have a sleeper in the organisation, he borrowed one of their security passes, and I made a copy so that it wouldn't be missed. Unfortunately, our sleeper would be recognised as in the wrong place since this is not his department. All we need is someone who can go in unrecognised. I've a purple set of robes, and a sound system ready.'

There was a long silence, broken at last by Allsopp. 'I can do it, sir, I know enough about church practice to pass muster, and they wouldn't know my face. Hopefully, they'd all think I was someone that they hadn't met yet. It's a big meeting.'

'He's not trained for this kind of work,' Sir Tristan objected.

'Who is? There's not much call for undercover monks these days.' Cooper shrugged. 'I think it's the best we've got.'

'I agree.' The PM stood up. 'Report back to Wilson as soon as there is any news, we'll meet at Number Ten tomorrow evening. Thank you, gentlemen.'

# Chapter 37

The Bishop opened his eyes slowly. There was a familiar smell; one that made him shiver: bombed buildings. He had been around enough of them during the blitz. Dust filled his mouth, nose and throat, thick black smoke, the metallic taste of his own blood. He was lying on some fallen masonry and various bits of plastic. But the wail of the ambulance siren was modern; not the ringing bell he'd known then.

'So, am I hurt?' he asked himself, for the comfort of hearing a voice in the darkness. He began to shift various parts of his anatomy. 'Just my left arm,' he murmured, 'and a gash on my head, judging by the blood on my face. Not three bad, although the mattress could be kinder.'

He lay there listening for a few moments. There seemed to be voices nearby, and a strange skittering, scrabbling noise that he couldn't place for a moment.

'Rex, what have you found? Good boy!' A voice closer to him now, and someone treading carefully over the rubble. A rescue dog. Best make a noise.

'All people that on earth do dwell, sing to the lord with cheerful voice,' the Bishop bellowed at his best reach-the-back-pews setting.

'I think we've found the Bishop, Sergeant. He's singing Psalm 100 at full throttle!' a Welsh voice said from overhead. 'Can you hear me, sir?'

'I certainly can.'

'Are you hurt?'

'Just my arm and a head wound I think. There's something heavy on the arm; I can't move it.'

'It may be a while, but we'll have you out as soon as we can, sir. Need to be careful how we shift this rubble.' A light flashed through a gap in the debris.

'That's great. By the way, I can see the light of your torch above my head.'

'Can you now?' the voice answered. There was a further scrabbling, a thud, and the little space in which the Bishop lay was suddenly full of bright torchlight. Above him, slightly to his left, there were two heads in silhouette, a German shepherd dog and a policeman.

'I am pleased to see you,' croaked the Bishop. 'You wouldn't have any water on you?'

'I'm afraid I shouldn't give you any sir, in case you need anaesthetic, sorry.'

'I'll live, unfortunately for those who wanted my silence.'

It took almost three hours to extricate the Bishop; his arm was pinned down by one of the large pillars that had held up the roof and on top of that was precariously balanced masonry. He emerged from his temporary tomb into the light of street lamps and the flash of cameras. There was a BBC news unit as well, covering their own story; he smiled to himself and waved to the cameras with his good arm.

Then a white-faced Archdeacon Wise appeared in his line of sight.

'Your Grace! Are you badly hurt?'

'Not at all. You'll cope until they let me loose again; I suspect a broken arm and a bit of a gash to the head – it looks worse than it is. I've had something for the pain.' The Bishop grinned at him.

'Shall I bring you anything at the hospital?'

'I'll let you know. Don't worry.' The stretcher was lifted and slid into the ambulance, the doors closed, the engine kicked in and the siren wailed overhead. Well, thought the Bishop, life is full of surprises. I never expected a ride in one of these today. His mother would have quoted the Chinese curse: May you live in interesting times. He closed his eyes and drifted off.

The paramedic beside him sprang into action; then smiled and sat down. The Bishop had fallen asleep.

Paul Markham left the casualty department wearing a variety of bandages. There were several newsmen there that he recognised, and he stopped to speak to them.

'Paul, are you ok?' Jimmy Rafferty pushed his way to the front of the crowd; his rugby player bulk was not easily resisted.

'Just cuts and grazes. They spent a lot of time picking out shards of glass and bits of plastic. But it won't spoil my good looks – the face is ok,' Paul grinned.

'That's a matter of opinion, mate.' Jimmy stood poised with his notebook in hand. 'Your version of what happened?'

'Tell you what, Jimmy; I'll give you an exclusive if you'll get me back home; Dan will be crazy with worry until I get back.'

'No problem, I'll get the Rolls.' Jimmy doubled away to the car park. The 'Rolls' turned out to be an ancient Morris traveller. 'Jump in,' Jimmy said, one eye on a traffic warden heading in their direction.

'Nice wheels.'

'She does me fine; engine's as sweet as a nut, and no-one even bothers to key the paintwork. Good in some of the places stories happen.'

They sat late into the night; a Guinness and a bottle of red between them on the table. Dan sat white-faced as he heard the details of the explosion. He'd had a terrible few hours until he'd tracked both Ruth and Paul down at different hospitals, whose phone lines had been overwhelmed with calls. But he did not interrupt his partner as he gave Jimmy the low-down on the True Gospel Church.

'But do be careful, Jimmy. They don't play by the rules. It may seem fantastic, but I'm sure they were at the bottom of today's bomb. The Bishop and I were planning quite a lot of dung-raking on air. They wanted us silenced.'

'Do you think a Catholic Belfast man would be put off by a few proddy bomb threats?'

'Probably not,' Paul laughed, 'but I had to mention it, in all fairness.'

'Anyway, it's one hell of a story.'

Sometime after midnight, Paul handed him over to Jimmy.

'Tell him your story, Dan. I think it's time you were resurrected, don't you?'

It was three a.m. when the meeting finally broke up. Jimmy headed to his office, Dan and Paul to bed.

Ruth lay in the hospital bed, drifting in and out of sleep. They had kept her in overnight in case of concussion. The nurse came and checked her every half an hour, which made it difficult to rest, but the thoughts that were going around and around her head would not allow her any peace at all.

Her mind replayed the scene in the ambulance again and again. She had finished the hymn. The man had lain back on the stretcher, suddenly vomiting blood.

He looked at the crimson mess, looked up at Ruth and said, 'Praise the Lord, Sister Ruth. I have given all in the cause of the truth.' He reached into his pocket and passed her a card. 'Return this to Brother Joshua, Sister.'

The paramedics turned the man on his side as he continued to vomit more blood, then passed out. The alarm sounded for cardiac arrest, she helped the paramedic as best she could. But the man was dead on arrival at the hospital.

Who had ordered the man to detonate the bomb? Could he really be working for the Five Hundred Group? The bloodstained card in her pocket was a weight on her spirit. She felt dead inside as she thought of all the misery caused by that bomb, all those innocent people killed and injured.

Ruth stared at the half-light of the ward, wondering if it was like the half-light she had been living in all her life, until at last, she slept. The nurse, on her rounds, pausing to see her regular breathing, and feeling the steady pulse, left her to a healing sleep.

## Chapter 38

Josh was still not used to wearing robes; he'd only worn his brand-new novice ones at the meetings for a few hours. He supposed women would find the flapping material round the ankles less distracting. There were several elders in front of him at the double doors. On each side of them stood a black-robed figure, who addressed each one as they entered. As Josh neared the entrance, his heart thudded. One of the black-robes was asking for a password, the other for the security card he had tucked inside his Bible.

He held out the card, swallowed his fear, and simply blurted, 'Brother Joshua.'

Incredibly, the black-robed figure simply nodded and waved him past. Josh moved to a seat near the back of the room, his legs feeling as though they didn't belong to him. Once seated, he took deep breaths to calm himself. Then he had the answer: this was the Joshua Group, the password? Brother Joshua. How he had been named Joshua by his father escaped his understanding, since he was the man who... no, it was definitely not a good time to think of him now. Perhaps it was divine providence, but it had saved his skin today.

Josh looked about him; there were a good number of the black-robed figures around, most of them standing, a bit like policemen at a football match, he thought. Perhaps that's what they are, church police. He took out a notebook, one that he'd bought at a True Gospel Church meeting, and noted down the thought. Then he wrote down the names of as many of the delegates as he could. There were many he didn't recognise, and wondered if there would be any use of real names at the meeting to come.

A tall white-robed figure strode onto the platform, 'Peace be with you, Brethren.'

'And with your spirit, Brother Joshua.'

'Let us remember our purpose.'

The whole gathering began to speak as one voice.

*Have I not commanded thee? Be strong and of a good courage; be not afraid, neither be thou dismayed; for the Lord thy God is with thee whithersoever thou goest.*

'Let us begin. First, Political Change. Brother Amos, will you begin the slides?'

Josh looked at the screen in astonishment. The church was launching its own political party. The manifesto that was being discussed was truly disturbing; he began to jot notes down as fast as he could, and then, with a start, looked around to see if he was alone in doing this; but he wasn't, people were scribbling notes as fast as they could. He found himself voting on the following issues:

- Naming the Party.
- Producing the Manifesto. The Ten Points for Truth.
- Selection and Training of Candidates.
- Publicity.
- Financial breakdown.
- Time plan.

The manifesto was the subject of lively debate, there were more than ten points suggested, and the votes were carried narrowly on some issues. Josh's head was buzzing with concentration when he felt the vibration of his mobile phone in his pocket, but daren't look at it to see who had left him a message.

Josh's notebook was sweaty in his hands by the time the meeting was closed in prayer by Brother Saul, and was followed by the recitation of another rather more chilling bible verse:

*'Whosoever he be that doth rebel against thy commandment and will not hearken unto thy words in all that thou commandest him, he shall be put to death: only be strong and of a good courage.'*

As the delegates filed out, Josh sat for a moment, waiting for the queue to diminish, when he noticed the black-robed figures exiting through a different door nearer the back of the hall. As the last of them disappeared, Josh sauntered across to glance through the glass. His sharp hearing picked up the leader's voice without difficulty. Josh moved toward the front of the hall, so that those in the room could not see him. He had a clear view of the dais on which the leader stood.

'Replacement, four two six; Group B; any proposals?'

Three men were led to the front, a black-robed escort with each. The escorts each spoke briefly, and then a vote was taken, one man chosen, the others led away.

'What was that about?' Josh mused, hurrying toward the exit as the last of the delegates were going out. Just as he reached the doors, a hand fell on his shoulder. It took all his self-control not to jump like a guilty man, but he turned around calmly.

A black-robed figure stood there, holding out his hand. It took Josh a moment to realise that he was holding out Josh's pen.

'Bless you, Brother; I would have missed this later.' Josh managed to keep a casual tone as he took the pen.

'A new commandment I give unto you, that ye love one another,' murmured the man, whose bare arm revealed a tattooed number forty-seven.

'Praise the Lord,' Josh replied to the best of his ability, smiled and turned away. Upstairs again, he longed for a stiff whisky but settled for a cup of coffee and several biscuits as he reported his findings to Inspector Cooper.

The Inspector listened impassively to Josh's account, making notes as he did so. 'Bit of a close shave at the door, then?'

'It was a bit hairy for a minute.'

'Providence or luck?' Cooper looked at him with one eyebrow raised, a half-smile on his lips.

'Whichever it was, I'm glad to have got away with it.'

There was a long pause as Cooper looked at Josh's notes.

Josh took another biscuit.

'There's a thing,' Cooper mused, pointing to a list of items found at the site of the explosion.

Josh looked at the list where indicated. Item fifty-one, a right arm, and shivered involuntarily. Cooper turned to his laptop and summoned up photographs of the objects found, and scrolled through them. Cooper stopped at one, enlarged it to full screen, and then zoomed in on a tiny patch on the forearm.

'Is that the kind of tattoo we're looking for, do you think, Allsopp?'

'Absolutely spot on, sir.' Josh swallowed the last of his coffee in a gulp and refilled his cup. His hands were shaking.

'So, someone from the black-robe-brigade was at the studio. Get onto the hospital and check if the man who was attached to this arm has survived.'

Several hospitals and phone calls later, Josh reported that the man in question was a Roger Saunders who had died on the way to the hospital. A Sister Ruth had been with him in the ambulance.

'Better and better!' Cooper rubbed his hands together, poured himself a coffee. 'Try the studio, see if he was a member of staff.'

A few minutes later, Allsopp put the phone down. 'He was a cameraman, sir.'

'Right.' Cooper downed the rest of his coffee in one, grabbed his coat. 'Let's go and see Sister Ruth.'

The hospital was gearing down for the night as the inspector's shoes echoed on the tiled floors. Josh's steps were lighter behind him; he was still wearing the sandals favoured by the true Gospellers.

Ruth was helping one of the older patients with his meal when they arrived. She smiled at them, and indicated a seat beside her. Josh found another seat and placed it by the bed.

'You're blessed that I'm still here; I was kept in overnight for concussion, but the doctor has only just been to discharge me and I'm waiting for my brother to collect me.' She continued spooning rice pudding into the old man's mouth. He seemed to be enjoying it, but Josh averted his eyes. He didn't do rice pudding.

'I wanted to ask you about the man who died in the ambulance on the way here. Did he say anything?'

Sister Ruth paused for a moment, a troubled look in her eyes. Then she continued plying the spoon. 'Yes, he did. First, he asked me to sing for him, and I did my best. Then, as he began to …to bleed heavily, he said, "Praise the Lord, Sister Ruth, I have given my all for the truth".'

Ruth put the spoon into the empty bowl and reached into her robe pocket. 'He also gave me this to give to Brother Joshua.' She held out the bloodstained card that had given her such a troubled night. Cooper took it carefully and placed it in an evidence bag.

'There is also something that Sister Josephine gave me at the True Gospel Headquarters. She had been doing some research for my father and passed it to me. She thought you should have it.' A canvas bag was slung over the back of the chair, and Ruth rummaged in it until she found a slim brown paper package.

'Here.'

But just as Cooper reached out his hand to take it, a black-robed figure shot through the ward and snatched it from Ruth's grasp. Before Josh had even reached the ward entrance, there was no sign of the thief.

# Chapter 39

Ruth sat for a moment, nonplussed at the speed of it, whilst the two policemen had leapt into action, chasing the thief. They returned a few minutes later out of breath and angry.

'Miss Diamond, do you have any idea what was in that parcel?' Cooper asked.

'No, I don't. I don't think it will be a good idea to talk to Sister Josephine, either. It might be difficult for her,' Ruth said, slowly.

'It'd blow her cover,' Brother Josh said.

Ruth looked puzzled at the phrase.

'Sergeant Allsopp means that it would draw attention to your friend,' Cooper explained.

'I see.' Ruth looked worried. 'Do you know anything about the 'Agenda for Change', Inspector?'

'Only what Sergeant Allsopp was able to glean this afternoon. Do you know anything about it?'

'No,' Ruth said, drawing her robes around her as if she suddenly felt cold. 'But I know where there is a copy of the whole document, at The Retreat. Would it be of any use to you?'

'I don't know whether it would or not,' Cooper replied, 'but I'd certainly like to eliminate it from my enquiries.'

Ruth rummaged in her bag and produced a mobile phone. 'Could you put your number in this for me? I can ring you when I have it and arrange for you to collect it somehow.'

Cooper took the phone and began tapping keys.

Josh suddenly remembered the silent call he'd had to ignore during the meeting, and took his phone out. When he'd read the message, he leapt to his feet.

'Alicia, my wife, she's having the baby. I must get back to her.'

'Right, good luck, Sergeant. There's a fast train to Salisbury in fifteen minutes.' Cooper smiled.

Josh didn't pause in his flight until he was safely on the train. He was unaware of the black-robed figure that leapt onto the train two carriages behind, out of breath and perspiring.

The Bishop was still slightly drowsy from the anaesthetic, but was determined that the nurse would listen to his request this time.

'Please, this is very important. If you won't let me phone, could you get a message to Inspector Cooper for me? Here's his number.'

The nurse on the desk beckoned her colleague over, and said something softly in her ear. Nurse one looked at the Bishop doubtfully, and then walked away briskly.

'What kind of an answer is that? And I thought the Almighty was obtuse sometimes,' muttered the Bishop through his teeth.

A few minutes later, the nurse returned with a familiar figure in tow.

'Why, thank you, nurse! White rabbits next?' The Bishop smiled, but the nurse was obviously not amused by the quip.

Cooper raised an eyebrow. 'That's not like you, Your Grace?'

'I've had the devil's own job to persuade them that I need to talk to you, but they insisted I rest. This is no time to rest, I said, there are vital things to be done!'

'Were you badly hurt?'

'Just a broken, rather crushed arm; it was caught underneath one of the pillars. It took them a while to sort it out; there's a pin where they took out the damaged bits. I hope they'll let me loose soon, but in the meantime, here's what I know. Got your notebook?'

Cooper sat and took notes whilst the Bishop talked, first of the programme that would have been broadcast, and the items that they had intended to cover.

'Look, beside my locker, the briefcase, there are some sheets of figures that we got hold of, finances, worldwide activities, the True Gospel College 'Rule of days' that's the routine students follow at the college, then more names of the vanished. I had a long talk with a Paul Markham whilst we were waiting to go on air, and he has someone he wants you to meet, quite soon.'

Cooper opened the case, and held it so that the Bishop could use his one good hand to rifle through the contents.

'Here, in this manila file.' The Bishop lay back with a sigh.

'Are you all right to go on?'

'Of course, just the flesh complaining. Now, Paul Markham, he wants you to meet Ruth Diamond's brother.'

'I was told he was dead.'

'No, he's alive but disabled. You should talk to him.' The Bishop indicated a side pocket in the briefcase. 'In there, a post-it note on my common prayer.'

Cooper lifted out the black leather book and removed the shocking pink note from the cover. On it was a name, address and telephone number.

'Do you think...?' Cooper began, but was interrupted by the nurse.

'I really do think you've talked enough, Bishop. You should rest now.'

'St Paul had it right – he called them a monstrous regiment of women!'

'Be careful, Your Grace, you'll find your tea unsugared.' Cooper stood up. 'I'll pop back and see you at some point.'

As the inspector moved away, the nurse pulled the curtains round the Bishop's bed.

The street was easy enough to find, but parking was another matter. He found a space in a side street and filled a parking meter with his small change. The steps at a front door part way down on the right had a zigzag ramp to one side. Cooper made a beeline for it, and rang the doorbell.

'Mr Markham, it's been some time since we crossed paths.'

'I had to find a bolt-hole with Daniel. This has proved ideal so far, but I think the True Gospel Church has better things to do than look for buried members. But do come in, Inspector.'

'Inspector Cooper, at last!' A blond young man in a wheelchair appeared in the hallway behind Paul.

Cooper stepped into the wide hallway. 'You must be Ruth's brother.'

'Got it in one, Inspector, come through into the sitting room – tea?'

'No thanks,' Cooper said briskly, taking out his notebook. 'Fire away. First, how do you come to be both dead and alive?'

Daniel laughed, and began to tell his story.

Two hours later, Cooper was back at the conference centre.

The Prime Minister looked up from his almost finished evening meal. 'Inspector, do come and sit down, I trust you have eaten.' He indicated a chair beside him. 'Wilson will be back in a minute. Daphne, this is the Inspector who has been working on all these murders and the church problems.'

'Pleased to meet you, Inspector, your reputation has gone before you,' she smiled, and Cooper was entranced. The woman radiated goodness. He shook her hand and sat.

The PM beckoned the waiter, 'Something for the Inspector, William?'

'We still have the smoked salmon, or the peppered steak, sir, or if you'd like an omelette we can do one?'

'The peppered steak sounds good,' Cooper said, realising that he hadn't eaten since breakfast. 'Do you mind if I fill you in on progress now?'

'Go ahead.'

Cooper summarised his day's findings, pausing only to tackle the steak, during which time he gave the PM the Bishop's file to read.

When he'd finished his steak and his report, the PM jiggled his knee for a few minutes, then, catching his wife's eye, changed to making notes.

Cooper took a long drink of water and refilled his glass. The PM passed him the list. Cooper read it through, nodded, and added a couple of suggestions to the ones already down. The PM smiled, and stood up.

'I'll get these things moving. How soon do you think you can get me the Agenda for Change file?'

'I'm not sure, Miss Diamond has to be careful, but I'm afraid it will be tomorrow at the earliest.'

'It can't be helped. Keep me informed.' The PM strode to the lift, followed by two plain clothes officers.

Cooper found himself alone with the PM's wife.

'Your reputation understates you, Inspector, do tell me about the '79 Series.'

## Chapter 40

Josh leaped from the train almost before it had stopped moving. He made for the steps to the underpass at a run.

Behind him, the black-robed figure had been prepared for his speed and had been ready as the carriage door slid open. Nevertheless, his target had reached the up incline before he caught up with him. This would be so easy, he thought, aiming for the back of the knees to bring the man down.

Josh reacted instinctively; his years of judo training took him into a forward rolling break-fall and back onto his feet, side-stepping quickly so that his opponent would shoot past him. Just in case, Josh stuck out a foot, but the man stopped too quickly. Almost as a reflex, his opponent had pulled a knife. Josh brought up his right foot in a smooth kick that made contact with the man's jaw, and he crumpled to the filthy floor in a heap of tumbled black cloth, the knife skidding down the slope behind him.

There was no one about, but soon there was the sound of running feet from above him. A uniformed man appeared at the run.

'Station security, sir. I saw him go for you, like, on the CCTV, but you sorted him real good.' He gazed down at the unconscious man. 'I've called the police, sir; they'll be here in a minute or so. Nasty, pulling a knife like that.'

Josh's heart sank. Time was ticking away. But he took out his warrant card and showed it to the security man. 'We'd best make sure he doesn't make off whilst we're waiting.' Josh pulled out his handcuffs and put them neatly on the wrists of the still unconscious figure. At the touch of the metal, he stirred, opened his eyes and began to struggle to get up.

Josh ignored him for a moment whilst he put the knife into an evidence bag, as people were beginning to come through the underpass from the train.

Together, the two men helped him to his feet, and with one each side, they led him up the incline toward the station entrance. Near the top of the underpass, they were met by Sergeant Barry and PC Hawkins.

'I thought you were in London, Sergeant,' Sam Barry grinned.

'I came back. The wife's in having the baby,' Josh said, his eyes flickering to the exit.

'Hope it's not another false alarm, lad. You'd best get off; we'll deal with sonny here and take your statement when you get back to the station. I know he mugged you from behind – I'll get the CCTV pics and run them through.'

'Thanks, Dan. Here, take this, it belongs to our suspect.' He passed him the evidence bag before sprinting up the rest of the incline and out into the station yard. His car *would* be at the furthest part of the car park. When he was finally sitting in his car, he took a long deep breath and telephoned the hospital.

An hour later, Ruth stepped off at the same platform, her blue robes not warm enough at this late hour and she wished she had worn her cape. Brother Saul had not been at the station to travel with her, but her ticket had been waiting for her in the office. The security guard gave her an odd look as she stepped out beside the taxi rank. A driver parked in the disabled bay across the road switched on his engine and lights and swung across to park at the kerb.

'Brother Adam, bless you for coming for me.'

'May His peace be with you, Sister Ruth. Was there another Brother travelling with you on the train?'

Ruth put her holdall on the back seat, and climbed in beside him. 'I saw no others of the Truth,' she replied.

'We'll await the next train, then, if he does not come, I will take you to The Retreat. Have you broken bread?'

'Yes, thank you, Brother Adam. I am neither hungry nor thirsty.'

Brother Adam returned to the disabled bay and switched everything off. 'Praise the Lord, you are unharmed, Sister Ruth.'

'I was safeguarded indeed; a pillar protected me from the blast, and I was able to help others once I was rescued. My ears and the cut on my head are still a bit painful, but the rest is minor cuts and bruises.'

'It's time for night devotions, Sister, let us pray.' Brother Adam led the prayer, and Ruth began to read psalm fifteen.

'Could you sing it for me tonight, Sister Ruth?'

'I will, Brother Adam.'

Ruth sang the psalm softly in the confines of the car:

'Lord, who shall abide in thy tabernacle? Who shall dwell in thy holy hill?'

They were both silent for a while after she had finished. Brother Adam broke the silence by saying, 'Psalms should really be sung; as they were in the Temple of old.' He gazed out wistfully over the car park, in which a man, obviously drunk, was staggering along between the cars. 'We seem to make so little difference to the needy.'

'I sometimes wonder how The Retreat would ever reach such people; for we keep ourselves apart from them.'

'But the Gospel is preached to them in the churches; surely that is enough?'

'My father used to say that the Gospel is better preached by actions than words. That's why he set up so many drug and alcohol rehabilitation units, single mother and battered wife centres. He thought it the outworking of Christ's love.'

'Your father was a very unusual man. He was able to disagree with my father and still remain on good terms with him. I wish I had that skill.' Adam sighed and looked at his watch.

'I'll go in and see if there is any sign of the Brother I was to meet. Wait here, Sister, I won't be long.'

He strode across to the station entrance and vanished. The latest London train was still standing beside the platform, but among the few stragglers, there was no sign of the missing Brother. He stepped toward the entrance, when a security guard spoke to him.

'You looking for one of your lot, sir?'

'I suppose I am. Have you seen him?'

'Fella in a black robe. Attacked a man in the underpass. Arrested for it, I'm afraid. One of your black sheep, Pastor?'

Adam was so shocked for a moment that he didn't reply. 'Thank you for telling me.' He hurried from the station and into the car, setting off for The Retreat at much more than his usual sedate pace.

'Is there something amiss, Brother Adam?'

'Yes, I must report to my father, I mean, Brother Saul.'

'But he is at conference in London.'

'I will still have to contact him.' He lapsed into the kind of brooding silence that Ruth recognised from when they were children.

Brother Adam was very upset.

# Chapter 41

Elizabeth had finished the batch of dough for the morning's bread. She put the dozen bowls in the airing cupboard that they used for rising and proving the loaves, setting the thermostat to low for the slow rising that made such good bread. She loved the yeasty smell and feel of the dough, imagining the homeless men at the shelter tucking into it.

Annabel was late tonight, perhaps there had been more to cater for this evening. She went to take the chain off the door ready for her return, leaving the door itself locked. There was a soft noise behind her, the door swung open, and Elizabeth's worst nightmare took living flesh. They had a key.

Two black-robes stood there. Before she had time to push the door closed, they had taken her by the arms and dragged her from the house and into a car that was parked at the kerb. She lost one of her slippers. Another robed figure was at the wheel. Her two assailants clambered in, one on each side of her. They smelt of the rough soap used at The Retreat. She shuddered. It used to make her hands chap and bleed when she used it for the washing.

Just as the car was pulling away, Elizabeth caught sight of Annabel walking towards the house. In the rear-view mirror, she saw her pause, pick up the slipper and look back at the car. Desperately, she yanked her arm free for an instant to wave. She saw Annabel's response. Elizabeth winced as the man who'd lost his grip on her arm wrenched it behind her back. But it had been worth it; she'd been able to let Annabel know what had happened.

Annabel stood at the kerb for an instant of shock as she held Elizabeth's slipper, still warm from her foot. It had happened at last; they'd expected it a lot sooner. She took her notebook from her pocket and wrote the registration number of the car with the tiny pencil attached to it. So now it was time to ask Inspector Cooper's help. Although she was terribly worried by her friend's abduction, she felt a sudden lightening of her spirit as she thought of talking to the Inspector again. He was a very comforting man, she thought; he gave the impression that things could be put right given time.

She hurried to the front door, which was swinging open in the wind. The first thing she noticed was the key in the door. It was shiny new. The smell of bread-making filled the air as she went into the kitchen to phone the number on Cooper's card.

'Hello. Police? Yes, I want to report an abduction. Yes, an abduction. My friend was taken away just now in a car. The registration number was... yes, I'll hold a minute. Yes, Sergeant. My name is Annabel Harman, I live at... but this is silly. Whilst I'm talking to you the men are getting away! There were at least two of them, they took my friend from twenty-nine, Hamilton Road. They were driving a black VW Polo, registration HJ64 VUM. Yes, of course I wrote it down.'

Sergeant Barry recognised the voice. What a cool and level-headed woman this was. If only there were more like it! No wonder Inspector Cooper had been singing after her visit. 'Would you hold the line whilst I put out an alert for the vehicle, Miss Harman?'

Annabel waited for what seemed like an age; aware of a radio playing somewhere nearby, before the Sergeant came back on the line.

'Miss Harman, thank you for waiting. There are several units on task now; I just need a few more details from you. Now, the lady's name?'

'Mrs Elizabeth Crouch, aged sixty-two, grey hair, wearing a navy skirt and blue pullover, might also still be wearing her cooking apron and cap; I don't see them here.'

'Can you think of any reason why she should be abducted, Miss Harman?'

'We've been expecting something like this for years. She's been taken back to the True Gospel Church. She's been out for some twenty years, but they've found her now.' There was a silence at the end of the line. 'Are you still there, Sergeant?'

'Yes, Miss Harman. Do you really think that the church would hunt her down and take her back? Like the Moonies?'

'No, not like the Moonies, Sergeant. Worse than that.'

Sergeant Barry looked at the knife in the evidence bag that Josh Allsopp had given him. 'Incidentally, were the men who abducted Mrs Crouch wearing True Gospel Church Robes?'

'Yes, Sergeant, black ones. They were probably members of the Joshua Group.'

'The Joshua Group?'

'The True Gospel Church Police, Sergeant. Think SS in church garb with fanatic zeal, and you have them.'

Sergeant Barry shivered involuntarily. 'Thank you, Miss Harman. I'll keep you informed of any developments. Your phone number?'

'Thank you, Sergeant. 017722 773257. Goodbye.' Annabel replaced the receiver. She'd done her best; it was up to the police now. She checked the airing cupboard on her way past; it was full of bread rising. So she would not have to do that. Whatever happened, the men must be fed in the morning. In the kitchen she began to clear away the signs of Elizabeth's evening's work. It was a process she called 'active worry', when something disturbed the inner peace, physical activity was a useful balm, especially when there was nothing else to be done but wait.

The car sped away into the night. Elizabeth sat bolt upright, memorising the route they took. She was the first to notice the blue flashing light of the police car behind them; keeping her face impassive, she spoke to the men holding her, to distract them.

'Could you release my arms? There's no need to hold me so firmly, I would be stupid to try and escape from a car travelling at this speed.'

The larger of the two men leered at her. 'I'd enjoy seeing you try it, Sister. You broke your witness. You deserve…'

'That will be sufficient, Brother Nigel. It is up to the council to decide her fate. Release her arms.'

Elizabeth breathed a sigh of relief as her arms returned to a more natural position and the blood began to circulate through her hands again.

'Step on it, Brother Neil, we have company behind us.'

Without a word, Brother Neil smiled like a child given permission to eat all the sweets he could manage. The little polo surged forward, faster than its manufacturers would have dreamed possible. The dual carriageway narrowed towards its end, Brother Neil overtook three lorries and a motorcycle just as he was running out of road. They lurched round the next bend on the wrong side of the road, narrowly missing a caravanette coming the other way.

The two men beside her sat impassively as the car's speedometer crept ever upward.

'Think we've lost them, Brother Elvis.'

'Return to safer driving, but keep a good pace. We can expect further police ahead as they inform others of our route. An alternative would be prudent.'

Without a word, Brother Neil took a sudden left turn on two wheels, bumping onto a rutted track. At a slightly slower pace, he skidded from side to side, avoiding the worst of the ruts and potholes. Half a mile along the track, Brother Neil steered right and put his foot hard on the accelerator. It was an odd road, Elizabeth thought. There were no lights, no other traffic, just this smooth expanse of tarmac. Then she caught sight of an old windsock, tattered but still indicating wind direction. They were on an old airfield.

The tarmac ran out and the car lurched through a gap in a hedge. The bright lights of a petrol garage came into view, and then they were back on an ordinary road again.

'That do, Brother Elvis?' The driver grinned.

'That will do nicely, Brother Neil.'

Elizabeth could hear an odd throbbing at the edge of her hearing, which had always been particularly acute. It puzzled her for a moment. Then she knew; it must be a helicopter. She glanced at the men around her. None of them seemed aware of the noise as yet. 'Let it be a police helicopter!' she prayed, fearing what fate these men had in store for her. Their attitude reminded her of her two boys, Calvin and Adam, long ago, playing war games. For fun.

# Chapter 42

Ruth stumbled out of the car at The Retreat, grabbing the handrail beside the door, which opened noiselessly to reveal Dr Harold on the threshold.

'Sister Ruth,' he said, stepping forward to help her, 'are you well?'

'Thank you, Doctor, I am simply very tired. I did not sleep at all well last night.'

Dr Harold beckoned Sister Barbara. Looking directly at her, he said, softly, 'Take Sister Ruth straight to her room; call me if you feel she needs my attention.'

Sister Barbara smiled and nodded. Taking Ruth's arm, and shouldering the carry sack Brother Adam passed to her, she took Ruth to her old room, helped her to undress and into bed. She was about to unpack the things from Ruth's bag, but Ruth, in sudden panic, shook her head, pointing to her pillow.

'Leave it until the morning, Sister, please.'

Soon, the light was switched off and a merciful darkness surrounded her. Ruth fell into a deep, exhausted sleep.

Sister Barbara took a chair, placed it outside the partly open door and sat, eyes closed, willing herself to wake in two hours to check her charge.

It was nearer midnight when the Volkswagen drew up outside The Retreat. Brother Amos was waiting beside the door; at the approach of the headlights, he had lifted the chains and turned the handle gently.

'Peace be with you, brethren.'

'And with your spirit.'

'Come, follow me.'

Elizabeth feeling the pressure of the gag around her mouth, was suddenly forced to stand on legs that were cramped from a journey trapped between two figures that had made no space for her. Brother Amos' words sounded so odd that she struggled to place them. Of course, they were the words of Christ's invitation to the disciples. What dark disciples were these? she thought, shivering in the night air. She had a distinctly chilly feeling that evil had taken flesh, walking beside her into The Retreat. Then she gave a wry smile; *Try not to be melodramatic*, she told herself firmly.

She did not notice her handkerchief fall from her pocket as she stumbled through the familiar front door.

The Retreat had changed little over the years; although now the paintwork was new, the corridors gleamed with polish, the curtains were thick, if plain, at the windows. She knew the stairs to the solitary wing; only twice had she climbed them before – both had been clandestine visits to speak to Calvin after some misdemeanour had landed him trouble again. Now, it was her turn. In some ways, it would be a relief; like waiting for the day of execution to come, the footsteps had finally arrived at her door, to bring her back to face the consequences of her action. As she sat on the bed in the bare room, the door closed behind her, she smiled. The years of freedom had been so worthwhile.

She knelt to pray, sat on the bed to read her evening scripture using the Bible from the bedside table. She was aware of the eye of the observation point, but pretended not to know of its existence. They would never let her loose if they thought she'd reveal their goings-on. She settled herself under the covers, wearing the rough cotton nightdress that she found under the pillow. She whispered into the darkness, 'Underneath are the everlasting arms,' and slept. The overhead light silently switched itself off.

Joshua found a parking spot easily at this hour of the night. The doors to the Maternity unit were well lit, casting a pale light out into the darkness of the car park. Josh took the path and the doors at a run, although some vandals had broken the lights along the walkway. The Nissen-hut shapes of the wards reminded him of the hospital's military history. Although the hospital had much brand-new building, this older part was still as it had been when he'd been here for his tonsils. He paused at a window marked 'Reception' and rang the bell. A few minutes later, a nurse appeared.

'Can I help?'

'Mr Allsopp, my wife's...'

'In the delivery suite. Her mother's there with her, and she's doing well,' she pressed a buzzer and the door beside her opened, 'come on through.'

Inside, after the greasy tarmac of the long corridor, the wards were bright and clean. Everything seemed to be taking place very slowly. How was she? Would she be angry that he hadn't made it earlier? He wanted to run down the corridor, but the nurse only walked briskly. Then he had to wash his hands, put on a clean gown and face mask, before, feeling slightly ridiculous, he was finally led into the room where Alicia and her mother Alex were.

Alicia looked up, saw him, and gave him that wonderful smile of hers. Josh felt his heart lurch; she was so lovely, even lying there with the mound of his child swelling her belly. She held out her hand, he took it in his, and his world was this room and this woman that he loved so very much.

Inspector Cooper hadn't quite finished his lemon meringue when his mobile rang.

The PM's wife smiled. 'I'll leave you to it, Inspector.'

'Thank you, ma'm. Goodnight.'

'Cooper.'

'Dan Barry here, sir. Thought you'd like to know we've got one of the True Gospel lot under lock and key. He tried to mug our Allsopp, which was a mistake, as you can imagine.'

'And?'

'Allsopp did one of his judo kicks and knocked him cold before he could use the knife he pulled.'

'So he's up at the Maternity ward now?'

'Aye, sir. Thing was, there's this package among the prisoner's things, addressed to you.'

'Brown paper, size of a CD?'

'Yes, sir.'

'Was this devotee wearing black robes by any chance?'

'Full length, wide sleeves with a belt to take the knives – three in fact, all the same design, a drawstring purse with a train ticket, four pounds twenty and a pocket scripture. Oddest thing was the pendant: a sword in the shape of a crucifix complete with a mounted Christ in silver.'

'Interesting. Did you notice if he had a tattoo on his right arm? It seems to be part of the genuine article.'

'A number, sir. Eight seven one.'

'Good. Whatever you do, don't lose that package, nor let any smartass lawyer or True Gospel official fix bail for the blighter. He doesn't sound at all safe to be let loose on the street. Oh, and Sergeant, would you ask the pathologist if the knives the prisoner had with him could be the type used in the ethnic cleansing murders?'

There was a short pause before Dan Barry answered, 'Right, sir.'

Brother Adam did not like using the telephone. He had only used one twice before. He hesitated before knocking the door to his father's study. He jumped when he heard a voice ask him to enter; he had not expected anyone to be there. He opened the door, to find Brother Amos at his father's desk.

'Welcome, Brother Adam, the Lord bless you indeed. How can I help you?'

'I was going to contact my f- I mean, Brother Saul. There is a problem.'

'May I help?'

Adam took a deep breath. Anything was better than using that telephone. 'It's the Brother I was to meet from the London train, sir. He was not there to be collected.'

'He was probably delayed. Perhaps you should return to await his arrival?'

'No, sir. He was arrested for attacking a man in the underpass at the station.'

Brother Amos looked up, his expression suddenly hawk-like. 'At what time?'

'Around eleven this evening, sir.'

'His number?'

'Eight seven one, sir.'

'Leave it with me, Brother Adam. I will deal with it.'

Adam breathed a sigh of relief, and hurried back to the front entrance. Just as he reached it, a small white object with an embroidered edge and initials caught his eye. He had not seen another like this for ... it must be twenty years. He stooped to pick it up and examine the initials more closely. EC: Elizabeth Crouch. Just as she'd always done it. It brought back a memory of a cut finger tied up with her handkerchief. He'd been seven at the time.

He drove home in a dream, climbed the stairs to his room and opened his top drawer. He placed the handkerchief he found there next to the bright new one he'd just picked up at The Retreat. They were identical, save that the one from his drawer was yellowing with age. Who was using his mother's handkerchiefs?

Alicia felt she could do this now that Josh was here. She set herself to push with each contraction now, as the midwife had encouraged her to do. Exhaustion had made her feel it was impossible to do any more without a long rest. The feel of Josh's hand in hers seemed to lend her the strength she needed to bring their child to birth. She could see the concern on his face as she groaned with the pain and the effort of it. Then just as she felt she would burst with the fullness of the head that bore down between her thighs, she felt a sudden loosening, as, like a cork from a bottle, the baby shot forward into the midwife's hands.

'Steady on there! That was a bit sudden!'

Alicia looked down at her baby and grinned up at Josh. 'What is it?'

'A boy.' The midwife placed him on Alicia's arm, where he looked up at her with deep blue, unblinking eyes. Then he sighed, and closed them.

'Isn't he supposed to cry?' Josh asked, anxiously.

'No, just breathing's enough,' the midwife said, as another contraction delivered the placenta.

A few minutes later, Josh found himself holding his baby son. He sat on the metal hospital chair with the tiny bundle in his arms, whilst beside him, Alicia smiled. He wondered at it all; could life be happier than this?

## Chapter 43

The ground was white with frost this morning. Saul breathed deeply of the fresh cold air in an attempt to clear his head. He was on his way to put flowers on Elizabeth's grave as usual on a Wednesday morning. He had returned at two this morning to find Brother Amos and Brother Joshua in his study. After the events of the day and the reports the men brought, Brother Saul had not slept well. They and the other two Joshua group brethren had been accommodated in the solitary wing, the other rooms being full. He had been puzzled; unusually, they seemed to have flour or some white powder clinging to their normally pristine robes. He turned the corner into the churchyard and paused in horror.

The churchyard looked as though there was a Boy Scout camp in progress; there were tents over a number of graves, policemen standing on guard at the entrances, and the sound of digging. As he watched, a van pulled away and another drove in close to the far gate beside the lane.

A voice broke into his trance. 'I'm afraid you can't come in here this morning, sir.'

Brother Saul looked up into a policeman's eyes. He wasn't used to looking up at people; this man must be very tall. 'What might I ask, is going on here? Don't they realise this is sacred ground, that it is an offence to disturb burials?'

'Of course, sir. But this is an official exhumation, the order has been signed and this is perfectly legal.'

'But morally inexcusable! Who is in charge of this abominable act?'

'Wait here sir, with PC Hawkins, and I'll find someone to speak to you sir.'

The men must have been busy for several hours under the tents that screened their activities from the public gaze. As Brother Saul watched another coffin was being lifted into a van.

The tall policeman returned with a man in plain clothes. 'Here is a man who can help you, sir.'

Saul found himself led away, invited to speak to someone at the station, and offered a lift in the most persuasive way. He looked back at the ruined churchyard, half stepped back towards it, looking down at the bunch of three white lilies in his hand.

'I'll place those for you, sir. Which grave were they intended for?'

'My wife. Elizabeth Crouch.'

The policeman gave no sign that that was one of the exhumations, just nodded and took the flowers as Brother Saul was helped into the car. On any other day, they would not have been able to persuade him so easily. The bomb, the demonstrations, and the things that Brother Amos and Brother Joshua had told him, all were clamouring for his attention. Would there ever be peace again for him?

At the pathology lab, extra staff had been drafted in, and the place was in organised upheaval. Dental records were to be searched. Causes of death established against the records of burials and death certificates.

'This one's all wrong, sir. Supposed to be a woman, mid forties. It's an old man, probably in his seventies, with bad arthritis.'

The pathologist smiled. There was definitely something fishy of whale-like proportions here. At least there would be no awkward questions about unnecessary exhumations if this continued.

Ruth had woken feeling refreshed. After breakfast, Doctor Harold had sent for her. When he had examined her and weighed her, he sat at the desk, looking over his glasses at her thoughtfully.

'You have gained a little weight, but you are still far too thin, Miss Diamond. Have you been taking the food supplements that I prescribed for you?'

'Yes, though I have missed them on days when I've been at the studio or singing.'

'You need to gain a good deal more weight before I'm satisfied that you are well enough to go back to full discipline. An eighteen hour day is too much for you. I am going to ask that you be put on convalescent duties. If you do go on a singing engagement, it must be all you do that day. When was the last time you menstruated?'

Ruth blushed crimson. 'I don't remember. It doesn't happen often.'

'That's because you are so thin that your body is unable to risk the loss that it would mean to you.'

'But that's what happens to people with eating disorders.'

'Quite right. Anorexia nervosa. You don't allow yourself enough food, for whatever reason.'

Ruth sat on the edge of her seat, feeling that the world was spinning out of her control. Her terrible secret was out. But maybe Doctor Harold had the answer. She said, almost in a whisper, 'I've had trouble eating since I was a child. My mother made me eat everything on my plate, even when it was cold and greasy. It often made me sick. Then it happened whenever I was upset. It still does, especially if I eat a full meal. It won't stay down.'

Doctor Harold said nothing for a while, thinking of what Miriam Diamond *nee* Crouch, would have been like as a parent to a sensitive child. Ruth watched him, anxiously.

'Don't worry about it, Sister Ruth, you will be fine. I suggest that you have several small snacks throughout the day to begin with. Then we will begin to increase the amount slowly, so that your body can become used to a full meal again.'

Ruth's large brown eyes were fixed on him, as though expecting condemnation.

'This is not a sin, Sister Ruth, believe me. This is a sickness, caused by things beyond your control. You will be well again, I promise. You have made the first step toward it today, by telling me.'

'And what penance must I do? Shall I go to Brother Saul?'

'No, Sister Ruth, you will not, there is no penance to be done. I suggest you spend the morning in the music room. Go.'

Ruth sat in the music room, her fingers on the piano keys. It had been a long time since she had done any practice. Her mind was skipping about, from the relief of the doctor's words, to the problem of the file she must get to the Inspector somehow. Leave it for now, she thought. There will be a way if God wills it.

Her fingers remembered the music. She played scales, arpeggios and her favourite Beethoven Piano sonata. Then she launched into a psalm, then into a piece from the Messiah.

'How beautiful are the feet of them that preach the Gospel of peace, and bring glad tidings, glad tidings of good things.'

Matthew stood at the door entranced until she had finished singing that piece, before he knocked. 'Peace be with you, Sister. Midmorning snack; Doctor Harold's orders.' He placed a tray containing a glass of milk, an apple, cheese and cream cracker biscuits on the piano. 'Can I also say thank the Lord that you're all right? I was out of my mind with worry all yesterday.'

'Bless you, Matthew, I am sorry. Things were a bit... unexpected. I can't tell you all of it, but I am well.'

Conscious of the surveillance, he dare not say more, and was forced to smile and leave, although he longed to gather her in his arms and hold her, just to convince himself that she was made of real flesh and blood, and not a figment of his imagination.

Ruth ate most of her snack before she realised there was a note under the plate. The surveillance camera lens was at this end of the room. She placed the tray on the window sill beside the piano and took a book of sheet music from the pile on the sill. At some point during the morning, the note beneath the plate had found its way into a book of sheet music and then into Ruth's pocket when she had used her handkerchief. Deception was becoming part of her existence, she thought.

At eleven, Ruth was delighted when the Music Master came in to give her a voice lesson. 'But only an hour, I'm told, you are still convalescent. Tomorrow, we must go over your scales and do some work on your Grade eight piano. I'd like you to do some advanced work.'

When he had gone, Ruth was surprised to find how tired she was. She followed the noon devotion and went to lunch. The note from Matthew seemed a lead weight in her pocket.

Elizabeth had woken with a start. The events of the evening before snagged at her consciousness like barbed wire on skin. Someone had left a tray of breakfast for her on a small side table. She sat up, gave thanks and ate hungrily, although the food and drink were cold. She had missed her supper last night. She looked for her clothes, but they were gone, replaced by a novice's yellow robe. She sighed. At least it was something to wear. She lay back on her pillow, in no hurry to find out what the day had in store for her. She wondered whether Annabel had managed to finish the baking on her own in time. There was nothing she could do about it if she hadn't. She closed her eyes, and then opened them in sudden surprise. Somebody was playing the piano. Somebody was singing a psalm in the most beautiful voice Elizabeth had ever heard. Then the voice soared into a passage from the Messiah.

## Chapter 44

Ruth should have returned to the music room after lunch, but she didn't. She was very aware of the weight of the blue room keys in her pocket; but even more aware that this needed doing before her nerve failed her completely. Most of the deacons were away and her plan depended on the security and store deacon being among them. Her heart thudded painfully as she went to the stores and security-room office and knocked on the door. It opened to reveal a novice.

Ruth swallowed hard. 'Peace be with you, Brother. I need to fetch something I may have dropped in the blue room when we were doing the Agenda files. Could I, perhaps, have the keys for a moment?'

'May the light of His countenance shine upon you, Sister. Unfortunately I am alone and cannot accompany you to the room until tomorrow. Perhaps you could return then?'

Ruth's heart sank. 'Perhaps, since it is an empty room and I only need to check if my baptismal ring is there, I might go alone, this once?'

The novice hesitated, glancing at an enormous pile of papers that he was working on.

Ruth knew he would be having a tough time; she had done a stint in the office and knew how the system worked; nobody would show a new person how things were done – they were under discipline to discover or work things out for themselves. It was a waste of time in Ruth's book.

'Perhaps you need some help with all that? May I assist you when I return?'

The novice grinned, gratefully. 'Bless you, Sister.' He handed her the keys.

Ruth tried to walk calmly to the blue room. Her footsteps seemed abnormally loud. Her hands were shaking as she put the key into the lock. The afternoon sunshine fell in pools on the polished wooden floor beside each window and little dust motes danced in the beams. Which radiator had it been? She stooped and made pretence of looking for her ring, quartering the room, looking behind and running her fingers under the radiators as she reached them at the end of each sweep. The file was there, right at the edge of the third one along. She knelt beside it and ran her fingers along the bottom of it, sliding the file under her cloak, standing and continuing her pretence of a search. She gave a satisfied grunt at the next radiator, holding up her baptismal ring with a smile, slipped it onto her wedding ring finger. She went via the ladies, where she placed the file out of sight on top of the old chain-pull cistern, for later collection, then went to help the poor novice with his filing.

The novice, Brother Andrew, was very grateful for her help; and she felt no qualms about breaking that rule. There were no observation points in the offices that she could make out. By the time she left, Brother Andrew had no papers left to file, knew how to do the work, and Ruth had put both sets of keys back on the hooks in the cupboard.

Ruth breathed deeply to steady herself. Part one complete; just the phone call and the file to deal with now. But she would do some more voice and piano this afternoon. The opportunity did not come too often.

At four, Matthew appeared with another snack. He coughed harshly as he set the tray down.

'That's a nasty cough, Matthew.'

'It'll pass. How are you doing?'

Ruth groaned, 'I feel stuffed!'

'You don't look it.' Matthew grinned unsympathetically, 'Bless you, Sister Ruth.'

'May the light of His countenance shine upon you, Brother Matthew,' Ruth replied, poking her tongue out at him out of the line of camera sight, knowing he could do nothing in return. He simply smiled and left.

She ate one of the ham sandwiches and slipped the other in her robe pocket. Her body felt uncomfortably full. The cake she left on the plate.

Adam waited for Calvin to appear; he was late as usual. He had placed the two handkerchiefs on his desk. It was possible, he supposed, for two women to have the same initial. But he had gone through the church directory and there were no others who had these initials still serving in the south region. Then there were the events in the churchyard. His father had said that the police had all the paperwork to authorise the exhumations. He'd had to accept it. But the sight of the gaping hole where his mother's grave had been, had given him quite a jolt. Did father know that mother's grave had been despoiled? If he did, he showed not a sign of it. He had been in his office ever since he had come back from the police station, not even emerging for devotions. Something was very wrong.

Calvin's bicycle appeared in the drive and Adam opened the front door. 'Bless you, Brother. How are your broken ribs now?'

'Bless you too, Brother. Very painful, thanks. What was so urgent?'

'Come in and I'll show you.' Adam stood aside as his brother came in and closed the door himself. 'In my study,' he said, pointing to the desk.

Calvin looked. 'Mother's handkerchiefs. So what?'

'This one,' Adam pointed, 'was in my chest of drawers until last night. This one,' he held it up, 'was on the front door carpet at The Retreat last night.'

Calvin picked it up. 'Could be anyone with the initials 'EC,' he shrugged.

'Surprisingly, there's no one else serving in the south region with those initials.'

'Then the directory is out of date. This is a new handkerchief.'

'Embroidered the way mother always did it?'

Calvin glared down at the scrap of cloth. 'But she's dead and buried. It can't be hers!'

'Have you been past the churchyard today?' Adam asked softly.

'No, Why?'

'The police have been exhuming some of our burials.'

'What? Does father know?'

'Father knows. But I don't know if he is aware that mother's is one of the ones they have violated.'

Calvin sat down rather heavily and winced. 'What's happening, Adam? All that we have worked for seems to be shifting. I feel as though we are caught up in an earthquake. It's not as though I've been totally committed, you know that, but it was always there, solid as certainty and sunrise in the morning. Did you hear it was a bomb? Sister Ruth could have been killed.'

'That can't have been anything to do with the church, Brother. The Eldership would never allow it.'

'Just like they'd never allow murder in morning service?'

'That's different; the church is under attack, it has always been so. The powers of darkness are most active where the Gospel is preached.' Adam looked out of the window at two blackbirds competing for ownership of the garden. *'Who wins Eden?'* he thought.

Calvin shrugged. Adam's statement did not convince him at all. 'I am worried about the Joshua Group. They have gained power and influence since Brother Joshua Adam set them up to keep discipline in the church. They have taken three of my men to headquarters recently. Only two of them came back. I have lost one to 'Special Duties'. What does that mean? Have they the right to do as they please?'

'We have no choice but to submit to discipline, Brother. But I want to go and see who is being kept in solitary at The Retreat. Do you wish to come with me?'

'Whom do you expect to find?'

'I don't know. I only know I have to look; I will have no peace otherwise.'

Calvin paused, staring long at the handkerchiefs, before picking the new one up and sniffing it. His expression changed.

'What is it, Cal?'

'It smells of *'4711'* cologne.'

Adam's heart skipped a beat as he took the tiny piece of cloth and inhaled the familiar smell that he associated with one person in the world. His mother.

'Let's go. Father is in his study and tasks are assigned for the afternoon. I have convalescence; I should be reading for my Deacon's examination. Ruth's lucky; hers is music, as always.'

'The Bible Study for tomorrow's meeting is nearly finished. I'm going to leave it.'

The brothers set off together, Adam slightly behind his fitter brother. The smell of an enormous clump of *Daphne Odora* drifted across the driveway as they passed the gate. Mother had planted them and had always cut some for the house during the late winter, to bring the smell of spring indoors.

## Chapter 45

Ruth sat on the closed toilet seat for a few moments listening. There was the occasional drip of water from somewhere near; a branch was tapping the window. But there was no sound from the other cubicles. She took out the little silver telephone. The battery was still good; she did not know how she was going to be able to recharge it without being observed, but maybe it would only be needed this once.

The little beeps that it made seemed to be played *fortissimo* to Ruth's tightly strung perception. A voice answered. 'Station Help Desk, can I help?'

Ruth spoke as loudly as she dared, hoping that the little phone would be able to pick up her voice. 'I have a message for Inspector Cooper, please.'

'Just a minute, I'll see if he's in his office – who's calling?'

'Ruth Diamond.'

There was the sound of further dialling, then a click; 'Cooper.'

'Ruth Diamond here, Inspector. I have the file.'

'Excellent. Now, how do we collect it?'

'Tonight, I'll bring it to the side gate beside Ash-leas Lane. Devotions finish at ten; I will try to bring it to you after lights out at eleven.'

'I will be there. You've had no problems?'

'Only indigestion.'

'You have my sympathy. Nervous tension, I expect. See you tonight; but if there's a problem, I'll be there same time tomorrow night. Be careful.'

'I will, Inspector, goodbye.'

Ruth rubbed her stomach to ease it; and with the other hand shifted the ham sandwich, the second piece of crumbed fish that she had been unable to swallow at lunch, and half the quiche from dinner between her robe pockets. They would probably not clear if she tried to flush them away. Or they might block the drains. She could bury them tonight, perhaps.

Calvin and Adam came over the river bridge, down Ashleas lane and rode along the side path, which was overlooked by the dormitory wings, normally empty at this time of day. They left their bicycles behind the shrubs near the fire escape.

'Follow me, Ad,' Calvin whispered, leading his brother to the back entrance and into the boiler-room, where he stripped off his jeans and T-shirt and put on his robe. Cautiously, he peered round the door, and then emerged, Adam hot on his heels.

'New handrails,' commented Adam.

'My fault,' Calvin replied, 'I fell down them.'

'Really?' Adam was unconvinced. His brother was as sure as a cat on his feet.

'As far as father is concerned, that's how I injured myself.'

Adam sighed, 'What were you up to that time?'

'Don't ask.' Calvin was at the top of the stone steps, peering through the partly opened door. 'Come on; act normal, in case anyone comes.'

The two of them emerged into the silence of the entrance hall, passed the main staircase and crossed quickly to where a corridor led to a much narrower flight of steps.

'Here goes.' Calvin took the steps carefully, standing to the side of each. 'These squeak; be careful.'

The wooden steps protested despite the care that they took climbing. At the top, they began to work their way along the right hand corridor, one on each side, peering into the rooms through the little spyglass set in each.

'Black Brothers in most of these, I'd say,' Calvin whispered.

'We shouldn't have come,' Adam said, 'there's no one here.'

'We are going to check the left hand corridor. As you said, you won't have any peace unless you know,' Calvin said, slightly louder than he'd intended. They both looked behind them, but no one emerged from the office set at the corner where the two corridors met.

Calvin dropped to his knees as he passed the office window that opened onto the corridor, not standing again until he had passed the glass-panelled door. Adam hesitated; this was absolutely ridiculous. But he dropped to all fours as his brother looked back at him and glared furiously.

It was the seventh room along that brought Calvin to such a sudden halt that Adam cannoned into him. He looked through the glass. A woman in a novice-yellow robe was sitting on the bed, reading. The two boys exchanged glances and each looked in again. It was Adam who turned the key that sat in the lock and opened the door.

The woman looked up, and her face lit into a smile of joy. Throwing her book aside, she ran to throw her arms around Adam. Tears ran down her cheeks.

'How lovely to see you.' Then she saw Calvin behind his brother, and gave him a hug of sheer delight. 'Has your father sent you?'

The brothers exchanged glances. 'No, Mother. We came because of this.' Calvin held out the handkerchief.

'I found it in the hallway last night. So we came to find out who else had handkerchiefs embroidered with the initials 'E C' and smelling of *4711* cologne.'

'We thought you were dead,' Adam said, unable to believe what he was seeing, 'all this time, we've been putting flowers on your grave, and father, too, every Wednesday. He puts white lilies.'

'We probably don't have long before we are discovered, so sit down and tell me everything. I have missed you both so much.'

'But where have you been, Mother? Why did they say you were dead?' Adam looked deathly pale, and his mother pushed him towards the bed.

'No fainting away on me this afternoon, Adam, we haven't time. I left your father. I couldn't cope with the Discipline any longer. I have been working and hiding ever since. Last night, two Joshua Brothers came and brought me back. Against my better judgement, I may say.'

Adam and Calvin sat in stunned silence as the bell for devotions sounded.

Ruth crept out of the door beside the boiler room and began to walk along the side path. Her shoes crunched slightly on the gravel, her fear making the sound seem like the feet of an army on the march. The bushes seemed like crouching figures, the moan of the wind in the ash trees like dead voices murmuring.

Then there came a low growling that Ruth could not place. Around the corner from the front lawn came the most enormous dog that she had ever seen, its fur shining silver-grey in the light of the crescent moon. Ruth just prevented herself from screaming by stuffing her handkerchief into her mouth. The dog began to lope towards her, the growl deepening in its throat as it advanced.

Ruth's hand brushed the heaviness of the food in her pocket. She pulled out the tissue wrapped bundle and shook the contents onto the floor. The dog hesitated. As it sniffed the food, Ruth stepped to the path wall and scrambled up a tree that grew beside it. Carefully, she trod along the flat top toward the outer wall, turning right towards the side gate. Before she was half-way along, the dog had finished all the food and was racing over the grass towards the wall. He stood beside her and began to bark. A figure appeared at the gate house and began to run towards her. Ruth took a deep breath and jumped from the wall into the lane, expecting to land on the uneven stones that passed for surfacing.

Two strong hands caught and steadied her. 'Come on, over here, out of sight.' Inspector Cooper hurried her into a thick patch of scrub, and they crouched in the darkness as the dog's handler scrambled up to look over the wall. After a few minutes, he vanished and called the dog to him. A few moments later, Ruth heard the squeak of the front gate.

'He's coming down to look with the dog!'

'Right, give me the file, and get back over the wall, high-tail it back to your room.'

Ruth handed him the file, Cooper gave her a shoulder to stand on to reach the top of the wall and then he melted into the blackness. Ruth ran straight across the grass that she hadn't ever walked on in her life and into the back boiler room. Gasping for breath, she leaned on the wall for a moment, feeling sick and giddy.

She was surprised to see Brother Adam come down the steps and make towards the door. He jumped, startled to see her there.

'Pardon me, Sister Ruth, but should you not be in bed?'

'That's true, Brother Adam. But so should you.'

'I have church business to do.' He turned to open the door.

'I wouldn't go out there if I were you. Someone has a guard dog. It is rather large and very fierce.' She couldn't resist a half-smile at his discomfiture.

As Ruth spoke, they heard a low growl outside the door. Someone tried the handle, tried to peer into the half-darkness of the basement. It was probably Brother Fred, the caretaker.

Brother Adam paled. They both held their breath until footsteps moved away.

'Perhaps I should go out the front way.' He began to climb the steps, but paused. 'May the Lord bless you, Sister. I recommend that you go to your rest.'

'I will, Brother Adam. I shall not remember that we met.'

He hesitated and then gave a half-smile. 'It will be difficult to forget such a meeting, Sister Ruth, but I shall not talk of it to anyone. Goodnight.'

As Ruth vanished over the wall, Inspector Cooper sprinted over the field and into the river; the ice-cold water came up to his knees. He swore softly under his breath as the chill penetrated to his bones. He waded as quickly as he could upstream to hide in the shadows under the bridge.

Only minutes later, the dog picked up his scent in the lane and followed it into the field to the water's edge. It cast around fruitlessly for a while and then loped back to its master. It seemed an age before they passed through the gate and closed it behind them.

Cooper stood there for a full three minutes before he climbed out of the near-freezing water beneath the bridge and clambered up to the lane.

'I'm too damned old for this sort of caper.' He squelched his way back to where he'd parked the car out of sight, wishing that he'd left it nearer. At least he'd got the file. Now he could get a bit of sleep. A glass of malt seemed to be necessary before that, though.

# Chapter 46

Wednesday

The start of the emergency cabinet meeting was a stormy one. The PM had asked for reports on the True Gospel Church from the Home Secretary, the Police Commissioner and the intelligence services. The armed forces report was to be ready by the afternoon, and another cabinet meeting was scheduled for the evening. Many of the ministers present resented the sudden loss of an evening when many of them were set to attend a reception at the Palace.

'Are you telling us that this is a matter of national security, Prime Minister? Surely a bunch of religious fanatics aren't worth a second thought?' Mrs Bradley, Minister for Health, thumped her glass on the table for added emphasis.

Stuart paused and took a deep breath before he spoke. 'Gentlemen, and Mrs Bradley, I would like the Police Commissioner to fill you in on the latest developments in this matter. We will discuss the implications of these matters when he has spoken and you are in possession of the facts.'

The Police Chief stood up. 'Mrs Bradley, gentlemen, I would first of all stress that nothing I am about to say should be repeated outside this room.

1. The True Gospel Church has been implicated in the worldwide and systematic murder of people of other faiths.
2. The Church has begun a political strategy known as 'The Agenda for Change'. The points they are pursuing are: (i) the abolition of all Sunday trading. (ii) The criminalisation of prostitution, lesbianism and homosexuality. (iii) The return of the death penalty for murder, grievous bodily harm, drug peddling, pimping and blasphemy. (iv) Only the teaching of Christianity to

be permitted in schools. (v) Darwinism is not to be taught. (vi) Compulsory Sunday worship. (vii) Children born out of wedlock to be brought up in the church. (viii) Unemployment benefit to be earned through workfare. (ix) New censorship rules; no nudity, sexual activities, extra marital or marital to be permitted in print, photography, film or sound narrative. No use of offensive language or blasphemy in any media. (x) No former felon to be considered for public office of any kind. These points are being pursued internationally.

3. There is a network of True Gospel Church agents in prime positions throughout the world. They are known as 'The Joshua Group'. They are organised in sections of five hundred. They are a formidable force of unknown capacity.

4. There are bombs hidden in major public buildings, often in the fabric of the buildings during construction. The bomb disposal squads have been working at night in order to keep the search as discreet as possible. To date, fifty-nine suspect appliances have been made safe. The bomb that was detonated at the television studios during the *Derek and Deanna Show* was of the same type.

5. The finances of the True Gospel Church exceed the gross domestic product of the five major world powers. They have enormous financial power.

6. We know that there are two True Gospel Members who are Prime Ministers, several judges and others who hold positions of power and influence. Have you any questions?'

There was a long pause before anyone spoke. Then everybody spoke at once. It took the PM some minutes to calm them all down.

'This is absolutely ridiculous, Prime Minister; nobody could take such an agenda seriously in the twenty-first century. It's positively mediaeval. They would never get such legislation through.' Mrs Bradley looked exasperated.

'I assume the right honourable member has read the latest on the Sunday Trading bill? Any more defeats like that one and we'll be facing a vote of no confidence. Yes, they seek controversial and repressive legislation. We will have to be well prepared to withstand the onslaught; our opponents are well organised, disciplined and tenacious. Do not, I repeat, do not regard them as half-baked religious fanatics. They are not stupid. I believe that this sect threatens human rights and civil liberties in a way that we have not seen before nor even imagined. Home Secretary, your report, please.'

Inspector Cooper had made half-dozen copies of the three CDs that had been in the package found on the knife-toting Joshua Group Member, by five-thirty that morning. He had tried without success to make sense of the data on the discs, had asked if there were any IT specialists available to help at short notice and been told that the earliest he could hope for any would be next week.

'Computer crime is a growth area, Inspector, I'm sorry.'

So the Inspector was in no mood to be gracious when Allsopp arrived at eight-thirty, looking hollow-eyed but happy.

'Morning, sir. What have I missed?'

Cooper threw a copy of the Agenda for Change file across to him. 'There's that; Ruth Diamond got it out to me late last night; go through it and mark the things that were passed at the meeting you gate crashed. Copies have gone to the PM, the Commissioner and the Chief Constable. We've recovered the package that was snatched at the hospital; your assailant of last evening had it in his possession. I've made copies, but the IT lot can't help me with the data on it until next week. I need to access this stuff now.'

'What about Robert? He helped with… with the Rex King case.'

Cooper looked up, sudden hope in his eyes. 'What about Robert! Why didn't I think of it?'

'Maybe because it's a little outside generally accepted practice?'

Cooper swore softly about accepted practice, and then said, 'Find out if he's free.'

Josh yawned loudly as he dialled his half-brother's office number. 'Robert? Yes, I know; seven pounds nine ounces in real money. No, we haven't. Listen, we need some help on some computer data – three CDs that hold information the Inspector's desperate to unravel – have you got the time to take a look? You will? Great. Yes, seven tonight, she'd be delighted to see you. Bye.' Josh replaced the receiver. 'He'll be round in ten minutes, sir.'

'Excellent. By the way, congratulations on being a dad.'

'Don't really believe it yet, sir.' Josh grinned.

'You will when it wakes you at three a.m.,' Cooper said, glumly. But he was smiling.

Fox had been torn about which to follow; but had decided on Mrs Bradley since she had protested so loudly; he'd had a superintendent who used to mutter 'methinks the lady doth protest too much'. It must be from some play or another. The pavements were busy with shoppers and he was able to keep quite close without being observed.

His quarry ducked into a department store. In the foyer were several payphones. Mrs Bradley made for the end one and began to dial. Fox moved as close as he dared. So this call was not to be shown on her mobile. He dug in his pocket for coins and lifted the receiver on the nearest phone he dared use. His skin was prickling with excitement. He strained to hear what the woman was saying. There was the sound of coins dropping, then...

'A 6 here, repeat, A 6 here. Code is Red, repeat, Code is Red.' Mrs Bradley put the phone on the hook and left. Fox waited for a count of ten before heading for a quiet spot to make his report.

As he waited for someone to answer the phone, he noticed a newsagent's sign board with a headline that made his stomach lurch. He jumped as a voice sounded in his ear. 'It's Bradley, she phoned from a landline in a store, said "A6 here, Code red". Check?' He listened as the message was repeated to him, then asked; 'Is there any fallout over the Clarion's lead story?' Fox listened for a minute, and then said, 'There will be, I only hope that it's not too bad. Cheers.'

He went to buy a paper and headed to a café to read the story over a coffee. He didn't take long over it; he emerged grim-faced and made for the Clarion's offices three streets away.

Matthew's chest hurt every time he coughed, but he couldn't go to solitary; he hadn't seen Ruth for ages. He was worried about the rumours that were spreading through The Retreat. What had Ruth been doing lately? What was going on among the Elders? He continued to peel potatoes. His head ached and his throat was sore.

## Chapter 47

Cooper had left Allsopp with Robert Gillman, his half-brother, bent over the computers. The street was one of many terraced pre-war houses that clustered around the disused gas station whose rusting bulk blocked much of the light on this side. There was an odour of fish and chips that seemed to emanate from the house walls.

The house he was looking for stood out; its door was painted a fresh bright green, the letterbox and doorknob shone as though just polished. He rang the bell. Almost immediately, Annabel opened the door, wiping her hands on a red checked tea towel. A smell of cooking flowed past her; bread baking, perhaps cakes; something meaty too. He hoped she couldn't hear his empty stomach rumble.

'Inspector, it's good of you to come round yourself. Do come in. Is there any news of Elizabeth?'

Cooper smiled. 'One, it's no problem, two, yes I will, three, yes there is.'

Her laughter was as uninhibited as a child's. 'Sorry, I do run on a bit sometimes.' She led the way into a large kitchen. Beneath the window to his right there was a scrubbed pine table, ahead, a large Aga threw warmth toward his chilled body. 'Do sit down, Inspector, can I make you coffee?'

Cooper sat on a pine carver chair, its red-checked cushions tied on with red tape. 'Thank you, white, no sugar, please.' He wished now that he had eaten some breakfast; he was feeling decidedly light-headed.

To his left, a kitchen sink, a window and a worktop covered with bowls and utensils. The red-checked curtains were pulled back to reveal two contrasting views; one of the kitchen next door, one of a beautifully tended garden in which snowdrops nodded and daffodils were in heavy bud. She brought his coffee. She had a cup of herbal tea.

'So, what's the latest news of Elizabeth?'

'We tracked her abductors by police helicopter. They took her to The Retreat.'

'I wouldn't have thought they would take her there – too close to her husband and two sons. Unless, of course, they knew she wasn't dead?'

'I've no idea. It's just that we haven't gone in to find her because the whole church is under investigation for other serious matters and we don't wish to jeopardise these enquiries. Before I make any decision on that score, do you think Elizabeth is in any physical danger?'

Annabel looked away from him, her gaze on the little garden. A robin was hopping about among the snowdrops. 'I'm not sure any more, Inspector. The effort of keeping discipline nearly destroyed her, you know, she was an emotional wreck when she came to me first. I did despair of her coming through it at times. To be honest, I think she is in more danger mentally than physically, but I don't know how things have moved within the church whilst I've been out.'

'To clarify the situation, we have been doing some exhumations at The Retreat cemetery. Certain things we have discovered concerning those burials mean we are extending our search there and to other cemeteries. There is also a proven link between the ethnic cleansing murders and the Joshua Group. So, with that in mind, do you think it's urgent to go in and rescue her?'

Annabel paused for a long while in thought. 'I don't know, Inspector. But what I do know is that Elizabeth would not want to be the cause of criminals escaping justice. I think she'd rather take her chance at The Retreat until you'd finished your investigation.'

'That's good enough for me. I must be getting back…' Cooper had tried to stand up, but a wave of giddiness made him sit back in his chair as the room spun sickeningly round him.

'Are you not well, Inspector?'

'I'm fine, really. Just rather a long time since I ate anything.' He grasped the table in order to gain some sense of stability.

She went to the Aga and took out a dish. She ladled lamb ragout onto a deep plate which she placed in front of him with a crusty roll and butter beside it. 'Eat,' she said, going back to the cooker and serving herself.

'But...'

'You need a decent meal, no 'buts' involved. There's no flesh on you.'

Cooper's resistance was lowered by his hunger and the lovely smell of hot food. 'Thank you.' He began to eat, slowly, savouring the meal. The lamb was tender, the bread rolls fresh baked.

She bowed her head and said a silent grace.

He looked up, embarrassed. 'I do hope I haven't been rude?'

'Not at all; I wouldn't impose my rule on you; you'll have your own.'

'I do remember a saying about Romans and Rome,' Cooper smiled.

'And how do you feel about the newcomers to our country? Do they follow this rule, Inspector?'

'No, they don't.'

'Yet they expect us to allow them places of worship, benefits, health care. But do they extend the same courtesy to us when we go to live in their homelands? No, don't answer that. I'm a little bitter about some aspects of missionary life.'

'What happened to you?'

'It's a long story. Suffice it to say that racism is not one-way, Inspector.'

'I know that only too well.' Cooper was beginning to feel better. 'Tell me more about yourself.'

Their talk began as though they'd known each other a lifetime. They finished the lamb, she brought a fruit compote and fresh cream to the table, her laughter filled the kitchen. Cooper felt something begin to thaw inside him as he looked into her eyes. They reminded him of emeralds.

'Maybe you could come round for a meal again? It's a bit empty without Elizabeth.'

'I'd like to,' Cooper said, before his caution cut in.

'There's only one thing that would gain you admission.'

'That is?'

'Remembering my name.'

'Annabel.'

'So you do know it. I was beginning to think I was easily lost among your case files.'

'It's not that. I could never forget...' Cooper stopped himself with an effort.

'I'm glad to hear it, Charles.'

Cooper's mobile rang.

Allsopp and Gillman were so absorbed that they didn't hear the door open, a policeman enter and plonk an envelope with an audible slap on Inspector Cooper's desk. 'Forensic report,' he said as the two men looked up sharply. 'For Inspector Cooper.'

When he had gone, the two young men sat down with a sigh. 'Coffee is what we need,' Robert said, stretching his long limbs.

'I'd go for inspiration, myself,' Joshua said, yawning, 'it must be something easy to remember, perhaps biblical?'

'It may be simple letter substitution. I'll do an analysis of frequency,' Robert began to tap the keys in the rapid way of the computer geek.

'Frequency?'

'Yes. The most commonly used letter is 'e' – so any symbol repeated most often is likely to be 'e' and so on through the alphabet. Didn't you do codes when you were a kid?'

'No. You were better off with gran than I was with my aunt.'

'True.' Silence fell as Josh went for coffee and Robert went on with the task.

'You got a Bible here, Josh?'

Josh took his out of the desk drawer and held it out.

'No, could you look at the first letters of all the books?'

'G,e,l,n,d,j,j,r,s'

'Stop there a minute. If that's the key, then a=g e=b l=c n=d d=e, could you jot down the rest of the first letters?'

'Do I include the Apocrypha?'

'Yes, put it in; we can always delete them if it doesn't work.'

The printer whirred as a page of text shot out. Robert picked it up and began to pencil in the alternative letters under the words. He reached out for Josh's finished alphabet and continued to write at breakneck speed.

'Ha! That's most of it, but we run out of books; some letters don't appear as the first of any book. Probably just randomised the rest. That'd make it a bit more difficult, except the end of the alphabet probably won't be too hard to deduce.'

'How?'

'Q's a good one, seldom occurs without a 'u' after it.' Robert was in his favourite puzzle to solve mode. 'This is beginning to make sense; there are words appearing out of the jumble, look.'

'That's great. But it's going to take an age to transpose all the CDs if that's how we've got to do it.'

'Leave it to me; I might be able to make some software to sort it.'

An hour later, they had the complete solution to the encryption. 'I'll be away to my office. I have some appointments but after I've sorted them out, I'll get down to working on the software. One CD should be enough. Antoinette will help.'

'Give her my best. She has become a fixture?'

'In my office, my home and my life,' he grinned, 'never thought I'd find anyone else who'd forget to eat whilst there was a computer problem to solve. In fact, she's worse than I am.'

'That's impossible,' Josh grinned, 'thanks a bundle. I'd better get on with my reports and then get onto the other discs just in case you can't cut it?'

'Bollocks, o ye of little faith! Bye for now.'

Josh picked up the telephone as Robert left.

'Cooper.'

'Sir, we've cracked the disc problem. Robert's taken one CD and gone to see if he can make software to unscramble it – by hand it's going to be quite a job.'

'Excellent. I'll be back as soon as I can, thank you,' he looked up at Annabel, 'I've got to go, I'm afraid.'

She looked as though lit from within, he thought. He longed to hold her warmth close, to kiss those lips, but some things just couldn't be. 'I'd like… I mean I wish…Sorry I've not time to help with the dishes…I must go.' He picked up his hat and hurried out of the door.

Annabel watched him half-running down the street and wondered what it was he'd like and what he wished for. She turned back to the empty kitchen. Activity was the best solution to vexing questions; there were dishes to do. What was it that so haunted the inspector?

# Chapter 48

Jimmy Rafferty had been up as early as Cooper that Wednesday despite his late night. It wasn't often he had a scoop; and this was dynamite. He smiled at the pun, and then went to read his proof copy again, although it would be too late to change anything. It would do. The photographs were brilliant; Stan Short had excelled himself this time. He had watched him manipulate the images; merge some with others until they satisfied him.

'Don't ever tell me again that the camera doesn't lie, Stan,' he'd chuckled as the images were printed.

'This is where photography becomes art, Jim, the truth and more than the truth; you wouldn't say that a painting lied, now, would you?'

'I've never felt the inclination to, no.'

'Well, what about tricks of perspective, changed angles, trees added or subtracted? No more and no less than I do.'

'I won't argue with you on that, but I hope they give us a full centre page spread with these.'

'I won't be holding my breath.'

Jimmy went to the back entrance to have a look for the first edition; it should be there soon. He lit a cigarette and leaned against the wall. He saw movement reflected in the office window opposite. His car was outside beside an unfed meter, but the man standing beside it was not a traffic warden; they kept civilised hours. Then the news van pulled up and three bundles of papers were thrown at the entrance to the alleyway. When Jimmy went to the entrance, there was nobody to be seen. He lifted out a newspaper. Yes! There it was – and a full page of photographs. Daniel and Robert had come out particularly well; Ruth Diamond looked pale, almost shrunken. Who did that look remind him of? Some singer who'd died, that was it. Jimmy went to get himself some breakfast and some change for the meter. The traffic wardens would be about soon.

The PM listened to the Commissioner's report impassively. Under the desk, unseen, his leg wobbled frantically. 'So the gist of it is; some of the burials don't match the gender and age of the name on the plot, and some show evidence that the causes of death aren't natural?'

'Yes, sir, it seems to be the same in all the burial sites we have visited so far.'

One of the desk telephones rang. 'PM. What? You can't be serious! Not Bradley! Right, will do. Thanks.' Stuart replaced the receiver with the air of a drowning man. 'Bradley's one of them, it seems. What do you suggest?'

'First, that she's unavoidably prevented from attending the next briefing, sir.'

'My God, yes, she mustn't hear the strategy. Even if they're wrong about her, we can't take the risk.'

'The other item is the press report, sir. There's been a front page exclusive at the Clarion; the headline is "True Gospel Church Revealed in its True Colours".'

'Yes, I read it. Edward. What should I do about that? It's just another news item, after all. The True Gospellers must be used to news coverage by now.'

'I fear there may be repercussions, sir. Remember, we haven't checked the newspaper offices yet.'

The PM looked pale at the thought. 'You don't think they would, not in the centre of the capital on a busy weekday?'

'I fear they would. We have already put out an alert. But the worst thing is, we don't know if, how or when. But most likely it'll be the newspaper office.'

'It's like the terrorists all over again – a recurring nightmare if ever there was one.'

Sir Edward sighed. 'It's always religion, it seems to me; Catholic, Protestant, Muslim, Jehovah's Witnesses; they all pass my fanaticism test.'

'What's that?'

'That they put their religious principles at a higher value than that of human life. Let brotherly love continue.'

The PM looked at his old friend in amazement. 'I didn't have you down as a philosopher-cynic, Edward.'

Edward shrugged. 'I just pick up the pieces. If that's all, I'll get onto the Bradley problem – liaise with Fox and his ilk to make sure we don't tread on one another's toes.'

'Thanks, Edward.' The PM stood up to shake his hand when the room was rocked by a massive, thunderous sound. The two men looked at each other and then the Police Chief ran from the room. Stuart went to the window. There were people running, and there was the mournful sound of sirens nearby.

Jimmy was on the telephone in his basement office when the blast shook the building and the line went dead. Masonry tumbled around him and he climbed under his desk; a mammoth pre-war oak thing that his father had left him. The harsh, heavy sounds of the building above him dying filled his head; dust choked his lungs and smarted in his eyes. Then he smelt the smoke. 'Jesus, it's Belfast and Iraq in one,' he swore inventively, and then listened. The worst of the settlement seemed over, the ensuing silence eerie until it was broken by the sirens and people shouting.

He emerged from his hiding place, took a torch from his desk drawer and shone it around. The door was gone under a pile of rubble, so he began to crawl slowly towards the place where the pavement window normally allowed him to see the feet of passers-by. He felt the sharp edges of shards of glass under his knees, found something to sweep them aside. Then his nose caught a familiar stink: gas. A main might have fractured, please God it was only a small feeder pipe. There was no waiting for help here. Out he must or a spark would char-grill him to a turn.

Fox grabbed the woman with the baby in the pushchair and threw them and himself to the ground behind a rubbish skip as the building just ahead of them exploded in a cloud of reddish dust. The noise was unbearable. Glass flew through the air and a rain of bricks tumbled about them, Fox crouched over the child, who was screaming. A man who had been just in front of them collapsed with a shard of glass in his temple and lay there staring open eyed at him. Then came silence, as if the very air had been deafened.

'Thank you,' a shaky voice said at his side. Fox took a moment to realise it was the woman he'd rescued.

'Think nothing of it.' Then he realised that the child had stopped screaming. She must have realised it at the same instant, and in sudden fear, knelt up beside the capsized pushchair to look. Fox was amazed to hear her laugh with an edge of hysteria in the sound.

'He's found his bottle. I'd tucked it in beside him when we left home.' She was covered in dust and had blood trickling from a graze on her cheek.

'Are you hurt?' he asked.

'I don't think so, you?'

'I'll live.' Fox lifted the pushchair back onto its wheels and looked down at the child. 'Nothing wrong there, then. I'll be getting off; people to help.'

The woman looked after him. 'And we don't even know his name, Nathan.'

Jimmy had managed to break out the rest of the window frame and squeezed his bulk half through the gap. The next obstacle was the grille that was set into the pavement over the window well. Part of a car had landed on one end and buckled it. Jimmy retreated to the office again. He needed something to bash the grille hard, knock it loose. But there was nothing. The smell of gas was getting more intense. He decided to get his head outside before the fumes got any worse.

'Hello? Is anybody there? Help!' Jimmy roared at the top of his voice. He kept it up for a long time. Then he ducked back inside for his sports whistle when his voice began to crack. He coughed and gagged, there was more gas than air in here now, he thought. Back, halfway out of the window, he began to blow blasts, short, long, short.

## Chapter 49

The PM had been on the phone to Isaac M'bele, the new US President. He had listened with concern as Stuart outlined his problems. When he'd finished, there was a long silence at the other end of the line, punctuated by the ticking of the President's watch.

'You got a real squib to deal with there, Stuart. Thing is, I got it too, only worse, since there's such a strong gospel element here anyway. There's no way I can move easy on them without tripping over the freedom of religion they got. Thinking about it: that 'Agenda for Change' is out of the same hymn sheet as the New Gospel Democrats are singing from. But, since you got so much on this sect there, I think I'll give the FBI chief a call. He'll liaise with your Commissioner. The leopard might have the same spots this side of the pond. Talk to you soon. Have a nice day.'

Stuart put the phone down with a sigh; he was very unlikely to have a nice day any time soon. He lifted the handset again, dangling it until it began to spin and untangle the twisted cord. Would God that all his problems could be unravelled as easily.

In Salisbury, Cooper was sitting at his desk surrounded by papers when the phone rang for the umpteenth time that afternoon. 'Yes?'

There was a muffled voice on the line. 'This is a bomb warning; the Clarion Newspaper Offices, New Street.' The line went dead.

'Damn these hoax callers! Just because there's been one in London!'

Josh looked up. 'Sir?'

'Bomb alert; Clarion Offices.' Cooper was already dialling the Superintendent's number. 'You phone the newspaper and warn them.'

'Superintendent.'

'Cooper here. Bomb warning at the Clarion Newspaper offices.'

'Damn. I'm short of officers already; I've around twenty tied up with the demonstration at the Cathedral, and there's been a pile-up at the Countess roundabout; a coach load of tourists for Stonehenge collided with a school bus on its way to the swimming pool.'

'I'll be ready to go if you need me, sir. Meanwhile, I'll get on to the other Clarion offices in case ours was a one-off genuine warning.'

'Right, bye.'

The newsroom was busy; they were doing a feature on the True Gospel Church in Salisbury, and raking out all the old files on them that they could find. The Sunday-Worship murders, the unexplained deaths at the colleges, the resurrected homosexual, and the London office bomb. There was also the demonstration outside the Cathedral against using a place of worship for secular concerts. Although the majority of protesters were in ordinary dress, suspicion was that it was True Gospel organised.

Tom Rafferty lifted the receiver, hoping there would be news of his father. 'Rafferty, news desk, can I help?'

'DI Allsopp, here, Tom. We've had a call saying there's a bomb in your building.'

'It's probably a hoax; someone watched the London news and wants us to sweat a bit.'

'We've got to take it seriously; think of the TV Studio and your London offices. Better be outside than in if there is one due to be detonated.'

'But the evening edition's going to press!'

'I think they'd like to stop that coming out – I'd wager you've a front page spread about the True Gospel Church again.'

'Damn them to blazes. But I'll get folks out, Josh. Thanks.' As he replaced the receiver, Tom leaned over and smashed the glass on the fire alarm point beside him and then put his wheelchair into fast forward towards the exit. He hated these slow Victorian lifts, but there was no alternative for him. He could hear people running down the stairs beside the lift shaft as he began to descend.

Cooper dialled again, 'Directory enquiries? I need the telephone numbers of all the Clarion News Group offices – not Salisbury or London; Southampton first?' He covered the receiver. 'Josh, take the other line and dial the first for me?' and so the two of them worked through the cities' Clarion newspaper offices, warning them of a possible danger.

'We'll look silly if there's nothing, but I'm not prepared to take the risk,' Cooper was saying as there came the sound he'd been dreading. For an instant, they sat motionless before leaping into action. They met the Superintendent on the stairs. 'I've already given a major incident alert; the emergency services should be on their way already. Take two from the desk with you and get down there. I'm on my way.'

The one-way system was in absolute gridlock. New Street was blocked with rubble and cars. A police sergeant at the further end was manfully attempting to divert cars into Catherine Street or St Anne's, but nothing was moving. Cooper had left a police constable to park his car and the rest of them pushed their way through the gathering crowd, ducking under the police tape.

'Sir, we're making some progress; I've got Sam Barry down the far end but things aren't moving. I'm sending traffic down the pedestrian precinct into Fisherton Street. The fire engines are stuck up Crane Bridge Road, but we got an ambulance through, and half-a-dozen paramedics have come in on foot.'

'Right, let's get some of this traffic out of the way – Josh, we'll divert some into the car stack until there's space in these other streets. You, Ames, Hawkins, see if you can't get the stuff moving down Catherine Street, Wilson, you head down to see if Barry needs a hand. Disperse this damned crowd as you go.'

Cooper got Josh started on the cars, and then went to see how many of the newspaper staff had escaped, chivvying gawkers as he went. There was another crowd in the entrance to the Mall. Cooper lifted his megaphone. 'Could everyone who has nothing to do with the newspaper offices, please disperse? Clarion Newspaper staff, please stay – who has the roll-call?'

A pretty dark-haired woman of about thirty pushed her way to the front, clipboard in hand. 'Betty Scammell, I've accounted for most of us. It's just Tom Rafferty, Pierre Simons and Jenny Tang.'

'Anybody injured?'

'Only cuts and bruises from flying debris, Inspector. There's a couple of paramedics seeing to them now.'

'Where would they most likely have been?'

'I think Tom Rafferty was in the lift when the bomb went off – he's in a wheelchair, Pierre was working in the rear offices, Jenny Tang is his secretary.'

'Thanks Betty.' Cooper breathed a sigh of relief as a fire engine finally made it through. He ran to the window. 'Just three staff missing, one male probably trapped in the lift in his wheelchair, two from the offices at the rear of the building are missing.'

'At least there's no sign of a fire,' grunted the fireman.

Cooper stood back as they got to work. The street was clearer now; two more ambulances had reached the scene, the crowds were dispersing. Then, through the thinning mob, he saw something that made his heart lurch. A figure in a black robe was making its way towards the back of the crowd in the Mall. Cooper hurried towards it; the figure quickened its pace. Cooper broke into a run. Black-robe took off at full speed, straight through Mother Care, knocking a display of maternity wear into Cooper's path. Cooper jumped over it, skidded, and regaining his balance, shot through the far doors into the street beyond. There was no sign of the black-robed figure. Cooper turned, looked in shops either side, moved to the other side of the road. A man in T-shirt and jeans who had been in the shoe shop emerged. In a holdall, he had a rolled up black garment.

In the London office basement, Jimmy Rafferty's head was ringing with the sound of the whistle that he had been blowing steadily for so long his lips were numb. He felt slightly sick from the gas fumes that seeped out around him, and chilled to the bone. There was a sound somewhere to his left. A teenager in a hooded top, smoking a cigarette.

Rafferty dropped his whistle to yell at the kid. 'Put that damned fag out – there's gas leaking down here, you bloody idiot.'

The figure looked around, not seeing where the voice had come from.

'I'm not bloody joking. If you don't step on that cancer-stick you'll damn well not live long enough to develop it.'

Something in Rafferty's tone must have penetrated. The youth put his foot on the cigarette and walked towards the shattered building.

'Cor, you're right, it don't half stink o' gas.' Two blue, innocent-seeming eyes looked down at Jimmy.

'Never mind that; can you help me shift this grille and get me out of here before the next idiot comes by with a spark?'

The kid was not strong; only about fourteen, and even with Jimmy's help, made no impression on the grille. 'We need a bit o' help.' He turned and sprinted away.

Jimmy watched him go with a feeling of abandonment.

Fox was taking a short breather when he noticed a young lad trying to get past the police tape without success. He wandered across.

'What's the matter, lad?'

'Just tryin' to get the cop to come wiv me – there's a man trapped round the corner.'

'Don't listen to him, mate, he's allus spinning yarns that one. Right waste of space, should be in school.'

The lad looked desperate, so Fox ducked under the tape, using the crowbar he'd been carrying as a support.

'No harm in taking a look, constable.'

The policeman shrugged. 'It's your time to waste.'

The lad's face cleared in relief. 'Come on, guv, 'urry – there's gas comin' out o' there.'

Fox quickened his pace.

Jimmy heard voices a few minutes later. Then a guy wearing a dirty lurid check coat and carrying a crowbar came into view. 'It's good to see you,' he croaked.

'Right, let's have you out of there.' Fox began to prise at one end of the grille. Only pausing to heave the car debris off the further end, he gave the lad another length of metal for the other corner. Jimmy pushed, they heaved. Sweat ran down the man's dusty bloodstained face. There was a sound of protesting metal as the grille lifted.

Jimmy fell forward as the weight shifted. The two outside fell backwards, the crowbar and metal strip tumbled noisily into the window well, and the grille clattered and rocked its twisted shape on the concrete beside them. Jimmy took the man's hands and he half scrambled, was half pulled from his prison.

'Run!' Jimmy gasped. 'Gas might go off at any minute.'

Jimmy was telling the chief fire officer about the basement gas leak, at the moment when a rescue worker sneaked around the corner for a quick cigarette.

## Chapter 50

Tom Rafferty came to in total darkness. He brushed dust from his face and his fingers came away covered in blood. He took a minute or two to orientate himself; then his mind cleared into sense and his eyes adjusted to the lack of light. Presumably, the bomb had gone off before the ancient lift had creaked its way to the foyer. The lift was tilted at an angle that left his wheelchair leaning against the metal sides, next to the control panel. The glass on the emergency phone was already shattered. He lifted the handset to his ear but heard no dial tone.

He twisted around in his chair for the bag that was slung on the back, taking out the mobile phone that was in the side pocket. Who to phone? Possibly the emergency number? He gave it a whirl. 'Police, please. Yes, my name's Tom Rafferty. I'm trapped in a lift at the Clarion offices. Yes, I'm on my mobile, the number is...' and he read off the number that he'd taped to the phone.

'Yes, I'll hang up now if you don't mind, to save my battery. No, only seem to be a bit scratched, yes, fine. I'm not going anywhere.'

That done, he settled down to wait, closing his eyes and taking himself in spirit to the white sands of the Wexford beach that he'd played on as a boy on holiday. His school friends were all there, still young and alive before they were involved in the troubles.

Cooper saw the Superintendent crossing the road at a run.

'Sir?' Cooper fell into step beside his superior officer.

'We had a call from the man trapped in the lift – he's not injured, I've spoken to the CIC of the rescue, but there's no news of other casualties.'

'According to the roll call, there's only three staff missing, the man in the lift, Tom Rafferty, and two who used the same office at the rear of the building, a Pierre Simons and a Jenny Tang. I informed the rescuers.'

'What's the most immediate problem?'

'Gridlock, sir, traffic blocking the access to the street. I've got men diverting some into the car stack.'

'Right, let's get down to it.'

Jenny Tang struggled to breathe with his weight on her chest. Pierre hadn't moved at all since the explosion. She could feel his blood sticky on her skin. Or was it her own? She wriggled her hand free, felt for his neck. It was cold. There should be a pulse just there. As she felt for it, Pierre's head lolled to the side. Tears trickled uncomfortably down towards her ears.

If only they'd taken notice of the fire alarm.

'It's only a drill,' he'd whispered in her ear, 'let's not stop now.'

'Perhaps we'd better…'

'Non! No, my love, I cannot leave!' He had continued to thrust himself into her with fixed concentration. His body was so lithe, so brown from the sun, his hair so blond, and his eyes so blue, Jenny had lain back on the inflatable mattress and closed her eyes, giving herself up to the pleasure of him.

Now, perhaps, he was dead. When she was found, whether still breathing or not, there would be the damning evidence of their miscreant behaviour. She could hear her headmistress saying the words in her head. She blushed at the thought. Pierre had been her first. Had been…her tears made little tracks on her dusty skin. She had to move Pierre, make herself decent at least. She began to wriggle herself free. The inflatable mattress had collapsed, leaving her lying on the wooden floor, which was no longer level. The desk had landed across Pierre's back; one of the metal chairs had been crushed under it. Jenny pushed hard one-handed against the desk, which fell backwards with a splintering crash. Some large chunks of plaster fell, showering her with yet more choking dust. At last she managed to sit herself up. She gave a cry of anguish as she saw Pierre's back. Two of the stainless steel chair legs had been driven into his flesh. She began to sob as she struggled to be free of him and his once beautiful broken body.

Ebb Crouch had been sleeping off a bottle of cheap whisky taken without food when the wall had collapsed on him. The central heating boiler had been on the further side of it, and boiling steam had erupted only yards from him. He could not have moved if it had come in his direction. Ebb was unaware of his lucky escape as he lay among the rubble of the wall, singing 'Amazing Grace'. He could still remember all the words, even stone drunk. He only wished he could forget the monsters that chased him into madness during his conscious moments.

Someone had obtained plans of the building. There was nothing further to be done but to let the experts do their work. Some of the ambulances had been called to help with the RTA casualties; two had remained on hand for the time being. Cooper headed back to the station, Josh at his heels. Robert had sent the decoding programme and the CDs back and the two of them sat for hours working through the information, copying the results carefully, and double checking. They sent copies to the various departments and to the PM. At six, Cooper stretched and said, 'Best get yourself off to your family, Allsopp.'

'I've not finished this lot yet, sir,' he said, indicating the piles of paper that seemed to breed on their desks.

'Neither have I. But I intend to leave it till tomorrow. I think it was Sir Francis Bacon who said: "If work is the greatest thing in the world, best save some for tomorrow."'

'Seems good to me, sir.' Josh grabbed his coat and shot out of the office before the phone decided to ring.

Cooper sat down and tackled another heap of papers. He stood up and looked at his flow chart, made and drank two cups of coffee. It would be good to see Annabel, he thought as he threw the plastic cups into the bin.

The road was deserted as he walked towards her home. He pressed the doorbell in anticipation of her warm smile. There was no answer.

'Damn, should have phoned first.' He scribbled a note and began to push it through the polished letterbox. The door wasn't locked, nor was it fastened with the chain. Cooper pushed it open, called Annabel's name. There were no lights on, and no sound, just the warm smell of bread making.

Cooper called her name again, and then switched on the light. He moved slowly, not sure what he would find. The kitchen was in darkness too. Perhaps she had merely gone out and forgotten to lock the door behind her? She had left her washed dishes to drain. He searched the whole house, thoroughly. Her bedroom walls were pale lilac, the cotton duvet, curtains and the rugs on the polished wooden floor all bore the same pattern of lilac flowers. He paused by the dressing table, lifted the bottle of her perfume, inhaled the smell and then put it down guiltily.

The only sign she had been there recently was the light on the cupboard. Inside were trays of loaves in their tins, rising. Batches of rolls jostled for space with hot cross buns. The smell reminded him that he was hungry. He was just about to close the door when his eye caught something unusual. Two of the buns' crosses were rather oddly shaped. Cooper pulled the tray toward him. They bore the initials 'J and G'. Joshua Group. Had she insisted on finishing her task before she was taken? He closed the door, remembering his mother's insistence that the bread dough be kept warm to let the yeast do its work.

He sat on a red and white checked kitchen chair in order to think. If it was the Joshua Group, they would probably have taken her to The Retreat. Perhaps he could contact Ruth Diamond somehow, to check? Perhaps a short text, late at night, would be unobserved? Who else could know where Annabel might be?

He stood and went to Annabel's phone. He dialled a preset number labelled 'Pastor'.

'Hello, Pastor John Black here.'

'Hello... Pastor, this is Chief Inspector Cooper here. I am at Annabel Harman's home. I found the door unlocked and there is nobody home. Might she be at some church function tonight?'

'Not that I am aware of. She was baking for the homeless shelter tonight.'

'That is well under way; someone will need to finish it if she doesn't return.'

'I rather feel that she's met the same fate as Elizabeth, Inspector. She thought it would happen one day. Shall I come with my wife and wait there, tend to the bread, and let you know if she should return?'

'That would be very kind, thank you.'

'It's part of my job, Inspector. I'll be there as soon as I can.'

Cooper stood holding the phone for a moment before hanging it back on the wall. Then, as he sat down to wait for the pastor and his wife, in the kitchen, his tired mind began to work overtime. Annabel's disappearance brought some hard questions bubbling to the surface.

Could it be possible to fall in love with someone so quickly? What was he thinking of? She would never have a relationship with a married man, her spiritual commitment; her honesty would be compromised if she did. He contemplated not telling her of his marriage. But that would mean she would expect marriage. That would either mean he would be a bigamist – and what consequences for his career if it were to come out? Then, how would she feel if he had betrayed her in such a way? Would she consider marrying him if he were divorced? He did not have any answers.

He sat staring at Annabel's checked apron that hung on the back of the kitchen door until it began to dissolve into abstract patterns of red and white.

## Chapter 51

Saul sat at his desk in the early dawn, his journal open in front of him. His eyes smarted and prickled from lack of sleep, his knees ached from long hours in prayer. Yet there was no peace, no sleep, no feeling of communion with his Lord. He lifted his pen and began to write.

It is only a few days since my faith was shaken to its roots. The Agenda for Change meeting was the beginning of this earthquake. As far as I understand it, Brother Amos and Brother Joshua have begun a markedly different agenda from the one my father began with so many years ago. They have embraced violence in the name of Christ, in direct contradiction to his instruction. 'A new commandment I give unto you; that you love one another'.

The Joshua Group has been murdering those of other faiths, seeing them as a threat to the gospel. I have had to accept the fact of it, but my soul is torn; am I to go to the secular authorities, reveal what I know and thus destroy all that we have built so far? There are also questions about members who have been called home. The police have been exhuming burials countrywide. I cannot come to terms with the desecration of them, nor can I accept what the police are telling me; that Elizabeth is not the one who was buried in the plot with her name on it. I am living a nightmare.

I have been to the police station several times. I believe that I convinced Inspector Cooper that I had been unaware of the discrepancies in the records and of the true nature of the causes of death of those buried.

Brothers Joshua and Amos came to see me in my study. Was it really only yesterday?

'We have much to tell you, Brother Saul,' Brother Joshua said, taking a seat. 'The bomb at the studio was set by us.'

'You set the bomb? But what about Sister Ruth? She might have been killed!'

'The hosts of the Lord camp round about the dwellings of the just. She was preserved, the Lord willed it. Had she not survived, that would also have been His will. It was necessary to prevent those ungodly men from slandering the church.'

I stared at him. I found it hard to believe what he was saying.

Brother Amos passed me a local edition of the newspaper. 'Look at the lead article, Brother Saul.'

The piece was full of the usual accusations about the Brethren, with some very imaginative twists. 'It's no worse than most things they write about us. That nonsense about Daniel Diamond is going to be hard to disprove, but we are used to this kind of thing, Brethren.'

'We have taken steps to avoid such things in future. The Clarion offices in London will be bombed, and if all goes well, the one here in Salisbury will follow. There is some discussion about other offices; the decision will be taken later today.'

I realised then with horror just how far the corruption had spread.

Brother Joshua's smile made me shiver. 'They'll soon learn not to write such defamatory things about us. Our discipline is our own affair; Daniel Diamond is a homosexual; he does not deserve any pity.'

'Are you telling me that it's true, what the newspaper says? That you tried to kill him and failed? Is that why there is someone else in his grave here?'

'Of course it's true. The only thing is, we don't actually know who it is in his grave; we thought we were burying young Daniel.'

'And the other burials?'

'Some brethren who were too old for service, some whose assets were needed to advance the cause, some who threatened to destroy the True Gospel Church by scurrilous accusations. They stood in the way of the truth.'

They stayed for several hours, going over their plans, trying to convince me that this is the right path to take; the church militant, the Army of Christ. I was relieved when the call to prayer came, and we went to the chapel. I was so relieved to see them go back to London.

They do not seem to understand the enormity of what they have done. They seem utterly convinced that they are doing right in all this. But to me it seems to be murder, more murder and other murders all in the name of the church. This is not the gospel of love. I made one decision yesterday after I heard the news of the London bomb. I warned Inspector Cooper by telephone about the one in town, thinking that nothing would be lost if it turned out to be an empty threat.

I have spent long hours thinking about what is to be done. I am becoming convinced that the end time is upon us; that Armageddon is due. The corruption of the church, the attacks from the world, the wars, famines and plagues such as Aids. What must I do to protect my children?

Saul lay down his pen and bowed his head. He was awoken by a timid knocking at his door. 'Come.'

The door opened and Adam and Calvin stood in the opening, looking very uncomfortable.

'Peace be with you, my sons. Do come in and close that door. How can I help you?'

The two looked at each other, then both began at once, then they both faltered to a halt. Then Adam swallowed hard and began again.

'Father, we would like you to come with us to the solitary wing. There is someone there who very much wants to see you before they are taken somewhere else.'

'Who is this person?'

'We think it's best if you just come with us. Then we can be sure that we are right, that this was none of your doing.'

On other mornings, Saul would not have moved, but the surreal events of the last few days had left him without an anchor, without confidence. To the astonishment of his two sons, Saul stood up and followed them to the solitary wing without any further question. Adam opened the door, and stood back to allow his father to enter.

A woman novice was sitting on the bed, reading. She looked up at him and smiled. 'Peace be with you, Brother Saul. The boys said they would bring you. I doubted they would be able to persuade you to see me. After all, I let you down very badly. I just wanted to say how sorry I am, have been, for that.'

Saul stood rooted to the spot, unable to speak for the tumult of feelings that were in danger of fighting their way through his self-control.

His sons looked at each other.

Calvin whispered, 'I'd say he had no idea.'

Adam went into the corridor and fetched a chair.

Saul sat in it with the air of someone sleepwalking.

## Chapter 52

The black Citroen had been outside the flat for some time. When the street was finally empty of people, four hooded and robed figures emerged. They did not knock. The first figure took a swipe at the door with a large metal implement which broke the lock and the door chain from the frame. The glass in the door shattered as it swung back against the interior wall. The men were inside and searching the house within seconds. There was no one there. One of the men kicked a hole in an inner door, muttering under his breath.

Another of them put a match to a firelighter and dropped it on the sofa. Within minutes, it was ablaze. The four figures moved in unison to the door, the car doors slammed and the car was gone. Inside the house, the alarm was shrieking and the sprinkler system was raining hard on everything.

Some distance away, Paul and Daniel's phone rang.

'They've paid you a visit, lads. They set light to the sofa, but the sprinklers have put that out. I suggest you stay where you are for the time being.'

'Here is the six o'clock news. There has been a second bombing at a Clarion Newspaper office, this time in the Cathedral City of Salisbury. Dominick Draper is at the scene, Dominick.'

'Good evening, Charles. Just behind me are the remains of the Clarion offices here in New Street, Salisbury. There are three people known to be trapped in the building. There was a warning phone call, giving no time or organisation responsible, but there are strong indications that an offshoot of the fundamentalist sect, the True Gospel Church, may be responsible. I have here the latest edition of the Clarion, which has gone to press despite the bombing.'

The newsman held up the paper, showing the headline: A Murderous Gospel? 'This is Dominick Draper returning you to the studio.'

'Thank you, Dominick. News is just coming in of further bombings this afternoon in other Clarion offices. We will bring you reports of them as they become available. It seems reasonable to suppose that they are targeted for their fearless exposé of the True Gospel Church and its activities. Here's our Religious Affairs correspondent, Howard Blithe.'

The Prime Minister sat in the cabinet room, his head spinning with proposals and counter-proposals. The Police Commissioner was standing again, pacing the room as he spoke.

'I am afraid that we shall have another incident like the Waco disaster if we aren't very careful. That six more murders and two bombings have occurred means that we dare not continue as we have been. But there is real concern that those in charge may turn their violence inwards if the sect is threatened. I propose that we mount a dawn raid, countrywide, on every one of The Retreats and Communities. We would hope that, with the element of surprise, there would be little time for them to organise any mass suicide or similar event. The discoveries at the various interment sites show that there are those among the membership who will not flinch at murder, even of their own membership. Our only problem is the shortage of manpower for such an operation.' The Commissioner sat down.

One of the Generals at the table stood up at the Prime Minister's nod. 'We aren't at full strength with our commitment overseas, but we could assist the police in this if we are required.' He sat down.

Another much decorated man in uniform stood up. 'It seems to me that we have no alternative but to assist the Commissioner in his plan. What is happening in the other EU countries, America, Canada, and New Zealand?'

The Prime Minister stood up. 'Gentlemen, I have waited for the outcome of this meeting before telling you that there are similar action plans proposed or underway wherever this sect has taken root. There have been murders, disappearances, questionable financial dealings and more, associated with the leaders of this sect worldwide. Although at grass roots level, there are many dedicated, deeply spiritual people who are unaware of the evil that is being done in the name of good. Our duty is to protect them as far as we can. If we agree the plan, all the raids will have to be coordinated so that no one group can warn another, allowing for time zone differences. It is going to be a logistical nightmare. May I ask for your votes, gentlemen?'

Hands rose around the table. 'The proposal is carried. Now, Commissioner, the logistics as you see them, please.'

An aide knocked and entered, giving a memo to the Prime Minister, who sat down. 'Gentlemen, I am sorry to announce that there have been three more bombs detonated at Clarion Newspaper offices in the last few minutes.'

Saul sat looking at his wife for some time, his mind and heart racing. There was no time to go into what had happened since she left, no time to discuss where they went from here. He struggled to put his thoughts into words. 'Do you think...? I mean, are you in any danger from the Joshua Group, Elizabeth?'

'I don't think they had intended to bring me here at first. But I see that the burial site is under police guard at the moment.' She did not sound at all worried about her fate, her voice calm and level toned.

Saul wondered at the changes in her, grasped hard at the thought that the Joshua Group had been hampered by the lack of a convenient and camouflaged burial spot. 'They might use anywhere. So how do we prevent them from taking you again?'

Calvin spoke into the silence. 'I have somewhere to take you, Mother. It's where I go when I need a little space. Sorry, Father, but I can't come up to the True Gospel discipline – I'm not made of the right stuff.'

Saul looked at his son with new insight, some pity for him, under the anger that came to the fore immediately. 'You were always a rebel, Calvin. We will speak of this disobedience at another time. Now, I believe it is urgent to take your mother to wherever this is as soon as we can.'

Adam said, softly, 'It might even be providential, Father.'

Saul was so out of step with himself that he didn't remind his son to call him 'Brother'. 'We'd best be on our way. Elizabeth, what have you to carry?'

Elizabeth smiled, stood up and held out her hands, 'Nothing.'

'It's not far away,' Calvin said, leading the way.

Matthew had missed Evening Prayers and meditation. Such absence was seldom missed, but Saul's attention had been diverted. So Matthew lay unnoticed in his bed, coughing painfully in between periods of restless dream-tossed sleep in which Ruth was alternately well and eating healthily, and nightmares of her being blown apart by a terrorist bomb.

Just as the Crouch family group were entering Calvin's refuge, three black-robed Joshua Group members came with their prisoner through the main doors, admitted by Brother Amos. Annabel was led up the narrow staircase to the solitary wing. It was fortunate that this trio were not the ones who had brought Elizabeth, so her absence was not yet noted.

So, worldwide, plans were made that would, if they were successful, bring the True Gospel Church leaders to justice. It might have been a complete success, except for the problem of the American General's new gold watch.

It was two hours before dawn that the soldiers surrounded The Retreat. Similar actions were being repeated around True Gospel Church groups worldwide. The sound of the bell for Morning Prayer was echoing through the valley as the men approached the perimeter walls. The Colonel watched the robed figures head for the chapel. This was the weirdest mission he'd ever had the misfortune to mount.

Inside The Retreat, Brother Amos was with Brother Saul in the office when the phone rang shrilly in the early quiet. Amos lifted the receiver.

'Brother Amos.'

'Brother Nathaniel. Armageddon, I repeat, Armageddon.' Brother Amos paled under his tan as the line went dead.

Saul paused at the doorway, on his way to the Chapel. 'Is all well, Brother Amos?'

'All's well, I will join you shortly, Brother Saul.' He lifted the receiver and dialled. 'Brother Joshua? Brother Amos. Armageddon, I repeat, Armageddon.'

Then he went straight to the storeroom to collect one of the crates marked 'A' in red, and carried it to the chapel. He returned and took the second one, and, stopping off at various points where overflow services were to be held; left two or three bottles of communion wine at each venue.

## Chapter 53

The service was being led by Brother Amos. Brother Saul looked as though his mind was elsewhere as he poured the communion wine into the glasses that were set into the trays that held them. Sister Ruth was singing unaccompanied as the Elders carried the loaves of bread to the waiting congregation. Each one broke a piece from a loaf, as it was passed around. It had always been a comfort to Saul to know that this celebration would be happening at this same time worldwide.

The Elders returned and began the task of carrying the trays of wine to the waiting congregation. Sister Ruth's voice soared into psalm one hundred, the choir joined in the descant behind her. In all the overflow rooms, the sound was repeated. The Elders returned to their seats. Brother Amos led the people in prayer.

'Now is the day of thy victory over sin and death...'

Outside, the men climbed the perimeter wall of The Retreat at the set time. What they did not know was that on the other side of the world, a certain General Bushman's new Rolex had been gaining time all night, and that his men had already launched their operation ten minutes too soon. A Brother Nathaniel, in his black robes, had been found holding a telephone.

Inspector Cooper had woken very early with an odd feeling of loss, of dread, perhaps of a departing dream, which stayed with him as he made toast and coffee. He was startled by a sound at his door, and he went to investigate. A square of folded white paper lay on the mat. He lifted the curtain. A shadow seemed to flit between the two houses opposite – there was an alleyway. He opened the paper, read its contents, and leapt into action. By breaking several speed limits, he was at The Retreat before dawn, parking his car in Ash Leas Lane and creeping silently amongst the soldiers who were in the process of scaling the wall. Where on earth was the Colonel? Suddenly Cooper found himself thrown heavily to the ground with his arm twisted up behind him.

'And what might you be doing here?'

Cooper knew that voice. 'Looking for you, Colonel.'

'Cooper! What the blazes do you think you're up to?' His arm was released.

'Bringing you this,' he held out the now crumpled paper. 'I've let the CIC know – seems someone's tripped up and the alarm's gone out. Armageddon; I don't know what the code means, but the message seems clear.'

'Don't drink the wine? Why not?'

Cooper's heart seemed to lurch painfully in his chest. 'Waco, Colonel. They drank poison.'

The two men looked at each other in horror. The Colonel lifted his radio and gave his call sign softly, and said, 'Whatever you do, don't let them drink the wine.'

It said something for the discipline of his men that not one of them asked a question.

'Are they aware that there is at least one guard dog?'

'Sure, that's been dealt with; it should sleep through the action. Come on, then, since you're so keen.' The Colonel and Cooper moved together towards the wall and scrambled over. Cooper was glad of the opportunity to do something; the thought of waiting at the Station to find out what had happened would have been purgatory to his heightened senses.

The Colonel went left to the chapel, shadowed by a dozen of his men. Others went towards the main house which was in semi-darkness. Cooper opened the main entrance door. A waft of incense and warm air greeted him. The hallway was empty. He tried desperately to remember where Ruth had said the solitary wing was. Yes, the narrow staircase. His ascent was marked by the banshee creaking of the old wooden steps. There were doors everywhere. But which was Annabel's? Would they have taken her to the chapel? Was she still here? Cooper peered into empty rooms; there were only tumbled bedclothes, doors left open. Then, one at the end, closed. He looked in, to see her sitting on the bed, head bowed, bread and wine on a tray in front of her.

She lifted the bread, and ate it as Cooper tried the door. It opened with a crash. Annabel jumped, her glass of wine slid sideways on the tray. She caught it deftly, raised it to her lips, smiling.

Cooper took two steps towards her and knocked it from her grasp.

'I don't mind being rescued, Inspector, but I think I might be allowed to finish communion first.' She was angry, her cheeks flamed red.

Cooper could not speak for a moment, his breath coming in short gasps. 'Not that wine, Annabel. It's the one called Armageddon.'

They looked in horror at the spilt wine, which bubbled and melted the varnish on the floorboards.

'I...' she began, and then she began to tremble violently. The tray slid to the floor with a crash.

Cooper sat beside her, took her in his arms until the trembling stopped. He hadn't planned to kiss her, but as he held her to him, looked into her eyes, smelt that freesia fragrance, he gently placed his lips on hers until he was sure that she was there, truly alive and his own body had stopped shaking.

Who was it that had said that stolen fruits are sweeter?

The Colonel opened the chapel door, sprinted over the red carpet to the front, his pistol at the ready. 'I have reason to believe that the wine you are about to drink is poisoned. I beg of you, don't drink it.'

A man in black robes launched himself at him, followed by several more. The Colonel ducked, the man took the full force of his head in the stomach. It became difficult to see for all the black robes that were swirling about. One of them pulled a knife. The Colonel brought the edge of his meaty hand down hard on the man's wrist and the knife shot into the air, falling, impaling itself in a pew. Oddly, the knife man doubled up and dropped to the floor, groaning. Several more of his attackers were similarly stricken. The Colonel stood up among the fallen, looked about.

The whole chapel was in turmoil. As far as he could see, some of the worshippers, mostly men, had already drunk the wine; they lay inert like so many dolls, their discoloured distorted faces showing that death had not come kindly to them.

Others were weeping. His men had done well, running along, knocking the glasses to the floor, calling to the ones they could not reach not to drink. Armageddon.

Then, from above him, in the pulpit, a woman's voice cut through the uproar.

'Peace be with you, Brethren and Sisters. We must be calm and of good courage. I do not know what is happening either, but I trust that the men who are here have come to help us.'

The Colonel looked up to see a slender figure in a blue robe. She was weeping openly.

The chapel hushed.

'It seems it would be better if we do not drink the wine, Brethren, and Sisters. Let us pray.' The congregation bowed their heads among the dead.

'Lord, we do not know what we must learn from this; we only pray that guidance be given us, courage be granted to us, and strength given us in our weakness. Amen.'

The people answered, 'Amen.'

The Colonel looked up in amazement at this lovely girl.

'What must we do, sir?' she asked, seemingly unaware of the tears that flowed down her cheeks and onto her robe.

The Colonel shook off the feeling that he was in some weird play. 'I'd like you all to stay where you are for the moment. My men will come and bring those who have been poisoned to the front...'

'The Brethren will assist you, sir. Come, Sisters, let us worship the lord.'

She began to sing, and the women joined in.

Surreal, thought the Colonel, truly surreal, as the words of the twenty-third psalm surrounded him, his men and robed monk-like figures carried bodies to the wide carpeted space at the front of the Chapel.

Elsewhere, there were others wakened at dawn that day: judges, police officers, MPs, summarily taken into temporary custody. Some, however, could not be found.

Saul could not believe what was happening in front of him. As usual, the men had taken the wine first, and he had not yet had his. He had wished to pray about the things on his mind over communion this morning. Now the chapel was full of soldiers in uniform, people, his children, were falling unconscious in the pews.

Then the soldier in charge had shouted: 'I have reason to believe that the wine you are about to drink is poisoned. I beg of you, don't drink it.'

As the man spoke, Saul was aware of a movement at his side. Brother Amos was running towards the side door. For a moment, Saul hesitated, and then followed. Brother Amos was in the car park, someone was already at the wheel of the car, engine running. Another man was loading cases into the boot. He and Brother Amos moved in unison to open the rear doors and jump in.

Saul moved in front of the exit lane to stop them. But they did not stop. His last thought was that he could hear Ruth Diamond singing the twenty-third psalm.

# Chapter 54

Matthew lay in a pool of perspiration. The walls billowed in a high wind that made his teeth chatter. Someone was coughing and moaning; the voice was familiar, so like his own, yet parched, as from a throat that longed for water. It should be prayers the bells had rung, but the clock on the wall swam in circles around the time; surely it was time for the breakfast bell? He should be in the chapel. With a tremendous effort, he rolled over in an attempt to get up. He crashed to the floor, and lay there, watching a woodlouse crawl along a crack in the floorboards. Then he slipped into darkness once more.

Cooper let go of Annabel, and sat gazing at her as though she were something he had imagined. Then the enormity of what he had just done struck him with full force and he looked away. 'I'm sorry, Miss Harman, I shouldn't have done that.'

Her low pitched laugh made him look at her again. 'What shouldn't you have done? Broken a perfectly good wine glass, ruin the varnish on the floor, or kiss me?'

Cooper shifted uncomfortably. 'The last one.' He couldn't help smiling.

'I don't think you need be sorry for that. I rather suspect I encouraged you, so if there's a fault, I share it.' She looked down at the fragments of broken glass, the blood-coloured liquid that had soaked into the wood. 'Look not on the wine when it is red, when it moveth itself aright, when it leaveth its colour in the glass.'

'That just about describes it, though I'd change it to *taste not* in this case.'

'It's a biblical text. It's strange, but I don't feel at all shocked by this. Perhaps it will catch up with me later.'

'I'll have to go, see if there's anything else I can do.' Cooper made towards the door.

'What do you mean? What's happening? How did you know about the wine?' She seemed suddenly to wake to the strangeness of the situation.

'I am here as part of a group that was to prevent ...'

'Armageddon,' she finished for him. 'Were they to serve that wine at communion this morning?' She looked at him in sudden fear and understanding.

'Worldwide.' Cooper said, abruptly, his mind refocussed.

She followed him into the corridor at a run.

The Prime Minister had not slept. He had been acutely aware of the passing of time in a night when the minutes played like a slow motion film. He was in his office at four thirty, sipping a large mug of tea and gazing at the radio. It was tuned to the BBC world service. No news had yet broken about the morning's operation. He opened the decoded True Gospel Church files that Inspector Cooper had sent. Methodically, he began to list all the appointments that would need to be made after 'Operation Eden'. It would mean a cabinet reshuffle. He opened his day diary and began to note things to arrange when his secretary arrived.

At six, the telephone rang. As he lifted the receiver his leg went into overdrive, but he was unaware of it.

'PM'

'Commissioner, sir. The operation went smoothly on the whole; not all reports are in. The one hiccup was that American General – his watch was fast, apparently and he went in too early and some were warned.'

'What happened?'

'Some of the groups were given a code word; 'Armageddon', which meant that the morning communion wine was to be a special reserve containing poison. Unfortunately, some churches have lost members as a result.'

'Any idea of numbers?'

'No, sir, but I'll keep you informed. Goodbye for now.'

'Bye, and thank you.'

The PM sat thinking of the political fallout that might follow the deaths. This was an aspect of politics that he hated. It wasn't simply a case of doing the right thing. It was trying to refute opposition and media allegations that could not be disproved. The facts of the bombings and the murders were good grounds for action. He sighed and went back to his list of new appointments.

Ruth had not eaten since noon the day before. She had led the members from the church into the dining room. She felt light-headed as she stood to say grace with the surviving congregation. After they were seated, she remained standing, in the place where Brother Saul usually addressed them.

'Brothers and Sisters in Christ. It has been a morning of great sadness for us all. These events are hard to comprehend; naturally our spirits will ask, "why does God allow such things?" The answer is not easy to find and I pray that we all stand firm in our faith during this time of trial. We know that our Brethren who have been taken this morning are safe in the eternal arms. We who remain must continue the work. For us, today, it means that we do those things that we would normally do, in an attitude of prayer. Today's text is "Be strong and of a good courage".'

She was startled when they all chorused, 'Be strong and of a good courage, in Jesus' name, Amen.' The hatches opened and the kitchen staff began to serve breakfast. Ruth's eyes scanned the faces behind the hatch; there was still no sign of Matthew. She went through into the kitchen and broke the rule of silence. 'Has anyone seen Brother Matthew?'

Startled faces looked round, heads shook, no.

Ruth ran to the sleeping quarters. Matthew's room was on the third floor, she took the stairs two at a time, peered through the tiny peephole. The bed was empty; the blanket had been pulled off completely. She opened the door. Matthew was lying on the floor, a pool of blood around his head. Ruth felt her heart thudding uncomfortably in her chest as she swayed on her feet, wishing she had eaten something. She knelt beside him.

Gently, she lifted his head. He was very hot. The blood was coming from his forehead, he'd probably cut it falling out of bed. His nightshirt was soaked in sweat. He coughed and began to murmur the words for Morning Prayer.

Ruth covered him with the blanket, put his pillow under his head and ran to the solitary wing to find Sister Barbara. She was sitting as usual in her room. But the empty wine glass beside her showed Ruth that Sister Barbara would not be able to help. She took dressings and ran back to Matthew. When she had washed and dressed his wound, she ran down the stairs again. There were still soldiers about.

'Sister Ruth.' It was Inspector Cooper with a woman she didn't recognise, in novice robes.

'Can you help me, Inspector? A man has fallen out of bed and I can't lift him off the floor.'

She was aware of their footsteps behind her as she raced back up the stairs. With one easy movement, the inspector lifted Matthew's inert form onto the bed.

'He's running quite a fever,' Cooper commented, pulling the sheet straight and throwing the blanket across the bed.

'He'll need a doctor. We'll need to phone,' she patted her pockets, 'it's hidden in my room.'

Cooper turned towards the door. 'There are some paramedics down in the chapel – I'll fetch one of them – it'll be quicker.'

Ruth sat heavily on the edge of the bed, the room beginning to spin around her.

'Are you all right, Ruth?'

'Never better,' she smiled wryly. 'I just haven't eaten for too long.'

The woman went out quietly. Cooper and a man in a yellow jacket came in to examine Matthew shortly after. The paramedic took pulse and temperature and listened to Matthew's laboured breathing.

'It looks like a really bad dose of pneumonia to me. We'll run him into hospital in the ambulance. I'll get my other half and a stretcher, won't be long.'

The woman returned with a large tray which she placed on the bedside table.

'Breakfast, anyone?'

'I need to go with Matthew to the hospital.'

'Not before you've eaten, young lady.' The novice was obviously new, forgetting to use the proper form of address.

'I can take you in my car later, Ruth, you must eat,' Inspector Cooper said.

Another voice echoed his. 'Yes, Ruth, darling, you must eat.'

They all looked at Matthew, who returned to coughing and muttering the words of Morning Prayer.

'I think that's carried, don't you?' Cooper smiled, reaching out to pour coffee into three cups.

Ruth bowed her head in prayer, as did Annabel, before eating.

Whilst they ate, two paramedics arrived to take Matthew with them. Ruth began to stand up but Cooper pushed her back onto her seat. 'It's more important for you to eat something. Now.'

Obediently, Ruth did as she was told, but her eyes followed Matthew as he was carried away. As they were finishing their cereal, a kitchen novice arrived with a pile of hot toast and more coffee.

Cooper's phone rang. 'Cooper.'

'PM's office here, Cooper; is there anyone at that Retreat who is taking over as leader?'

'I rather think there is. Why do you want to know?'

'Just that there are a lot of leaderless groups that need someone to help them pick up the pieces after this morning's events. The Retreat there was the main headquarters in the UK apart from head office, Joshua Group, which is closed at the moment.'

'Sister Ruth Diamond has stepped into the breach here. What do you need her to do?'

'Contact the other church groups; get them to continue as normal with the help of those who have come in to help them. Many are refusing to cooperate with the military or the police. Once they are working with us we can finish searching for hidden bombs in their buildings. There is a possibility that one of them might think it right to destroy themselves and the group at this time.'

Cooper looked at the frail figure of Ruth and wished that things had been different for her sake. She wasn't the strongest body in the gym. 'I'm sure she will help you in any way she can.'

'Right, can you take a list of the most urgent situations so that she can begin there?'

Cooper took out his notebook. 'Fire away.' He wrote the names down that were dictated.

'That's the lot for now, Inspector. Thank you.'

Cooper shoved the phone back into his pocket and finished his breakfast, not hurrying so that Ruth had finished eating before he spoke again.

'Sister Ruth, there is a rather demanding job that the Prime Minister's office has asked you to do since you seem to be able to lead the group here. Do you feel well enough to tackle it?'

Ruth looked up at him, her eyes dark rimmed with lack of sleep, and smiled. 'The smoking flax He will not quench, and the bruised reed He will not break. What do I need to do?'

## Chapter 55

Adam had decided to share communion with his mother instead of attending Morning Prayers with his father. He knew as soon as he began to swallow the wine that something was very wrong with it. As he dropped his glass, he reached forwards with a tremendous effort and knocked his mother's glass from her fingers. His head struck the edge of the table as he went down and he lay half-conscious, aware of his mother's horrified expression as he struggled to breathe. He did not die straight away, not having taken much of the wine, which was worse for those watching.

Calvin had run into the room as Adam fell. 'Oh, my God, I'm too late!'

Elizabeth woke from her horrified trance. 'He saved me, though. He may yet live, God willing. We need some help.'

'There are ambulance people here. They served that wine at Morning Prayers too.' Their eyes met, unable to comprehend the horror of it.

'Go on, Calvin, hurry! Where are these medical people?'

Calvin ran from the room, lifting his robes clear of his feet. Elizabeth knelt by her son, lifting his head onto her lap, putting pressure on the cut above his ear with her handkerchief.

Footsteps echoed on the concrete floor as Calvin returned, followed by two men carrying a stretcher.

'He's still breathing; fortunately he didn't drink much of the wine. But he hit his head on the table,' Elizabeth stood aside whilst the men lifted Adam onto a stretcher, gave him oxygen, and carried him outside to where another man had driven an ambulance close to the doors. Elizabeth and Calvin followed.

'Can you make your own way to the hospital? We've another patient on board,' the paramedic said, as they slid the stretcher in beside another.

'No problem,' Calvin said, taking his mother's arm and guiding her round the back of the building. There was a shiny gold VW beetle parked in the back of the barn. 'Hop in, Mother.'

Elizabeth did as she was told. 'When did you learn to drive? Whose car is this?'

'That's not important for now, Mother. What's worse than everything else is that father has been hit and badly hurt by a car. They took him to hospital. Brother Joshua was driving.'

Elizabeth wondered if she were dreaming and would wake up in a moment. But then Calvin's bleak expression told her this was all too real. 'How on earth did that happen?'

'I saw him try to stop Brother Amos from leaving. Brother Joshua and another man were already in the car; they drove straight at him, didn't even try to stop.' Calvin's hands tightened on the wheel.

'I was afraid of something like this. How are things back at The Retreat?'

'We have lost many of the Brethren. It was the rule of men drinking first – many of the women were stopped from drinking by the soldiers who stormed in on the service.'

'Soldiers?'

'Yes, truly, Mother. Then Sister Ruth got everyone to calm down. She was amazing.'

'She's as tough as Miriam, that girl, but has her father's gentleness. How did she do it?'

'Led us in prayer, then, when I slipped out after father, I heard her singing the twenty-third psalm.'

'Such amazing grace,' said Elizabeth, 'she's so real in her faith.'

'Unlike me. I was only spared because I overslept this morning. I was at the back of the chapel with the women.'

Joshua awoke to the sound of a crying baby. His wife was already half-way out of bed. 'Go back to sleep, dear – you didn't get much rest last night.'

'Neither did you.'

'It'll pass. It won't take long to get a routine established,' she said, lifting the noisy little bundle from the cot beside her

'What time is it?'

'Half past nine.' She put the child to her breast, and the wailing stopped.

'I should have been up hours ago! There's a lot happening today!'

'It'll happen without you for once.' She leaned over to kiss him.

'I suppose it already has. I missed Morning Prayers too.'

'It won't kill you.'

'I suppose not. You are simply beautiful, did you know that?'

Ruth sat in Brother Saul's chair. Inspector Cooper was at the desk beside the computer, she was on the telephone. Her head was reeling as she heard from some groups who had lost most of their Brethren. She repeated the message she had given to each, grasping at the words she had used at breakfast grace. Some groups were insisting that she give the authority code. She could not convince some without it.

'Our Brothers and Sisters in Christ, this is the message from us at The Retreat; cooperate with those who have come to help us. They may not be of the faith, but bear them witness by your strength and fortitude. It has been a morning of great sadness for us all. These events are hard to comprehend; naturally our spirits will ask, "Why does God allow such things?" The answer is not easy to find and I pray that we all stand firm in our faith during this time of trial. We know that our Brethren who have been taken this morning are safe in the eternal arms. We who remain must continue the work. For us, today, it means that we do those things that we would normally do, in an attitude of prayer. Today's text is "Be strong and of a good courage". This message will be sent by email to all churches today.' She listened for a little longer, gave some directions to yet another leader, and hung up.

Sister Annabel brought in a glass of milk, some biscuits and two cups of coffee on a tray. There was a carton of the food supplement as well. 'I found this with your name on it in the kitchen, thought it would be useful on a day like this.'

Cooper looked up at Sister Annabel with a smile that transformed his face. Ruth looked at him, startled by it. The smile was caught and reflected back as Sister Annabel gave him his coffee. 'Thank you, Miss Harman.'

'All part of the service, sir. Sister Ruth, will you be leading the morning meditation at eleven, or would you like someone else to take it?'

Ruth looked nonplussed. There was now a shortage of those who could lead such a group. 'I'm not sure who – I'm nowhere near finished here.'

'I could do it. I'm afraid these novice robes aren't the ones I used to wear. When I left, I was wearing lavender as a deaconess. If I can find one to fit, I could fill in for you.'

Ruth stared at her in amazement. 'I remember you! But you died...' then understanding dawned. 'Just as my brother did.' She stared down at her glass of milk as though it held the answer. 'Could you do that for me, Sister Annabel? Be strong and of a good courage.'

'And may the Lord guide your footsteps, Sister Ruth.'

Ruth grinned suddenly. 'I need it!'

Annabel smiled as she left the room.

Cooper was tapping away at the computer. 'I've sent your message to all the churches in the directory. How many more have you to do from the PM's list?'

'Six.' Ruth sighed, taking a long drink of her milk, consulting a list of numbers, and dialling again. 'I only wish I had the authority code.'

Cooper continued to access emails on the computer, printing off some, answering others. It was going to be a long morning.

Outside, the weather was turning wet and windy. Joshua group member C361 was leaning against a wall in the rain. There would be coffee inside. But it wasn't for him, not today. He had been in prayer for hours, not knowing whether his instructions should be carried out. He longed to go into the chapel, things always seemed clearer in there. But the soldiers and police were everywhere, spoiling the sanctuary. Apart from all those who had died that morning. Should he have died? Had he been spared to do his appointed task? He knew exactly where the equipment was hidden. But there had been no word from headquarters, no code given. It was a great responsibility. And, to add to his confusion, Brother Benjamin's daughter had taken the lead at Morning Prayers and at grace at breakfast. Surely, that was wrong, since St Paul had said: 'Suffer not a woman to teach?' But was leading prayer teaching? Brother Benjamin had always insisted that the letter of the law was so different from the spirit of it. But how to know what was the spirit of it? He shivered as the rain soaked through his black robes.

## Chapter 56

Brother Saul lay wondering why his room had suddenly become pale blue with flowered curtains instead of walls. He was unable to turn his head, but by moving his eyes he could just make out these things. There was also a strange smell and odd noises that didn't belong to his mornings.

'Saul?' Elizabeth's face came into view.

Perhaps I'm dead. That would explain it. But no, it wouldn't – Elizabeth had not died.

'You're in hospital. You had an accident.'

So that was it. The events of the morning came back to him in over-bright colours. Those men, people he had thought of as friends, his Brothers; their betrayal of all they had worked for.

'Don't try to talk just now. We only need one thing, dear. There is a need for the authority code so that someone can deputize for you whilst you are here.'

Saul tried to remember how to make words. With a tremendous act of will, he mouthed, 'Who?'

'There aren't any Elders left; we are managing with deacons and deaconesses.'

'Adam?'

Elizabeth's eyes filled with tears. 'In intensive care.'

Saul tried to think; who could take on the task? 'Who have we lost?'

Elizabeth held up the list.

Saul's eyes read, but his mind refused to believe that so many of his children had gone. There was no one to take over, no one at all!

'Nobody left,' he croaked.

'There is someone managing very well in your absence.'

'But not me.' Calvin came into view. 'I would be a disaster.'

Saul couldn't help smiling.

'Sister Ruth has shown remarkable courage and leadership qualities. After you left, it was chaos in the chapel; she calmed everyone down, led us in prayer, and sang a psalm.'

'I didn't imagine it, then; twenty-three.' Then he realised what they were saying. 'Not a woman! It can never be a woman.'

'Then who do you suggest, Father?' Calvin asked, 'She's better fitted for it than I would ever be.'

'She has trouble following discipline.'

'Sometimes our Rule of Discipline, spirituality and common sense part company, Saul. There are many things that we need to put right amongst us, and that is the first.'

Saul looked up at his wife. She was not the same woman who had left him all those years ago. He wasn't sure he liked this new, self-opinionated Elizabeth. 'No.'

'Then it will have to be given to me, Father, although I know I am not suitable.'

Calvin was right, there was precious little choice. 'Pen, paper.'

But Saul's hand was beyond his control, so he dictated the number whilst Calvin wrote the authority code on the back of Elizabeth's list, lay back and closed his eyes. 'Needs must when the devil drives.'

Calvin went straight to the telephone and rang Ruth. 'The code, Sister Ruth, I am giving it to you to use. Have you got a pen?'

Inspector Cooper and D I Allsopp had been back in their office all afternoon. Despite the officers they had working with them on this, the parameters of it were astronomical. The fall-out from the morning's work alone had left them with a huge pile of paperwork. There were all the murders linked in to the Joshua Group, few of which were going to be brought to trial now, since so many of them had died. There were one or two left who might yet be charged. The ones that had left the scene of the hit-and-run outside the chapel were being followed at a discreet distance. Orders were out to arrest any one who was wearing black robes. There were two from The Retreat unaccounted for. Cooper didn't want to think too hard about the consequences of this;

would it be bombs, suicides or murders? The clock edged past six.

The door opened. The Superintendent had come down the stairs without a sound. 'Cooper, it occurs to me that you'll need a lot more help with this church stuff: the murders, the burials, the poisonings and the bombings. How many staff do you have on this?'

'There are five of us, sir.'

'You'll need a few more than that. Right, you can have the main meeting room. I'll get it set up for you in the morning.'

'Thank you, sir.'

Cooper and Allsopp both breathed a sigh of relief. 'Let's go home, Allsopp.'

Annabel had been waiting outside Cooper's home for two hours. She was reading a good murder mystery, which kept her from thinking too hard about what she was doing there and why. When she saw him climb wearily out of his car on the driveway, she opened her car door, locking it behind her, feeling as though she were burning bridges.

He saw her. His face lit up, then that shadow filtered out the light. 'Annabel.'

'Charles. I need to talk to you.'

He led the way into a tidy but unlovely sitting room. Above the fireplace though, there was a beautiful painting in oil, on canvas. She stood in front of it.

'Andrew Marsh; Sunflowers,' Cooper said, 'can I get you a drink?'

'Yes, please. I'll have a white wine if you have some.'

'I'd have thought you teetotal.'

'Drink a little wine for your stomach's sake?'

'That's the opposite of the one I heard someone use this morning. "Look not on the wine that is red that moveth itself aright," or something like that?'

Annabel laughed. 'It's true – so many scriptures are contradictory. We just need to be aware that we were given a brain for a good reason.'

Cooper pulled the cork on a bottle of white and poured two glasses. 'Sit down then. What did you want to talk about?'

'Us. The way I feel about you. The way I think you feel about me.'

Cooper stared down at his glass of wine for a long time. 'It's difficult.'

She sat quietly, sipped some of her wine. 'Tell me.'

'A long time ago, I was married to a beautiful woman. We were very happy until our daughter, Jessica, was born. She had a breakdown; not just the ordinary sort, she became psychotic. I tried for years to keep her at home. But her illness got worse. One Christmas, on leave from the hospital, she attacked Jessica with a knife. Jessica walked out of my life that night and I didn't see her for many years. I didn't know whether she was alive or dead. My wife had to be sectioned. She has been in hospital for twenty years. She will never be able to live a normal life. She doesn't even know me.'

'So that is the shadow that crosses your soul every time you see me?'

'Yes. So, you see, it's impossible, you and me.'

'Not at all; it's just that we need to talk about what we are going to do and how we will go about it.' She put her glass down on the coffee table, moved to sit beside him. 'I'd very much like you to kiss me the way you did this morning.'

Cooper felt as though he moved in slow motion as he took her in his arms.

# Chapter 57

Ruth had been using the authority code as Brother Calvin had instructed her. It had seemed wrong, but all that morning when she had tried using her own name, all her messages had been returned invalid. So, stiff and tired, longing but unable to go to the hospital to see Matthew, she had gone to the evening meal, only to find herself led by Brother Calvin to the head table.

'Brothers and Sisters, it seems to you that God has called me to this place?'

'Amen, Sister Ruth, Amen.' The people looked to her, smiling.

'Very well. I have here a list of our brethren who have been called home. I shall read out their names, and then we shall stand in silent prayer for a minute.'

The names sounded like the tolling of a bell as Ruth's musical voice read them. During the silence, several could be heard weeping.

'Lord, for all Thy goodness to us in all things, we thank Thee. We beseech Thee that tonight we will be comforted in Thy love. We thank Thee now for this food, this drink, bless it to our use, we pray, in Jesus' name, Amen.'

She managed to eat quite well, although her every muscle seemed to ache. Her mind churned around the needs of these people. When all had finished eating, she stood up.

'Brethren and Sisters; it is a very different world we face today than the situation the church faced in the time of our Lord. As his disciples, we must be ready to seek the spirit, not the letter of the word. I ask you to support me as we move to bring the light of spiritual truth to our own hearts and to those around us. I ask you all to consider this as tonight's meditation.

'We are Brothers and Sisters in Christ. In accordance with the regulative principle, we have traditionally followed the rule of appointed tasks, some exclusively for the brethren; some exclusively for the sisterhood. If you have decided to make this change and appoint me your pastor, ask yourselves how this will affect our Rule and our Discipline; first, in the administration of the sacraments, second, in the running of The Retreat, thirdly, in the appointment of tasks. In your meditations, make notes of your thoughts. Bring them to your groups in the morning. Your leaders will lead you in prayer and discussion on these points. In the meantime, I will ask my Brother deacons to administer all sacraments, my Sister deacons to assist me in the administration of The Retreat.'

Miriam stood up. 'Sister Ruth, do you feel it is right for you to be taking this position? It is written, "I suffer not a woman to teach".'

'Sister Miriam, I am asking everyone to seek guidance in this matter. I simply ask you to consider what you feel constitutes 'Teaching' in our discipline today, according to the spirit, not the letter, of the word.'

Miriam pursed her lips angrily. 'This is not for any of you to decide. The scripture is plain. Women shall not teach.'

A Sister at the back of the hall spoke loudly. 'Look what has happened with the men in charge!'

There was an awed hush in the dining hall.

Ruth bowed her head, desperately seeking guidance.

And then, into the silence, came the sound of someone singing the words of a psalm.

'Behold, how good and pleasant it is for brethren to dwell together in unity!'

The choir joined in, one by one, swelling the sound, until almost everyone was singing. Someone beckoned Ruth to the front, and she took up the solo, the choir leading the four part harmony.

Miriam slipped away, angrier than she had ever been.

Calvin followed her.

The psalm ended, and again Ruth led them in prayer.

'Lord, we ask that you guide our footsteps aright. May the Lord bless us and keep us, may the Lord make his face to shine upon us, and give us His peace. Amen.'

Miriam took the side path around to the chapel, Calvin a few steps behind. He nearly cannoned into her as she collided with a figure that was climbing over the side wall. Calvin hardly recognised him; his black robes were very wet, his hair clung to his forehead, his face and hands were blue with cold.

Miriam snapped, 'Brother Simeon, what are you doing here?'

He looked at her, wild-eyed. 'Seeking the answer, Sister Miriam.'

'The answer to what?'

'Armageddon. The fall of Babylon the Great.'

'What do you mean by that?'

'It's not for you to know, Sister Miriam; it is for the brethren to make such decisions.'

'I think it's time you had a hot shower, a change of robes, and something to eat.'

'This is not of the body, but the spirit, Sister. I don't expect a weaker vessel to understand such things.'

'There are some things that are obvious even to a woman, Brother Simeon. Go and consult one of your brethren instead of wandering about in the rain. That's good old-fashioned commonsense.' She would not have spoken to a Brother in this way on a normal evening. It was, of course, Ruth's appalling behaviour that had driven her beyond self-control. It was too cold and wet to stand about out here. She must speak to Brother Saul. But how to get to the hospital?

Calvin let her go; more concerned about Simeon's intentions than he was with whatever Miriam had in mind. He watched as the man seemed to reach a decision, and then followed him past the boiler room and down the steps to the cellars that ran the length of the buildings. Plans were underway to turn this area into useful meeting rooms and stores. Calvin had once thought of using it for his own ends, but had rejected it as too cold and dark. He didn't particularly like rats either. There could easily be rats down here. The boiler room was warm, dry and light. No contest. Calvin shivered as he stepped into the blackness.

The man ahead seemed sure enough of his direction. He scrabbled around on a shelf near the door and switched on a torch that he must have stored there. Calvin followed the beam of light. He found the words of a hymn running through his head: 'Lead, kindly light, amidst the encircling gloom'. Probably not a kindly light at all: Simeon had sounded quite unhinged when he was talking to Sister Miriam.

Some distance in, the man paused. He played the torch over a handle set into a rusty looking tube. Calvin had seen something like it before. There were wires running towards the central supporting pillar, and others that snaked out of sight.

'Should have replaced this ancient stuff with something a bit more powerful,' muttered Brother Simeon, examining the equipment. Then, placing the torch on the floor, he knelt beside the thing and began to pray.

'Guide me Heavenly Father. A spirit of evil has overtaken your church. Is it Thy will that Thy servant destroy them before the evil spreads to others? Thou knowest I have wrestled long in prayer, guide me, Heavenly Father.'

Calvin suddenly knew with a terrible certainty what it was that Brother Simeon had been delegated to do. He was only too aware of the recent explosions through watching Adam's television news. He shuddered as he thought of all the Brethren and Sisters above, going about their concerns. Then he thought of Ruth, and his heart turned painfully in his chest.

'Whatever happens, not Ruth', he found himself praying for the first time in years. He had no weapon. He dropped to his knees, felt about on the floor as he crept towards the kneeling figure. His fingers closed round a piece of wood, he lifted it, and, half crouching, ran softly towards the kneeling figure.

The man stood up as Calvin approached. Calvin's foot knocked something, Brother Simeon swung round. Calvin aimed at the man's head, his piece of wood crashed down on the man's shoulder as he ducked sideways, the wood split in two, leaving Calvin with half the length in his hand. The rest of it clattered to the ground, striking a metallic note from the detonator as it went.

Brother Simeon pulled a knife, raised it and threw it straight at Calvin, whose forward movement alone saved him from the blade. Brother Simeon pulled a second knife as Calvin stumbled, and, remembering his many flights from the bullies all those years ago, let himself fall and rolled sideways as the man's arm came down and a knife flashed through the air again. It skidded across the stone flags and came to rest beside Calvin. He picked it up.

The man suddenly changed direction, heading back to the detonator. Calvin scrambled to his feet. The man paused, grinning, with his hands on the detonator handle. Calvin ran forward, tripped over some cable, and fell.

'In Thy name, o Lord!' Brother Simeon cried out and then bent to push the handle down.

Nothing happened. Dazedly, the man looked around, jerked the handle down once more. Calvin lay, knife in hand, with two cut ends of cable in his fingers. He had remembered who Brother Simeon was: his ex-school bully, Barry Dobbs.

# Chapter 58

Calvin was scrambling to his feet when Brother Simeon realised what his opponent had done. With a shriek of rage, he reached under his robe for yet another knife. Calvin reacted with a desperate somersault to his left. The knife caught his left leg a glancing blow and skittered away into the darkness.

'How many knives does he have?' Calvin wondered.

'Enough to remove an irritating little obstacle to the Lord's will.'

Calvin realised he had spoken aloud. He kept his gaze fixed on the knife in his opponent's hand. 'Perhaps you are the obstacle and I am the instrument of the Lord's will, Barry Dobbs.'

'Who are you, how do you know my worldly name?'

'I remember you only too well. Your favourite trick was jumping on my back in your studded boots.'

'It's that snivelling little wimp, Calvin Crouch, isn't it?'

'Not a wimp, Barry. You're on your own now. No five against one here.'

'You deserved all you got.'

'You are just a puffed up self-important bully, Barry Dobbs.'

'I'm Brother Simeon, remember that. I was chosen for this task!'

'By leaders who have abandoned you, and who have murdered many of your group as well as decent members this morning?'

'Lies! It's all an evil plot to destroy the church. You must be part of it!'

'It seems to me that you are the one about to destroy a large chunk of the church, Barry. If I hadn't been here, many more of our Brethren and Sisters would now be dead and the building above us destroyed.'

'Armageddon! The last battle has begun!' Barry spat the words and ran at Calvin.

Calvin sidestepped neatly, holding out his right foot to trip Barry, who crashed forward with a sickening cry and a thud. Barry staggered to his feet, blood dripping from his arm. He must have fallen on his own knife, but without pausing to gather himself, he ran at Calvin again. Calvin grabbed the knife hand with all his strength and began to squeeze the fingers against the handle. Barry jerked his whole body backwards. The knife blade sliced into Calvin's hand as it was pulled through his grasp. He gazed down at the wound in horror, and then looked up as his opponent threw his knife again. Calvin's sidestep was just too late as the knife found its mark in his shoulder. He fell backwards, crashing to the floor as Barry launched himself at him in a rugby tackle. Calvin waited until he was almost upon him before lifting both his legs, his feet making contact with his opponent's stomach, his momentum carried him forward, to crash head first onto the floor behind Calvin, who got to his feet with a tremendous effort of will. The blood was dripping down his arm from his shoulder wound.

Barry Dobbs lay inert, a gash on his forehead showed where his skull had made contact with the flagstones. He had been unable to protect himself; his injured arm had given way, his other hand, still holding the knife, had not been enough.

Calvin pulled the knife from his shoulder and pressed his good hand against the wound. There was a small square of light from the doorway, he staggered towards it. Nice to win against one of the bullies, he thought, though he'd had a long wait.

Reggie Foster and Willie Murgatroyd had met in the boiler room to discuss what to do, since there was to have been an outing to the races in the morning, but neither of them had been able to speak to Brother Calvin all day. They had been out in the shrubbery for a smoke, and were coming back in when they met Calvin staggering down the corridor, bleeding profusely.

'My God, guv, you don't half get yourself knocked about and no mistake.' Willy caught Calvin as he began to fall forward.

'Been stabbed,' Calvin said. 'Ambulance.'

'Cor what?' Reggie said, taking out his brand new mobile phone and pressing numbers furiously. 'Ambulance, please. A man's been stabbed. Yes, The Retreat in – oh, you know where. Right.'

'Tell them main gate, you'll have to get someone to open it.'

'Main gate, please. Yes, that's what I said, a man's been stabbed. Police? Right. Yes, I suppose so.'

Willy had laid Calvin flat on the floor and put an old robe used for rags under his head. 'Need something clean to press on the wound, mate, you got anything?'

Reggie looked about him, then headed for the gent's – returning with the roller towel. 'This do?'

Willie grabbed it and placed it over the wound. Calvin looked very white indeed. 'He's making a bit of a habit of this lately. Only just recovered from breaking his ribs.'

'Who do I ask about opening the gate?'

'Go to the gate lodge and tell Fred; but be careful of that dog of his, it's a nasty piece of work.'

Reggie ran, still wondering at the way his life had changed about; fancy him agreeing to have the police along.

Ruth had been staring at the same piece of paperwork for the last few minutes, unable to make word contact between eyes and brain, when the telephone rang, startling her from her stupor.

'Fred? I mean Brother Fred, yes, what can I do...?' She listened with horror as the gatekeeper told her of Calvin's injury. 'Where is he now? The boiler room corridor. I'll be right down.' Adrenaline surged through her as she ran down the main staircase, across the hall and down the steep steps, grabbing the new handrail to steady herself.

'Brother William?'

'We're down here, Sister Ruth. He's bleeding badly from a chest wound. Brother Reginald had a phone and called the police and an ambulance.'

Ruth knelt by Calvin's still figure. He'd always come off worst in fights. 'But how on earth has this happened?'

'Search me, Sister Ruth. He comes up from the cellar like, bleeding, says to call an ambulance. Don't know why he'd go down there – he's got a real thing about rats.'

'Looks as though he's been rolling around in the dirt, fighting. Did you see anyone else down here?'

'No, Sister, me and Reggie was outside like – we was looking for Brother Calvin.'

'So you were having a smoke.'

Willie looked away in embarrassment.

'Well, you would certainly have seen anyone coming out of the back entrance from the shrubbery. So, whoever it was is probably still in the building.'

The sound of the ambulance and police sirens interrupted them. Reggie ran along behind the ambulance and arrived in time to open the door for the two paramedics.

Sergeant Sam Barry spotted Reggie right away. 'How do, Reggie, what have you been up to this time?'

'I've been a model citizen, Sarge. Phoned for the ambulance and the police,' Reggie grinned.

'Stone the crows! You'll be taking holy orders next.' He turned to the paramedics. 'Anything I can do?'

'No, we just got a line in and some fluids. He's lost a lot of blood, so we'll just get him back to the hospital at the double.'

'Did you see that wound in his hand?' Sergeant Barry asked.

'That's nasty – thanks. We can't let him lose more blood if it can be avoided.'

Ruth stood back as the hand was quickly dressed and the stretcher lifted. She leaned against the wall as the others went out to the ambulance. Something, maybe a noise, made her look round. Her heart skipped several beats as she saw a robed figure stagger towards her.

'Brother Simeon? Are you all right?'

'What providence! I have the means to cleanse the church of this evil.'

'What on earth do you mean? But, you're bleeding badly. You must have it dressed; there's an ambulance outside.'

'I don't need an ambulance. Just my knife to cut away the rot that has infected the church; pride goeth before a fall, Sister Ruth. All your self-advertisement, singing and taking the lead in worship. It's evil. I'm appointed to prevent it.' He swayed a little and then stumbled towards her.

Ruth saw the knife as he came into the light beside the stairway. She swung herself round on the newel post and up three steps before swinging one leg back over the handrail behind him. Straddling the banister, she kicked him hard in the back as he shot past. He stumbled and fell heavily. His head made sickeningly loud contact with the boiler room door.

Ruth hopped back over the rail and down the steps, cautiously, in case he was feigning unconsciousness. She dropped her handkerchief onto the knife and took it from his hand. The outside door opened, revealing the stocky figure of Sergeant Sam Barry.

'Sergeant, I think I have your victim's assailant here. This is his knife.'

Sam Barry stood amazed for a few seconds at the sight of the frail-looking girl and the prone figure.

'Davina and Goliath?' he asked and then stooped to turn the figure over. 'Breathing's ok, pulse, ok, some bleeding from that wound; right, best check for more knives – they tend to have a few about their persons.' There was only one knife remaining in the belt. 'He's been losing a few.' Sam rolled the inert Brother over, pulled his hands behind him and secured them with a pair of handcuffs.

'I wonder if he's the only one left down in the cellar?' Ruth said, shivering now with shock.

'I'll check.' Sam called for a second ambulance as he went along the corridor. 'Shouldn't you wait for some help?'

The outside door opened and another policeman came in.

'Good timing, Perkins, let's check out the cellar in case they're breeding knife wielding monks down there. Could you put the knife the lady's holding into an evidence bag on your way by?'

Perkins dug in his pocket. 'Typical, Sarge, you never have any with you.'

'No need to; you bring them.'

Ruth stood in the dimly lighted corridor, wondering whether life would ever be peaceful again, whether she would be able to erase all the nightmare images that had etched themselves deep in her memory. There was a dreadful scraping noise behind her, and then the two policemen reappeared.

The Sergeant held up a rusty key, 'I've locked it for now; we'll need to come back again and take photographs in the morning. There's quite a Guy Fawkes situation in there.'

Ruth was too tired to work out what he meant.

Brother Fred appeared at the door. 'I'm just doing my rounds, locking up, Sister Ruth.' He stopped abruptly when he saw Brother Simeon lying on the floor. 'I thought the injured man had gone?'

'This is the other one, Brother Fred. Is the gate still open for another ambulance?' Ruth asked.

'No – I'd better nip back and wait for it.'

Everything seemed to be happening in slow motion to Ruth, whose eyes dropped black curtains of exhaustion every time she closed them. As soon as the men had all gone, she climbed the stairs back to her own room. She was surprised to see the light was on.

Sister Annabel was sitting, waiting for her. 'Sister Ruth, you look absolutely worn out.'

'I feel it.'

'Time for some TLC,' Sister Annabel said, lifting Ruth's robes from her shoulders and wrapping a towel round her. 'There's a bath run for you.'

Ruth hadn't the energy to protest as she was helped into the scented warmth of the bath, was washed like a child, towelled and led back to the bedroom. Sister Annabel poured hot cocoa from a flask into two mugs, passing one to Ruth.

After that, Sister Annabel poured scented oils into her hands and massaged Ruth's tight shoulders until they relaxed. She sprinkled lavender oil onto the pillow. Ruth lay down, fearing that sleep would never come to her again.

But Sister Annabel put a small silver thing beside the bed and pressed a switch. The sounds of running water, birdsong, the winds in the trees filled the room. Ruth dropped into a healing sleep.

Sister Annabel crept away, pausing only to put a 'Do Not Disturb' note on the door.

## Chapter 59

Miriam had waited for the bus, hoping that the few coins she had in her pocket would be enough for the fare. But when the bus had finally come, the conductor had said, 'We don't want none of your sort on my bus, thank you. My niece was in that building your lot bombed.'

She watched the bus disappear into the darkness. What bomb? Probably some vicious rumour spread about the church again.

She started to walk. When she had covered a half mile, an ambulance passed her, lights flashing, followed by a police car. She stopped then, uncertain what to do. The only place they could be going to was The Retreat. She shrugged and continued to walk. Not long afterwards, the ambulance came past again, rocking on its wheels as it turned the corner before the main road.

When the second ambulance passed her she hesitated again, but kept going once more. After all, the ambulances would go back to the hospital, where she was going. Unfortunately, she would probably have to wait until the morning to see Brother Saul now. But she would try anyway. The rhythm of walking had lulled her into a meditative state although she was tiring and her feet hurt. Her sandals were not made for long distances.

The town lights were a welcome sight. She was passing a pub when several drunks emerged. One of them spotted Miriam, and staggered towards her. 'Gi'us a kiss, darling.'

Miriam stepped back in horror. The rest of the group laughed. She didn't know whether to try to walk past them or to cut across the road away from them. The first man held out his arms. 'Come on, luv, don't be shy now.'

At that moment, a car drew up at the kerb. 'Sister Miriam, get in, quickly.'

Miriam scrambled into the car, seeing only that the woman was wearing novice robes. 'Thanks be to God that you came by, Sister?' She found herself shaking with shock.

'Annabel. It's not safe to wander about at this time of night, Sister Miriam.'

Miriam peered at the driver. 'Don't I know you from somewhere?'

'It's a long story. Where can I take you?'

'I was going to the hospital. I want to speak to Brother Saul about the hasty changes that are being made at The Retreat. I tried to get a bus, but the conductor wouldn't let me on. Some rubbish about a bomb set off by the church.'

'That too, needs some time to tell. One of the bombs was set off in the studio where your daughter was appearing. Didn't you know about it?'

'There was some gossip; I don't listen to such things.'

'Might I suggest that you come to my home for the night and we'll go to the hospital first thing in the morning? It's unlikely that you'll get to see Brother Saul at this hour of the night.'

'I was so upset, I didn't stop to think. I could sleep on a chair somewhere. Or maybe I should go back to The Retreat?'

'It's late. I expect Brother Fred has locked the gate, let his dog out and gone to bed after all the excitement.'

'I saw two ambulances and a police car in the lane.'

'Yes, it was Brother Simeon. He had a fight with Brother Calvin.'

'Calvin was always less than self-controlled.'

'On the contrary, I think he was very self-controlled about it; Brother Simeon was not behaving at all sanely from what I hear.'

Miriam remembered how agitated Brother Simeon had been, standing out in the rain, making no sense whatever. 'He was probably suffering from shock.'

'We all are. Your daughter is amazing, but it's taken its toll of her strength today. She really didn't need the stabbing on top of everything else.'

'I am afraid that my daughter is suffering from the sin of pride. I knew no good would come of the contract with that Waterman; now she seems to think she's above discipline.'

Annabel pursed her lips and changed gear rather energetically as she approached a roundabout. 'Sister Miriam, your daughter is one of the most disciplined members of the True Gospel Church. She never puts her own needs first. She has amazing strength and courage; just think how she calmed everyone down when people were dying all around, and panic was beginning to spread! Can't you see that?'

Miriam was silent. Nobody had ever spoken to her like that, except her husband. Her thoughts spun around out of control. She shook her head. 'I can't think about it now. I suddenly feel very tired.'

'I'm taking you to my home.'

Silence reigned in the little car until Annabel pulled up outside a little terraced house. She put a 'Resident's Parking' disc onto the dashboard and got out.

'Here we are. Follow me.'

Miriam followed obediently into the little house. She was greeted by warmth and the familiar yeasty smell of bread making.

'Come into the kitchen, I'll make us some cocoa.'

A voice from the stairway called out, 'Annabel?'

'Elizabeth! I was looking for you at The Retreat.'

'I've been at the hospital all day, with Adam and Saul. They're both rather poorly. I came home and did the bread for the morning. I phoned Pastor Black and he said he has been doing the bread in our absence. He's glad the experts are back. His efforts weren't as good as ours, apparently.'

Annabel ran to her friend and held her in a warm hug. 'It was good of you to do that, especially when you have so much on your mind.'

'It helps to keep my mind off it. You know, action, not anxiety. But where have you been? I thought you'd be here.'

'I was bushwhacked too, by a bunch of black-robed thugs, but not for long, I was rescued by Inspector Cooper before I had taken any wine.'

'Thank God for that. Sister Miriam, how lovely to see you.'

'Sister Elizabeth? Is it really you?'

'Reports of my death were slightly premature, I'm glad to say.'

Miriam followed the two women into the pretty kitchen and sat meekly drinking cocoa whilst they began to explain. She listened, amazed as they told of the actions of the Joshua Group, the kidnaps, the bombings, the unexplained deaths and the deaths that weren't deaths at all.

'So, you see, we don't know who was actually buried in the grave marked with my name. The police are investigating that, and several others.' Elizabeth finished with a sigh. 'It all started out with such high hopes for the future. When I think of all that's happened, I wonder any of us is still sane.'

Miriam gazed into her cocoa, on which a skin was beginning to form. Made with all milk, she thought: what extravagance. But she had to admit, it was just what she needed. A question was beginning to form in her heart, not her head, and she was very afraid of asking it.

# Chapter 60

Ruth woke and stretched out comfortably, feeling relaxed and refreshed. Until she remembered what had happened. Then she noticed the time. She had missed Morning Prayers! She leapt out of bed and scrambled into her robes. When she opened the door, she found a sister was sitting, meditating.

'May the Lord be with you, Sister Ruth. I am Sister Lydia. I am to take you to your office where the kitchen staff will bring you breakfast.'

'But, Morning Prayers!'

'Brother Jacob led that today; he says he trusts that was in order. We were unable to find Sister Miriam.'

Ruth sighed, wondering what her mother had been doing instead of leading her meditation group. No time to worry about that now, though. She turned to close the door behind her and saw the notice left by Sister Annabel last evening. 'Right, let's find breakfast.'

When she had finished eating, Ruth began the tasks she had set for the day. Allocating new responsibilities was a priority since so many had been lost. How to know which person was best fitted to do each task?

Sister Lydia came in. 'May the Lord be with you, Sister Ruth. I have some things that I feel you should know, now that you have the responsibility of managing much of our work.' She went to a corner of the room and pressed a catch. What had appeared to be a bookcase swung open to reveal a small room. Walls were lined with television screens. On them, the life of The Retreat was being played out.

Ruth stared at it in shock. It was one thing to suspect surveillance, quite another to see the evidence of it. 'How do you know of this, Sister Lydia?'

'I helped my husband, Brother Robin, as his helpmeet, with the computer, secretarial work and monitoring systems. I was under discipline of speech, of course.'

*'Told to keep your mouth shut'* thought Ruth. If this got out, it would cause a riot. Aloud, she said, 'Can we turn it off?'

'Turn it off? Yes, we can, but…'

'Let's do it, shall we, except for those that watch the outside of the building. It would be good to be aware of intruders.'

'As you will, Sister Ruth.' She bent and threw several switches until only the outside ones remained flickering. 'If you need help at all with the computer files, I knew as much as my husband did about managing the system.'

'That would be a great help, Sister Lydia. Do you know if the treasurer's wife was in the same position with her husband's responsibilities?'

'Sister Martha? She used to correct mistakes made by Brother Aidan, bless him. He was still under instruction when Sister Hope and Brother Harold were taken home. Shall I ask her to come to the office?'

'Please, could you?' Ruth watched her go, and realised that many of her problems would be solved if there were more of the women able to step into their husband's shoes. Then the penny dropped; of course, wives promised to be helpmeets to their husbands. Of course, it was in the rule of married discipline. How much she had to learn! A niggling question was struggling to the front of her mind; yes; where on earth was Miriam?

Miriam had woken with a start to the smell of baking bread. For a moment, she couldn't remember where she was. Then all the events of yesterday came flooding back. She closed her eyes and groaned. 'Discipline,' she muttered, and got out of bed to pray. It was a terrible struggle for her to find words to express her turmoil. She knelt there weeping for a while; something she had denied herself since the week after Benjamin's death. Someone knocked on the door.

'Come in.'

Sister Elizabeth came in with a tray of breakfast, which she placed on the bedside table. 'Bless you, Sister Miriam; we're making the bread for the homeless shelter and we thought you might prefer the quiet up here. There's no hurry.'

Miriam ate, washed and dressed in yesterday's soiled robes. She contented herself by brushing off the mud as best she could. She carried the tray to the kitchen. It was like a bakery at full capacity: rolls, loaves, currant buns, pies, and tarts covered every available surface. The two women were wearing white aprons and caps and singing whilst they worked.

'Good morning, Sister Miriam, I trust you slept well?' Sister Annabel greeted her.

'Yes, thanks be to the Lord. But my spirit is troubled by the things you told me last evening. May I help?'

'Of course, there are lots of dishes. We put the china stuff into the dishwasher and hand wash the tins.'

Later, a van arrived and they loaded trays of baked goods into the back. Miriam was taken aback when the driver, wearing jeans and a T-shirt, introduced himself as Pastor John Black. The three women followed by car to the 'homeless' shelter. Again, Miriam was astonished; over the door was a name. 'The Ben Diamond Shelter for the Homeless.'

'What's the matter, Sister Miriam?' the pastor asked.

'Ben Diamond was my husband.'

'I am very pleased to meet you indeed. We would never have been able to begin this work without his help.'

Miriam stared after the pastor as he carried a tray of loaves into the shelter. Did I know my husband at all? she asked herself, as she followed the pastor inside. The room was enormous, lined on three sides with bunk beds. Men were making beds, someone else was busy pulling curtains to screen them, others were setting trestle tables, yet others were carrying great pots of tea to those already seated at the tables. A queue was forming beside a large serving hatch where porridge was being ladled into bowls. Miriam caught sight of Elizabeth and Annabel in the kitchen and went to offer her help. After all, it was better than thinking. Her mind was spinning ideas like a force ten typhoon.

Her attention was caught at one point by an old man who came by singing a hymn under his breath. She stared at him, the face was familiar.

'Morning, Sister,' the man said, cheerfully, holding out a nicotine stained hand, 'Ebb Crouch at your service.'

Miriam's head swam. Ebenezer Crouch? But he was dead, wasn't he? 'Are you Saul's brother?'

'Yes, ma'm. But he disowned me a long time since. Black sheep of the family.' He passed by as the queue moved along towards the serving hatch.

Miriam made a decision. 'Excuse, me, Mr Crouch, I think you ought to know that your brother is in hospital. He was hit by a car.'

For a moment, she saw shock in his eyes, and then he chuckled. 'It's our time to be in the wars. Someone blew the building up where I was having a kip.' He waved a bandaged arm. 'But I got off lightly enough. Thanks, though, ma'm.'

Soon after ten, they left the shelter and headed for the hospital. Annabel and Elizabeth went to see Brother Adam, Brother Calvin and Brother Matthew, whilst Miriam followed the bewildering maze of corridors to men's surgical.

When she arrived, she was redirected to intensive care, where she found Saul surrounded by equipment. Saul lay with his eyes closed, breathing shallowly.

She sat to wait beside his bed. An hour later, a figure shambled into the ward.

'I thought I'd best make my peace with him,' Ebb Crouch said, taking a seat beside her.

At the sound of his voice, Saul's eyes flickered open. 'Ebb? Is that you?'

'Yes, Saul. I hope the other chap looks worse.'

A half smile creased Saul's lips. 'Not changed, then?'

'No, just the same old me. But I've been working in that shelter for the homeless for a few years now. Still have the odd bender, but I'm mending.'

'Ebb, I just want to say I was wrong, I'm sorry.'

There was a long pause.

'You still there, Ebb?'

'Yes, Saul, I'm still here. The only thing you were wrong about is thinking you could change me. That's down to me, always was.'

Saul began to laugh, weakly. 'It's taken me too long to learn it, Ebb. Even with my own son.' He closed his eyes, appearing to be asleep again for a few minutes. 'Is Elizabeth here?'

'She will be soon, Brother Saul,' Miriam said, 'She's with Brother Matthew and Brother Adam.'

'Sister Miriam.' Saul struggled for breath, and the monitor next to him began to bleep loudly. 'Tell her I love her and I'm sorry, I got things very wrong.'

Staff hurried to his bedside, Ebb and Miriam waited outside as they battled to bring Saul back to the living. Some time later, they stood back, packed away their equipment, and covered his face.

Miriam bowed her head for a moment, then, when she raised her eyes, found herself looking into the bloodshot blue eyes of Saul's brother.

'Thanks for telling me, Sister Miriam,' he turned and walked away.

Dazedly, Miriam walked through the maze of corridors towards the main entrance, hoping to find out which wards Brother Matthew, Brother Calvin and Brother Adam were in.

She became aware of a young man speeding towards her in a wheelchair, and stepped aside to let him pass. But he skidded to a halt, and reversed, looking up into her face.

'Mother.'

Miriam stood as though turned to a pillar of salt to match that of Lot's wife.

'Mother, it's me, Daniel.'

Miriam's iron self-control snapped. She bent and put her arms around her son. When she could speak, she fired questions at him. 'Why? What happened? Where have you been?'

Daniel laughed. 'This morning I've been to the physiotherapy pool for a swim. It keeps me fit.'

'But, Daniel, I thought you were dead!'

'I know. But I couldn't let you know what had happened. Look, come with me and we'll have a coffee and a herbal tea and I'll explain.'

Miriam followed her son towards the hospital canteen, sat sipping her herb tea and just looking at his face whilst he talked. Her sense of reality had shifted from north to south over the past two days, so the story of why he had been 'dead' for so long, and how he came to be disabled, seemed not to matter at all.

She thought: *For this my son was dead, and is alive again; he was lost, and is found.* A dozen fatted calves would not be enough to celebrate this.

Then she saw Elizabeth and Annabel come in. Elizabeth sat at a table looking dazed.

'Excuse me, Daniel, I must ...comfort Sister... Elizabeth.'

Annabel saw her approach and beckoned her across. 'It has been a trying afternoon for our sister. Her son Adam and her husband Saul have been taken home.'

'I am so sorry for her loss.' Miriam did not know what else to do, so she went to Elizabeth, stood awkwardly beside her. 'I am so sorry for your loss, Sister Elizabeth.'

Elizabeth looked up, but seemed not to register that Miriam had spoken. She lowered her gaze to the table, where she was drawing circles in spilled tea with her finger.

Helplessly, Miriam returned to her son.

'Bad news then?' he asked.

'Yes, Brother Saul and Brother Adam have been called home.'

Daniel paled. 'Adam was a good man. He will be a great loss to the church.'

Miriam was surprised to find herself crying.

Daniel moved his chair around beside her and held her whilst she wept years of pent up grief.

'I don't have any answers any more, Daniel. I don't know what is right and good anymore.'

'That's the best place to begin, Mother.'

# Chapter 61

## *One Month Later.*

Ruth stood up to end the memorial service with prayer. The sea of faces no longer worried her as much; but still her stomach turned as she began. The great sweep of the Albert Hall was filled to capacity with a mixed congregation outnumbered by robed figures; unfortunately, the majority of the True Gospel churches now were women after their recent losses. In the front row sat her brother Daniel, next to his mother.

'Lord, we beseech thee as we move into tomorrow that we do not forget those we have loved and lost. We pray that thou wouldst guide thy people in the truth; that thou wouldst enable us to understand our Brothers who are called to a different path. Enable us to learn from one another; that we might grow in grace and in the knowledge of the truth, which is greater than any one of us is able to comprehend in its vastness, as is the love of Christ, which passes all understanding. In His precious name, Amen.'

There was a thunderous 'Amen' from the congregation.

A Bishop came up beside her, and led the congregation once more in prayer. 'O, Lord, we thank thee for our Sister Ruth, who has begun a good work: in ministry of word and song. We pray that as Brothers and Sisters in Christ, we may work together in harmony to preach the Gospel of Truth; in the name of the Father, and of the Son, and of the Holy Ghost, Amen.'

A line of ministers walked up to the front and linked hands. The Bishop took Ruth's right hand, Pastor John Black her left, and lifted them up. All along the rows, others linked and raised their hands.

'Together in Christ!' Ruth said, as all hands were raised.

'Together in Christ!' roared the congregation. 'Amen!'

Ruth signalled to the choir and they began the medley of hymns and psalms they had prepared as a recessional for this service. They were augmented by choirs from other churches and the sound was superb, although they had only had one rehearsal as a complete choir this morning. Archdeacon Wiseman was ecstatic at the organ.

Sister Josephine pointed her baton in Ruth's direction and she began her solo part from *Handel's Messiah*. The acoustics were astounding.

*'How beautiful are the feet of them that preach the Gospel of peace, and bring glad tidings, glad tidings of good things.'*

Nobody was leaving. The music continued unabated for the whole programme. In the silence at the end, someone began to clap, until the applause spread throughout the hall.

After a few moments, Ruth held up her hands for silence. 'Brothers and Sisters, go in peace. As you go, let the songs of Zion lighten your hearts.'

She sang a chorus she had learned as a child, and the choir and congregation took it up:

*'Thy loving kindness is better than life,
thy loving kindness is better than life,
my lips shall praise thee, thus will I bless thee,
I will lift up my hands unto thy name.'*

As the people finally began to leave, Ruth led them in one song after another until the last of them had filed through the doors. But the singing did not end there. It echoed in the streets outside, in the coaches that people entered and along the streets where local congregations walked together.

The little group of ministers knelt together in prayer for a few moments, led by the Bishop, before they followed the rest of the congregation into the daylight outside.

Inspector Cooper, Joshua Allsopp, the Chief Constable and Fox joined them. They were to have dinner with the Prime Minister.

When they were all seated around the dining table, the Bishop said Grace. To end the silence that followed, Cooper asked, 'Is it all's well that ends well?'

'What do you think, Edward?' the PM asked.

'We can only hope so. It's going to take quite some time to tie up the loose ends. The exhumation enquiries are well underway, but there's a tremendous amount of work to do yet.

The finances are a nightmare to untangle.' The Chief Constable looked thoroughly fed up.

'There are the murders too, don't forget,' Fox added.

'How could we ever forget those?' Joshua said. 'It was bigotry turned excuse for summary execution. It was a shame on the church.'

'It's not the first time it's happened. Don't ever read *Fox's Book of Martyrs* if you want to sleep well at night. Burning each other at the stake and such like; pregnant women too. All out war, whichever had the upper hand at the time,' the Chief Constable said, grimly.

'Why burn them?' asked Joshua.

'The church was not supposed to shed blood,' Cooper said grimly.

'Seems a bit on the hypocritical side,' Fox said. 'I wonder if the Fox concerned was a relative?'

'Go back far enough and we're all related, I'm told. The True Gospel lot had one thing right; we are Brothers and Sisters,' said the PM.

'Cousins many times removed,' grinned the Chief. 'I only know that when religion goes wrong, it goes very badly wrong.'

'Human nature, sir, it wears a thin skin over its uncivilised past,' Cooper said. 'By the way, have they tracked down the hit and run driver that killed Brother Saul?'

'There's a lead in Spain. It'll be some time, but he'll be caught,' the Chief said. 'They haven't caught up with Brother Joshua yet, either. But Brother Amos Firth comes up for trial in August for fraud, mostly. It's been difficult, to say the least, to unscramble the activities of the Joshua Group. Quite unsavoury, some of it. If it weren't for the meticulous computer records they kept, we wouldn't have proved anything at all. The problem is that Brother Joshua Adam's computer was found immersed in the central fountain at headquarters. Much of the most damning information must have been on there. It must have been soaking for several days.'

'So that means that much of the information on it has been lost?' the PM asked.

'We've not had any luck with it so far. We'll just have to use the evidence we have to go to trial.'

'When exactly in August is the trial set?' Cooper asked, innocently.

'It'll be late in the month, why do you ask?'

'I've put in for a month's leave.'

'Never! You have to be forced to take your entitlement. What wind of change has brought this about?'

'I'm getting married,' Cooper said, smiling broadly and turning away.

'Verbal bombshell or what?' the Chief said.

'Excellent,' said Allsopp, grinning at his boss.

'Another good man down,' Fox said, morosely.

'It happens to the best of us,' the PM said, 'now, Sister Ruth, I wanted to talk to you about the 'Agenda for Change' if you would. Could you spare an hour or two to discuss things with me?'

'Of course I can. There are new paths that I want to lead the Church into, with their knowledge, input and consent.'

'I give you all a toast, Ladies and Gentlemen; 'To the new Agenda for Change.' They raised their glasses, just as the first course was brought in.

Much later back at The Retreat, in a dining room, Miriam, Ruth and Daniel were drinking cocoa, Miriam looked across at her daughter.

'I want to leave The Retreat, Ruth.'

'But Mother, what will you do?'

'I'd like to work in the shelter for the homeless that your father began. There is to be a vacancy to cover during Sister Annabel's honeymoon leave, so I will be of great help to Sister Elizabeth.'

'It's just such a sudden aftershock, Mother. You always seemed so contented at The Retreat,' Daniel said.

'Not really. I embraced the discipline looking for some inner peace, I never found it. But working at the Homeless shelter, I am doing something useful. I feel alive again after all this time.'

'You won't make them finish their greens will you, Mother?' Daniel grinned.

Miriam looked at him sharply and then her face relaxed into a smile. 'I wasn't always a wise parent, was I?'

'You did your best, Mother,' Ruth said, and a weight lifted from her heart.

Miriam looked at Ruth again, not knowing what to say. She swallowed hard. 'I'm sorry, Ruth. I got it very wrong with you.'

'Following the letter of the law, not the spirit – that's been the major failing in the teaching and the discipline all along, Mother. As you were led, so you did. Blind guides were never any use except in the fog.'

'That's no excuse.' Miriam dropped her eyes to the floor.

'Pobody's Nerfect,' Daniel said grinning as his mother tried to unscramble the words. 'Pobody's Nerfect.'

## Chapter 62

'I'm going to be a taxi driver,' Calvin announced. 'Reggie, Willy, Ricky and Mick are joining me. We've got our eye on a place in Salisbury – the owner's about to retire to Greece next year. It's time I turned an honest penny.'

'I didn't know you liked driving,' Ruth said.

'My father did, but wouldn't let me learn. He had other plans for me.'

'It seems rather odd, since we often needed someone who could drive.'

'Discipline, Sister Ruth, discipline. It's good for the soul,' Calvin said, in an accurate imitation of his father's voice.

'What will you do, Ruth?' Calvin asked.

'What I am doing, Calvin; I'll help run The Retreat and continue my singing. Perhaps do some composing if there's time when The Retreat returns to something like normal. As for anything else, I'll have to wait and see.'

'It's a leap year next year if you're still waiting then,' Calvin said. 'I've an early start tomorrow, goodnight everyone.'

'So you have really stopped the arranged marriages, Ruth?' Miriam asked when Calvin had gone.

'No, I have not, Mother. It has been a subject of meditation. After long discussion and prayer, the church membership has decided that, if a disciple wishes it, the Eldership will seek guidance and a marriage partner for them. Otherwise, it is a decision for the individual after prayer and guidance from their parents or of the Eldership if the parents are no longer with us.'

'It sounds a very dangerous move to me,' Miriam shrugged, 'but if that's what you want.'

'Mother, it's not a matter of what Ruth wants; it's what the church itself decides that is important, surely?' Daniel pointed out.

'The regulative principle should apply!' Miriam snapped.

'That won't hold any holy water, Mother. There's no scripture that says we should arrange each other's marriages. Just that we should not be "Yoked unequally with unbelievers",' Daniel said, angrily.

Ruth looked at them both. 'Time we were asleep, I think.' She stood up and took the tray of empty cups into the kitchen, shivering as she thought of marrying Amos Firth. That he was her 'chosen' marriage partner had made her physically sick. She went up into the men's wing and along to Matthew's room. The day had been so hectic that she hadn't been able to see him at all today.

He was sitting up in bed, looking very pale and thin, the angles of his face were sharply outlined by the bedside light. 'Welcome, Sister Ruth,' he smiled.

'And how are you, Brother Matthew?'

'Much better for seeing you. I was let out for a walk this afternoon. How did it all go?'

Ruth smiled contentedly. 'Amazingly well. The Prime Minister wants to discuss the Agenda for Change with me later this week.'

'I'm surprised you have time to waste on an ordinary mortal like me.'

'I can spare you a few crumbs of my day,' she laughed. 'But that's not what I came to tell you. I have the keys to your home. The Sisters that were there have returned to The Retreat, and the children are here. They are to go to ordinary schools again.' She placed the keys in his hand.

He looked at them for a long time. 'This key ring with the lion on it was my father's. It's a bit worn down, but still visible.'

There was a silence between them.

'Do you want to go there? It is, after all, yours.'

The news that Matthew's parents had been buried at The Retreat cemetery hung, unspoken, between them.

'Yes, Ruth. I need to go there. It will lay some ghosts. And I also want to know what it was that father had hidden in his safe all those years ago. Will you come with me?'

'Of course I will. After Morning Prayers tomorrow, I'll ask Calvin to take us in his car.'

'I heard Calvin had passed his test.'

'He'll be a fully paid up taxi driver soon. He's obsessed with cars.'

Matthew was overcome by an enormous yawn.

'I'd better let you get some sleep, goodnight, Brother Matthew.' She leaned across and gave him a very unsisterly kiss, which he returned with enthusiasm.

Next morning, Calvin dropped them outside the house before roaring away in his shiny gold VW. Matthew stood at the gate for a moment, looking up at the window that had been his bedroom all those years ago.

'It's not changed much; they kept it in good repair, I'll give them that.'

'The furniture's a bit weather worn, though,' Ruth told him.

They went in down the familiar two steps into the hallway. Matthew's head began to spin; memories leapt out from every picture on the wall, each chair, even his father's desk was still where it had always stood. 'This is weird,' he said, coming back through from the dining room, 'it's as though it's been preserved, like a museum of my childhood. Only the colours have faded.'

When they had been through all the rooms, they came back to the study safe.

'Let's open it.' Matthew's hands were shaking. 'Did you ever hear that there was a tribe that believed that the longer a letter lay unopened, the worse or the more powerful its message was?'

'Matured, like wine?'

Matthew lifted down the cuckoo clock and set it on one side. Behind it, the wallpaper showed the outline of the clock. Matthew pressed the place where the pendulum had marked the wallpaper. There was a click, and he was able to push a panel aside and reveal the safe. As in a trance, he turned the knob and the door swung open. He lifted out the bundles of papers and several little boxes, and laid them on the desk. A small key fell to the floor and Matthew put it in his pocket.

'I'll find out what that opens later.'

They sat together reading the documents for a long time. The only sound was their breathing and the ticking of the clock.

Matthew broke the silence. 'My parents' wills are here.'

'And a good deal of information about the Joshua Group's activities, the missing members and what we now know were murders.'

'These floppy disks must have a lot of information on them; we'll need to give them to the police.'

'Not if I have my way,' said a chilling voice from the past.

They swung round.

'Brother Joshua Adam!'

'This gun is loaded, so don't think of making yourselves martyrs. First, I'll have those papers. Put them in this bag, with the boxes; I want everything that was in that safe.' He threw a supermarket carrier bag onto the floor beside them.

Ruth couldn't believe the change in him; his face was unshaven, he was wearing a poorly fitting suit and a purple shirt with an ill matched pale orange tie. She found herself mesmerised by the gun in his hand and the cold, calculating look in his eyes.

It didn't take them long to put the contents of the safe into the bag.

'Thank you. It took you rather a long time to come back, Brother Matthew; I would have expected you to be here in a couple of days. You kept me waiting.'

'I had pneumonia.'

'Shame. Now, go down to the cellar, both of you.' He motioned with his gun.

They had no choice but to do as he said. Neither of them was strong enough to take him on. The cellar was rather different from Matthew's memories of it; there was little rubbish in it now; there was a computer on a desk, filing cabinets, and a telephone. Joshua Adam tore the cable from the wall and threw the phone into the hall above, not taking his eyes off them for a second. He opened a cupboard door, pushed Matthew into it and turned the key.

'Sit.'

Ruth sat on the office chair whilst he bound her to the seat, wrapping her arms tight to her sides.

Joshua Adam bounded up the stairs. 'Have a nice death,' he grinned, closing the door and locking it.

'What did he mean by that, do you think, Matthew?' Ruth said as she heard the front door slam a few minutes later.

'He wanted to say something to worry us, no doubt; any chance of opening this door?'

Ruth pushed the office chair on its wheels with her feet to the cupboard. 'My arms are bound to my sides, Matthew. I'm going to see if I can reach the key with my teeth.'

Try as she might, she could not turn the key at all.

Then they heard it. The sound of water trickling under the door.

'He's left the taps on in the kitchen! Matthew, is there a drain in this cellar?'

'No, it used to flood in the winter. There was a pump somewhere that we used, to keep it off the boiler.'

Ruth's heart was thudding painfully as she thought about their plight. Only if she could release Matthew would they have even half a chance of escape.

She pushed the chair with her feet so that her back was towards an edge of the brick wall. She began to rub her bonds against the sharp edge of the brick. It was going to be a long task; the rope was quite thick.

'What are you doing Ruth?'

'I'm trying to fray the rope tying my hands against an edge of brick wall. I can't move them up and down much and I have to hold the chair steady with my feet.'

She heard him thump the cupboard door with frustration. 'I wish there was something I could use to force this door from the inside. But the damn cupboard is full of stationery.'

The water was rising steadily.

She returned to her task, trying to get some purchase, but it was difficult to apply any pressure. She had taken the skin off her wrists by trying to hurry.

Her eyes kept flickering back to the water pouring down the steps as over a waterfall. She had always liked the sound of running water. Until now.

## Chapter 63

Ruth's eyes scanned the desk. She propelled herself wetly back to it and leaned down to pick up a pencil with her teeth and sloshed back to the cupboard, almost tipping the chair over in her hurry.

'What are you doing?'

Ruth could not answer. With all her strength she pushed herself up until she could push the end of the pencil through the head of the key. Then she pushed down on one end. The key would not budge. She let the chair down onto the floor and rested. The water was already several inches deep.

'Ruth, what are you doing, are you all right?'

'Mmm.' She lifted herself and the chair again and put the pencil through the key head from the other side, and pushed in the other direction until her teeth ached with the effort. The pencil snapped. Tears of frustration pricked her eyes. She pushed her chair back to the wall and began again to try and fray her bonds. Time dragged, she sang to herself as she moved her hands up and down until her arms and shoulders ached. The water was up to her knees.

'Matthew.'

'How are you doing out there?'

'I am trying to fray out the ropes round my hands, but I don't know how much effect I'm having; I can't see what I'm doing. I am exhausted and the water's rising very quickly.'

'Can you think of anything else?'

'I did try to lever the key round with a pencil but it snapped.'

'Take a rest from the ropes and have another go at the key with a pen or pencil. It might just work.'

Ruth's chair moved sluggishly in the freezing water to the table, where she took another pencil in her teeth and pushed back to the cupboard. She dropped the pencil and had to go for another. The water was creeping past her waist. Back at the cupboard, she tried again. Patiently, first one way and then the other, her mouth was filled with the taste of chewed wood and pencil lead.

'It won't budge,' she said, her voice muffled by holding the interminable pencil between her aching teeth.

And then, with a sudden click, the key turned, the pencil twisted and grazed the roof of her mouth. She let it drop into the water as Matthew waded from the cupboard, blinking in the sudden light. 'This is getting rather too deep for comfort. Well done, darling.'

'Quickly now, untie me, I have to telephone.'

'But Joshua Adam took the telephone out.'

'I've got my mobile in my top pocket.'

'Your mobile?'

'Yes, just untie me. Before the water reaches my phone.'

Matthew did as he was told, feeling as though he was in some horrible temperature driven dream from which he would wake in a minute. The water had already reached his waist and covered the first eight steps. There were thirteen steps to the top. If it takes forty-five minutes for the water to cover eight steps, how many minutes would it take to cover the other five?

'We've got thirty minutes at best,' he said, dully as he worked his cold fingers into the wet knot at her back until it was finally loosened. He saw with a pang of regret that all her efforts had done was to skin her wrists and only frayed the rope slightly. He wondered at her inner strength. 'All done.'

'Thanks.' She immediately pulled her phone from his pocket and wiped her fingers on the still dry top of her robe before dialling 999. She was shivering so much that her teeth were chattering.

Cooper was just going upstairs for some late breakfast when the desk sergeant called him back. 'It's that girl, the singer, at that Retreat place. She's just called 999 and says she's trapped in a cellar. Some joker called Brother Joshua Adam pulled a gun on them, shut them in and turned the taps on. Dan Barry's on his way with Hawkins to the house. It's in Odstock village.'

'Any news of where the gunman went?'

'No, not yet. She's given us a good description of what he's wearing.' The Sergeant passed him a slip of paper. 'He took some papers that had been left in the safe by Matthew's father before he died. She said there was a lot of evidence that you needed.'

'Great.' Cooper headed for the other set of stairs and hurried to the Superintendent's office. It was very important to catch Joshua Adam before he destroyed the things he had taken, or did some demolition work using explosives.

Dan Barry put his heavy weight against the back door of the cottage and it splintered away from the locks on the inside. He fell down two steps into several inches of water.

'You okay, Dan?' Hawkins enquired, stepping gingerly into the murky liquid.

'Course I am.' He scrambled to his feet and waded along the hallway. The water was flowing strongly under a door part way along, just opposite the kitchen. The other end of the hall had two steps up to the door to match the rear entrance. Hawkins went into the kitchen and turned off the taps.

Dan rapped at the door. 'You in there, Miss Diamond, Mr Farnsby?'

'Yes, thank God you're here. It's too creepy watching this water rise. And we're freezing.'

Dan tried the door. There was no key. Presumably there was a flight of steps beyond this door. He didn't fancy falling through this one. 'How deep is it?'

'There's plenty of time yet.' Ruth's voice was rock calm.

'It's reached the eleventh step of thirteen,' a man's voice replied.

'I've turned off the taps,' Hawkins said.

'That's the best news I've heard this year,' Matthew said.

Dan went to find some tool to prise the door open. He returned with a crowbar from the tool shed. 'Stand clear, you two.' He put his considerable strength to one end of the crowbar until the door parted company with the lock.

Two bedraggled figures stumbled out into the hallway.

'Thanks,' Ruth said, flopping down onto the stairs. Matthew leaned against the wall, blue with cold.

'Towels, Hawkins. Dry clothing,' Dan Barry said.

Later, at the station, Matthew gave Inspector Cooper the key he had found in the safe.

'Hmm. A safety deposit box key. I think we'll keep a few men at the cottage for a short while, in case the man was looking particularly for this.'

Back at The Retreat, the following morning, they had a visit from Inspector Cooper. 'We have our man in custody. How are you both after your cold dip?'

'Matthew has been a bit off colour. Wading around in a flooded cellar isn't the best thing for someone recovering from pneumonia.'

'Well, this should cheer you up. We have enough evidence now with the facts that your father had left us in the safe to convict both Joshua Crouch and Amos Firth of causing death by dangerous driving, fraud, and conspiracy to murder.'

'I'm just pleased that he's not likely to set off any more explosions,' Ruth said, with feeling.

'Well, young Barry Dobbs won't be leaving prison for a very long time once he's fit to stand trial.'

'That's a relief. We thought Calvin wouldn't make it for a while,' Matthew said.

'That safety deposit box key, by the way, has revealed a great deal of money, several bank account numbers and some jewellery. We shall be looking to find the rightful owners of these things in due course,' Cooper said.

'If they are still with us, Inspector; if not, we will endeavour to find their relatives,' Ruth said. 'I still have nightmares about the deaths at the church and that enormous mass funeral we had to hold.'

'On another subject entirely, Miss Diamond, will you do me a favour?' Cooper asked.

'If I can.'

'Would you sing at my, I mean, our wedding? Annabel and I would like it very much.'

'Of course I will. I have a television series to do on Sundays for eight weeks soon. Mr Waterman is rather pleased with himself. Just give me the dates and the music and I'll do my best.'

'Miss Diamond, your best is good enough for me. Thank you very much.'

'Thank you, Inspector,' they chorused, as he went out of the door and drove away from the building that had seen so much misery. Strangely, though, he felt that there were no ghosts there. It was already a place of peace. He changed gear to drive up Ash Leas lane. Lowering the window he smelt freshly cut grass. He sang softly as he drove back into town to buy some freesias.

# Characters

True Gospel Church. (TGC)

Saul Crouch. White robe. Retreat Pastor.

Calvin Crouch. Red robe; disciple, gardener. Son of Saul and Elizabeth.

Adam Crouch. Green Robe, Elder, Son of Saul and Elizabeth.

Elizabeth Crouch, Lavender robe. Chef. Saul's wife, mother of Calvin and Adam.

Ruth Diamond. Light blue robe, choir, lavender flashes; deaconess.

Miriam Diamond. Lavender robe, deaconess, Ruth's mother.

Daniel Diamond, Red robe, Disciple, house maintenance, Ruth's brother.

Benjamin Diamond, Green robe, Elder, Church finances, Ruth's father.

Matthew Farnsby. Red robe, disciple, chef.

Amos Firth, Purple robe, teacher, headmaster, theological college.

Annabel Harman. Lavender Robe. Chef, Ex TGC member.

Joshua Adam (Crouch). Saul's cousin. White robe, Headquarters manager, TGC discipline; leader, Joshua Group; TGC 'Police'.

Sister Josephine, Lavender robe, assistant to Brother Joshua Adam at HQ.

Brother Robin. Navy blue. Deacon. Treasurer, Retreat secretary.

Sister Lydia. Lavender robe. Helpmeet to Brother Robin.

Sister Barbara. Lavender robe, TGC nurse. Deaf.

Brother Simeon, Black robe. (Nee Barry Dobbs, School bully) Joshua Group member no 361.

Doctor Harold. TGC GP.

Calvin's Group: Blue striped robes. Reggie Foster, Mick Murgatroyd, Ricky Murgatroyd, Reggie Foster, Yellow robe.

Hope Briggs. Lavender robe. Church finances.

Harold James, Green robe. Church finances.

Roger Saunders Black robe, cameraman, bomber.

Police Commissioner/ Chief/ Edward …

Inspector Charles Cooper. DI Josh Allsopp. DS Melhuish. DS Sam Barry.

Sergeant Dan Barry. WPC Tullish, WPC Morris. PC Hawkins. PC Ames. PC Perkins.

Other Church Ministers. Bishop Gerald Maitland. Archdeacon Bertie Wise.

Methodist, Revd John Black. Catholic, Father Murphy, Free Church, Pastor Macgregor, Rabbi Solomon.

At Number Ten: Prime Minister Stuart. PPS, Wilson. Mrs Bradley, Minister for Health, Joshua Group member A6.

MI5 Agent Fox.

School Bullies: Ginger Foster. Barry Dobbs, (Bro Simeon) Bobby Parrish.

Oliver; psychiatric patient. Dr Hall, psychiatrist.

Solicitor: Nigel Bishop.

Music Agent, Max Waterman, his PA, Diane.

Journalists Paul Markham (Daniel's Partner) Dominick Draper, TV news.

Clarion: Jimmy Rafferty, Tom Rafferty, Stan Short, News photographer. Jenny Tang, Pierre Simons, Betty Scamell. Howard Blithe, religious affairs correspondent, TV.

Missing TGC Persons: David and Anne Farnsby. Mr and Mrs Jacob Reed. Mr and Mrs John Kirkham.

Their Children: Matthew Farnsby, Jacob and Martha Reed, Steven, Thomas and Rebekah Kirkham.

Paramedics, David Davies, Willy Foley.

Muslim Girl, Ayesha Muktar, Her cousin, Ahmed. Guy, her boyfriend.

```
                        Crouch.
        Saul Peter.                    Elizabeth Mary.
        _____
        |                                         |
        Adam Peter.                     Calvin Paul.
```

```
                        Diamond.
        Benjamin Daniel.               Miriam Ruth.
        _____

        Daniel Matthew.                 Ruth Dorcas.
```